Praise for *Fight for Your L...*

"*Fight For Your Long Day* is an original, witty, uncom
now: Homeland Security shadowing us, poverty, espec
of adjunct English instructors, the 'war on terror' inv
around hopelessness for too many. Kudera has the co
the mainstream culture, but he locates some heroes to. ...ant first novel."

—Joan Mellen, author of *A Farewell to Justice* and professor in the graduate program in creating writing at Temple University, Philadelphia, Pa.

"Duffleman is the overeducated Everyman for the age: his acute eye for detail and his ironic twist on reality take the reader on this 'A Day in the Life' journey through contemporary America and its moral ambiguities, anxieties, and occasional delights. These last must be taken with a smidgen of horseradish to remind us that even imagined sweetness can be sabotaged."

—Don Riggs, associate teaching professor in the English and philosophy departments of Drexel University, Philadelphia, Pa.

"Cyrus Duffleman, dedicated foot soldier of the faculty, aims high but faces frustrations and dangers every teaching day. With humor and real understanding, Kudera's novel unflinchingly exposes key paradoxes that lie disturbingly at the core of American academia today."

—Anthony Zielonka, French and comparative literature, Assumption College, Worcester, Mass.

"Wow ... Talk about bursting the myth of teaching as a noble profession. Mind-numbing bureaucracy, stifling political correctness, and subsistence-wage pay ... this should be required reading for anyone considering a career in academia."

—Iain Levison, a comic crime novelist whose published works include *A Working Stiff's Manifesto, How to Rob an Armored Car*, and *Dog Eats Dog*

"Like a subway-scholar Ignatius J. Reilly (*A Confederacy of Dunces*), adjunct instructor Cyrus Duffleman channels the rage of the academic underclass. The torments Duffleman suffers chasing across a light-rail and campus-common Philadelphia show an acute eye for all the absurdity and humiliation doled out over a long day of academic piece-work. Alex Kudera's novel makes lemonade out of the knowledge economy's stingy share of lemons, eking every ounce of catharsis owed to veterans of the core curriculum's front lines."

—Justin Bauer, books columnist, *Philadelphia City Paper*

"Are you teaching semi-literate pre-capitalists who will soon be earning more than you ever will? Are you lorded over by self-important, market-minded college administrators with Cadillac health plans and six-figure salaries while you wonder if you'll be assigned enough courses next semester to pay rent and utilities? Are you so fed up and desperate that you'll cling to any fantasy, even one that could get you fired? Do you feel forsaken, not just by academia, but by literature itself? Well, finally there's a novel for you! *Fight For Your Long Day* is an adjunct college teacher's version of *One Day in the Life of Ivan Denisovich*. Read it in your book club, give it to your pals, assign it to your gulag work crew, uh, I mean 'your class' ... "

—Eric Thurschwell, former adjunct instructor of college math, barely employed calculus tutor, and comic writer published in *Philadelphia Stories, Eclectica Magazine*, and other literary places

"Duffleman's misadventures will make you laugh out loud, shake your head in dismay, and nod in recognition on every page. I just might have to steal something from this book."
—Aharon Levy, fiction writer whose stories appear online and off in journals such as *The Sun* and *ecotone*

"*Fight for Your Long Day* presents simmering discord and strife through the eyes of Philadelphia denizen Cyrus Duffleman, a college professor who endures the bureaucracy of academia, and the irony of pervasive ignorance throughout higher 'education.' Kudera's sense of place perfectly evokes the city through sensory details. One can almost smell the cheesesteaks and hear the mumbled epithets whispered behind the scenes in the City of Brotherly Love."
—South Philly resident Andrew Breslin, author of *Mother's Milk*, available from ENC Press

"Kudera takes you behind the stately ivy-covered walls of the typical college campus and tells it like it unfortunately is for today's faculty and students."
—Linda B. Nilson, Ph.D., author of *Teaching at Its Best: A Research-Based Resource for College Instructors*, Clemson University

"The qualities that draw one's attention to Alex Kudera's prose are lucidity and [his] satirical vision. . . Kudera's particular talent is manifested in creating, rigorously . . . the American postmodern world in order to reveal its malfunctions and common places, verging on the grotesque and absurd."
—Daniel Dragomirescu, editor-in-chief of *Contemporary Literary Horizon* magazine, a multilingual and international literary journal based in Bucharest, Romania

Testimony of Adjuncts

"It's McUniversity where 'part-time' professors are paid like Wal-Mart clerks, teach ten courses across multiple campuses—and if that doesn't work, there's food stamps. Welcome to the world of Cyrus Duffleman. And he's invisible. It's like a 'diverse' society of so-called normal people where most of the labor is performed by lepers. The tenured can even look Duffy in the eye and act like he's perfectly fine."
—Joseph A. Domino, adjunct instructor, composition and literature, Boca Raton, Fla.

"[Higher] education is labor intensive. Like beer, or bread, or furniture, it has to be crafted. It can't be manufactured without a drastic decline in quality. To obtain the best result, exacting standards must be applied, according to long-standing and time-tested traditions for what counts as good education (or beer, or bread, or furniture) rather than calculations about market forces. . . [W]hat the adjunct system teaches us is that there's a conflict of interests between education as traditionally construed and the business model as it's currently understood."
—Peter Winston Fettner, multidisciplinary adjunct and philosophy graduate student, Baltimore, Md.

"The adjunct instructor is typically underpaid, overworked, and without insurance. Each semester, all the adjunct instructor does is help a university's students learn more. It doesn't seem like a fair trade."
—Isaac Sweeney, adjunct English faculty and freelance journalist published in the *The Chronicle of Higher Education* and http://www.insidehighered.com, Verona, Va.

Alex Kudera

Fight for Your Long Day

a novel

ATTICUS BOOKS

Kensington, Maryland

An Atticus Trade Paperback Original
Atticus Books LLC
3766 Howard Avenue, Suite 202
Kensington MD 20895

ISBN-13: 978-0-9845105-0-4
ISBN-10: 0-9845105-0-8

Cover design by Jamie Keenan

To the millions of adjunct instructors, contract workers, unpaid interns, migrant laborers, minimum wagers, indebted students, and all others preyed upon by the piece or the pound—desperate to survive, going without, and enduring the global charade

"Man was born free, and he is everywhere in chains.
One man thinks himself the master of others, but remains
more of a slave than they."
~ Jean Jacques Rousseau, *The Social Contract*, 1762

CHAPTER 1

SAFELY ENSCONCED ON THE HOME FRONT

Even on his long day, Cyrus Duffleman enjoys the fact that he can sip strong coffee and watch TV news before leaving his apartment five minutes past the opening bell of the New York Stock Exchange. The conga drummers living above his tiny studio own a satellite dish, so this is his free cable and time of the day. As he owns the most meager of holdings and no retirement plan, the green and red arrows of the futures markets are only a peripheral concern. What seems more of interest, and even shamefully soothing in its routine, are the news-crawler updates on soldiers, civilians, and "enemy combatants" who are maimed, killed, or otherwise blown apart in battle, while shopping, or by suicide bomb. The dry plains of this Middle-Eastern desert lie far, far away but indisputably dominate Duffleman's era and psyche. Over there, the bad news is always happening the night after or the previous day, the time zones never part of Cyrus's expertise.

Although he knows such analogies could be unpatriotic, tasteless, or even criminal, he sees himself as a foot soldier on the front lines of America's knowledge-based economy—the degree-granting, price-gouging four-year university. His war is not so much on terror, and only occasionally and tangentially on drugs; rather, the battleground lies in the classroom where the strong survive to reap their reward in the form

7

of middle- and upper-class lives and lifestyles while the weak perish into the poverty of high school diplomacy. For the cannon-fodder majority, the inability to pay educational loans is the only lasting sign of ever having attended college in the first place.

Each week, Duffy (mostly, but upon occasion, a potent Duff or unpredictable Duffler) guards the gate at four institutions, and on his long day, Thursday, he teaches or tutors at all of them. Backed only by commercial, catastrophic health coverage, he stands alert to all kinds of student complaints, parried blows, fits and elbows, verbal shots fired from the back rows, the baseball-capped white-boy section, where blank inscrutable faces stare back at his writing classes. Whether or not it is truly the age of information, or in fact, the age of terror, as his televised leaders claim, he is certainly a guardsman of the noble, hegemonic power of the time, a sentry at the door of the baccalaureate degree. His would-be warning to all who dare pass: "Read and write until you have piercing headaches and weighty paper or plastic bags under the eyes, a fat lump of gut precisely antithetical to the torsos of ancient Greece or Rome, and an education just slightly obsolete in this age of technologically enhanced cleavage and visual display."

But succumbing to the virtual moment—that wide world of in-text solicitation and file-attached aggression; websites informing of and advocating for all manner of breasts and bombs—he assigns no more than twenty pages per class. Duffy accepts his adjunct status and pay, choosing to ignore the fact that most college instructors earn less than sanitation engineers and public bus drivers, and significantly less than sales professionals and accountants, never mind the management types in pornography and terrorism. This information is easily accessed by his site-surfing students, and so, to the googling masses, he is the messenger worth ignoring, dismissing, blankly smiling at, flirting with, or worse if it would help the grade, and in his most paranoid vision, shooting. But by most legal interpretations, concealing weapons on campus remains beyond the pale, so he never wears his bullet-proof vest to the classroom, the souvenir his sister's husband purchased for him the holiday season following the twin-tower attacks. After all, some students are paid for—by parents, grandparents, merit- and need-based grants—and even for the majority, the huge loans loom so far in the distance that apathy as much as antagonism is the undergrad's response to his lectures and tedious essay assignments.

At times, the absurd sums noted on each semester's billing statement lead students to believe their teacher must be one of the wealthy reapers of financial rewards. After all, he is the "Professor," that middle-aged pale mass at the front of the room, even occasionally dressed entirely in corduroy. In the conservative-family scenario, he is seen as the exact same rich, liberal professor up at that state school the old man has imagined, growled about, and warned his kid against: "Just smile at all that bullshit. Act like you agree, grab your B, and fuck him in the ballot box 'cuz he and his tenured buddies don't know jack shit about the real world." But Duffy has pride, and so he rarely if ever discloses to a class of nineteen-year-old debtors his actual wages—a meager pittance that would make the overly loaned feel even worse. Instead, during his daily tour of duty, he ignores his personal squalor and his aching discs and arches, the remedying physical therapy several thousands out of reach.

Now at 9:28 a.m., Duffy succumbs to his couch, clean-shaven and a moment removed from his second toilet sitting, one less than his morning norm. He never dresses until the very last moment of morning calm but stays in worn gray boxer-briefs and a white undershirt, his back sunk deep into the middle of the couch, which is already malformed from this daily habit. With his calves propped up and resting flat atop a short breakfast barstool used alternately for food and his feet, he stares at the twenty-inch television screen.

Today, the tube projects an image of a slow-paced speaker, a man of short words and long pauses. "I'd like to introduce you to a man." Pause. "He was an able man." Pause. "Er." Pause. "He is a solid man." Pause. "He is a man who helped lead the war on terror." Has Duffy mistakenly changed the channel to a children's educational show? Is an adult reading to small children with some other matter on his mind? Back to televised reality, he hears, "And I will miss him." Alert again and out of his early-morning, absent-minded reverie, he recognizes that indeed he is breaking fast with the President of the United States of America, his articulations living proof that all of his messages to students about proficiency and expertise in reading and writing and speaking as the best path to the lofty perches in our sacred land are, well, er, um, perhaps just a bunch of bunk.

The national-news types bid all a fond farewell, the image of the President disappears, and commercials follow. Sincere actors and toll-free numbers attack and molest him. Duffy has no truck with incontinence pads or toilet-bowl cleaner but at this time of the day wishes their advocates would let him be. After the raised volume and carefree jingle of a supersized McBreakfast, the local news blasts its energizing beat. The reports on gun crimes and fires fought can flood his brain with adrenaline and nostalgia, and these two natural highs are usually enough to get him off the couch and out of the apartment.

"Good morning, Philadelphia. In the news at 9:30 a.m., graft at City Hall, dead deer in Fairmount Park, murder in North Philadelphia, a fire in Logan, but now for our top story, the Under Secretary of Homeland Defense is in town today to dedicate Liberty Tech's Institute for Homeland Security, the first structure built for their multibillion-dollar Graduate School of Defense Technology. Live at Liberty Tech, here's our very own Brenda Glontz. Brenda?"

Duffy stares at the black steel and glass structure surrounded by a concrete and cement campus that is his second school of the day.

"Good morning, Don. Here we are in front of the new Institute for Homeland Security, part of the new William Winsome School of Defense Technology, and I'm joined now by one of the benefactors who made this graduate program possible. Let me introduce Lawrence Neal O'Connor. Mr. O'Connor, many benefactors on college campuses name buildings after themselves. What made you decide to honor the fortieth President of the United States of America?"

"William Winsome was a great man. He ended the Cold War and brought peace and prosperity to the American people. He's a dying breed. We wanted to honor the man."

The announcer pauses, as if stunned by the direct praise of the dying breed, the dead President. Then, after a moment, Brenda Glontz turns to the camera, smiles, and says, "Don, back to you."

The benefactor, his news lady, and the black glass and steel architecture disappear from view, replaced by earnest Don, whose smile has turned to a slight but solemn frown.

"In other news, overnight, the animal killer of Fairmount Park has struck again. We go live to the scene of this latest gruesome tragedy. Earl."

A green woodsy area overwhelms the screen, and Duffy feels relieved that his cement future has for the moment disappeared. Replacing anchor Don is reporter Earl Watkins in a yellow rain poncho, with a background of animal-rights protestors shouting, "Hell no, we won't go!"

"There has been another gruesome discovery in the Fairmount Park section of Philadelphia. Two joggers, running together to protect themselves against the Fairmount Park serial rapist, came upon three dead deer lined up together in the middle of the jogging path. Each deer had been shot in the side by what looks to be the kind of arrow shot from a bow. Two were found dead, and the third one, tragically, died as veterinarians from the Park Outreach program were arranging transportation out of the Park to the Collegetown Animal Hospital. Now police are cordoning off the scene with yellow crime tape." The camera pans away from Earl to a few cops in the background who appear to be taping trees in slow motion, either milking the overtime pay or instructed to wait for the job to be caught on film. Then, back to Earl.

"As you can see behind me, this latest killing has brought people out to Fairmount Park today. Animal-rights activists are protesting what they feel is the police's failure to protect the wildlife of Fairmount Park. I have here with me now Julian Door, leader of a group called the People's Revolutionary Animal Protection Party. Julian, what does your group think about these horrible crimes?"

"Horrible crimes is right, sir. These are crimes against humanity here, sir. We demand immediate increases in police protection for our animal brethren making their home in Fairmount Park. The squirrels, the deer, the occasional possum, and raccoon—all deserve our protection. We wouldn't be here healthy today were it not for the ecosystem, and it is up to all of us to work together to ensure the survival of all species. Man can cause extinction, but man can also make the difference. We are planning a march on City Hall later today, 3 p.m., to let the mayor know we will not tolerate this kind of animal abuse in our city. We demand justice! We demand animal rights!"

The crowd in the background shouts and screams, following their leader. "We demand justice! We demand animal rights!" They wave their signs and hop up and down, dreadlocks aflame, making their point known. Duffleman, suffering from low caffeine levels and ten years of adjunct drudgery, is shocked to see people so full of energy so early in the morning. Door. Julian Door? The name lingers in his conscious state; it means something to him, but he can't place it this early in the morning. Perhaps this boy Julian was one of his former students? There were always a few of the protest ilk, particularly at Urban State— where, he notes, he is due to teach in thirty minutes.

Oh shit. 9:40, and now 9:41 a.m., according to the time and temperature on the blue background just above the stock-quote corner of the screen. To meet his Tuesday–Thursday schedule, he needs to be out the door at 9:35 sharp to arrive at his first class in a timely fashion. Now he is six minutes late.

Channel changer in hand, Duffy shoots dead his screen, springs from the couch, shot-guns his tall glass of tap water, and swallows the last half cup of lukewarm coffee, praying he receive not the shits while sampling public transportation. After throwing on a gray and worn-thin wool sweater and stepping into functional beige khakis, finally socks, shoes, and deodorant in case he forgot, he darts around his tiny two-room studio, searching for his umbrella, which he remembers he has been unable to find since the start of April. But he sees from his window that it's only drizzling, and he lowers each window to two inches so as to let in air but keep out any watery gusts during the day. He turns off the coffee pot, and checks to make sure the toaster oven is switched off. Then he glances down at the oven knobs as he presses firmly against the refrigerator door to test its airtight seal, steps back to the bathroom to make sure the toilet water isn't running but as he does so, in double-checking the coffee pot, he sees the milk is still out on the counter, and so he returns it to the refrigerator, rechecks the oven knobs with his left hand as he firmly presses the fridge again with his right, and then double-checks the radio despite its silence as he returns to the bathroom and finds all fixtures secure, and not a droplet of sound. He opens the tiny bathroom window as wide as it will go, admires the branch that has been growing off the plastic window sill—a tree seed and soil apparently found its way to the perfect humidity of a window by the shower—and then moves back to the bedroom to double-check the computer switch and the back window—where the terrorist or burglar would likely sneak in—and finally grabs his jacket and book bag, walks out of his apartment door, and locks it behind him. As he takes two steps down the stairs, he realizes he has forgotten his granola breakfast bar and peanut butter 'n cheese cracker snack, the two items he needs to save three dollars on snacks from the food carts around campus. So he fusses with his key, reenters the apartment, grabs the snacks, eyes the coffee pot one last time, lowers his hulking bag to the floor as he tosses on his jacket, lifts the bag, and then locks the door, hurrying down the steps before he can remember to check anything else.

Outside, where the drizzle has picked up to a steady, light rain, he gets wet and checks his watch. 9:44 a.m.

Duffy has no time for the calm ride of the slightly out-of-the-way suburban trains, so he rushes for the subway, pacing as briskly as possible without falling on his ass. His shoes are an investment; they are made of a synthetic material used for "walker" models, with good traction and better arch support. He fondly recalls paying twelve extra dollars to buy the pair with waterproofing. As he marches forward, head tilted down enough to avoid puddles but still see approaching pedestrians, his glasses catch the water. A constant drip from the upper rim of the frame plops down just below each eye.

At a quarter to ten, not many are out walking, not in this rain, most having already made it to work, and not yet prepared to venture outside for their morning smoke. In the underpass below the trains, Duffy indulges in thirty yards of dry. As he returns to getting wet, to his left, he passes the Drew building, where they award generous stipends for fiction, poetry, and plays. His terminal degree states that he has a "Masters" in the so-called "Fine Art" of creative writing, and he applied years ago, long before the seven deadly sins of literary blockage—daily drudgery, anxiety, low self-esteem, depression, lack of talent and ambition, and above all, laziness—stole away any chance he had of concentrating for long enough to produce anything even loosely resembling a work of art, or tight and tidy enough to be considered that marketable commodity, "the contemporary novel." Even in his overworked state, he still remembers to brood and mutter bitterly each time photos of smiling prize winners are published; from Duffy's perspective, there seems to be something politically correct, connected, or insubstantial about every finalist. Who has ever heard of writers smiling so widely? These winners could not be writers worth reading. Awash in envy, he sees it all as one steamy lump, a movement of the ordinary produced by the educated but scared; the winners' writing takes less risk than a political front runner in a national election. He could admit that it shows far superior craftsmanship than his endless comments on student essays, all he could claim as his own *oeuvre*. Such self-crunching honesty doesn't make him feel any better, and so, with no time to stare at the imposing gray marble, Duffy trudges on.

Just as he briskly approaches and then dexterously stops at the red light at the corner of 21st and Market, a huge SEPTA bus headed west on Market plows past, drenching him from his knees to his shoulders with a shockwave of rainwater. Gathering his wits, he feels grateful this bonus soaking doesn't come with muddy sprinkles on top. When he crosses, looking both ways, Duffy bravely fingers the bus already a block away. Past the firehouse and the adult book center and peep shows—whose bright red neon distracts him for only the briefest of seconds—he begins the steep descent to the 22nd and Market eastbound subway-surface platform, hoping, as he does so, that he encounters only sane people below. Although the new gourmet market has brought the middle class—yuppies, buppies, two-earner families, and trust-fund slackers—back to this station, particularly after work, Duffy remains cautious. Interaction with the half clad, salivating, mentally ill, or emotionally disturbed is more than he can handle, particularly at such an early hour. That each day includes an inordinate amount of interaction with himself makes life troubling enough.

After a slow, careful, one-step-at-a-time descent of the deep cement stairwell, his glasses fog up entirely with the temperature change. A trolley's distant squeal transforms to a roar and culminates in a screeching halt; in his haste to progress, he at first shoves and nearly pushes down an elderly woman he cannot see, but then holds her up until he can steady them both. A moment for a deep breath and then he makes sure that she boards safely ahead of his oafishness, all the while apologizing profusely and at last stepping up and into the crowded car. With a tissue from his jacket, he clears his glasses to see the huge driver staring at him menacingly because he witnessed the entire episode. He absorbs the driver's glare as acknowledgement that he is the worst kind of middle-aged white man in control of the universe—the kind who would run down an old lady in pursuit of daily bread, and no doubt take more than his share.

So Duffy returns the look with sad eyes expressing the guilt of millions, perhaps his paternal grandfather's buried bones in the mix. At most 37.5 percent Jewish—and rarely feeling like much more of a man than that—nevertheless, culpability for this crime against humanity, this near toppling of a senior citizen, washes across his brow. For a moment, he imagines he knows what it is like to be black. Or even poor. He then recalls that by data gleaned from several surveys he tilts toward poverty or at least a lower quintile, so he shakes his head vigorously as if such brisk exertion could shake out such race- or class-based understanding of the world. He then slides his monthly pass through the slot and turns to meet his fellow passengers.

Posture-poor and folded into most of their seats, overweight brown and black Philadelphians abound, the drab colors of rain jackets and sad or expressionless eyes presciently complementing the rainy day. But there are also careerist, high-thread-count African Americans and others standing near the front, most of them appearing more erect and fit than the slouching writing instructor. He pushes past a few thin Asian girls he often sees in Center City, of varying economic classes and regions of origin—South or East or Southeastern; Pennsylvania, New Jersey, or Asia—most fully hyphenated and a few of ambiguous first language or visa status, but all in tight blue jeans or professional attire. As a people, they appear to have lives and diets; they do not cluster together, and so an attitude of individualism appears alive underneath their name brands. He pauses to marvel at these tender morsels of accessible flesh—packaged tightly in designer wrap—and for a moment feels privileged to bear witness to the Freedom of the West.

But to Duffy, alas, such fruit is forbidden, and with his throat dry and stomach rumbling, he damns himself thrice over—first for seeing so much ethnic difference; second for being such a filthy old man; and third for daring to desire the prohibited in a way that could get him tortured or maimed by radical fundamentalists. He squeezes through the packed-in passengers to find himself wedged between an enormous black woman and a middle-aged hippie. The latter is ostensibly a white male without a harem or wife or clutter of exes, the poorer kind, perhaps laid off, disabled, idled, or otherwise ignored on the employment rolls. Duffy senses that he sees one not unlike himself. Despite this shared life experience, when his nose gets stuck in the hippie's long locks, he feels disgusted and angry. He can smell the pungency of unwashed dreads. Days, months, even a decade would be possible, and overpowered by this evil wafting, he can barely appreciate or even feel the shock of terror over the arousal he feels from the huge woman's bosom thrust forward and flopping down into the small of his back. Forced to stare downward, Duffy cannot ignore the bald fact that the hippie rides without shoes, sandals, or any other footwear to protect his tan and yellowish heels and toes from the God-knows-what of public transportation.

At 19th Street, a few depart, or pop out as the doors open, and Duffy feels himself rearranged like one of the candies in a gumball machine. He winds up briefly on a tight-jeaned lap—Vietnamese or perhaps Laotian—who with long nails pinches his neck, the sharp pain succeeding in driving him off and vertical again, this time his face six inches from the hippie's beard. In the beard, he sees every manner of refuse from the ages, the red of tomato-sauce stains, a fleck of silver, protest posters from decades ago, all in thick-knitted tufts of light brown and gray. When he moves his eyes up and away, the hippie smiles directly at him. Is it a knowing look? Congenial? Conspiratorial? Lewd?

Duffy isn't sure but doesn't have time to find out, as the trolley lurches to a halt at 15th Street. He is among the last to pile out, just behind a purple-dreadlocked crusty punk whose perfect cleavage under army camouflage reads "college is a scar" until the last half letter renders visible the fact it was a "scam" all along. Into the dirty, dark cavernous central pulse of public transport, he is but another cow in the common herd. Nevertheless, as an individual, he is cautious and nimble in foot placement, seeking to avoid water puddles and the multitudes of gum droppings both fresh and aged. Good soldier and obedient commuter, he follows the others up the filthy, blackened cement steps and around the bend—two ninety-degree rights—toward the Orange Line, the North-South Broad Street Line.

As he descends onto the Market Street Elevated Line's underground Center City platform, he sees a huge pinkish pale cop holding the leash of a seated German Shepherd. The dog has soft, innocent eyes—antithetical to his master's reputation as a mean-spirited boy in blue. They are there to protect America from violence—both imported and domestic—but no Americans stand anywhere close to their defenders. As he walks past the dog and cop, Duffy glances at the various commuters striking their poses at ten in the morning. One is seated with a cup of coffee, another stands peering at a folded newspaper. A pitch-black obese man in a brown-cloth Kanga hat stares back, reminding him it's safer to stare at the ground. No one likes being stared at, particularly not in the subway, particularly not by a sad, sallow stranger. Eyes to the ground and plodding forward, Duffy is nagged by a severe urge to pee.

To fight the bladder that be, he picks up his pace—he is, after all, on the verge of arriving more than the permissible five minutes late—and marches on. The corridor narrows everyone to single file, commuters trudging one behind the other, weary, sluggish soldiers who cannot keep the beat. Pungent smells of stale coffee, perspiration, cheap perfume, and old urine compete for notice in the corridor. And then worse, ominous scents hit him, like the shit is about to go down, so strong in his nostrils that Duffy's ecstasy knows no bounds when the corridor widens once more, and an almost jovial newspaper hawker shouts out, "Deer lynched in the park, American troops dead again, read all about it, two papers for a dollar." Somehow, the Philadelphia newspaper salesmen have been selling two papers to the same customer. For a dollar you could get two copies of the *Daily News* at a savings of twenty cents total, an *Inquirer* and a *Daily News* at a savings of ten cents total, or two *Inquirers* at no savings at all. Although he has read that math is an obsolete language—public-school children handed calculators instead of Cuisenaire rods—and that the *Daily News* is said to be written on the third-grade level, and the Inky only the fifth, he has trouble fathoming who would be buying into such a scam. In the age of the Internet, who would be reading both newspapers, or requiring a copy of the exact same thing? Nonetheless, as he passes the vendor, a lady says, "Two *Daily News* sir," and he sees her handing the man a crumpled bill.

Duffy weaves around another beefy cop—this one *sans* Shepherd and more menacing to account for this lack—and turns down a narrow flight of stairs, with unwashed white tiles for walls, revealing a permanent rainbow of underground grime. Graffiti gets professionally washed away but some dirt and water stains last forever.

On the subway platform, he passes a blank-faced wall of black teenagers, none of whom look old enough to be out of school at this hour. Maybe in another time, another community, a caring adult would talk to the boys, find out if they're late or lost, warn them against truancy, and perhaps even offer them cab fare, a SEPTA token, assistance in getting to school or calling a parent. But these days, today, the "student" could have a temper or carry a knife or gun, or even an acutely contagious STD according to televised news. So he leaves such inquiry to the cops, who are presently occupied striking their own pose in the war on terror. He paces past, and finds a small gap on a metal bench between two students with eyes stuck in their books. In the mornings, these studious ones cramming in the subway give Duffy a bit of hope for the future. Sometimes he sees one with a novel, deeply engrossed in its contents, possibly even unassigned reading for pleasure. Now, on the cramped bench, he is forced to look straight ahead, in this case at a large yellow sign depicting people in jeans and sneakers with cardboard boxes shoved over their heads. "Labels are for packages," the large lettering reads. Duffy, so fagged, doesn't get it. His early-morning hunger pangs for something easier to understand. He glances left to see supersized ads for bright red burgers and fries and then right, yet more ads for treating anxiety and depression. "If you or anyone you know is suffering . . . "

Then the roar approaches, the train doors open, the masses depart, and those like Duffy, headed to North Philadelphia, surge into each car and fill up the seats. Through the opposite window, he sees the yellow sign's smaller print: "Embrace difference. Embrace America." He looks around desperately for dissimilar citizenry whom he could hug or even offer the seat he is about to sit in; he aims for nonwhite but is willing to settle for female, older, younger, or overtly happy. Establishing no eye contact, on second thought he concludes that an act of goodwill would only draw more attention to difference. For packages, right? So he plops down, relieved that only a few students are left standing. Five local stops later, along with most other passengers, Duffy files out and through the turnstiles of the Cecil B. Moore station. As he passes through, he checks the clock behind the SEPTA ticket salesman. It is 10:10 a.m., which would not be so bad if his class were not a five-minute walk from the station. He stumbles up the crowded steps and then picks up the pace, fast-walking as best he can, feeling the familiar ache in the left hamstring, his would-be jumping leg if Duffy could defy gravity just one little bit.

On the first floor of Barron Hall, he rushes into the men's room to find both urinals busy, one with a student rep for the videogame-obesity generation, and the other with the sort of old fossil who'll just lean against the porcelain and let her drizzle for days—a scary reminder of what the latter years could be like. Duffy finds a stall vacant save for a boat-sized bowel movement left floating for the next fellow to see. Disgusted and suppressing the simultaneous urges to howl and heave, he pisses straight down, like a marksman gunning for old brown sides rusting in the harbor. He forgets to flush, exits the stall, and breathes again. At the sink, he turns the hot water on full blast, feeling dirty and thus especially disappointed when all he gets is a lukewarm trickle. The soap dispenser fails to produce the pink ooze he can see in its packet, so he lets his hands soak under the faucet, admiring all the more his ideal form of government, the democracy in action of Urban State University. After shaking and rubbing his hands under the warm, faint breath of the sanitization system, Duffy returns to the stairs and ascends to meet his fate.

CHAPTER 2

AN URBAN STATE OF MIND

Striding in with his head down, Duffleman removes his soaked outer garment—in theory waterproof and in practice a charcoal-gray synthetic jacket. He hurls his hulking, roach-brown book bag from his right shoulder onto the faux-wood surface of the old, metal-legged desk. The bag sits there, motionless, straps up and zippers down, not unlike a fat, frozen bug just stunned by a swatter. For a moment, he stares warily at the bag as if expecting its tiny legs, or zippers, to move on their own accord.

After extracting materials essential to this Urban State experience, he inhales, exhales, and turns to face the firing squad, his first audience of the day. Establishing eye contact, he tries to force a grin onto his tired face. Some students fidget, and some frown at him for his lateness. Still others smile, most likely not because they like him but because they learned to do this long ago—or recently, say in this class—to create a favorable impression so as to influence the authority and improve the grade. Influence enemies is how some of his colleagues see it, but Duffy remains ever hopeful the students are intent on winning him as a friend.

Although his transcript states that his doctoral coursework is in Comparative Literature, the class is called Business Writing. Most of the available adjunct work is in precollege and freshman composition, or classes with titles such as Technical Writing, Business Communications or Writing for the Corporate World. Unlike so much of today's English department, this latter group includes neither a radical worldview nor a political agenda. Rather, these courses teach clarity, focus, and agreement; that is, agreement with the boss, customer, colleague, and any other affable capitalist who could conceivably cross one's path to corporate enlightenment. They are classes designed to meet the needs of a college population intent on achieving material security without any heavy lifting or personal ownership. The will to keep dry, more than to snag power, dominates the contemporary college scene.

The career goal pervading all of Duffy's campuses is to gain entry to the professional class, to represent in words, images, or numbers any tangible good or intangible service—for example, a synthetic leather basketball—or perhaps as a professional to aid in the healing of some such adult consumer after having enjoyed the basketball to the point of physical injury, perhaps a sore back or busted groin, or maybe to write or sell or account for a policy insuring against such catastrophe with synthetic leather, or, for the acutely ambitious, even perhaps to represent said victim in a court of law, entrusted to sway the sampling of the masses known as a jury toward the decency of the injured client and the legitimacy of the complaint; but above all, the goal is to not spend one's post-baccalaureate adulthood up to ten hours a day and six days a week, for seven dollars an hour behind the counter ringing up the synthetic leather basketball for some eager, preadolescent consumer. Sewing the ball together is the only fate worse. The third-world factory—whether in Gary, Indiana or Jakarta, Indonesia—is decidedly for suckers. Even downtrodden Duffy knows teaching as an adjunct is better than working at a factory. Even his students perceive this is so.

To be fair, compared to his other places of employment, Urban State students appear less receptive to this college as capitalist-in-training model; in fact, many can and will argue stridently against the global movement of plastic and all of its debt and conveniences. In the concrete folds of North Philadelphia, an egalitarian tradition perseveres, and so the tenured types could wear their radical hearts on their sleeves—beige or brown, elbow patch and corduroy—without causing too much of a stir.

A small portion of the students even arrive on campus gift-wrapped at the Financial Aid office from the marginalized neighborhoods and do-not-drive zones the professors seek to restore or avoid. But with total costs for state residents last seen sprinting past 30,000 American dollars per year, most of the students come from enough affluence to express sympathy but not identity with the subjugated, and Duffy doubts that he is precisely perceived as part of that caste. The students paying their own way—the overworked, tired, and tapped out—drive aged automobiles from distant, lower-tier, pale if not sickly suburbs and appear more worn down than their teacher. He imagines they search for free parking on the campus periphery, city blocks occupied entirely by underrepresented real estate and abandoned black people.

This morning Duffy draws a triangle on the board, draws four parallel and equidistant horizontal lines through it, and so produces the pyramid of Maslow's Hierarchy of Needs. He writes from the bottom to the top— one section at a time—"Survival" and then "Safety and Security" and then "Social/Group/Belonging" and then "Self Esteem" and finally "Self Actualization." He doubts very much they will explore and achieve this highest-level need by the end of class, but he is conscientious enough to include it in the lesson.

Post-chalk, Duffy turns to face his heterogeneous students, clothing and skin of dappled hues. With so many consuming twenty credits while working thirty hours per week, most appear exhausted with one far-column soldier fast asleep by the window. Still, a few seem awake, perky even, alert, and ready to go. For the first time in his long day, he speaks.

"So, ladies and gentlemen, on the board is Maslow's Hierarchy of Needs." Duffy offers a brief explanation of each need, trying to explain with examples for all five. For self-actualization, he describes running marathons, painting pictures, doing things not for money but for personal exploration and fulfillment. He forgets to include slapping down plastic to pay for textbooks while carrying a full load of classes or enduring a long day as an adjunct instructor at four urban campuses.

"Now let's explore the needs we meet when we go to the voting booth. In America, are we voting to satisfy survival needs? Safety needs? Belonging?"

"What if we don't vote?" As usual, the Afrocentrist in the middle left side of the room responds first. She often gets her two cents in before Duffy has even said anything. Occasionally, she'll send a shout out as he walks in the door, before class has begun.

"Well," and then he pauses; he can't quite believe this outspoken woman is not a voter. Her agenda sways between slapstick and Afrocentrism; although the former seems faithful to its heritage, derived from centuries of ethnic-minority, stand-up comedy, the latter appears notably similar to European socialism or communism. Regardless of its origins, it stinks of ideology.

"Okay. Pretend that you do vote. Or pretend that if you were to have interest in voting, you'd have needs that would drive your decision behind the curtain."

"You ain't wanna hear what these folks doing behind the curtain!" The Afrocentrist shrieks after her booming witticism, her "funny." Duffy hears whispers of disapproval from the class's polite, tight-jeaned, well-manicured, and preprofessional African American women. This group has come to his aid before; they seem destined to function within the system, to work effectively if underneath some better compensated lighter-skinned person in long-lasting, stable careers. They earn their A grades and seem in possession of an optimism and bright future that has eluded their instructor.

"Surely some of the other students in class are serious about what happens in the voting booth."

"You can't get sex out the voting topic. Ain't been someone to vote for since they lynched Slick Willy for getting his lyin' lips caught in Monica's oval office!"

The Afrocentrist and her immediate posse—young men mostly, who surround her periphery like a not-so-secret service—burst out laughing, and then the chuckles, grimaces, and guffaws spread slowly in ripples until they blanket the entire room. Baseball-capped white boys awaken from morning reveries of inaccessible supermodels to contribute loud laughs, and even the appropriate A-earning girls join reluctantly but soon cackle and moan, with one caught in a loud and irregular honking noise.

Duffy enjoys the Afrocentrist's wit too. He considers her an ally in her good moods and a terror in her bad ones. The Afrocentrism itself may be doctrinaire and stifling, but he is grateful for her presence and her help in getting other students to pay attention. Now he is curious.

"Just by a show of hands, and please don't tell me for whom, how many of you have cast a ballot in at least one election? I mean, how many of you have voted in your lifetime?"

The laughs have simmered down, reduced to the occasional hiccup and giggle, but only three hands are raised, including the Afrocentrist's, which makes sense because she is most likely ten years older than the others. (With her vast flab she out-dufflebags the Duffler himself; he suspects she outweighs him by at least eighty pounds.) Oddly, the silent, motionless girl—sitting with excellent posture and staring straight ahead—has her hand raised, as does the goody-two-shoes in the front, the leader of the preprofessional black women's caucus. This one can raise her hand without altering any other aspect of her facial expression or body—34B-25-36 and with enough understated makeup for a face that should do for corporate America. Duffy remembers the time she combined slight scorn with a sly smile when she caught him adrift too long in her stacks.

"Come on, now. I know more of you vote."

As if in pain, a bunch of hands ascend to crooked-elbow, partial extension, perhaps a baker's dozen or so. Duffy completes a quick, silent count and estimates that more than half the class has voted. Not bad at all, he says to himself, remembering full well that he has taught other classes where but one in five are voters, and of course some freshman sections where even after November only a single student has voted.

"Good, good. We have an aware citizenry in the classroom. Now let's use the same brain power that gets us voting to evaluate why we vote in terms of Maslow. Work in groups of two or three for five minutes."

To his pleasant surprise, nearly all of the students engage a partner or two, and begin the task at hand—the most beneficent of teaching tools, the small-group discussion. Only a few of the nonverbal baseball caps sit staring ahead, not finding the topic relevant or interesting enough to stimulate a ninety-degree turn to the right or left, and then engage in conversation. Duffy would like to think of them as the strong silent types, but realizes it is a major weakness in their résumé dossier if they genuinely have nothing to say.

Seated, he scans his roll book. He has given back half a dozen short assignments already, and knows all of their names. They are, for the most part, present.

A wee bit later, uncertain he has given them a full five minutes, but to prevent himself from putting his head down flat on the desk, he closes ranks. "Okay, let's bring it in. In what ways does voting meet our survival needs?"

"Gotta vote so those muthas don't take away our food, air, water, and shelter. They's folks out there today who ain't got them basic needs met." The Afrocentrist has an ability to speak grammatically correct English but parades her passion for Ebonics. She comes correct, easily employing even pre-MTV slang to express her authenticity.

The A-earners of the Af-Am women's caucus murmur in agreement, and even the baseball caps out in white-boy land keep from smirking. These five or six in the back represent the new, improved class size, innocent tuitions sacrificed to ensure that the Cadillac health coverage of Urban State's various top administrators, tenured professors, and union types would remain in place even as the adjunct instructor—in this case, Duffleman—sinks under the weight of more grading. All the same, he is happy to note that at least for this section, this morning, as a group, the students refuse to denigrate the indigent, the dirt poor, or the homeless.

In a good mood now, he determines to encourage participation. He'll call on the first silent ball cap who establishes any eye contact whatsoever.

"Dave?"

"Yeah." Not much, but a start.

"Which needs do you focus on when you vote?"

A long pause. "Well, I'd say all of them really."

"Can you elaborate?"

"Isn't it obvious?"

"Could you explain why it's obvious?"

"Everyone wants all those things you were talking about. When they vote they think of which guy is going to help them get the most." The boy crosses his arms over his chest, squeezing his fists into their opposing armpits in triumph. He stares defiantly at Duffleman, who stares back, meeting the boy's confidence in motivated self-interest with a silent, pensive look while self-flagellating for not feeling more grateful for the two complete sentences.

And so he averts his eyes and scans the room for a second contestant. "Phil, what do you think?" Another baseball cap. And he doesn't think much.

"Bill, what's on your mind?" Nothing. Three strikes and you're out, Duffy.

With nowhere else to turn, he backpedals around and behind the desk, and from his book bag produces his trump card. A bit early in the class to unveil the ace of spades, but Duffy is on an all-out mission to encourage inspired student discussion, particularly from ones who rarely if ever speak in class. Forget the baseball caps, there must be others out there yearning to try in-class participation, fifteen percent of their grade.

What Duffy delivers is a caricature of President Fern, sent to him as an advertisement from a left-of-center political magazine. He can sometimes light the lamp by regressing to their first language—that of pictures, not words—and so he holds the face high and walks laterally across the room, pausing so each column of students can get a close look. The sideways stumble and stride, while sputtering from either side of his mouth, has become one of his specialties over the years.

"So, class. What do you see? Take a close look. Take a few notes. Look for as much detail as possible."

As Duffy waddles across the room, the various states of Urban students squint and squirm to look at the picture.

The Afrocentrist shouts out, "It's the President shoved in a 'big ol' cowboy hat so you just see his racist smirk!"

"Yes, very good. What else do you notice about his face?" Positive reinforcement gives him a chance he'll hear from more than the extroverted.

"He's smiling," adds a sincere-sounding fat boy close to the front.

"The cowboy hat is covering his eyes," just-the-facts another girl.

"That boy can't see shit and he's happy. He flyin' blind!" The Afrocentrist folds her arms over menacing cleavage and raises her head high with a satisfied look.

The class is silent, as if genuinely considering the blindness of the President of the United States of America and how it relates to their present circumstances, their teeter-totter existence of student debt and middling grades at a middle-tier, four-year university. Duffy suspects that in fact half the class is spacing out, pleasantly staring ahead but not taking in much of this charade. They're thinking ahead to weekend plans—alcohol and sex if they're lucky—or math exams like "College Algebra" that desperately need to be passed before graduation, or perhaps merely which three-dollar, food-truck lunch—yes, possibly just cigarettes and a diet coke—will satisfy their midday cravings. The essential wants come first; consideration of the political situation can wait. Maslow indeed. Duffy sighs aloud.

Breaking the moment, out of the void—the hallway, that is—a bright-colored whirl blazes into the classroom. This late arrival in dreadlocks stretches his arms wide as if rushing into announce the arrival of enemy combatants upon Urban State cement. Before Duffy can note that his bright orange and yellow striped rain parka looks a tad familiar, the intruder explodes: "That motherfucker is decimating the planet!" He grabs the ad by lunging at his teacher who slides away, wrenching his lower back in the process, longingly imagining the yoga and stretch routines he failed to perform a few hours earlier. The Rastafarian rain dancer's face turns from bright pink to beet red. He stares down the political advertisement. "I hate that motherfucker. I hate that man!" He begins ripping the page to shreds.

"Word up, white boy!" The Afrocentrist, in ecstasy, enjoys the show, shaking her groove thing just a bit, rocking her chair just slightly to and fro.

"This motherfucker deserves to die in pain!" The dreadlocked boy reaches behind his rain poncho, and produces a sky-blue American Spirits cigarette lighter. He scampers to the corner, and over the rusted brown trash can, starts burning the caricature of Fern in effigy.

"Let's burn this motherfucker down!" adds the Afrocentrist on back-up vocals. She picks up her rocking rhythm. "Man, this wanna-farian got it right. The prezatarian deserve to go down, sendin' Americans off to another Vietnam 'n shit."

The dreadlocked boy stares up at the Afrocentrist with an extremely serious look. As solemn as Moses, he commands, "Sister, there is work to be done."

The Afrocentrist shrieks and bursts out laughing. "Okay, homey, you my white homeboy now!"

"The men he sends off to war will never be the same. Thousands dead, thousands physically wounded. And their emotional lives? And what kind of environment are they coming home to? One polluted by the irresponsible waste of monolithic corporations, cleaned up, if ever, on the taxpayer's dime?"

"Word to Massa Rasta!" The Afrocentrist ceases her rocking, settling the chair back to earth.

Duffy has more or less been cowering, unnoticed, in the front corner furthest from the trash can. By his own admission, not the most professional pose, but with no binding contract or health benefits, his safety and security come first. The dreadlocked boy burns one strip at a time, and Duffy can see there is no real harm to anyone's person here. Indeed, he sympathizes with and even admires the radical gut of this student. He remembers similar feelings from his college days, an impulse to improve the conditions under which the common man suffered, although he was more likely to snuggle up to Rousseau or Marx in the library than to burn the President's smug mug in public. And although now he lives paycheck to paycheck, feeling oneness with the masses in the check-cashing line every other Friday, thoughts of philosophy remind him of the main way in which he fails to connect with his students. Where he is theory, they are practice. He contemplates. They do. Even as a senior in his undergraduate days, Duffy could only dream of petting the soft locks of a kind, gentle coed, and now he comes to work five mornings a week, imagining full well his students have even been fucking on weekday nights.

Feeling safe, he plays off dreadlocks to see if he can regain the attention of his charges. "Julian makes some good points." Even as he says the boy's name aloud, he realizes this is in fact the famous Julian Door. The outspoken radical boy in his Business Writing class is also the protestor interviewed on the local newscast earlier in the morning, back when Duffy was but a lump of flab frozen to his couch. "It was kind enough for him to join us after a long morning protesting for animal rights in the rain, all the way over in Fairmount Park. Now let us take his present inquiry further. What will the damage be to our returning soldiers? Can you put it in terms of Maslow's Hierarchy of Needs?" He moves his left arm back to the triangle on the board, hoping to reconnect the classroom discussion to his lesson of the day.

"If you're dead, you can't satisfy any needs." This comes from a deadpan baseball cap in the middle of the room. Again, like tiny waves, giggles and grins spread from the center of the room to the periphery. Only the silent, motionless girl, third row from the front and second column in, sits straight up in her chair, as if she were being hypnotized by Julian Door and his firefight directly in front of her.

The Afrocentrist hoots, "I heard that." Even as they emit a chuckle or two, a few students try to suppress their remaining laughs in respect for the dead.

Julian Door, now finished burning Fern, stares at the middle of the room in distrust, unsure of the intentions behind the dry wit—is it gallows humor or a malicious slam at the poor and disenfranchised who fight on the battlefield? When the student recognizes that he has been standing in front of the group since entering the room, he looks guiltily at his audience and then slides into the front-row seat two chairs in front of the motionless girl. The radical leader's smooth transition to cooperative undergrad surprises Duffy, but Door proves equally adept at orating from a seated position:

"It is true many will die. Too many. But the ones who return alive may have it even worse. They'll be too traumatized to achieve even their basic survival needs."

The students nod and murmur. Duffy experiences the decency of the group.

Julian continues with confidence: "Did you know that at one point in time, half the homeless in America's cities were veterans of war, mostly Vietnam?"

The murmurs and nods grow more fervent.

"Amen," adds the Afrocentrist, but softly this time, respectful of the class's new mood of reverence.

But a baseball cap rebuts: "Oh come on. We're not fighting the Vietnam War." Despite the daily media blast of the Middle East's chronic bad news, the true patriots—most likely numbered among the few Republicans on campus—police the class discussion to make sure that students don't compare the jungles of 'Nam to the deserts of the Middle East. Different terrain entirely, and Fern and Rysenschat are not Nixon and Kissinger, and let's not forget that Kennedy and Johnson led us into Vietnam. In fact, it was Clinton who failed to protect our territorial integrity, our daughters and borders. To an extent, Duffy appreciates the fact that these conservatives know some of their history, although it is unclear if this contrarian view at Urban State was not merely a partisan perspective force-fed in some faraway suburban dinner table or small-town civics or history class.

"Did I say we were fighting the Vietnam War?"

"Amen," adds the Afrocentrist. "Word up. Well, did he?"

"Your type always says you aren't comparing it to Vietnam, and then you turn it around and compare it to Vietnam!" The baseball cap looks angry. Your type. Liberals? Radicals? Bolsheviks? Fags? Duffy's type too? He can't help but feel indicted by the baseball cap's wrath.

"Well, what d'you think happens to returning soldiers? Does Uncle Sam give a shit about their mental problems?" Julian fights back.

"That is so exaggerated. That's what *youse* always do in this argument. My Uncle Sam, my real uncle who lives down the shore, came home and was just fine. He went into real estate in the late seventies and now he's a wealthy man. The war didn't destroy him. If anything it made him stronger." Herr Duffleman cringes at the misuse of Nietzsche although he has heard Shaquille O'Neal abuse the full aphorism on national TV.

"With redlining, black Vietnam vets couldn't start no business back then. How they gonna do it today if one in two black men between sixteen and sixty-four can't find no job? Folks even afraid to hire vets 'cause they think they all crazy! That's the city-ation I'm comin' from." The Afrocentrist folds her fat forearms over her breasts and frowns. Her stats cause Duffy to consider all the blank, sad, or angry faces he experienced during his morning commute. The black men, aged sixteen to sixty-four. *There but before the grace of God goes Duffleman.*

"That's exactly it," adds Julian. "Your uncle probably had family to support him and fall back on. He came home and he wasn't alone. I bet he got family money to start the business."

The baseball cap turns a shade redder than his spring farmer's tan, the latter interpreted as a sign he has been to the Jersey shore in early April. Perhaps he is just another poster child for *the* vacation spot for Philadelphia-area white privilege and tradition. But not wanting to give up on the all-American rags-to-riches version of the land of possibility—yes, the American Dream—Door's opponent switches relatives and leaps back one generation. "When my grandpa came home from World War II, no one was there with a handout. He worked his ass off at three jobs until he saved enough to start his own bar. He didn't come back from the war bitchin' and moanin' about lack of opportunity."

"White boy, what you tryin' to say?" The Afrocentrist looks enraged. She turns to her left to stare down the baseball cap whose face affirms willful belief in his own devil's advocacy.

"Yeah, what the fuck? Are you trying to say soldiers returning home aren't sacrificing for our country?" Julian inches out of his chair, as if he might walk over to the once white but now beet-red patriot in the blue baseball cap.

Duffy appreciates Julian's and the Afrocentrist's version of American reality, and yet he cannot help but feel touched by the baseball cap's tales of family overcoming the odds to achieve the dream; for a brief moment, he gets lost in nostalgia, the primal longing for the poor immigrant as marginalized European in the land of plenty. His imagination extends not far from his own ancestors: sixteen-hour days at the Triangle Shirt Factory or eighteen-hour shifts churning slop into sausages in Chicago meat-packing plants. And then he switches back to sympathy for the plight of the Afrocentrist's people—as a twenty-first century Philadelphian, in some odd sense, these were more Duffy's people too. His fluttering mind rests at the understanding that these conflicting sympathies and concerns are essential to his own predicament.

"It's better to be a soldier who fights in a war!" These loud piercing words hang in the air, hovering over the room for all to hear. Everyone sits still. As the group digests the thought, the chorus begins to shake their heads and voice dissent. Duffy scans the room; he has an odd hunch, but he wants to be sure.

"If you go to war, you come back and get treated like a hero unless you die. Soldiers get treated better than deserters and hippies, the people who vote for peace. It's better to be a soldier." The motionless girl has spoken.

The chorus of dissent grows to a steady humming sound. *That ain't right, girl. What's her problem? Why'd she open her mouth anyway?* Few in the classroom agree that it is better to be a soldier stuck in a jungle or desert facing an enemy he might not see, never mind experience any personal animosity toward, or even understand at all.

Duffy does an unusual thing. Not wanting to silence forever the motionless girl, he does what he tries to do with many student comments. He co-opts them, alters their ingredients, and rearranges the tone and meaning; he aims for something thoughtful, useful, perhaps even good, or at least not unabashedly malignant. This time, in doing so, he even remembers her name.

"Thank you for participating, Eileen. I believe what the young lady is trying to say is that in some wars, returning veterans are treated with great respect and decency. I don't believe we have to see this as 'these people were treated better than those people'; however, it is true today that we have seen great fanfare in small towns and cities across America where young people fighting in the Middle East have made it home safely. And perhaps this is as it should be. One problematic aspect of the peace movement during the Vietnam period is that hippies and peaceniks—allegedly—would greet returning soldiers at airports with boos and hisses. And although many journalists and historians refute that these events occurred, it is said they would release some of their anger over the Nixon administration's policies on the returning soldiers themselves."

He can hedge with the best of them, but it is all the blue ball cap needs.

"Yeah, that's what I'm talking about," two-cents the blue boy. "They're all traitors."

Now the Afrocentrist has had enough. She shifts her large body causing her desk chair to waddle. But she is willing to risk her balance to extend her left hand to the point where she can quickly grab the bill of blue's ball cap and slam it down over his face. He screams in astonishment. Then fear. Then pain. She is falling face-first toward the boy but is unwilling to compromise and let go. As she extends toward him, falling out of her desk chair, she grabs his right shoulder for support.

"Damn, black bitch," he shouts out in pain. "That's my throwing arm."

Duffy suspects it's used more for tossing than throwing but immediately rises to the task: "There will be no language like that in this class!"

The Afrocentrist scoffs as she topples to the floor, at the last minute loosening her mighty mitts from the fragile conservative. "Too late now. I got a lawsuit 'gainst this school, and your name is gonna be on it. You encouraged a racist environment!"

The white boy, having learned never to hit a lady, scowls in astonishment and stifles a few sniffles, even a tear.

"How'd I do that?" The Afrocentrist sees fear in Duffy's eyes, so she goes in for the kill.

"That poster you showed us is racist! It's a parody of the President's whiteness. You got us thinking in terms of race in the first place. You show us that to encourage racism. You like these fights!"

"That's what they do. Niggers. First they spit in your food. Then they show you the blade!"

The class is stunned into silence. It is not every day they hear the n-word and certainly not in the classroom. The same appropriate girls who have been muttering tsk-tsk at the Afrocentrist's proclamations now direct their disapproval at this motionless girl, this newcomer to class participation. The girl sits there pleasantly, her neck and head still fully upright, her slight smile evincing satisfaction after well-chosen words. She then offers verification, further proof she can speak:

"First, they spit in your food, then they show you the knife. They put it against your neck so you feel the blade. I never should have paid his rent in the first place."

Duffy's knees jerk in response. "Eileen, whose rent? Can we avoid the foul language? What are you talking about?"

"My black boy. He put the blade to my neck. He raped me." The whispers of disapproval return; it is unclear if they disapprove of speaking aloud of race or rape, combining the two, or something else altogether.

Could it be the black women's disapproval of black men chasing white women? Duffy hears "knife" and "rape" and resists an urge to duck behind the desk.

"Dag! Homegirl got raped by a brother!" Back in her seat, the Afrocentrist shows all the physical symptoms of ecstasy—not the drug, but the emotion, experienced from her ability to interpret these messages as well as the content itself.

"Fuck you," says Eileen, speaking to the Afrocentrist without moving her neck. "My parents told me that if I slept with dogs I'd get fleas. So they were right. But so what? I hate them too."

"Bitch, you ain't gotta get in my face about it!" Now the Afrocentrist appears angry and hurt. "Shit, white bitch think she know about black men. Who you sayin' got fleas?"

"First they show you the blade, then they spit in your food. I slept with a black dog and got fleas." With a matter-of-fact tone, Eileen redelivers her mantra.

The Afrocentrist storms out of her desk chair, apparently intent on raising the level of dispute from verbal to physical, but in doing so, the wobbly chair flops over, causing a large crash, crushing her foot, and causing two separate drinks—coffee and OJ—to fall over in the back row.

"Motherfucker! Lawsuit again!" As the Afrocentrist shifts slightly to avoid her midsection's girth, and stares down at her foot, she slips on the converging orange and black mixture seeping out from the fallen cups, now a sea of burnt orange swelling over the dirty linoleum floor. Head first, she crashes. Her shocked instructor stares at the floored student and resists another urge to duck and cover. Some students gasp and cringe, but others laugh and go along with the vaudeville act turned violent; these are good Americans who attend to their education as custom dictates, but also *schadenfreude* purists who believe in a good chuckle at life's expense. For Duffy, the whole business leaves him longing for escape; he turns to the window and notes how the mood has put a damper on the lessening humidity and clearing skies, what is fast becoming a pristine spring day.

Eileen interrupts again. "That fucking black bitch is taking his side! They show you the blade, and then the others take his side." She starts scratching her arms like she is plagued by a swarm of mosquitoes. "They all stick together. Then you get fleas."

The dreadlocked protestor rises to help the Afrocentrist. "Who has a cell phone?" commands Julian. "We need to call an ambulance." He is nimble and sharp-witted, and unlike his inert instructor, a man of action. "Call campus security. Ma'am, are you okay?"

Julian's poise in the face of adversity helps Duffy regain his composure and evaluate the scene. By the way the student addresses her, he is reminded that the Afrocentrist is significantly older than the others, a woman closer to forty than thirty, speaking from experience as much as rehearsing an ideology. Poor schools, passed over for promotion, redlining, high-interest rates on cars and appliances, she has lived in the post-civil rights version of segregated America. She could possibly be older than her teacher.

Eileen shouts, "Serves that black bitch right," and then storms from the classroom.

At last springing loose from his own paralyzed state and seeing other students assist Julian with the Afrocentrist, he stuffs his belongings back in his book bag (adjunct rule number one, never leave anything behind), grabs his jacket, and chases after Eileen. "Young lady, young lady, please slow down." Thirty paces out of class, down the ugly gray, faux-marble staircase, and out the side door, she does slow down for him. In fact, she holds the heavy steel-framed glass door open, as if waiting to meet her professor outside. She lets go with Duffy two yards away; he extends his right hand and winces with pain as he catches the door before it slams in his face. In a light mist undetectable from the classroom, he joins Eileen on the smooth stone surface of a small courtyard past the side exit.

"Young lady, Eileen, may I call you Eileen?" He knows he has already but hopes his question passes for concern and decency.

She nods hastily, as if pitying Duffy, and the extent to which he seems out of sorts with one of her type. And indeed he is lost, an adjunct instructor who received no training whatsoever in how to handle her kind: the silent and wounded whose anomalous voice includes sex crimes, racism, anger, and pain. Is she reporting the truth or experiencing psychosis? He hasn't a clue but knows where they keep the local experts on these matters.

"It sounds like something is bothering you, Eileen."

"They spit in your food and rape you and tell you you're no good! Of course, something bothers me!" She glares at him, and even at the two yards' distance he has kept for his physical safety, he can see it in her eyes. It is the glare of madness. In his own family, he has a history of mild mental illness—a fine blend of anxiety and depression—but now in Eileen, he recognizes something familiar but much more severe. She may be from the same tree, but much further out on the branch. Her perch appears perilous, but he is the one who feels overwhelmed.

"Eileen, perhaps you need to speak with someone about this. I'm just a teacher."

"So you take my parents' side too! I knew it. First they sharpen the blade, then they spit in your food, and then your teachers call your mom!"

"But, Eileen, I've never spoken to your mother."

"Yeah, right. They spit in your food and fuck you, so then your parents, who fucked you over first, can get your teachers to fuck you too. My parents are the ones who made me go to school in the city. I told them this is what happens when you go to an urban campus. They show you the blade and make you beg for fleas."

"Young lady, I am not the right one to speak to about these matters. You need to see counseling services. Follow me." Somehow, as if inspired by Julian Door, Duffy seizes the moment and becomes a man of action.

He strides forward, and miraculously, she follows, ranting and rambling behind. Counseling services are not far away, just a city block or so from his classroom. Down the beige and brown brick pathway, cars prohibited and classes in session, Duffy leads and Eileen follows, her loud ranting reduced to a soft babble. But less than fifty yards from Sucher Hall, she darts in the opposite direction.

"Mister, thanks, but I'm going to call the cops on you for talking to my parents."

Her pace is quick, but even as she rushes off, she stares back at her teacher, as if daring him to chase after more troubles than he can possibly understand. His first impulse is to break in her direction, but soon she is lost in the massive throng of Urban Staters just arriving to campus and enjoying the rain's end. He needs to pick up a cold fruit drink full of calories and vitamin C, walk back to his department for a short office hour, check e-mail in his shared office space, and then, twenty minutes later, his Liberty Tech class begins sooner than he would like. But because he already strides in a direction opposite his office, Duffy decides to complete the mission.

At Sucher Hall, he strides down the elegant black stone marble steps to the basement. An original campus building, Sucher's walls consist of authentic brown stones, even covered with ivy vines, not at all like the blah brick-and-cement uniformity he usually teaches in. He imagines that the classical arts and sciences were once taught where now the counseling services lobby boasts leather couches and chairs atop plush wall-to-wall carpeting. Downstairs for the first time, he learns that at Urban State the crazy and their counselors receive far kinder treatment than the enrolled but sane students trapped in classrooms with ugly, aged desk chairs and dirty, gray linoleum floors.

After a brief interaction and failed explanation with an imposing push-up bra at the front desk, Duffy collapses onto a firm, black-cloth couch opposite a beaming bald counselor in a maroon leather chair. Only a wooden-framed, glass coffee table protects him from the therapist. Michael Zuegma. Cyrus Duffleman. I'm glad you could stop by. Nice to meet you. And how may I help? He delivers everything he knows about the case of Eileen.

"Are you fucking her?"

"Hell no!" Duffy's brow crinkles in rage, even as his heart flutters in fear.

"Just checking. No worries, you have confidentiality here unless her parents sue us to break it. But no worries, they'd sue the university long before they'd sue you. The attorneys know that even tenured professors aren't worth a shakedown. They go for the endowment or a chunk of tuition revenue. The bold ones sue the state that funds public institutions like ours."

Duffy's look of savage fear slowly dissipates until it is replaced by a sense of guarded neuroses. He worries. Three years ago, he wandered in alone but left a bar with a former student, an emaciated atheist on the verge of graduation. He had taught her the previous term, and felt no attraction to her whatsoever, a condition abruptly altered when she rejected unintertwined fellatio, tore off his khakis and her denim, and jumped on top of him instead. He hardly moved after that, terrified she'd get pregnant at first but then experiencing tremendous exhilaration and relief as she whipped out a square plastic package, with her front canines tore it at the corner, and with left hand only, firmly delivered its message over the Duffler's shockingly stiff edification. Sober the next morning, he fought off a severe headache and vowed never to "go there" again. His vow has been aided and abetted by the slow encroachment of his aging, its signposts of burgeoning gut, neck flab, wrinkles in the brow, sadness under the eyes, his entire face awash in his staple-crop guilt, altogether warning away the younger crops. Staying overworked—attending to four or five posts all at once—forces him, in his fatigue, to refuse even the easiest offer of company. Not that one is extended.

He returns to the present and stares back at the counselor.

"So what seems to be the problem?"

"*Her problem,*" corrects her instructor, craving distance from any involvement, "seems to be that she was raped at knifepoint by her black boyfriend before he went off to fight in the war. Or at least that's what she told us in class."

"She said all that in class?" Counselor Michael's sober deadpan reveals not a hint of belief or doubt. Like vodka, it reveals nothing at all.

"Well, not directly and clearly." Oh how Duffy craves a stiff drink.

"Then how?"

"In spurts. And repetitions. She kept repeating, 'first they spit in your food' and 'then they show you the blade.'"

"If that's what she said, then how do you know the rest?"

The question means Duffy is still part of the *problem*, and the intense heat of Michael's eyes arouse the full weight of his internalized guilt—the deep-down stuff, submerged well below sea level, the rust and barnacles he'd been taught long ago to attribute to sexual deviance at the core—but as always, this feeling of implication manifests itself far removed from any sexuality at all. He needs to know his wanting or not wanting to have sex with Eileen is not the reason he has wound up discussing her condition with counselor Michael. But aided by Zuegma's stern look, he feels implicated in her mental illness. Somehow he is guilty, to blame, at fault, not part of the solution, once more the adult failing the child. He must suppress this instinctive guilt, keep it bottled below, play the game, and act professional. It is far too early in his long day to admit to anything defamatory, criminal, or perverse. He vows to tread water and float on the surface, bob and weave while beasts from the deep attack from below. Flaccid as a banana peel, he could resist.

Duffy returns to the eyes that have never left, wondering for a brief instant how much time passed when he was inside his own head. A split second? A full minute? Enough time for the counselor to classify him as a full-fledged lunatic or merely the standard absent-minded professor? He decides to try his luck with a first name.

"Michael, she spat out the whole thing, eventually, first the blade, I mean first the spit, but then all of it. She said it aloud to all of us. But not to all of us really. She was shouting directly at me but responding to an Afrocentrist, my best participant, seated behind her. Do I need witnesses?"

Zuegma stares, his eyes intent, seeing all. He must be a rapist at the poker table. Duffleman swallows the guilt of his inappropriate or at least untimely thought.

"Oh, no, not at all. I see. It must have been a very disturbing outburst for you." Duffy feels incredible relief, the guilt at least momentarily drained from his system, grateful that good counselor Michael's tone has changed to consolation, to sympathy. Like a specialist in infections, his words suck clean the pus wound.

"Yes, very disturbing. Very loud, scary actually." He settles into the couch and relaxes his posture. He experiences comfort.

"Yes, I understand." Michael nods kindly, graceful in his knowing calm.

"So what is her condition, doctor? What should I do?"

He prays that when the doctor interprets these words, he will not be reading into the equation, as if Duffy asks in coded language for his own diagnosis. In his world of literary interpretation, he now demands the literal, surface level, and stares ahead anxiously, intent on avoiding the symbolic layers.

"Well, have you or the class felt physically threatened?" Duffy exhales a huge sigh of genuine relief. The doctor is talking about Eileen as the patient.

"No."

"Well, did you suggest she seek out counseling services?"

"I had her on the way here, but then she dashed away just as we approached the door." Pray Michael doesn't interpret this as Duffy's inner woman afraid to fully let herself out by running away less than fifty yards from the door of psychotherapy. He would handle all that another time, in retirement perhaps, but not today.

"Good. You've done what you can. All you can do is try to guide her here. In the past, many teachers have walked in with their patients, I mean students."

"Oh."

"If she hasn't been violent then there's nothing we can do. We can get the police involved only if there has been a physical threat to herself, a teacher, or a classmate."

"The police?" He pictures the beefy cop and German Shepherd from his morning commute. Man and dog on terror alert. Eileen obstructed his classroom, but Duffy doesn't see her in an orange jumpsuit. "The girl is mentally ill!"

"Everyone wants to play doctor," mutters counselor Michael.

"I just meant we don't need the cops." Duffy sighs heavily, exasperation from brow to chin.

"Yes, yes, of course not." The counselor returns to his reassuring voice. "The cops are only for forced institutionalization."

"Institution?" Duffy waxes Foucaultian as he pictures the mentally ill chained to their beds, injected at all hours, howling at the moon until lobotomized into tranquility. Maybe okay for himself in a few years, but not at all applicable to one of his charges. "Can't we just help her? Can't you come get her for me?"

"Help her is what we both want to do. But it is against school policy to enter the classroom and physically remove a student."

"Can you just go to the room, and ask to see her?"

"Well, it's not explicitly against Urban State's policy although it is strongly discouraged by our department as we find that very few students we make contact with in such a way actually admit themselves to our program. They tend to feel singled out, and are in fact more likely to reject counseling services."

Fuck the rationality of everything passes through Duffy's mind and he hopes not his parted lips, but all the same, he is starting to catch on to the program here. Counselor Michael is like a new class, another environment, with another set of variables—replacing his usual circumstances of poor lighting, skeptical students, and missing chalk. He tries to adjust. He waits. And then it clicks. These are free, voluntary counseling services, and so far Duffy is the only one who has volunteered to discuss his concerns.

"It's all so awful. The girl needs help! What can I do?" Duffy turns to rapidly twirling a front lock of hair, like a madman from a Russian novel.

"I can see this is really bothering you." Counselor Michael sounds sympathetic again.

"Yes. Yes, it is," and Duffy can barely choke off sniffles and tears. He is ready to hug the horse. His hair twisting ascends to full knotting and yanking and then just as abruptly subsides.

"Have you had trouble of this kind before?"

Regaining his composure, he considers the question. He remembers all manner of mean, obnoxious, failing, weird, or unpredictable students but nothing at all like this.

"No, nothing like this." He looks up at his interrogator. "I've never dealt with overt madness in the classroom."

"Well then, welcome to the world of mental illness!" Counselor Michael beams at his client. A deer caught in the headlights, Duffy returns an odd smile. He has never considered himself altogether foreign to this world, and his first instinct is to silently clarify, "Oh, I've been here before, not to these services in particular but to the world of which you speak." Michael's broad smile casts a glow upon the couched and cringing instructor. The tension builds, and then Duffy bursts out into sick convulsions of teary laughter, the contagious kind that soon has both men in mad guffaws, deep belly whoops, and final snorts and giggles.

Counselor Michael is the first to calm down. "Well, I'm here if you need to talk about it."

Duffy suffocates his last stragglers. He gulps. He tries to stare soberly back at the counselor. He is beginning to see the long and short of it. From Counselor Michael's eyes projects the information that Adjunct Duffleman is presently in therapy, something he has avoided his entire life. He is unsure of how to handle this sudden realization, whether to submit fully, lie down on the couch, or to resist—maintain an upright posture, to stare back into Zuegma's dilated pupils, as if they are two reasonable professionals—the two men, not the eyeballs—discussing a case together, *her* case and decidedly not *his* case, the two of them decidedly not doctor and patient. Duffy prays he can resist throwing himself on the floor and begging counselor Michael for some meds. At least somewhat sober reason returns and he isn't even sure if this kind of therapist can prescribe anything at all—isn't that only for psychiatrists or have the rules changed? Finally, with resolve, he regroups, as a man who doesn't have the time to find out about his condition. His long day in particular is no day to investigate his way-overdue analysis.

"Michael, you know, thank you for your time." He attempts the calm soundings of the professional plague sweeping the nation. He stands, bangs his knee against the counselor's coffee table, squeals like a wounded pig, and hurriedly in half steps limps toward the door.

"Are you okay?" Counselor Michael's pupils widen even further in astonishment, as his voice reveals real concern for both the mental as well as the physical patient.

"Yes, dammit, yes. My bad knee," mutters Duffy as if there were only one poor joint in his life. "That's all, thank you."

As gracious host, counselor Michael rises from his leather chair, steps to the door, opens it wide for all of humanity to visit, and gives as sincere a smile as possible, as much as a madman's madman can.

Duffy tries to return the smile, desperately suppressing his pained expressiveness, which manages to creep in as slightly flared nostrils.

"The students have amazing resilience," Michael adds, partly consoling, partly condescending. It's okay man, *I'll pretend this wasn't therapy for your own self esteem.*

"Yes they do." Grabbing the last words, Duffy gasps in pain and then rushes for air.

CHAPTER 3

AWAY FROM THERAPY AND THEN SOUTH AND WEST

Outside, limping briskly away from psychotherapy, or whatever that was, Duffleman checks his watch. 11:17 a.m. When he rushed out, he must have been only forty-seven or so minutes into class. He considers going back to the room to check on the Afrocentrist, but he trusts she is in good hands with that young boy, Julian, a take-charge type, who might get ahead in this world. He imagines Julian even earning a salary protecting the animals, the environment, the black people, or even part-time instructors of university English.

So instead, Duffy limps as fast as he can back to his office. He picks up steam as the pain in his knee dissipates and he regains his hazy sense of an independent self. As he strides, he vows a return to routine; he'll gather his departmental mail, check e-mail messages, let the undergraduate chair in on the case of Eileen, and reassert his right to a quiet hour in a cramped office with but two other names on the door.

In the process of purchasing his orange juice, he regains some confidence by returning the food cart's overpriced breakfast bar to its proper place as he remembers that he has brought his own from home, one of two dozen purchased at discount in bulk. Ah, *the man who can save a dollar can save a life*, or is it the other way around, and what exactly does the proverb mean, and where did he read it? Montesquieu? Not

Nietzsche? Some daily rag's quote of the day? A freshman essay? No worries, its recollection somehow contributes to his self-esteem, and so by the time he reaches Althusser Hall he feels almost forty and slightly normal, waiting at the elevator among the masses of undergraduates seeking a lift to a higher floor of enlightenment. His usual claustrophobia from the crowded floor-by-floor elevator squeeze lacks its bite today, and Duffy uses the delay to meditate on how he will approach his immediate supervisor.

At all costs, he must not come across as unnerved by the incident; to keep his job, any of them, he must show he can handle his students, in all makes and models, regardless of their irregular categories and conditions, be their illness mental, physical, emotional, or socioeconomic. Course descriptions and syllabi count, but his first duty is to control the situation. And yet his bosses will need to see some emotion; for if he comes across as too calm and rational about the matter, it may appear that nothing is to be done because nothing seems to be too terribly wrong. Above all else, he wants to wipe his hands clean. There ought to be someone else in this university who can take charge of the matter. Disheartened to learn that the counselor could not swoop in and grab her, and certainly of no mind to call the cops on the poor girl, he cannot imagine that the mentally ill should be left entirely under the jurisdiction of an adjunct instructor of the English department, educated in creative writing and comparative lit, teaching a class in business writing. The university must offer a full-time job and health benefits to an expert, someone, somewhere in this vast labyrinth of a not-for-profit higher educational facility, who attends to such extreme moments of education, thus ensuring that the cheap labor, the teachers, could meekly subsist and go about their specialized duty, which is, at least presumably, to effectively educate the remainder sane enough to function within the societal confines of normal classroom behavior.

By the tenth floor, Duffy has breathing room, and so he strides out of the elevator in a civilized fashion, not at all like the students who slid, popped, and fell out floors below. On second thought, he feels better off eschewing this false bravado of upright posture and firm gait—if he were to appear too forward-walking, or positive, he risks allowing the tenured faculty to see him as content, dumb, happy, perhaps even barefoot, and yes, with his gut pregnant-looking adjunct working for scrub wages *sans* benefits. He cannot bear to allow them this view of him. At the same time, it is risky to keep the rich, landed gentry convinced they should pity his condition. He doesn't want them overwhelmed by a sense of guilt at the sight of his poverty and sadness sulking down the corridor. Most often, a meek smile and gentle approach to interacting with the tenured is enough interaction, but even here lies danger, for it is unclear how these job-secure professors would interpret any facial expression at all. And so, by Duffy's estimation, the best way to navigate the English Department is as an invisible man. To have the permanent faculty pay him no mind at all ensures that nothing he does produces in these touchy teachers any emotion whatsoever. When all else in life fails, he could still focus on the American cultural rite and obligation of putting forth effort to keep his job. To get rehired remains an adjunct's end in itself.

So he slinks toward the mailroom, trying to disappear, sucking in his midsection to further reduce the possibility of detection. He keeps his eyes slanted forty-five degrees toward the ground; head down and no eye contact means no chance of communication. In the mailroom, he finds his slot among the hundreds for English professors, graduate students, fellows, other adjuncts, and administrative assistants. Just one knowledge worker among the masses, he reaches in and pulls out five sheets. All are departmental or university-wide fliers, advertisements for this reading or that reminder; the top sheet is the Memo on Respect for Religious Observation in the Classroom, which quickly and oddly enters his psychic churn as an image of the Rastafarian whiteboy and the Afrocentrist, buck naked, dancing around a fire in the middle of his classroom, roasting the offending ball-capped pig stuck high above the heat.

Duffy madly darts his head left and right, praying no mind readers have trespassed through his less than PC, rather catholic imagination. Both coasts appear surprisingly clear. Relieved when the vision passes, he makes another grab and feels something harder shoved toward the back. There are two actual letters in his slot—each with a stamp and filled out like regular mail. He finds himself in the rare position of having received not one, but two pieces of personal correspondence. A light blue envelope and a forest-green envelope, both are in the shape of greeting cards. He decides not to press his luck by opening either one; instead, he stuffs them in the left back pocket of his trousers, leaves the mailroom, and averts all eyes down the hall to the undergraduate English department.

At first, Duffy hides his body and exposes but one full eyeball and a third of his head as he peers into see if his boss is at home in the offices for undergraduate English. At the desk, he sees a work-study student—dark and delicate, of the Desi diaspora—stapling forms together, no doubt another paper reminder, mass circulated to faculty, mass thrown away or recycled straight from each mail slot. A few students sit and stare at course-listings booklets, searching for that perfect complement to a career track—that intriguing liberal-arts course. Some of these are no doubt the few and proud English majors, those seeking to go where no man save the odd Duffleman—and, yes, truth told, millions of other lost souls—have gone before. Whenever he catches himself grumbling about the illiteracy of "students these days," he must remember that Urban State has over one hundred English majors per undergraduate class to its credit. Even Liberty Tech, Urban State's practical peer, has added the major to its curriculum. Not quite an escape but the retreat to the humanities is alive and well! Duffy shudders in fear.

Beyond these hole-in-the-jeans-and-nose types lounging in the lobby area, Duffy sees that his boss, Harold "Call me Harry" Van Oyle, is indeed at home. His obesity sits two-thirds obscured behind a fat, oak desk, covered with thick clumps of paper inches deep and even atop the computer monitor and keyboard. The life of the tenured overseer of undergraduate-course instruction is no easy one; the combined overflowing paperwork and overeating fat man fills the office as if it were the six cubed feet of storage space the city provides its homeless. Duffy likes Van Oyle but fears the paperwork swamp and the boss's spittle known to fly at random during any conversation. The unique feature of Van Oyle's "spray it while you say it-ism" is, at times, how far the spittle flies when the course disher sits silently, pie trap shut.

Duffy lumbers past the work-study migrant and straight for the boss's open door.

"Harry?"

Van Oyle looks up, squints through his bifocals, and chirps, "Hey Cyrus. What can I do for you?" From eight feet, Duffy should be safe from the spray. But due to the seriousness of the matter, he is prepared to brave the sea.

"May I have a seat for a moment?" In his head, he estimates the chair opposite Harry's on the other side of the desk is still four feet from the spit factory, enough room for most human error.

For a moment, Harry appears disturbed by the request, as if prevented from slaying a goat because a berry gatherer has just interrupted his more important travail. But then he chirps, "Sure Cyrus, have a seat. What's up?"

Duffy slides into the chair opposite Van Oyle. He tries to exude the confidence of a man able to handle his charges; the coordinator should see an instructor who looks calm and in control.

"It's about a girl."

"I see." Van Oyle nods ever so slightly. Duffy sees lust in his eyes. In fact, the boss's wise leer seems to imply it is always a matter of the bedroom even if it seldom occurs there. Duffy detects a tiny thread of spittle slinkying out of the far-right corner of Van Oyle's mouth. He'd like to resist this fusion of topics; sex and saliva should remain as separate strands of discourse. At least at this early hour of a working day.

"She told me she was raped by her boyfriend."

"I see." Now Van Oyle almost glows, nodding repeatedly and solemnly, as if he has heard this before. "How'd you get on that topic?"

"She screamed it out; she sounded angry."

"What did you do to make her mad?"

Van Oyle's glow wanes. Duffy sees he has gotten off, quite easily, on the decidedly wrong foot.

"No, I mean she screamed it out, *at* me, but *to* the whole class. Everyone was there."

"Wow! What'd you do to make her so angry she'd yell at you in front of the whole class?" Harry's fleshy mug shows concern for the children—all of the students in English classes and specifically the one the Duffler has wounded.

Duffy wishes he could start all over, reenter from the hallway, or perhaps somehow have decided wisely not to come at all. "It has nothing to do with me. It seemed like a reaction to class conversation about race."

"That's tough material for undergrads, Cyrus."

Duffy feels a brief shock of moisture snap him just below the left eye. He tries to ignore the moist gift, his mind transfixed by Van Oyle's baby blue tissue box, half hidden below a stack of papers. Would the boss be offended if he were to ask for a Kleenex?

"I once had a kid whip out a starter pistol and shout he was prepared to use it if necessary." What Duffy doesn't need at this moment is an anecdote about a more serious threat trivializing his own problem. But Van Oyle continues, "Of course, what your situation reminds me of is the girl who flopped on my desk looking for a father."

"Whah," is all the lesser man can manage, as he wipes with his balled fist, just as another spit sniper grazes his right ear. As a survivor of Van Oyle's graduate seminar, Duffy is acclimated to the greater man's tangents.

"She was pregnant. Seven months. Looking for a Daddy and figured I'd do as good as any." Ten to fifteen years Duffy's senior, Van Oyle is lucky to be alive; in the seminar, he introduced himself as a survivor of severe maladies—the trifecta of stroke, heart attack, and cancerous polyps, found in his colon, detected in a palliative stage. Thrice defiant at death's door, and protected by tenure, Van Oyle could shoot the breeze in any direction he pleased. Along with the spit juice, one could never know what would egress next from behind his yellow and pink curtain of teeth and lips. "She told me she'd do everything necessary to make me happy, and she gave me a look like she meant it."

Van Oyle appears caught in reverie. Duffy experiences the tingling of terror down his spine as he finds himself wondering if Van Oyle grows a bone from the memories of seductions past. Duffy would like to keep matters professional and memories under the desk and out of view; he omits an audible sigh when Van Oyle returns to his supervisory role.

"Okay. Let's go over this again. You've got a girl in class screaming she was raped by her boyfriend. Did you think of taking her to counseling services?"

"Yes, I tried to do that but she wouldn't go."

"So you did the best you could. No worries."

"But the girl is a disturbance to the class. Something is wrong with her. I'm not a psychiatrist, but I could tell the girl is not okay. It's possible she really did get raped by her boyfriend at knifepoint, in which case this is a criminal matter."

"Well, maybe we should call the cops?" Even while trying to maintain an anxious look equal to the severity of the problem, Duffy can't help but feel relieved Van Oyle is trying to help, and for the moment, even doing so without salivating.

"The counselor I spoke to at services said that they do that when the student is a genuine threat to herself or others. It seems extreme to call the cops when she hasn't threatened anyone physically. If she is mentally ill, then the rape at knifepoint could even be a fictive incident. Or the rape could even be the trauma that triggered the mental illness."

"Hmm." Duffy spies what could be a dangler. "I see."

It doesn't seem to register to Van Oyle that his adjunct instructor leads the charge here, while the boss lags a step behind him in each turn of discussion. On paper, if it came to documentation, it would appear the opposite, mirroring in fact their publication record. Van Oyle's prolific scribbling of literary texts—short stories, film theory, critical analysis— surpasses his massive production of spittle, and this quantity in print amazes and intimidates Duffleman. Harry is a kick-ass writing machine while Duffy has no publication credits at all on his curriculum vitae. Thus, in Van Oyle's frothy presence, he feels meaningless and soft. Truth be told, he has never composed a CV; he uses a two-page resume full of the minutiae of part-time employment if he needs to search for more of it. In a publish-or-perish world, Van Oyle has produced text and made progress while Duffleman stagnates in student concerns, an academic dying on the roadside. To V.O. and his C.V. go raises and health benefits; to the lesser man, a life grading papers.

As an exclamation point, a long, thin strand of Harry's good stuff now dangles from the left corner of his lower lip. "Hold on, Cyrus. I'm in over my head here. Let me go talk to Seward."

Van Oyle rises, and as he does so, Duffy is amazed to discern no old harpoons and netting stuck in the backside of this white whale of a man. He does see high waters, mud-brown slacks three inches off the shoe, and underwear posted an inch above the belt. Van Oyle waddles out of the room, leaving the teacher alone and at peace, with no audience at all to impress with patience and reasoning skills. He breathes in deep and exhales with a sigh half the size of Van Oyle's office. He looks around at the papers all over the desk, the two wall-sized windows beyond Harry's wide, wooden chair, and then over at the walls of bookshelves to either size. It is tempting to walk to the window, peer below, and gaze down at all the kinds of Urban Staters mingling under a spring sun that has burst out fiercely, in defiance of morning rain. But this would seem too odd, if the department chair and undergraduate secretary were to return together, and find an adjunct gazing down below as if it were his office, and not a greater man's. They would no doubt take him for an imposter, a "wannabe" as the students coined it, and only further the suspicion created by his contract status. Duffy knows his story would be less likely believed because he is among the office sharers of the lowest rung and thus seen as less capable of communicating or understanding anything at all. Van Oyle might be a fat idiot who compares genuine student problems to his tales of sexual seduction by pregnant coeds, but as such, he lacks the capacity to look beneath his status for knowledge or understanding.

So he slides a few inches down in the chair and waits for fate to return in this matter, wishing he would remember to wear a watch so he could see precisely how close he is cutting it to winding up late for his Liberty Tech class at one p.m. For a moment, he considers peering behind Van Oyle's desk to see the time on his computer screen, but should they walk in and catch him in this act, the consequences could be extreme. So instead, he slides in and waits and finds himself in the process of trying to remember the third line of a childhood prayer—Jewish or gentile, he is unsure, but he craves more than the 62.5 percent chance it includes a concept of heaven—when Van Oyle returns with Dr. Seward.

Duffy has never met Seward and so he fears the worst of the natural habitat—a feminist with talent, ambition, and lefty politics who will see in his subsistence-wage status the failings of the capitalist system, and yet blame him for his own problems because he is part of the patriarchal structure of society; in fact, he is a classic type, a white man handed everything and amounted to nothing. Beat a dog when he's down, as they say, and better yet, reclaim the cliché from the patriarchy in the process.

Van Oyle squats in his seat; Seward stands and looms over both men, but Duffy must admit she looks kind and perhaps motherly in a nonsmothering way.

"So Harry tells me you are having trouble with a student."

"It's not my trouble, really, but the trouble she seems to be having. She shouted out in an extreme way about being raped at knifepoint by her boyfriend. It seemed far beyond *normative student discourse.*" His life sentencing to the prison house of business comm is a fate more obscure even than the ghettos of English comp, but in the department chair's presence, he feels obliged to toss in a bit of academic jargon.

"So she said those things to you at your desk?" Dr. Seward's tone and brow show genuine concern. For his student or for her teacher? It is hard to say.

"To the whole class, not just to me."

"So did you take her to counseling services?"

"She wouldn't go."

"In the past, some teachers have guided their students to counseling."

"I tried but she resisted. She ran off before we got there." Duffy feels like a man who has repeated himself too many times. First counselor Michael, then Van Oyle, and now Seward. Each time the inquisition implies he could have done more and reminds him of the dangers of going public about anything.

"Well, it sounds like you've done all you can." *Ah, relief.*

"But what do I do about the class? Her comments were entirely out of order and racist too. I was shocked. Generalizations about all black people based on this horrible experience, that perhaps drove her to insanity, or perhaps due to her insanity this event she has entirely invented." Duffy rushes his words and hates himself for delivering a run-on fragment in place of a sentence; nevertheless, he feels more confident that he is the diagnoser and not the diagnosed.

"Well, if she's been violent, you can call the police."

"But she hasn't been violent. There should be someone at this university who can remove her from the class. Not the police. Someone must have a job or function like this at the university."

"Well," and now Dr. Seward adopts an administrative tone, "by law, we cannot remove students from classes they have enrolled in unless they have committed a criminal action of some kind. The students have legal rights to attend our courses. We're a state university that provides opportunities for nontraditional students."

By seating a class of thirty in front of a guy paid for the course from the tuition's share of just two? How the other twenty-eight get their money's worth is what Duffy would love to know.

"So there is really nothing that can be done. What happens if this girl routinely impairs my ability to teach the class?"

"Then, we can have campus police remove her as an obstruction to teaching the others."

Seward has all the answers, but Duffy, slow learner, is catching on. Unless he calls the cops on the girl, he's stuck with her in class. Her rantings were so disturbing that he feels immediate dread at the prospect that she would stay and continue to participate in this way. He isn't paid enough for such hassle and pain. But before he gets visibly angry and verbally abusive, he remembers his top priority is to appear as if he can handle the situation. Duff must play the man capably in charge of his charges, so he sucks in, smiles, and delivers.

"Well then, thank you for clarifying my options. I wanted to bring this matter to your attention, just in case this particular student, or perhaps another, complained about the situation. If she speaks out further in such an inappropriate manner, I'll again attempt to guide her to services. Up until this point, she has been silent, so if she returns to this previous behavior pattern, then she will be no trouble at all."

He doesn't want to minimize the severity of the situation, but he feels he must show calm and resolve. He might be paid peasant's wages, but he needs to be as strong and confident as the king. Under the desk, his anxiety leg, his left, thrashes about like a rodent's tail caught in a trap. He sees Dr. Seward return his smile, evidently pleased with his final thoughts.

"Very well, then. I appreciate the fact that teaching brings us into these difficult situations, and I admire your willingness to reach out to help this student. We in the profession must remember that this dedication to student concerns is a primary motive for our choice to teach at Urban State."

"We in the profession," Duffy interprets with subtitles: you of the six-figure Department Chair's salary, and me of the two-grand-per-course adjunct instructor's pay. Then, he prays a Red Sea of shame that his thinking in crass dollars hasn't washed across his face. But he is almost out of the situation, and as with the meeting with the counselor, he has a chance to extricate himself from any thoughts that he is the one who has the problem. Both times, he went to address *her* problem, and both times, he feels lucky to escape without ranting, yelping, getting fired, whining, begging, or otherwise blaming it all on his mother.

"Well, I just wanted to be sure I addressed this matter with the department. Thank you for your time." He stands up, nods politely, and ignores the *known known* that he will be instructing a psychotic girl for the rest of the semester. A bit of pee trickles out at this thought, and he can only hope its stain fails to mark his pants. He'll check in the lavatory on a foreign floor, not this administrative one nor his own.

"Nice to meet you. Thank you for expressing your concerns."

"See ya, Cyrus," chirps Van Oyle, seemingly oblivious to all that has come to pass.

Duffy walks out into the main room, where the nose rings are still perusing course guides. A particularly anorexic bleached blonde stares up at him, blank more than mysterious, but that's all. In her eyes, no pity for his fortieth birthday or acknowledgment of his basic predicament. He experiences a strong urge to about-face, reenter Van Oyle's office, and get it off his chest. He'd give the two of them a piece of his mind on just how much hypocritical bullplop it is that adjuncts are the cannon fodder in this preemptive strike against the confused, alienated, or otherwise disturbed that Urban State steals from with college-catalog lies of wealth and career. Duffy kills himself with worry while those two stroll into graduate seminars and pretend to know a thing or three about Lyotard, Lacan, or some other sacred cow, kosher or not.

And the Duffler does it!

But as he turns the knob to reenter, he hears their voices. He stands frozen at the door; their words are soft but audible.

"It doesn't sound like he plans to sue, and as long as she isn't told to leave the class, she won't have grounds for a lawsuit either."

"Okay, our bases covered then," chirps Van Oyle, just as chummy with Seward as he was with Cyrus moments ago.

"One good follow up," replies Seward, "is to check with Michael Zuegma in counseling. See if he'll tell you anything about the nature of his meeting with the instructor. Anything he can tell us without breaking patient confidentiality. That typically is interpreted as dealing with content, so just try to find out about tone. Was the instructor visibly angry or emotionally disturbed? He seemed particularly calm just now, but he could have been faking it to keep his job."

Seward's acute ability to discern layered text is disturbing. This is not the same woman he left in the office moments ago, and yet it is her voice. He experiences a reverence, an awe for a woman like this so acutely aware and in charge and able to function on multiple levels. He feels a slight sexual awakening, turned on by the strength of her words, stiffening in his trousers he prays the anorexic girl cannot sniff out from her seat.

"Will do," chirps Van Oyle. "I'll call him pronto." Duffy imagines a strand of Van Oyle's finest spittle shooting her in the eye.

"Good, I'll inform our legal department, discuss the case, and refine our strategy. Over at Rural State, they let a similar situation go unchecked until it got out of hand. The department chair was forced to resign, the student died, and the adjunct in question walked off with half a million dollars in an out-of-court settlement. We certainly won't let that happen here. You must understand we're under tremendous pressure from Dean Ghod to save money for research and recruitment—our costs must be controlled."

Duffy jumps back from the door, visible wood or no, and strides away, out of the department clearly intent on covering its own wide ass, with just a momentary glance over at the anorexic girl. She stares at him as if he is an exotic fish and not a tenuously employed fellow nearing forty who could stand to lose a few. Or twenty. In the main hallway, he hooks a left and heads down the stairs to his office on the eighth floor.

So this is what it has come to. He goes to his boss to discuss the issue, and ends up as the object of a legal discussion that recognizes him as the possible problem rather than the responsive and responsible teacher he once aspired to be. Van Oyle and Seward are not his friend or mother. They are two tenureds with their own problems—fiscal, medical, mortal—and orders from above. They see him as a legal threat to the institution and, by extension, their economic well being, which depends upon the vast discrepancy in earnings between the tenured elite and the adjunct remains. If he were to sue, say, under the name of unfair working conditions, he could no doubt bring attention to this socioeconomic inequality in the college-teaching profession. But would he have any realistic chance of winning the case? Would a lawyer work on a contingency basis? Would society see it as just another frivolous lawsuit, or would "the people"—a jury, that is—side with the adjunct? Does society want the person who teaches college to their kids to earn a fair sum? A so-called living wage? Perhaps per hour a buck or two more than gas-station pay in South Dakota?

Duffy feels hurt and confused. Being seen as a potential traitor to the department is more painful than the peasant wage he receives. The whole thing makes him feel dirty. They know the adjunct is a legal threat because they are alienating his labor, stealing from him to pad their own superlative pay and benefits—German-sedan health coverage and expense accounts for books. They sacrifice the guard dog to feed the overstuffed pigs at the trough of tenure, and then the pigs have the nerve to invite the peasants to departmental holiday parties, where, with a straight face, they offer gourmet sandwiches and middling wine. He feels a sharp pain in his side—heart attack, appendicitis, or merely a psychosomatic reaction to his basic predicament?

Duffy ignores the pain and pushes through to the stairwell and descends. At the ninth floor, by the slender window, he sees the memorial to the fallen student. According to notes graffiteed by the window, some left with dried flowers—pale yellow and lavender, Mirag John leaped out and ended his beautiful life, while yet a young man full of intelligence and goodness. Duffy has passed this memorial many times over the year since the fatal fall occurred. Now he wonders if this Mirag had anything in common with insane Eileen. From all the notes on the wall, it sounds as if he went much more gently into that good night, and of course, Eileen is still—to the best of his knowledge—fighting it out among the living. Duffy finds it disturbing that a young man chose death at such a young age, and yet he is grateful the courageous suicide floating down from a mammoth concrete edifice took his own life and no one else's. Such grace under pressure is quite unlike all these suicide bombers "keen on death as you in the West are keen on life." He has read these words online and in print, and because he has not felt "keen on life" in years, he wonders whom the speaker refers to. Have these terrorists even been to our country and seen how depressed or mediocre most of us feel? Are they so deceived by our TV advertising that they think of us as an entire society of keen livers? An optimistic spleen to every woman, man, and child?

Duffy recalls reading about the angry zealot with the thick rims and thicker beard who taped these words for the world's media outlets. According to a detailed article, he was a Kuwaiti school teacher the one day but radicalized the next. On September 11, just like President Fern, he was reading to the second grade. He joined Bin Laden's group soon after, and was immediately designated a PR man for his literacy and English. Duffy cannot imagine an English teacher in America making such a sudden leap to head of public relations at Altria or the Republican National Committee. Perhaps no leap at all was possible for most of those marooned in the field of education. But this man stared calmly at the camera and said, "We are as keen on death as you in the West are keen on life." And this is above all else, rather disturbing.

Beyond all talk of War for Oil, or American imperialism propping up Saudi royalty while ignoring human rights in the kingdom, or Israeli tanks keen on Palestinian collateral damage, this unnerving sense of sacrifice permeates the whole Al Qaeda movement. Whereas Duffy can still resent his subsistence wages and regret his service as university peon, these men embrace a similar position. These soldier-servants of Allah believe in their cause while Duffy is skeptical at best about his mission. Self-actualized within their group movement—aye, an oxymoron—they are the opposite of alienated labor. Say what you would about Al Qaeda as a brainwashed cult, these men seem relentless and content to blow themselves up while taking down others, most often fellow Muslims, but also occasional big hits against major Western cities: two towers' worth of America and more recent attacks—major and minor—around the world.

Departing from thoughts of Muslim mass murderers, Duffy returns to earth, albeit the ninth floor, and stands and stares at the photograph of Mirag crazy-glued to the wall. Myron Seligman, an emeritus aged sixty-nine years and housed across the hall, popped into his office two days after the photo appeared.

"I bet it was retribution," hissed Seligman. "One of our 'true patriots' mistook this Mirag for an Arab and did him in by pushing him out the window. Some of the kids at this school are thugs, racists who'll use any excuse, especially 9/11, to commit violence. We teach them the written word, but all they know is this." And toward the window in Duffy's shared office, Myron extended his open palm in a way that made leaping out seem almost inviting.

Seligman's racism is oriented toward the black students, whom he sees as pseudo-literates at best, and nonreaders most of all, but Duffy wonders if Myron has paid attention to the burgeoning ignorance of whites on campus as well. To use another's tragedy to express your own racism seems odd and unfortunate, but of course, today, in the classroom, Duffy has heard even worse. He'd prefer to remember the young readers he has witnessed on his morning commutes.

Now, at the photo by the window in the landing, he can't help but take a closer look to see if the boy has any Middle Eastern features whatsoever. Mirag appears to be a South Asian American with a wide, warm smile. He is in front of a chocolate-iced cake with candles; presumably, the photo is of his birthday, as the wall suggests he lived twenty-one wonderful years spreading peace and goodwill. Duffy imagines a traditional home, and this Mirag discovering a secret untraditional craving in his heart that was too much for his parents to bear. Maybe love for a black woman? Or a white man? Or a deep-felt desire not to take up medicine as his parents' dream had been for him since before he was born? Who could know what this Mirag wanted for his life? The notes on the walls were of appreciation for the life he lived, not the future he denied himself.

To Duffy, to choose death, and go it alone, now seems so much braver than the Mohammed Attas of the world who aim to take thousands of innocents with them, or the Palestinian "suicide" bombers who inject themselves with all sorts of HIV and Eboli and hepatitis, with the goal of finding some miserable checkpoint security force, and taking down one or two at once, and hundreds more in the aftermath. The Muslims in the area are just as at risk of contracting the AIDS virus, and yet these men write poems before their end, expressing no remorse, and even joy at the potentially successful mission, as if suicide, murder, and spreading deadly disease were all the natural outcome of refugee camps. And wasn't it mainly old ladies carrying vegetables who died in these attacks? Do the Muslim and Jewish grandparents infected by HIV and blown apart in "battle" get access to any of the virgins promised to the martyrs in heaven? Idle musing on suicide and murder helps Duffy gain perspective on his own less tragic condition in the 10:10 a.m. class. If only he could prevent Eileen from taking her own life, then he will have done a *mitzvah*, a good deed, something his father's father would appreciate.

Once more, Duffy whispers a few words for this Mirag he did not know and then slides away, descending one more flight, and with just a step into the hallway of the eighth floor, opens his office door. He and his two officemates share a sliver of corner space with a window; compared to the panopticons that adjuncts commiserate in at other universities, it is a generous blessing to cohabitate in sixty square feet of occasionally private space, with a potted cactus, two full-sized filing cabinets, and a panoramic view of northern Philadelphia. As he closes the door, he thanks God his roomies are not around, and with the lights off, drops his book bag onto the ugly, beige linoleum floor, and slumps into the cushioned, puke-green office chair. He depresses the power button, and the old but functional computer checks files and scans for viruses while he shuts his eyes for a moment of rest. He has seven minutes to be alone in the room. It is his office hour, his time for the students, but he feels no remorse closing the door from the public good. Five minutes of down time on a long day will do wonders for his mental state, and the students know e-mail is his preferred method of communication. He keeps his eyes closed. He relaxes and breathes.

A few minutes later, he raises his eyelids, gobbles down his breakfast bar, and pops two ibu and an extra-strength acetometaphine after opening his orange juice. He finds the most global letter in the alphabet, and clicks the big, bright blue lowercase "e." His first order of Internet business is to check his e-mail. Every September at each school, he reads policies explaining that all e-mail interactions with students must be completed with university accounts—no doubt, so the higher-ups can read them, and reprimand, fire, or refuse to rehire if need be—but Duffy's busy schedule precludes checking separate accounts, so his four university e-mails all channel to the greater hegemony of Web-based gmail.

He punches in his password and arrives at the inbox. A hundred and three new messages, but it is a relief to recognize that the lion's share are spam concerning affordable antidepressants, penile supplements, educational software, "no money down" women from Turkey to Tajikistan, and other random advertisement-laced "journalism" he can never figure out how to unsubscribe to. But one targeted mark among millions, the mass mailings amplify his feeling of anonymity.

Ugh! Global sex and death, his classroom anxieties, and the loneliness of his celibacy combine to overwhelm him; the pain is unbearable. In defiance, the Duffler furiously surfs through the mix of sex and romance spam. He closes his eyes, clicks, and responds to "Svetlana Novascotia"—giving up his date of birth and social to a virtual hottie offering cooking and companionship and claiming residence somewhere between Vancouver Island and Nizhny Novgorod. When reason returns, he kicks himself in the brain for allowing his lonely self to succumb to such an overtly fishy phishing scam. Checking his trousers, he is thankful the information release left no visible stains. Phew.

He deletes the remaining junk mail and is left with a dozen or so messages. Skimming through, at a quick count, perhaps five appear to be from students. Immediately recognizable is muffdiver23@hotmail.com, a student so overjoyed that his instructor does not mind receiving messages from this address that he e-mails at least twice a week. Duffy believes he comprehends its meaning although he cannot recall a single similar slang term from his own day used for this form of giving. Along with muffy, he also reads:

jld37@libertytech.edu

juliansdoor@urbanstate.edu

Franklin.Andrew.Hamnett@libertytech.edu

yourevening@ivygreen.edu

As tempting as the last message sounds, in a world where AT&T and General Motors are said to be major players in the pornography industry, the e-mail could be mass marketing from the university and not some overtly flirtatious coed mocking his long bout of going without. The one above it is the one that matters, now that he recognizes this Franklin. He points, clicks, and the message appears:

As G&R said, it would have been simpler to use a gun . . . hey prof, hope you're enjoying the rain, and praying for the sun.

—Frank of the First Rank

Franklin Andrew Hamnett, aka Frank of the First Rank, and just Frank to Duffy, is one of those curious students who just doesn't quite fit in. Now a fourth-year junior at Liberty Tech, an ROTC boy from a small white town in the middle of the state, he was sent to Iraq during the first wave of the war, and saw battle in Tikrit. "A rush," is how he described it when he ran into his former teacher early in the winter quarter. Now at the start of his second quarter back on campus, Frank has been home six months, and Duffy knows he is having trouble with civilian life.

He taught the soldier during his freshman year, and didn't particularly like him, but somehow he'd wind up running into the kid and engaging in conversation. Frank seemed a little lost, a little lonely, and even though he at times acted as the conservative police during Duffy's introduction to liberal guilt branded as English 101, somehow he has grown to sympathize with him, still not really liking him much, but sort of seeing him as a boy in trouble, out of place, and a bit needy. So many of the students at Liberty Tech are from much wealthier backgrounds, the kid who joins the army to afford college deserves his concern.

As for the current e-mail message, Duffy doesn't pretend to understand it. It could just be the cool college kid kind of message—raw cynicism explored and violence alluded to via the World Wide Web. He cannot imagine anything to say in response, and so he returns to his Inbox and clicks the "Juliansdoor" e-mail. It's a very polite, perhaps a bit officious, rundown of all that transpired in class after he left. Julian's tone is tolerant and respectful. He understands his instructor has been having a very hard day; therefore, it is perfectly understandable that student interaction would trouble him and that completing a full class session could be beyond his means. Duffy cringes at Julian Door's implying that he ended class early because he couldn't handle the situation. Or is he suggesting Duffy's myopic focus on Eileen was inappropriate? Maybe Julian sees her not as ill but as a racist, part of the problem, and decidedly not the solution?

Duffy tries to recall how much of her insanity occurred during class, and how much was revealed outside in the hallway and during their walking together toward counseling services. He will need witnesses from the classroom in case anything negative is reported by students about his handling of the situation. Julian may be a responsible agent for social change, but it is unclear if he understands precisely what his teacher had to handle back there. The Afrocentrist certainly wouldn't take his side, and so he'd have to comb the chorus for allies. Surely among the mumbles and moans of disapproval he could find students who saw the situation as he did. Students willing to come to his defense if need be. Or maybe they were already plotting to remove him from the classroom?

Removal seems unlikely. The low pay ensures that it would be difficult to find a replacement, and most qualified adjuncts are already as booked as possible and exhausted this late in the spring term. Besides, he comes to work each day—yes, he attends—and this seems to be enough to keep his toehold in the cliffs of higher education. About the adjunct world, Woody Allen's "Ninety percent of life is just showing up" is on the mark. After skimming Julian's documentation of all services rendered to the Afrocentrist in her injured state, he feels grateful for the update. Yes, the student leader is a good, capable man, no mere dreadlocked demagogue raging against The Man for TV fame. He cannot imagine a Van Oyle or Seward spending so much time caring for another unless it led to sexual partnership or career advancement. That this thought could stem from his own selfish nature occurs to Duffy but not so emphatically as to send him searching again for escape in the fake love of the phishing scams.

He has time for one more message, and so, despite the spam snafu, he clicks the "Yourevening" e-mail. As he does so, his fear of downloading porn hits him so hard in the chest he gasps for air. What a fool to take such risk on a public computer shared by three and linked to a system that could read the entire hard drive. And just as soon, reason returns because the ivygreen.edu domain seems to warn against this; at worst, it should lead to nonprofit, educational pornography. He points, clicks, waits, and reads:

> Can't wait to hear the story of the dove in your coat, professor. ☺
> See you this evening for further illumination under your shrewd
> pointers. We've all been babbling about your cossack, Cyrus. ☺

Perplexed at first, phobic next, and thirdly aroused, he finally laughs aloud at the absurdity of the situation. Apparently, Allison Silverman from his night class at University on the Ivy Green has changed her screen name. He should have known it would be something like this. She has been flirting with him in an aggressive but jocular manner all semester. The evening course at Ivy Green is Duffy's late-night treat and last class of his long day. This chance to teach literature is his just reward for wading through the quasi-literacy and not yet broken dreams of his daily excursion through higher education. Ivy Green imported genuine elite-level students—some even with intellectual curiosity and passion for reading—and once per year, in the spring semester, Duffy teaches a course in the "Twentieth Century Eastern European and Russian Short Story." Dead Jews for Living Long Islanders and other Wealthy Americans—tasty morsels of Kafka, Schulz, Singer et al, and of course, tonight's heaping spoonful of Isaac Babel. All in translation, which Duffy—in French, semi-literate at best—requires as well. Tonight, they would be discussing Babel's "The Story of My Dovecoat" and "Guy de Maupassant." The latter in particular is racy, charged writing and Allison Silverman is getting an early jump on the spirit of the stories. She is the typical, busty, "be fruitful and multiply," suburban lawyer's daughter so common to Ivy Green, and yet there is something a little off about her. Perhaps she is a bit too needy for attention, and her insistent flirtation couldn't possibly be genuine. As any phishing victim would, Duffy still experiences occasional sexual hope, but he knows who he has become: a lumpish man soon to be forty, his only natural asset an ample head of hair a shade lighter than the full growth covering his pale fish belly. And an adjunct at that, a man with no job security, who could easily be removed from the employment roles by not being rehired for the next quarter or semester. There would never be any reason required for dismissal because for adjuncts there is no formal firing. No union protects his interests; he is surrounded by students, tenured faculty, and administrators too busy with their own survival to see it from his point of view—the poor, alienated man of middle-aged malaise seeking succor in returning the advances of the flirtatious undergrad. Legal daydreams are Duffy's consolation prize; at least Allison Silverman must be over eighteen.

He checks his watch, and sees it is time to depart. Waiting to log off and restart, Duffy wonders about the strange communications he receives from these students. Julian Door, the Afrocentrist, Eileen, Andrew Hamnett, or Allison Silverman; aside from the obvious, a grade or a letter of recommendation, he has no idea what these young people want or need from interacting with him. Did they see him as a potential father figure or a role model? Could he be a friend? Or is he merely a stooge, providing the students a good laugh and leaving them thankful there are those in worse shape—older, slower, and with far fewer years left for acquiring wisdom or wealth? It is all a puzzle, but in a strange way, these offerings of words keep him from feeling so hopelessly lonely.

Duffy grabs his book bag and heads for the elevators, thirty-seven minutes before his Liberty Tech class. Because he is riding down during the middle of an Urban State class period, the Althusserian lift arrives quickly this time. When the thick, steel doors open he is greeted by the wide smile and flabby girth of Professor Solomon O'Shea. Beside O'Shea, the elevator's other occupant is a thin, young woman he recognizes but cannot quite place; nevertheless, the scene of O'Shea alone with a skinny one reminds Duffy of recent departmental history.

As a tenured professor and department chair before Seward, O'Shea mixed power with job protection. As a generous leader, he advanced the careers of female graduate students by providing them with Platonic wisdom in exchange for a glimpse, or rare groping, into their physical world. He had moved in briefly with a particularly young, acutely seduced girl two years back, and then moved out and back in with his wife and their daughters, the eldest two years younger than the student. At the time, it was rumored he tried four forms of therapy—single couch-style psychoanalysis for him, plus two partner therapies, one each for his wife and the young woman, and then *gestalt* style for his entire family—and it was certain he was removed as chairman of the department. But the grad student maintains her stipend in the Urban State PhD program in English literature, and she hasn't sued anyone, not even the school or the state, and so Solomon O'Shea kept his good job, and its generous salary, and continued to write volumes on Henry James and Herman Melville, disseminating his knowledge into the next class of twenty-somethings and riding the elevator with whomever he pleased.

Three in the shaft offers either polite smiles or tension; Duffy engages in both as the elevator descends to the lower level exit. It finally smacks him on the brain that he recognizes the girl as the genuine South Philly waitress who came across as a bit too earthy to be enrolled in a graduate school of English literature. He remembers talking to her six years ago at a graduate-student mixer. He was fully enrolled in the comp-lit program but hopelessly lost in his second-year coursework and terrified of exams on the horizon; she was fresh from the streets, or some undergrad institution, excited to be entering the world of higher learning. The conversation was something to the effect that it was all hopeless according to her, and you seem bitter according to him. No, it must have been the other way around, and he never saw her again after that exchange over hot wings and beer in the downtown bar. (The grad school has enough funding for social events that it could pick up two pints for anyone in attendance with proper ID.) And now she has apparently advanced to the point where she is soon to be the last duchess, albeit briefly, of mid-fifties roundman Solomon O'Shea. Duffy can't help but wonder how he does it. Is it just the power of tenure? His honey-tongued poetry? Or does he have some secret to his success that could be applied to the life of any man, no matter how mortal or meek his station?

All three of them walk off the elevator and stride to the back exit, which is closer to the suburban transit line. After such a full morning, Duffy has no interest in the Broad Street subway, Philadelphia's transport for the young and disenfranchised. Indeed, Eileen's racist rant has amplified his own worst ideas about dogs and fleas, and so he decides to take the commuter rail to 30th Street Station, and then to Liberty Tech. He just can't stand the thought of passing by those sullen, black teens; his inalienable tendency to imagine these alienated youths as violent criminals is too strong now. Duffy desires the bourgeois experience of passing through town on the suburban trains.

His happy elevator acquaintances are walking in the same direction, and so, as a threesome then, they stride as a horizontal marching line, away from their monolithic cement phallus, Althusser Hall, past the low-rise public housing, and toward the commuter rail. Duffy feels as awkward as a tired man can, a great urge to yawn, and an even greater urge to stifle any yawning in front of a superior officer. After all, he may have threateningly bad breath by now. The skinny graduate student walks between them, and Duffy cannot help but think of a moving version of Robert Frost's "Mending Wall," and once again it is the neighbor hurriedly replenishing the wall with the necessary balls and loaves. He toils in the barren fields of Business Writing and English Comp, and yet these smooth rocks of literature are sent sailing from cow country to smash him in the brain.

Three is a crowd, but on this beautiful spring day, Solomon O'Shea smiles, as if nothing is unusual about their less than holy trinity. "I hope you are in good spirits these days."

Duffy imagines that these young grad students experience full vaginal orgasm every time Solomon uses expressions like "good spirits" around them. Good spirits? He hasn't even had a good beer lately, never mind hard liquor to wash away the pain. How in hell should he answer this one?

But O'Shea is kind enough to save him from responding: "You're getting enough work aren't you?" This redirects the orientation of the question, away from the fires of male competition—*Yes, we both can see I'm double the man you are in both rank and girth, and that indeed you'll probably never get laid even once from the likes of this plaything here, whereas I can return time and time again to the fresh field of the entering class of graduate-degree candidates*—and toward the more humanist plea, *realize kind sir, that there are men sleeping on the streets and working behind countertops so your situation is not so grave; your adjunctry, after all, is salary and decidedly a step above shift work.*

And so he responds with a meek smile, "Why yes, plenty of work. Today is my long day, but what a beautiful day for strolling about town."

Duffy is given spirits, and he counters with a stroll. Should he have said ambulating or traipsing about?

"Yes, the perfect day for a *pilgrimage*," responds O'Shea, pronouncing the last word in aged, almost Chaucerian English. The grad girl beams. Is she certain she has just heard the clever utterance of genius or willing to grin at anything in hopes of getting ahead? Duffy doesn't have time to assess motive, and at the entrance to the suburban trains, he breathes a huge sigh of relief when his two "colleagues" move for the elevator to the right, and the platform for trains departing from Philadelphia.

Duffy takes the stairs—sixty steep steps of concrete—to the trains returning to Center City. His quads quiver and his hamstrings ache as he slowly climbs toward his afternoon classes at Liberty Tech; en route, he prays the physical exertion causes no brief enuretic seepage in his pants. He hears a train arriving above and would hurry to see if it is on his side, but with his fat gut laughing in his face and an overstuffed book bag pushing down on his spine, he has no strength for such quick movement. When he arrives at the platform, he sees the train is one departing the opposite way, and there stand O'Shea and his little T&A, his skinny TA, that is, with perfect timing, the last to board. No outstanding visible display of affection, but as O'Shea allows the twenty-something to board just before him, he gently but firmly with his right flat palm fully on her bottom, pushes his little helper forward, and holds his hand there just a bit too long for innocent chivalry. More than aroused or disgusted, Duffy stands in awe. Opposite platforms, opposite lives. No frolic in the sack on a weekday for the lesser man. But as he waits for his train to arrive, for the first time on his long day, he does indeed appreciate the shockingly clear blue sky, and what is fast becoming a perfect spring noon.

Boarding his own train, Duffy walks to the front car to find an empty seat facing forward and by a window. As assbackward is his life in some if not most areas, on the commuter rail from Urban State to Liberty Tech, he genuinely enjoys the forward march of progress. Down the aisle, he passes students with headphones and multicolored hair, fat men and briefcases, and an elderly lady shriveled up like a prune who smiles widely to show off her edentulous state. Duffy knows staring is inappropriate, weird, and even dangerous, but he cannot resist it during these moving breaks in his day. He could only imagine what fellow commuters saw in return—nostrils sprouting fluffy patches of hair with dark duffle bags below the eyes, a death gray where pink and yellow—healthy hen colors—should be. Topsoil in shades of brown with the solid white strands appearing here and there, like the singular pale elderly subsisting in a browning nation.

He smiles back at the aged charmer and passes on to finally succumb to a free window two-seater three rows from the very front of the locomotive. Instantaneous, pain-free death in a head-on collision is the positive way to see it. The train moves and Duffy admires the passing housing projects, dilapidated residential blocks, and vacant lots of gone if not forgotten North Philadelphia. And then an oasis of contemporary homebuilding, an almost brand-new cluster of government-subsidized, two-story, three-bedroom homes, the antithesis of the high, concrete prison-like projects of years past. Before Duffy can envy this affordable housing for the procreating, working poor, units far superior to his own, the slums return in full flourish—ugly brown brick, unwashed and uninviting, graffiti all over walls, storefronts, and even the doors of some homes. He sees black-grate bars anywhere possible and too many plastic bags sealing off empty spaces where home and car windows should be. A strange aspect of his reality is that residents of this area qualify for state or federal health coverage, insurance superior to Duffy's commercial, high-copay HMO. If they get sick, they can see a doctor for free whereas if Duffy were to keel over in front of the classroom he'd be admitted to an emergency room but left with a bill worthy of bankruptcy court. He has also come to see that most of his African American students at Urban State are from the suburbs or more affluent sections of the city. They grew up far from such utter abandonment, and are just as likely as their white peers to be alienated by, or even terrified of, the entrenched poverty surrounding campus.

As the train descends into the underground, Duffy closes his eyes for a five- to seven-minute nap before the natural light of the sun awakens him as the train emerges into daylight around 20th and Market. Only today, he regains consciousness early at Suburban Station by some loud black women yapping it up over what smells distinctly like fried chicken. Registered Democrat and leaning left on ninety-three percent of the issues according to online self-assessment surveys, he can document a good-liberal voting record; he is certain he is not supposed to smell what he smells or hear what he hears—fried fumes and finger-licking conversation. But resistance is futile. Although he is tired, poor, hungry, and certain there is a NO EATING sign in every car of the train, Duffy surrenders to the invasion of their lip-smacking, good-time talk. The stench fills the chamber. His cavernous gut roars for fried meat.

"Can't be too safe, is what I say."

"Amen. We in Iraq, this muthafucka in charge gonna get us all killed by retaliation. You got to be careful."

"You know Earl who live down the way?"

"Yeah."

"Well, he got these thick-ass bars on every window. They keep out burglars, rapists, every kind of crook, and even terrorists for nothin' extra. The bars can stop someone from breaking a window if they try to smash a car into your house!"

"Word."

"And the best part is if they plant the bomb in your house, you just pop out the bars and jump out the window. Even a child can do it. The man came to the house to teach Earl's boys how to do it."

"Sharonda, ain't no A-rab terrorist gonna bomb Earl's house. They go for politics and big business; natural white folk habitat. They ain't interested in a poor janitor like Earl."

"But he's the head janitor now. He's with the school district."

"Please Sharonda. Girl, you too much."

And then after a long pause, the two burst out laughing in mutual glee at Sharonda's funny. With the exaggerated guffaws, bits of the Colonel's favorite recipe are visibly ejected from their mouths and into the air, one piece finding a perfect hiding place, crash-landing into Duffy's ear. The food attack sends him scavenging for snacks. Searching his stuffed satchel, he gets lucky and finds a few aged chocolate kisses at the bottom of a crammed pouch. He unwraps and gobbles down one at a time.

As he finishes the last kiss, he wonders if the conversation were all for show, if like the Afrocentrist, these chicken women had access to multiple Englishes but favored a form of Ebon-glish for public display. Could Duffy be one of the few in town limited to one tongue? It is too much to fathom within the day's time constraints.

The train emerges from underground, and he is greeted by the strong sun now shining down on the City of Brotherly Love. He stares out at the Schuylkill, a river as polluted as they come, and yet, on this perfect day, the odorous water hosts sun dances on its surface. Standing, gathering his book bag, he slowly ambles back the way he came, up the aisle to the nearest exit. The train comes to a halt, and Duffy exits into a nearly empty platform dappled with sunshine passing through the partially open ceiling. He descends the escalator and passes the ticket office, Dunkin' Donuts, the newsstand, and Auntie Anne's Pretzels before heading down the sloping marble path that leads to the middle of 30th Street Station.

As he enters the main atrium he discerns that something is not right. The huge open section he usually walks through is cordoned off; thick-necked law enforcers with ferocious-looking German Shepherds stand guard, preventing hundreds of onlookers from pressing forward past the ropes.

Alone in the middle of the protected area stands a black briefcase.

So this is it, the real deal. Duffy has always imagined getting blown to bits in a crowded public space as the most anonymous death available to contemporary man. Although he imagines his own demise on a sickbed in his squalid, overpriced but convenient, two-room studio, at least he could expect to get some visitors at the end. The landlord and the bill collectors wouldn't stay away, and he figures a few of his adjunct associates, particularly the kinder, gentler, elderly women, would swing by to pay their last respects. His sister and her husband live in the wealthy western suburbs, but he expects she would come too in the end, although he realized long ago she finds his relative squalor so extremely upsetting that he seldom calls for fear of her having to deal with his chronic "situation," which is frankly, in her words, "depressing as hell."

Now, he sees none of this need concern him anymore. Here is the briefcase, the bomb, the proverbial shit about to go down and take Duffy with it. He blesses the Good Lord that the vociferous fried-chicken women stayed on the train, perhaps to one day successfully defend against a terrorist attack on their own home by purchasing at the same security-bar outlet that has served Janitor Earl so well. He briefly envisions himself enskied in a white sheet; he floats to the heavens high above where he meets similarly clad men who look vaguely familiar. He squints but cannot discern if they are Saudi terrorists in garb after a completed mission, the KKK fresh from a cross burning, or the innocent among us who have transcended to extend their lives as God's angels. Eyes open but not of this earth, Duffy trips on his own two feet; it is a miracle he manages to maintain his balance while snapping out of it.

Back to perceived reality, he considers a duck and cover, as useless as it could be, but then notes how odd it is that much of the crowd of commuters, loiterers, and lunch seekers—the general population of the 30th Street station—surges toward the ropes and not only in other directions. Why aren't the masses abandoning the building? "Three, two, one. Action!" A bright powerful light basks the suitcase in a fierce, conical whiteness, and a famous if middling Hollywood actress, B grade at best, shimmies out in the shortest miniskirt allowed for a PG rating in any state of the union. She presses her ear against the case, listening for the click, click, click, her facial expression so maternal and caring, one would presume she were attending to the beating heart of a baby on life support.

"And CUT!"

And that's it. Nothing at all seems to have occurred, and so the boys in blue and young stagehands remove the ropes and allow people to pass through what was a danger zone just seconds ago. As he plods forward and picks up his pace once more, Duffy receives a glossy one-page flier promoting this sizzling summer miniseries to be. He breathes a sigh of relief, pleasantly amused even, that his potential destruction is in fact only Philadelphia once more pursuing its dream of becoming the Hollywood of the East.

CHAPTER 4

CARRYING OUT THE COPIER AND THE UNDER SECRETARY OF HOMELAND DEFENSE

Duffleman ducks through the hallway of the Liberty Tech English and philosophy department, deploying the same strategy here as at Urban State, trying to avoid eye contact so as to avoid conversation. Past noon, with his teaching overload, he rarely feels a need for extra talking, particularly not on his long day with all the work ahead. He has come to the department to copy materials just before class, a job for which he will sometimes spend his own cash—at a Kinkos or Staples—to avoid people he knows. In the worst-case scenario, just like Urban State, these conversationalists may be his superiors, and expect him to show enthusiasm for work and happiness concerning his squalor. And if he shows overexertion, fatigue, duffle bags under the eyes, they could take it personally, as if he were frowning at them and not the terms of his basic predicament. It reminds him of his very first job, at the Urban Outfitters on the Ivy Green campus, and how the lowliest employees, the minimum wagers, were the ones expected to greet the spoiled students and the company's own visiting corporate types with the most enthusiasm. The America of Duffleman's résumé enjoys its bottom rung dumb and happy, or at least faking appreciation for the scraps thrown from the tables of the fully compensated shareholders, those with stock options, profit sharing, partner, or tenure.

At the turn of the millennium, when President Fern took charge, this feeling of a just economic stratification intensified, and the CEO formerly known as president of Liberty Tech began to do his best to uphold unwritten national policy by providing his Main Line mansion with spectacular new additions while declining cost-of-living raises for adjuncts and other menial employees. To his estate he added a sun room, greenhouse, tennis court, swimming pool, and his most recent plan is to build a small, bucolic back nine on an adjacent lot he would have Tech purchase. His new-addition policy was implemented soon after 9/11, and inaugurated when he had Liberty Tech pay for a safe house deep under the mansion that would provide him and his trophy wife, and even her poodle, twenty-five years of food, shelter, clean air, and water in the event of catastrophic terrorism. Liberty Tech even employs half-a-dozen well-compensated administrators to oversee the add-ons and incorporate them into the university's five-year strategic plan. In fact, Tech keeps droves of administrators in all the important fields—sports marketing, customer service, fundraising—while maintaining one of the worst ratios of tenured faculty to adjuncts on the entire East Coast. With so few tenured professors in English, at least it means Duffy has fewer faces of power to avoid.

Now with his head down, he plows forward, occasionally sidestepping shoes stomping his way. He progresses to the copier room, where just as he looks up, he nearly falls into a guy in a blue workman's uniform blocking his path. The man has the massive industrial-strength copier on a four-wheeled flatbed.

"Where are you going with that?"

The fellow turns just slightly, eyes on the task at hand. "Lease is up buddy. Gotta get her back to the shop."

Duffleman lets the disappointment soak through.

"Excuse me, buddy, we gotta get by."

"Oh, er, of course," mutters Duffy. As he slinks out of the copier room, he hazily recalls a departmental memo that notified him of this tragic loss.

The memo was written as an exciting positive, Liberty Tech boldly embarking on a brave, new eco-friendly course. The CEO wanted a wireless, paperless universe, and the photocopier had gotten the axe. Duffy recalls that no one said a word about it in the last meeting of the Freshman English program, as if no one expected anything less from Liberty Tech. Freshman English—a national curriculum whose bedrock was the photocopied additional essay, a professor's favorite left out of the current anthology—would suffer in silence as the technology crowd conquered the campus.

No copies for Duffy today, but before leaving, he moves further down the hall to check his mailbox and find three documents—a direct deposit slip for March that has apparently been sitting there over a week, the weekly flyer reminding all and sundry of the ease and access of purchasing online the Freshman English program director's textbook, and an updated Spring Schedule revealing he has lost his second section of Monday-Wednesday-Friday English 103.

His first thought is horror: *How in hell am I going to pay my rent?* His second thought is to go beat down the door of the program director. His third thought is hardly of surprise, and fourth, he realizes he must order the director's textbook for future classes to make sure this doesn't happen again. *Fuck him* is Duffy's conclusion to the five-thought outline as he crumples up the flyer. He must have said the words softly but aloud because a fortyish horse-face smiles slyly at him as she slithers around him and out of the mailroom. The entire course pay, 1980 American dollars, comes to only 1,437.93 after the war lobbyists and other pork apostles take their cut; split three ways for the monthly deposits within the quarter, and it's little more than what men in suits put on a credit card after a client dinner. Just one dinner's worth is all he has lost, hardly anything at all. And so, Duffy silently slouches toward the elevator.

He passes the men moving the monolithic, industrial-strength copier out of the hallway and onto the service elevator. Fleshy, fat, union types—crack exposed where it counts—but for this job, they are both wearing black-leather, lower-back support systems with dual-use technology for recreational purposes. Made by Nike, the silver lettering exposed. Duffy briefly considers inquiring about their wages, maybe shouting, "Excuse me, gentlemen, but as part of my commitment to the capitalist educational model, I'm doing a survey on remuneration," or, "Yo! How much that gig pay?" But he thinks the better of it and merely shuffles past, head down but unable to resist a sideways glance at the silver Nike swoosh.

At the elevator, an almost octogenarian he has known for years greets Duffy's hello with, "Young man, remind me of which class you are in?"

He considers explaining that he too is preoccupied, alienated, if not senile, adjunctry, but then thinks better of it. And so he lies. "I was your student in freshman English three years ago, Dr. Pasteur. I really enjoyed your class."

He expects his colleague to beam with pride, but instead he turns and stares, an all-out eyeball attack on Duffy's nose, a look of inquiry showing that Pasteur is trying desperately to place the face. The older man moves his head closer, less than a foot from the younger instructor, and in this adjustment, a tiny nose follicle is set adrift; it catches onto to his upper lip, teeters there like a seesaw plank, and then is lost to gravity's will.

Or perhaps the final descent is caused by the arrival of the lone working elevator? Duffy holds the doors open for his elderly friend, and they move to the back wall. Just before the doors close, a small clan of students leaving class bum rushes the elevator, smushing Duffy and his codger colleague into a back corner. Duffy is stuck awkwardly with his head down, realizing if he straightens his neck he could start a domino reaction ending in an elevator riot. But by tilting slightly to the left, he can stare longingly at the front where more room appears. When the doors close, comments ensue.

A three-inch pink halter top covering full ripe mounds of succulent teenager, both lower and upper boob exposed, goes off: "I hate it when they go all feminist like that 'n shit. And assignin' all them papers too. Dag, she think her class like the only one we take. And her breath stink."

Duffy's nose is forced to within inches of his older associate, and he can smell the stale musk of age. Pasteur's scent drives him to consider his own fate, that he too could live his last days as an under-deodorized worker-professor, some forty years hence, shoved in the back of a rusty lift by rude young people, unable to place names and faces, but still instinctively drawn to purchasing the proper number of pens and grade books, wandering into assigned classes no more than twelve minutes late. Death is distant, but the eternal purgatory of the instructor's existence looms ahead. Duffy can't help but wonder which of them is more sex- or sleep-deprived.

He gasps at the stench of elevator steel and intermingled bodies.

Another student continues, "Yeah, I noticed she stink. Worst though was this time we had Docta Whathisname down in the basement with no windows. I swear the man ain't know what soap was and probably thought deodorant was some French colony in Africa. He'd be talkin' about the oppressive state and we'd be IM-in' all class long 'bout his oppressive funk. Why them hard-ass teachers that make you read 'n shit always the funkiest is what I wanna know?"

The remaining students, the polite audience, burst out laughing and nodding. "I know what you mean" and "I know what you're sayin'" and "Word" and "Word up" and even an "Amen" from a solemn character in a beige summer suit and soft blue bowtie. Duffy wonders what that student's deal could be. Running for student government? A compassionate conservative or of the Nation of Islam? A gay thing? Or some combination of all of the above?

Duffy moves his nose from his squished mate and squints to see the more fully expressive malcontents. Through the crowded elevator, he cannot see the male student's face, but when he looks down at an angle, he can see the boy's jeans, hung low off his hips with red boxers exposed above, and an extra-wide white tee shirt neatly tucked into the boxers, as if he had tried for formality but had merely misunderstood his parent's directions. Just then the elevator stops and the doors part, and as students push out, Duffy sees the tattoo on the talking boy's neck, and just as he surmised, the boy is pinkish pale. The What-Up-Yo White Boys arrive from suburbia and small town alike, rich with black slang but not always bereft of their conservative values—"I told the bitch I ain't want her to get the procedure"; they act high on America's dreams and perhaps other hallucinogens, and are strong on defense, or at least strongly defensive—about their clothing and tattoos and earrings and above all the longer-lasting dress of whiteness itself. For a moment, Duffy considers the whale of it all, but then, with the cork popped, he and Pasteur are poured out like aged wine into the world.

He ducks solicitors selling credit cards, vacations, Free-Baraka hoodies and tees, soft pretzels, water ice, and newspapers advertising Lyndon Larouche, Ron Paul, or communism in three flavors—Maoist, mocha chip, or Mexican. He bobs and weaves with his head down, focusing on students' hips, to track their movements, and thereby avoid their sudden turns and twists left and right. But then, just before the main square, a wall of bodies blocks his forward progress. He moves laterally to his right but finds the path sealed by flesh; he is stuck standing with no forward lane available. Glancing back to his left, he catches a glimpse of pink halter-top boobs and a hairy pale hand on the small of her back, the tips of the fingers disappearing under the matching miniskirt. He sees it is the Eminem-alike from the elevator, with presumably her digits scrawled on his arm, just below his faux prison brand. With nowhere else to go but up, Duffy raises his head to enjoy the glorious sunny day that has erupted overhead, bright blue cloudless skies in place of the morning storm clouds. The necessary antidote to April showers.

In an upright position, he can see in the distance a podium on a stage surrounded by thousands of Liberty Techers and other Philadelphians. There, glistening under the sun, two men in Armani are on the mike, with others in dark glasses and thicker but less expensive suits on all sides. Duffy squints and sees that the trophy that one of them holds is in fact a machine gun, and that his thickness appears to be from a dark vest; in fact, these men are not dressed formally at all. They stand stormtrooperish in dark military uniforms tucked into shiny high black boots. Duffy suspects they wear bullet-proof pajamas underneath. Looking more closely at the two Armanied guys in the middle, he sees none other than Liberty Tech's CEO president and what must be the United States Under Secretary of Homeland Defense. Duffleman immediately and instinctively experiences raw fear at the sight of a man in charge of protecting him from "terror."

A woman dressed in casual PR trots up the steps and onto the makeshift stage. On her way to the microphone, she passes a small, older gentleman who Duffy notices for the first time. He squints and sees it is the benefactor interviewed on the morning's televised news. "May I have your attention," she shouts into the mike looming a foot above her nose; the image is not dissimilar to a short woman fellating an NBA star. With the audio on too high, her voice disappears into screeches and ear zingers. Two students jump up to adjust the mike, and two of the guards impulsively cock their weapons. False alarm. It seems only a few in the crowd notice this security glitch. They test for sound once more, and move the mike down to the woman's chin.

Duffy hears clanking and shouting over to his right. Dreadlocks, tie dye, jeans holed at the knee, an anarchist where a preprofessional should be. These are protestors like none he has seen before at Liberty Tech; he wouldn't have known they existed here. Now they chant, almost in unison but not quite so, perhaps to emphasize their belief in discord. On a placard raised high by a protestor, inviting others to join in, Duffy reads the chanted words:

> War on terror is in error
> > No more defense contractors
> Our country needs tractors
> > Jobs, training, schools, and books
> We don't need your terror crooks
> > Hey, hey, ho, ho,
> Edward Cliff has got to go.

As a writing instructor, Duffleman appreciates the sheer badness of the poetry. The word that stays longest in his brain is *tractors*. He wonders how the protestors arrived at the need for increased spending for agricultural machinery. He considers that he hasn't seen a working farm in many years. He remembers a tractor from his childhood, at five years, a kindly, elderly farmer in blue work shirt and overalls, hoisting him up onto his lap and placing him in front of the wheel for some mock driving. A day in the country for an urban kindergarten. "Son, this is what made your country great," said the farmer. This image of greatness stuck through his schooling from kindergarten choice time where he'd always play farmer, through his high school identification with Jefferson the agrarian, to his undergraduate rebellion into Socialist realism and boy-meets-tractor glory, to his graduate schooling in comparative literature, often enough emphasizing the humble and yet heroic common man the world over. And now the common farmer is hardly the average American, but Duffy feels quite usual among this sun-basted throng.

He stares back at the stage at the current symbols of American greatness—two bureaucrats without armbands but wearing wealth and power on their sleeves. Duffy squints to see the CEO head for the microphone and believes he spies a little white tag still on the CEO's cuff, the kind found on suits in the discount rack. Liberty Tech's leader shows proficiency in adjusting his own mike. He speaks.

"We at Liberty Tech, as proud Americans, are extremely excited to have here today a man who is leading our country boldly into the twenty-first century. He is a tough man, a veteran of war and the tough-minded policies necessary to keep our country safe. He is a righteous man who stands on his own two feet and knows the difference between right and wrong. It is my great patriotic pleasure to announce that the United States Under Secretary of Homeland Defense, Edward Cliff, is here today to help us in our dedication of our Institute for Homeland Security. He is here today to help us announce completion of our two-billion-dollar baby, the futuristic missile-defense technology that will lead Liberty Tech to the head of the class in defense instruction in this new century. Ed Cliff, please honor our campus and our newest department and edifice with a few words."

Tech's CEO president raises his hands high, and begins clapping slowly, football-stadium style, encouraging the audience to pick up his beat. Duffy hears a decidedly lukewarm response, as if only slightly less than half the audience participates, perhaps exactly mirroring voter representation in the 2000 presidential election.

Ed Cliff seems not the least bit deterred. He moves to the podium and slightly adjusts the microphone.

"Thank you, CEO Tsvilikakis. Thank you, staff. Thank you, students. It is my great honor to be here today to celebrate the completion of the Institute for Homeland Security. The technology developed within this building—the first of many to be built for your new Graduate School of Defense Technology—will protect America, and everyone affiliated with this campus should be a proud American today. Your campus is going to keep America strong and free in the twenty-first century!"

Like a calming lullaby, a nostalgic tune he has heard before, the Under Secretary's words pass through Duffleman; he is cast adrift from the crowd's common purpose to peruse once again the periphery. Beyond the speaker, he can see the completed building. It has been a work in progress for two years now, its noisy construction often interfering with Duffy's intros to composition and literature. He has taught quite a few spring courses where the sawing, drilling, and hammering outside mandated closed windows that in turn produced an extremely humid take on literary analysis. But now the building is complete, and its black metal frame and glass shooting up from the earth and above all the other older buildings gives it a brilliant majesty. It commands attention as the center of campus, the natural loci of all things Liberty Tech. The building's brightness causes Duffy to squint and then turn quickly away, sun splotches in his eyes as he moves his head fully to the shadier left; there, he can't but help notice through the glare the motion of two arms wielding what appears to be a large stringed instrument familiar to him. His brain quickly inventories and checks off what the instrument is not—violin, cello, guitar, ukulele—and just as he arrives upon the conclusion that it is indeed a long bow, the quiver vibrates with the shot, and Duffy watches the arrow disappear.

The Under Secretary of Homeland Defense hovers with the feathers protruding from his left ear, and the murky discolored arrowhead protruding from his right. He looms, now more stern and opaque than usual, as if it's all part of a deadpan Halloween greeting, a faux arrow through the head to treat neighborhood moms greeting him at the door. But it is April on campus, yet not April Fools' Day, and he is a dead man teetering to the left and right, not unlike a weeble-wobble save for the fact that he now slides over and falls first to the (political?) right, and then headfirst down. The CEO of Liberty Tech cries in horror at this collapsed mannequin ruining his shiny shoes. The protestors cease chanting, and stare instead, mouths agape. The sun blazes.

Pandemonium ensues.

The dust clears and Cyrus Duffleman feels more grateful than ever to stand on the periphery of life, in this case among the outer fragments of the common herd, which allows him to briskly walk away from the terrorized masses and hop onto a bus. He swipes his SEPTA pass and walks two steps in toward the back to see a bus-full of soft-eyed, flabby, mainly older African Americans, not quite as exhausted or physically fit as they could have been fifty years ago when blue-collar graveyard shifts were available and not yet automated away. Today, few of the passengers appear headed for any work at all; rather, en masse, they sit motionless in a Wal-Martized economy. Overwhelmed by the local results of global markets, Duffy promptly departs two blocks down. Just as the doors are closing behind him, he hears the simultaneous song and squeal of cell phones from inside the bus; no doubt, passengers are getting alerted to the most current event, that of the fall of the Under Secretary of Homeland Defense.

At the light, during a lull between tsunamis of violent traffic, Duffy hustles across the street and over to the senior building on campus, the First Building as it was named in an age of progress and F.I.R.E. Hall as it has been called since the naming rights were sold. He begins his ascent to an aged wing of the fifth floor. On the long winding flight of stairs, pausing to drink from his water bottle, he sometimes questions whether F.I.R.E. 572 lies not at the end of the longest step walk available on a contemporary American campus. Every other vertical journey of his long day will include visible elevator access, and he wonders if a disabled person has ever sued the school for such sin of omission or if he has overlooked an aged freight elevator hidden somewhere in this wing. At the fifth floor, gasping as usual, he leans against the wall as he stumbles toward the classroom; at the water fountain, he pauses to fill his bottle but also bends down to savor the arc of cool but metal-tasting liquid. He places his hand on his chest to await a less rapid beat and then shuffles into class three minutes late.

Over half appear present for the second day of spring quarter Critical Reading and Research. These must be the students who got here early enough to remain completely ignorant of any tragedies outside; they have turned off their cell phones, following directions from orientation and the first day of this class. Duffy finds it remarkable that they choose the immediacy of passing a class to the larger crossroads of terror, defense spending, university funding, and now the spectacle of political assassination. Of course, with so many of his own problems, Duffy has no energy left to concern himself with dead secretaries, under or not; he hopes that his task of surviving will go easier if he can forget he saw anything unusual at all. *Just do your job, Duff. Teach.*

The students sit in desk chairs of cheap black, rubberized plastic on silver support legs, pencil doodles from decades back engraved in the flat, laminated wood surfaces. While Duffy fights with his book bag's zipper, they wait in silence and watch their professor fail a procedure described as opening one's carrying case and removing the contents.

"Just a minute, er." With full concentration applied, he carefully unsticks the zipper and removes photocopies of the day's reading along with his roll book. He slides his chair backward toward the green blackboard, moves the cheap metal desk, and settles in as far from the students as possible, the furniture barricade his last defense.

"So, please take out the handout from the first day."

He has already given them something to chew on, a short favorite, Richard Meyer III's "Assembly Line Americanization." Having just begun a third quarter, the spring quarter, of their freshman year of college, the students are beginning to see that although Liberty Tech started three weeks into September, now it feels like they are enduring a lot more than their high-school peers who chose schools with traditional semesters. Whereas their friends are almost finished their second and final semester, these young Liberty Techers must now complete a third quarter, five more classes, and they are stuck at Tech until mid-June. They seem none too happy about this matter, and particularly displeased with the third leg of required Freshman English. To top it off, they have endured five flights of stairs to wait for this sloppy joker at the front of the room.

Duffy has endured this annual obstacle many times before, and now he watches as the students move in slow motion, descending upon their book bags and removing the handout as if it pained them to lift a few photocopied pages into the air and onto their desks.

"So after reading 'Assembly Line Americanization,' what do you think about Henry Ford?"

A number of hands shoot up in the back, the pale, pinkish palms of suburban Philadelphia and small-town Pennsylvania. These students are dressed in Flyers jerseys, Phillies caps, and assorted other clothing and hats bearing sports insignia.

"He was a great American who gave immigrants everything."

"They owed him their lives."

"He was a patriotic man."

"And the article showed they were grateful, unlike today's immigrants who mooch off the system and hate us."

"This country needs a good dose of Henry Ford today."

After his recent history with psychosis and murder, Duffy is relieved to listen to the minor prejudices of nationalism and anti-immigrant speech. Later, he'll count it as class participation, which comprises twenty percent of the final grade. He even tries to sympathize with these students—many of whom are from Pennsylvania's Alabama, the red counties lying between Philadelphia and Pittsburgh—and to understand their frame of reference, their background as a sum total of experience, as his business communications textbook would say. Surely it is the parents, teachers, and little league coaches of this last frontier of homogenous white America that deliver these students to Duffy with these biases firmly in place. And yet, he cringes at these first responders, the proud and true Americans selectively interpreting the text. The article depicts at least two sides to Ford's Americanization program, and yet these students, who have only skimmed for what they want to hear, seem to have remembered only the enormous pay raise of the five-dollar day, and the flag-waving ceremony at the end.

Two kinds of conservatives are drawn to the business major at Liberty Tech. First are the genuinely naïve, true patriots, often small-towners, admitted despite lower SATs, but nurtured on an undying faith in the capitalist system. And then there are their sharper, sharker brethren, more common to some suburbs, eighteen-year-olds who are already so practical, cynical, and business-minded—willing and wanting to extract as many dollars from the world with as little effort as possible—that the idea of learning to read, write, and think, perhaps only for reading, writing, and thinking's sake, seems like a complete waste of time. Perhaps this latter group sees the written word for what it is, a weak, dying symbol being replaced by the stronger, more virile image. The image, of course, they could use to turn a profit. At times, Duffy would try to impress on them the importance of learning the written word to become a manipulator of these all-powerful images as opposed to someone manipulated by them. The advertisement creator as opposed to the consumer of advertised crap. But this lesson did not always seem to sink in, and besides, isn't that why they will be consuming marketing credits next year? As too many Liberty Tech freshmen see it, the entire content of first-year writing—with its leftist pity for the alienated worker, the woman, the weak—is a complete waste of time.

"Did anyone understand the article to be both positive and negative?"

A front-row girl's hand shoots up. It is a student whose parents were born in Southeastern Europe, and brought her here as a seven-year-old. Duffy has taught her in the previous quarter and is grateful she has signed up for his section again. She seems to possess a genuine intellectual curiosity, and she *reads* much more conscientiously than most of her native-born peers. The irony of this difference is that judging by the heterogeneity of student last names, the latter are but a generation or two more American than this European-American. Indeed, at times, Duffy has taught rooms full of first-generation Americans, so he has seen the dramatic diversity of their intellect, taste, and reading comprehension.

Now he smiles widely as he calls on the girl.

"Meyer is showing the two sides of Ford's program. Although he is offering them a good wage, he is forcing assimilation upon them, forcing them to conform to his demands. It is almost like paid slavery."

Paid slavery, an odd idea, but one Duffy can identify with in consideration of his own worker-drone status. He appreciates her use of complete sentences.

"Very nicely stated, Ilana. Let's see if we can develop the idea of the two sides." As Duffy turns away to face the blackboard, he suppresses the need to apologize for the view of his wide flabby ass. He glances down at the board's silver tray to find a single eraser and not a flake of chalk. The most privatized campus of his long day, which in theory should be the most efficient, offers these repeated instances of missing necessities. No photocopies and no chalk—the authorities are intent on forcing Duffy into the twenty-first century and all its e-technologies, and yet the room is devoid of digital projectors and Internet access as well. He could only suppose that teaching tools for freshman comp are not a priority for the efficiency experts. But rather than turn the missing chalk into a business lesson, Duffy turns back to class hoping his look of exasperation is not misinterpreted. He wants to encourage class participation as much as possible. And he is in luck, as today, the true patriots are juiced up and ready to perform.

"Aw, come off it. No one told 'em they had to work here."

"Are you saying you would do whatever your boss told you? Dress any way he made you? How would you like it if Bin Laden conquers our country and you have to spend five hours a day chanting the Koran?"

"The American flag is a symbol of the freedoms Osama hates us for. Ford is making these immigrants wave it for their own good."

"Yeah, he's reminding them of who saved their asses."

"Shut up and do your job, and be grateful America let you in."

Duffy stares back at the next America, young people raised on 9/11 and love of the red, white, and blue. An assembly line a thousand miles away and one hundred years ago has become a "here" of contemporary debate, tribal turf in need of defense. The intensity of jingoistic anger is painful and perplexing. Although these boys say they love America's freedom, it seems as if they are imprisoned in a blind patriotism that refuses to recognize any of America's weaknesses, the soft spots in the underbelly of capitalist democracy. False promises of forty acres and a mule have been replaced by fifty million uninsured. Their own progress jeopardized by Liberty Tech's for-profit mentality that granted the students calamity-coverage subsisters for instructors, an army of Dufflemans surviving by teaching six courses plus tutoring each term. But this is lost on the conservative boys; many of them may even presume Duffy rolls in the dough as a college professor. So a guy like him better love America too because any criticism would be biting the hand that feeds.

While the border patrol shouts down the immigrant girl's recitation of Emma Lazarus's "tired, hungry, and poor," Duffy spies between opposing points of view—sitting in the middle of the room, that is—a boy paralyzed with an intensity of anxiety strewn across his brow. His face shows the pain and fear of a civilian caught in the middle of a battlefield, as if instructor and immigrant attack him from one side and the back-row Americans from the other. His stare lingering a moment too long, he recognizes the boy from Freshman English 101 in the fall. For that class, he attended roughly half the sessions, said nary a word the entire time, but managed to complete something double-spaced for each of the essays, and so Duffy granted him his escape with a D. Good enough for Liberty Tech credit but not good enough to transfer, which is what most D students would prefer to do. They get discouraged and want to move on. From speaking with students, he has learned it is not unusual to attend two or three schools on the way to a bachelor's degree these days.

Back in the moment, Duffy wracks his brain, desperately trying to remember the boy's name. He is a Justin Something or Jonathan Somebody, but as hard as he tries, he can't produce an exact name he could pronounce with confidence. If only the boy had participated, handed in a few more journals, the name would come to mind. As usual, Duffy feels left with a rough draft, just a small glimpse into the undergrad's life, important details missing like an essay returned incomplete. He has an urge to halt the class, and welcome the boy back into the fold, ask him how his winter quarter of English 102 went, but with the verbal onslaught nearly out of control, such a timeout proves impossible.

"Yeah, who the hell are you to tell us what to do with our immigrants?"

"Yeah, what gives you the right? I bet your parents weren't even born here."

The immigrant defending immigration looks a bit flustered, outnumbered by back-row Republicans and tired of parrying their repeated, dull blows. Duffy admires her willingness to debate, to raise her hand in class, and fight off the discontented hordes of Liberty Tech; nevertheless, he knows he needs to rebalance the terms and conditions of battle, and he surprises himself when he does so, aiming to turn the tables on the true patriots.

"Young men, were your parents born here?"

"Yeah."

"You bet your ass."

"You better believe it." Affirmative cacophony is the back-row return fire.

"How far back can you trace your own family? Where were your grandparents born?"

The noisy troops simmer down to nothing too soon. Duff is puzzled by the absolute silence, but then he understands.

"You don't know where your grandparents were born do you?"

Duff waits. From under a red Phillies baseball cap, he sees a slight nod of assent. Flyers Jersey merely stares back blankly. Others keep their eyes diverted, growing a darker shade of red. Their heads down or to the side, as if something scary or embarrassing were occurring beyond the window.

So he turns to the immigrant girl and asks, "Do you know where your grandparents were born?"

"Two of them. The rest I'm not sure."

Duff regards Jonathan Somebody caught in the middle. His look is still largely of fear, with some slight relief above the eyes. Although his face expresses recognition of the emotions around him, it is difficult to say if he is listening.

Knowing full well that lecturing could lead to his being described as an "asshole" on student evaluations, nevertheless, Duff decides on a history lesson.

"My father's father was a Russian Jew who escaped the violence of a pogrom back home to arrive here safely in 1906. He was nine. Many in his family hoped for work in the New York City's garment district, so they changed the family name to Duffleman; they knew Duffel, Belgium was where the heavy woolen cloth was produced. Knitting and sewing in sweatshops was women's work, so as soon as he was old enough, thirteen, he moved to Chicago with an older brother and went to work full time at a meatpacking plant. He swept pig parts off the floor and down a drain for reprocessing as wieners and sausages. These were long fifteen-hour days; it was filthy work and he stopped keeping kosher. He came home to his flophouse reeking of dead pork, so he kept a low profile and tried to blend into the wood-plank bed. At night, he would dream of the Five Dollar Day, but it wasn't available to him because Henry Ford discriminated against Jews. In 1917, he ran away from home and enlisted in the army. It was a chance to see the world. Have adventure. Kill some Krauts, a Russian's natural enemy. They discovered his age nine months later and gave him an honorable discharge. Back home, he was still a nobody, so it was right back to the sausage factory for Abraham Duffleman. But he worked hard and showed enough promise that he met and married my mother three years later. She was unusual, half-Jewish, half-gentile, a mix ahead of its time although quite prevalent by the 1930 s, when Hitler came to power. She had a Jewish nose and blonde hair, was born in Poland but moved here in infancy with her parents. My grandfather wound up starting his own kosher meats processing plant, stayed in business twenty years until he was laid to waste by the Great Depression. Sometimes market forces control the man."

The students stare at their instructor; they are unaccustomed to immediacy in the classroom, anyone who would dare speak of his origins and attribute ethnicity to noses and hair. Although Duffy often feels like an imposter, a foreign agent, there are times like the present one where, for better or worse, even with five-eighths of a foot in his mouth, he is someone they can bear to pay attention to.

Jonathan Somebody looks like sausage-factory work threatens his own future, but the other faces show awe, respect, and even visible reverence. So Duff continues.

"Over on my mother's side, my grandfather, a Slovakian potato farmer, met my grandmother, of Irish ancestry, and of course, accustomed to men of potatoes. They settled in an Irish section of Philadelphia. Slovaks were rare, but generally accepted as similarly downtrodden peasants from Europe. My mother met my father in 1959, at a college mixer in Philadelphia. Their parents struggled mightily to survive in the new world, and they were both the first in their families to attend college."

He pauses. It is time to throw the mike back to the audience.

"Are any of you the first in your family to go to college?"

Just one of the back-row Republicans raises his hand to half mast, a sheepish look crawling over his face, as if being a trailblazer is something to be ashamed of.

The immigrant girl also has her hand up. She offers, "My father has a PhD in industrial engineering from a university in Moscow, and my mother studied flute at a conservatory in St. Petersburg. I'll be the first to get an American degree."

Duff wonders if the others can even fathom that this means her parents are far more educated than their own. Part of the patriotic brainwashing seems to include the idea that degrees from other countries are meaningless or soft. But maybe they know better. They've seen that half the doctors, scientists, and programmers they've met come from other countries. They are anti-immigration because they know foreigners are desperate and smart; they work hard, grab the good careers, and leave the less driven and more native coughing in the dust. The patriots know they can't compete. It occurs to Duffy that he can't compete either. The brilliant, exotic post-colonials having seized half the tenured posts in the humanities, and the Duffler is three-stepping the adjunct shuffle. But he is too satisfied with his message to stay down for long.

"So I suppose they work as terrorists here?"

"Exactly." The immigrant girl seems pleased by the irony whereas Jonathan Somebody's look of paralyzed fear intensifies as if he understood the literal meaning alone. Duffy resists the teacher's impulse to explain, "That was a joke. I didn't mean to imply that her parents were terrorists." Of course, that could be for Jonathan Somebody's good—or at least good for his comprehension—but it could further alienate the back-row Republicans, further cause them to think he regards them as idiots. He looks back there and sees they have returned to their jaded, relaxed postures. "Yeah, right," they tacitly state. "Tell me another one, Teach."

For a moment, Cyrus Duffleman experiences genuine pleasure. He has reached that certain level, that dignified position, of actually feeling like something he has said has gotten through to the students. A message delivered. *Duff has taught the class.* This feeling of bliss soon subsides as reality sets in. Turning his grandparents' stolen lives into instructional material captivates the audience, but he knows he has wasted his riff on their immigration far too soon in the quarter. In a way, he pilfers from them the same way America has stolen from its immigrants throughout the centuries—by promising a dream, alienating their labor, laughing at their comedy routines on stage, while profiting from their disenfranchised status.

Just then, interrupting his latest bout of self-flagellation, a kid comes tearing in, a half hour late, out of breath from the steep steps. Duffy has an instant flashback to Urban State and Julian Door's audacious interruption of class and his subsequent pyrotechnic display. Returning to the present moment, he hears the kid cry out, "They killed him. The terrorists got him. Shot him on stage with an arrow."

Although he was witness to this deed, Duffy finds himself as surprised as his seated students. Like the 9/11 event itself, when he first thought he was watching a movie, he must see the image or hear the news a third or fourth time before the message registers. Back then, he remembers experiencing some real fear, a slight suspicion that a Philly skyscraper could soon be targeted unless poisoning the Broad Street subway was next, whereas today, he feels no fear at all. As a good inhabitant of the post-9/11 age of terror, he should be at least briefly paralyzed with fear, no? But all he saw was a targeted assassination. They want the leaders, not the minions. For better or worse, Duffy feels safe.

"Murderers!"

"Who'd they kill?"

"We gotta keep their kind out of the country!"

"Had to be Al Qaeda. Those crooks."

"Those damn liberals think we're not even at war. They'll get us all killed."

"It's all fuckin' Michael Moore's fault!"

The runner breathes in heavily, almost hyperventilating, perhaps a preasthmatic, his blubbery middle heaving in and out, the student's heart and stomach tributes to Liberty Tech's rich institutional food. He inhales, exhales, and sputters out, "Right on campus. They got the Under Secretary."

It registers.

"We gotta do something!"

"We gotta get out of here."

From the back row, Flyers Jersey reaches underneath his red, white, and black uniform and pulls out a small, silver-gray metal device. He is packing, carrying a piece. "One of them messes with me, and I'm ready." Duffy resists a strong urge to shit his pants and dive beneath the desk. The students, even his peers among the back-row Republicans, turn and regard him warily. Good Americans, they know the evening news is about disgruntled students and workers shooting up everything around them. But Flyers Jersey senses the fear and says, "Jeez, guys. You're with me. I'm not gonna off you. I got your back. If you're proud to be an American." And he turns to squint meanly at the immigrant girl and then his instructor.

Duffy feels creeped out but also negligent for not explaining what happened at the beginning of class or better yet cancelling the session and sending them all home to hide under their dorm beds. An assassination is at least as grave as a girl's psychotic cursing and ranting, so Duffy owes them at least an early ending, what is fast becoming the theme of his long day.

But before he relents to their escaping, from education and the enemy, Duffy assigns two critical pieces for the next session. One concerns sexism and anti-feminism in American marketing and advertising, the other the tobacco company executives' duplicity and how they rationalize their career of helping to spur on death for millions every year. He looks around the room and notices for the first time the silent partners of today's class, several young women in globs of lipstick and mascara, their look midway between professional and trashy. He notes with dismay that the immigrant girl pancakes it on more than any. He sees boys and girls with the jaded and hardened looks of smokers. He knows they have no higher conscience—or feel they cannot afford to express one—when it comes to earning a living. For in the past the common reaction to the tobacco-executive piece has been, "It sounds like a good job with high pay and company perks. How do I get one of those?"

"Now, no worries. This sounds like a targeted assassination. They aren't after all of us. Just the big shots. No reason to panic. Just leave the classroom in an orderly manner and return to your dorms. Call *the rents* to let them know you're safe." He cannot explain it, but Duff feels secure as he combines authority and hip lingo in what he says. "We'll all be fine. We'll meet here next Tuesday. Come prepared to discuss the readings. Good job today."

Just like that. He brooms them. The immigrant girl and the preasthmatic boy are the last ones to leave, and they each linger around the desk, as if they have a special request. But like many shy freshmen, they wait for the teacher to speak first. Duffy wants to thank the immigrant girl for participating and for seeing both sides of the issue. Instead, forgetting his train of thought, he finds himself lost in her formidable cleavage. She catches him, and he quickly averts his eyes first to the floor, then to her face. She seems amused more than angry. He has noticed that this tendency to linger too long in the taboo neighborhoods of proper eye contact has gotten worse over the past few years. Horny and alone, he could even find himself staring momentarily at student crotches, gender neutral, in the middle of class, out of the corner of his eye, even a few on the far-seated periphery. So many dull, dead, repetitive clichés came from their mouths, it is as if he were exploring for their better selves, their vibrant, living parts.

The immigrant girl just wants to tell him she read the feminist advertising piece in high school and really enjoyed it.

"Thank you," he whispers to her as she leaves the class. Shame flushes his brow.

"Ah, sir," says the boy, finally having caught his breath. "Could you tell me what I missed?"

Oh how Duffy hates this question! It causes him to imagine the exhausting task of repeating the whole show while fearing there might not be anything of import once all the tangents and interruptions are removed. Give me the summarized version in ten seconds please, is how it sounds. "You missed class" is his instinctual reply. But the freshman will look devastated if he delivers this truth. Or worse, they will begin to spout out long, detailed apologies and excuses, clinging like a small mammal until he absolves them of their sins. No matter what the crime, they have the audacity to demand this forgiveness.

But this time around, remembering to show extra kindness to a young child who has just witnessed a violent death, he says calmly, putting effort into keeping his eyes on the sad, puffy face, "We reviewed and discussed 'Assembly Line Americanization.' If you show me your notes on the text, I'll be glad to review them with you."

"Well, er, I didn't really take notes."

"Did you read it?"

The boy solemnly shakes his head sideways. "No, sir" he mumbles at the floor.

"It's okay. It's been a long day for you already. Go back to your dorm and call your parents. Let them know you are safe, and then get some rest. Show me your notes next week after class."

"Thank you, professor." The boy seems genuinely grateful for such consideration. He smiles as if this small act of letting him off easy is what he experiences as true decency. Duffy is a guy cutting him a break. And then the boy turns and lumbers away.

Duffy is about to turn off the lights when from the corner of his eye he spies a green-gray crinkled paper, lying innocently alone in the far right corner of the back row. He feverishly darts his head to and fro, making sure no one else is around. Then, like a starving man craving grain, he dashes upon the found cash, ignoring all manner of stiff joints and muscles as he flies on all fours, ape-like, to the crumpled bill. A dollar? Or would this be the Duffler's Five Dollar Day? Or even a ten spot or twenty? Saliva drips off his jowls as he pounces on the lost cash—only to discover it is merely a tissue left behind by a phlegm-heavy undergrad. It is moist and green-gray with a hint of yellow ripple. It would have been just too much work for the poor, hungry student to toss away his waste, so in shame, Duffy, with pinky finger and thumb touching as little as possible, nabs the offending mirage and discards the tissue.

And then he gathers his belongings, turns off the lights, and shuffles out of F.I.R.E. 572.

As he descends the black marble steps, down from the furthest perch of Liberty Tech's higher education, he hears someone bounding up the steps from below. When he arrives at the first landing and turns to continue, he sees Frank Hamnett standing post-leap on the next landing below. As slow as he ambles, Duffy stops as well and shares a moment of indecision with his grimacing student. The two maintain this long pause together, one half a stairwell below the other, the mutual acknowledgment of men frozen in time. The teacher is about to raise a hand, and offer a friendly greeting, when the student turns suddenly, cat quick, like the trained soldier he is, and leaps back down the stairs. In just a moment, Frank is gone from view. It is just as well. Duffy is too battle weary to endure another student concern. Thankful for this precious time on his hands, he decides to go kill it at the train station.

CHAPTER 5

INSPECT YOUR PACKAGE AT THE DOOR

Walking back toward the train station, Duffleman pushes through crowds of concerned citizens. He sees faces full of fatigue and apprehension but no overt displays of panic and fear. The National Guard and Philly cops are everywhere. He hears a loud megaphone repeat in an ominous drone: "All Amtrak trains are closed. SEPTA trains are running with a two-hour delay. The green and blue lines are running but all parties must be searched. We apologize for the inconvenience." It occurs to Duffy that he has witnessed a major assassination and arguably the most significant event of his life. Unlike his daily efforts to educate the city's youth, this political kill appeared to be a perfect success. He finds it strange that he chose to teach through the experience, as if nothing unusual was going on. Is he that far gone? Unable to turn away once he has begun plowing through his long day? Or in some sick, twisted way does he enjoy teaching that much? Does it merely take his mind off graver realities like the day's tragedy or those reported daily online and in print? Is he not the average American intent on hating his job? Or is he genuinely afraid of not teaching, worried he would be unable to conceive of anything to do with his time? It is all more than he can fathom, particularly on his long day. One thing he knows is keep moving, keep moving on the long day, and it helps him ignore the basic predicament.

Yes, the basic predicament is in part caused by the long day, but to recognize this fact now would only make things worse.

The boys in blue are now performing full searches of all people entering 30th Street Station. As a result, few seem to be taking advantage of the opportunity to commute by rail or eat inside. He imagines the paranoid masses—yes, a people he is not wholly apart from—already expecting the train station to blow up or a terrorist attack against a local skyscraper. The average American might not read the papers or political magazines, but from seeing Cliff, Fern, or the veep on national TV, he or she must know that Al Qaeda always plans sensational, simultaneous attacks. The assassination has to be only part one. More is to come. Big media instructs that this is so.

In a short line, he finds himself waiting behind a postal employee and a dark-skinned man in a turban. The two give each other a wide berth, and Duffy is left wondering who is stereotyping whom—the presumably South Asian man, presumably a Sikh, in fear of the legendary serial-killing postal employee? Or is the postal employee keeping his distance from the turban, this otherness a certain sign of the terrorist, a hat bias that is part of the new and improved racial profiling? Or maybe they are just good Americans, practicing their distance categories, allowing a neighbor some elbow room.

Duffy would like to believe the latter as he pushes past the heavy, glass door with its gold-painted bronze frame. The policeman in charge of checking his overstuffed bag appears perplexed by its contents. He looks first in the main chamber, furrowing his brow as if he has never seen so many thick textbooks and student papers before. He takes out each book and pages through the contents, pausing at a few photographs of attractive female CEOs in the Business Writing textbook, and finally for a blonde, spreading the book wide as if he were staring at a centerfold. The textbook is chock full of images selling the idea that America's corporations are all about the multinational, equal-opportunity, antidiscriminatory accrual of wealth; yes, technocratic but tolerant profits for all genders and hues. Duffy sees the illustrations as a kind of corporate pornography, but the policeman gawks at the thirtyish blonde in professional skirt suit, stockings, and heels like she is a genuine hottie. He chuckles just a little, adds a slow whistle under his breath, and moves on to Duffy's photocopied story packet, which in turn doesn't capture the cop's attention. The officer ignores the Business Ethics Reader that Duffy uses for Critical Reading and Research, and then he grabs all of the papers, and begins flipping through them one after another. The pile is huge, and the policeman does Duffy the good service of slipping in his mad flipping so that too many sheets fly all over, some onto the marble floor of the station, a few rebels floating to the cement walk outside the station's entrance. Thinking fast, the Duffler scurries madly about to pick up his lost treasures. He is thankful most fell inside, and the wind blows hardly at all, and so he soon gathers his paper grading, if not in order, at least clumped together.

"Er, sorry about that buddy." The policeman shows genuine compassion, not because he has to grade all of those monotonous sheets, but because he had to stoop to pick them off marble and cement. It is clear the officer has ascertained that his is the exceedingly more important job.

Despite noise and commotion all around him, Duffy focuses on the cop. After shoving the papers haphazardly back in the bag, the officer moves to the smaller pouches and compartments. Duffy watches the officer battle with five years' worth of notes on scraps, tiny ends of lifesaver wrappers and assorted paper bits, cough drops, old keys, unsharpened pencils, worn and faded business cards from a large variety of brief acquaintanceships, and broken watches from semesters taught long ago. The cop is persistent and conscientious, and so after leaving no meaningless odd or end unperused, he goes last to the bag's tiniest pouch.

He unzips and stares down at the white powder that appears on the two fingers and thumb he moved into the area. His eyes meet Duffy's with the death stare. From major media outlets, everyone in America knows that mysterious white powder, what would have been presumed baking soda in the 1950s, cocaine in the 1980s, is now invariably the killer ingredient, anthrax. Duffy, good citizen and TV viewer, shares the cop's moment of paranoid panic, both frozen and trying not to breathe. It occurs to Duffy that he has had this massive, roach-brown book bag on his person for most of the day, in fact most of the life, and so it is unlikely anyone could have planted anything inside. He racks his brain to remember what the powder could be. If it is anthrax he has no idea which colleague could have planted it there. He is almost certain his status as ignored adjunct has been enough to avoid personal conflicts with peers. The students are a different matter, their strong emotions unpredictable and scary. Could it be a radical from Urban State or a conservative from last class? Flyers Jersey sends scary signals for sure. The officer recovers his calm, and resumes the search. He peers into the tiny compartment, moving its unzipped sides as far apart as possible with just the tips of his fingers. He opens it so only he can see, chuckles again, and then allows Duffy a peak: several small, broken pieces of childhood innocence. It is white chalk, what he placed in that area many months or years ago. The fractured pieces would have come in handy last class, if in fact he had remembered they were in his possession.

"Why ya got chalk in the bag?"

"I'm a teacher, sir."

"Yeah, but ya makin' a mess of ya bag."

"I'm sorry sir."

The cop stares skeptically at Duffy. How could any sort of teacher be so much of an untidy man? He just stares, evaluating the sum, the mess of him all, the pouches under the eyes, the garbage in the pouches, the stranded white soldiers in Duffy's hair. And then he nods ever so slightly, Philly style, indicating that it is okay for the perp to pass through.

"Thank you, sir," and Duffy nods twice, doing just the slightest Chinaman's stooping bow.

As he shuffles into the station, Duffy turns toward the noise, and he can see the man in the turban and another policeman stuck in a loud exchange, nose to nose, the cop's menacing deadpan matched by the South Asian's fierce alacrity with emotionally loaded nouns.

"Liberty."

"Yeah."

"Freedom."

"Uh-huh."

"The Rights of Man."

"So?"

"I am with you, man! These fires are burning in my soul!"

Duffy finds something sick and sordid about the immigrant's need to recite aloud, like a trained seal, the clichés of a nation although his motivation is surely survival instinct and his need to gain entry to the station. Immigrant rule number one is to assimilate in every way possible—to say anything to survive and prosper. And although he can appreciate and even acknowledge his own obeisance to this rule, Duffy wants desperately to quash the brazen stereotyping that stabs him in the brain, that only a man owning American gas stations would recite such bland jingoisms for the boys in blue. And so with relief, he leaves these patriots behind.

Once inside, Duffy sees a few professionals left over from the lunch crowd, but most have left to return to work or home or anywhere with all-day televised cable news. Seated at the remaining tables are the indigent men he prefers the company of anyway. The business people, men mostly, sit and gab in such a harsh, cynical way—against corrupt CEOs, idiot liberals, the crimes and bankruptcies of black athletes—that it is often painful to be subject to their bitter discussions. The homeless men, on the other hand, usually sit alone and quiet, just like Duffleman.

He passes the sullen and mostly black crowd of *isolatoes*, each with a dark-green circular table to himself, some sitting with a newspaper, others with a coffee or pint milk carton. A particularly old man mutters to himself, a strand of saliva hanging off his lip while he sways from left to right. The next table down, a woman sits with three huge shopping bags, one on each remaining chair as if they were her afternoon bridge partners. As Duffy passes, he can see a violent red rash on her pale neck, not unlike fire-damaged skin. Turning away in revulsion, he grabs a used newspaper from the free rack, walks past the nonsmoking area, and around the corner to wait behind a single customer for his coffee from Dunkin' Donuts. As he waits, he skims the paper, opens randomly to a few pages in, and sees a short article titled, "Black Unemployment Up in NYC." He reads that according to a recent study completed at a CUNY campus in the Bronx, only one of two African American males aged sixteen to sixty-four report that they are employed on a full-time basis; in parentheses, he reads that "full time" is counted as thirty-three hours per week. So this is where the Afrocentrist got her information. The daily newspaper. This study contradicts Federal unemployment statistics that list African American male unemployment as roughly double that of the overall unemployment rate but still only thirteen to fifteen percent. "The numbers are troubling," says New York City's mayor. "We need to find jobs for these men."

"Next please." Duffy looks up from the paper to see the small woman, Indian or possibly Bangladeshi, ready to take his order. He feels an immediate pang of guilt at having imagined the turbaned man as a gas-station owner. No one to beg forgiveness to so all he can do is correct himself. Yes, this is the real immigrant's experience, selling doughnuts for chump wages, earning less than the panhandlers who rove around and outside the station.

Pleased with his internal compassion, he places an order: "I'd like a Boston creme doughnut and a medium coffee with milk and sugar." She retrieves the doughnut, placing it with a wrapper in a Dunkin' Donuts paper bag. Then, she moves to make his coffee, and after she pours the hot, black liquid, she reaches for the half and half. Duffy sees this and says, "Milk, please, milk."

She takes the quart container, and gestures up with it, saying, "Milk. Milk," smiling at him as if to say, "Be happy because I am going to pour the milk."

"No," he replies, "milk, not cream."

The woman turns away, exasperated, and calls to someone in the back, in a language Duffy cannot understand. Returning to the paper, and on the same page, in an adjacent box, he reads an Associated Press report from a politically neutral, economic think-tank. The story states that while four million immigrants have gained employment in America in the last four years, at least one million U.S. citizens have lost full-time positions.

Back to the coffee purchase. A supervisor appears, also South Asian. He is dressed not in a Dunkin' Donuts uniform but in a long-sleeved white Oxford under a company tie with brown and pink stripes. As if he has heard this conversation hundreds of times before, he asks, "You want milk?" As soon as Duffy nods, he retrieves the other carton, the milk carton, hands it to the woman, and then returns to the office. She smiles and pours in the milk, too much in fact, but Duffy doesn't say a word for fear of further delaying his coffee fix. She can count money just fine, and she smiles when she sees that he has handed her exact change. "Thank you," she says.

Duffy can't help but make the connection from the woman working behind the counter to the newspaper stories he has just read. Are African American men losing out on jobs to immigrants who don't speak English? He wonders if this woman is a legal employee, or if she is being paid five dollars per hour under the table. *Under the counter*, he corrects himself. Couldn't one of the homeless men in the train station bag doughnuts? Somewhere is there not one among the millions represented by the one in two capable of pouring coffee and counting money? Since his earliest high-school history classes, Duffy has wanted to believe in the American Dream as the immigrant's dream, just as it was for his grandparents, the hardworking and brave who defended the country, and asked for little more than a chance to subsist, to survive. And yet, he wonders if the tables of homeless men, or fifty percent of the black people crammed onto the bus, would have a better chance of subsisting if fewer immigrants were paid shit wages for the menial labor of the land. Duffy even has a sense that his red-American Liberty Tech students know a white America where Caucasians were similarly unemployed, underemployed, full time at the lowest rung—pumping gas or cleaning toilets—or buying goods with food stamps from minimum-wage immigrants working behind the counter.

And yet, he has read articles explaining how increased immigration and immigrant employment produce economic energy and create jobs for everyone. Cities were not zero-sum games where one fellow swiped another's coffee-bean opportunity, but rather like the espresso machine itself. Vibrant metropolises heat up a bubbling froth that is then poured into the world for everyone to share. But Duffy, sad binary thinker, cannot shake the zero-sum view of the world, and he wonders at times when he too would be replaced to return home for good to his simple one-button, four-cup, auto-drip coffee maker.

Yes, the decline of the white American, or when the black man would ever be President or free, or at least employed and insured, is too much to contemplate, but precisely the kind of thing he finds himself worrying about in transition in the middle of his long day. His own mediocre catastrophic health coverage is but a sad afterthought, a coda to his immediate concerns; what he worries about is the health coverage of others.

Duffy finds an empty place in the homelessness section, tosses the paper onto the plastic, green grate table, dumps his bag, removes his jacket, and slouches down low in the chair. He enjoys the fact that with his dreamy, vacant look he can blend right in. Even with his paper grading sprawled across the table, few seem to recognize him as more than a transient. He remembers waving and smiling at a tenured old maid of Liberty Tech, Dr. Vonda Crenshaw, when she wandered past him one time in this part of the train station. Boldly, he smiled and waved at her, but she returned a look more of disgust than horror, sure she was being saluted by an untouchable. Another time, he was sitting reading the papers, with an empty Styrofoam cup, the remains of his coffee his only companion, when a businessman in a dark suit suavely slid out his right hand in passing, and tossed in two shiny quarters. Duffy let the coins lay where they were, and sure enough, once one suit contributed, they all chipped in. On that particular day, even after two rounds of coffee, he left with a $13.37 net gain—all in change save for one mangled bill.

Today Duffy returns to the front page to skim the morning headlines. He sees a short piece on the Under Secretary's visit to Liberty Tech. The article notes that he attended the university twenty-seven years ago when it was an all-male institution for future businessmen and engineers. In fact, according to the article, the current Tech CEO and the Under Secretary were fraternity brothers back in the day. "Two proud Liberty Techers made good" is how a quoted Liberty Tech press release put it.

"I'm glad to be back," says the political appointee to Homeland Defense.

Duffy feels odd reading an article that quotes a dead man as living in the present. If the American government were a deck of cards to the terrorists, then surely someone from their ranks could now claim ownership of at least the Jack of Clubs. On the other hand, in a monolithic American bureaucracy, it is hard to say for sure that such a recently created department would carry such weight. Perhaps the Secretary of the Department of Energy or Education or Labor would be a bigger hit? Duffy remembers reading that the Chinese American Secretary of Labor, one Ethel Chin, is on record as stating that developing-world sweatshops—no, not only ones full of Chinese women—are of no concern to the United States government. If these terrorists were sincere in their intention of righting American imperialism's economic wrongs, then maybe she's the Queen of Spades?

"I was the queen of Manhattan in my day."

Duffy peers up to see the old lady, her thick shopping bags hovering over him, already stacked on one of three empty seats at his table.

"Young man, is this seat taken?"

He looks about and sees that much of the seating area is empty, including her previous spot, but he cannot imagine sending this poor, frail woman, this old bag, yes, off to sit by herself, and so he says with uncommon cordiality, "No, no. Please dear, sit down."

The red-rash dowager smiles widely, revealing more gaps than gold caps and yellow stains. "How sweet. There's just no kindness among the younger generation today."

He imagines that she has met some of his students.

"They never offer a lady a seat. All a lady wants, really, is a seat, just a chair, and perhaps a chance to exchange a few words."

Duffy—mid-sip—nods as vigorously as possible without spilling his coffee. He indulges a bit too much and brown liquid sprinkles downward, seeping into his worn gray sweater. It is so old anyhow, not good for much more than waxing a car, and he wonders why he didn't just buy a new one yesterday. After five years of daily wear, perhaps it is about time.

"These young people are so selfish. They don't care about us. All they do is listen to that music, dream about money. To hit the big time, they blow up buildings."

Duffy hasn't linked the music to the money or the destruction of architecture but perhaps she is onto something.

"When I was young, I was a Hollywood actress, but I always cared for other people."

Ah yes, he muses, the former actresses. He often wonders where the theater coeds disappear to after decades of waiting tables. As if by magic, a dried flower and stem appears from behind her right ear.

"I'd send a dollar to my mother whenever I could. I'd wave and say hello to kind, old ladies." Somewhere in the back of her mouth, she finds a molar, and using the stem as a toothpick, she sets to work.

Duffy tries to smile as sincerely as possible. For a moment, they make unwavering eye contact—two spent soldiers enduring the early afternoon after a full day's worth of morning skirmishes. And then the dried flower is out of her mouth and returned to her ear.

"You look so kind and gentle sir. Would you like to know the lady's name?"

A tad unsure if this is conversation or a pick-up line, Duffy replies, "Sure. What's a lady's name?"

"A lady's name is Lucia Starr. Do you recognize it?"

He cannot say that he does, so instead he says, "It sounds familiar."

"It's from the 1950s. I was big then. I played opposite all the usual suspects. They came in droves. I accepted their flowers."

Duffy nods.

"But what do I have to show for it?"

The woman pauses, letting the question hang, and Duffy supposes this is indeed his cue. It is his turn for words. He considers the full ramifications of this Lucia Starr, and all the Lucy Starrs of the world, how they start off young and romantic—a beautiful freshly plucked flower—and wind up stinking and homeless, adrift in a menacing, global economy. It is all he can manage to mutter, "I'm sorry a lady has fallen on hard times."

"Son, you look so nice. So kind. I have a business proposition."

He prays this involves cash, not sex.

"It isn't very difficult but you see I need someone to watch my bags, just this valuable one in fact, while I go to the bank." She produces a faded pink plastic bag that appears to have slight rips and scars along its sides. Tiny holes the treasure might fall out of? "Since it's so valuable, all I ask is that you give me five dollars for a deposit. When I get back I can pay you ten. Perhaps more if you like."

Duffy hasn't done business with anyone since his dabbling in retail sales—home appliances to be exact—as a luckless employee paid on commission; his firing led him to retreat to grad school. All he can think to say then, "If it is really just a dollar or two you need, something to tide you over . . ."

"I'm not asking for handouts. I don't want your money. I need a business partner."

"I don't have five but I can offer you one."

"Sir, I'm sorry but I need *five* for business."

"But all I have is one. Would you like it?"

"Well, if you insist."

Duffy reaches deep into his right pocket, where he holds all of his money, identification, and credit cards. He never carries a wallet but has become adept at reaching in and pulling out bills, cards, or change alone; depending upon what was required, his fingers could feel paper, metal, or credit-card Braille.

The only bill he remembers is an old crinkled one, but what he finds is stiff, firm, unwrinkled paper. He pulls it out, his last fresh twenty of the week, what is due to take him through Friday afternoon. The old dollar escaped at Dunkin' Donuts. He can't part with the twenty no matter how needy the case, so he reaches deep in his pocket for remaining change. He collects one quarter, one dime, one nickel, and two pennies. He has forty-two cents; the number is no believable answer to any question in Duffy's universe, but as a net worth it makes perfect sense.

"I'm sorry dear, but this is all I have."

With a guilty look, he hands her the change, but the woman returns sincere gratitude.

"Oh you must not have common blood at all," she says weepy-eyed. "You're not at all like the other young people I meet these days."

It is then that he realizes that whereas he has been thinking of his students as the young people she referred to, she has been including Duffy's age group.

He sees there will be no getting her out of the chair, never mind the bags, no matter what lip service she has paid about going to the bank, so he decides to rise and recuse himself from further service.

As he does so, she continues, "Yes, so kind. So kind. Not like the others. Sir, please, could I come to your apartment and take a shower? Look how filthy a lady gets these days. They make me wear these rags, and I can never take a shower."

Duffy imagines this woman nude in his filthy bathroom. Yes, perhaps the two were made for each other; he sees her standing tall in his bathtub, tearing out the window's tree branch, and using it to wash her nether regions. The image causes him to heave and gasp so much that he forces himself to imagine a clean kitchen to fight off regurgitation.

"I'm sorry, I'm just too busy and . . ."

"Please, sir, please. Look at this filthy rag I'm wearing."

"My place is a mess, and I've got to run."

Lucia Starr begins to cry real tears. But Duffy is a man of business on his long day—he has overcome so much already. If he were to waste even more time dealing with the wounded and broken, he risks becoming economic road kill himself.

"Don't worry, Lucy. Your break is just around the corner. The movie producers will call again."

"Oh that's so sweet, darling. You're such a kind man, not like the others."

"There's still time for a Hollywood Ending," Duffy mutters to himself as he departs from the table. He walks past the lady, and promptly sits down two places beyond. He can't imagine her turning around to find him. With her bags, she looks entrenched for the duration.

As soon as he slides into his new place, a lone businessman, smoking what appears to be an unfiltered cigarette—a Chesterfield or Lucky Strike, almost an anachronism even if big tobacco won the last election—says from a table over: "It's sad how they wind up, yeah, but right now the government has greater fish to fry. We've gotta use all of our resources and go after *them*."

Duffy reorients himself to terror discussion, in these times, a conversation that anyone with ears could wander into at any time. His eye contact is enough response for this fellow.

"Yeah, they got one of our best and brightest today."

Best and brightest? Duffy can only assume he is talking about Ed Cliff, and he can barely restrain a loud yakking noise. To be an Under-anybody under any political regime requires intelligence for sure, but Duffy has doubts. He didn't see Cliff as positively evil, but he certainly wouldn't see him as among the "brightest." He isn't sure he'd classify him as bright at all.

"Is he dead then?"

"Didn'ja hear? They shot him with an arrow right on stage. Over at the college. Dead with one shot. Right through the ear."

Duffy hasn't the time or energy to articulate any vivid recounting of the event so he instead responds, "I heard on the news he was down."

"Well, now you know he's out. We gotta get after them. We need to send more troops over there to do this right."

That is how the pro-war Americans describe it. Them. Over there. The "them" and "there" loose ideas, representing any number of enemy combatants, any number of countries. Duffy has heard from the right wing before; he knows short and vague is the best way to avoid an exhausting argument with a pedantic blowhard. Republican numbers are thin in Philadelphia, but the species is by no means extinct. In fact, due to local corruption in the Democratic machine, conservatives seem to be gaining a foothold.

"The fact that they're trying to kill our boys, even as we speak, is proof we gotta be there."

To himself, Duffy considers the possibility that if we hadn't gone in and taken out the "evil dictator," and then stayed around to get shot at, they wouldn't be trying to kill "our boys." He has read that "our girls" are over there too, although a student from several years back, who had served until honorably discharged, completed a long report for class stating that eighty-three percent of the female soldiers bound for Kosovo in the nineties got pregnant to avoid that war. Duffy was skeptical of the figures then, unsure if the student were only offering his sexist take on the new army policy of full integration of women. But from his own full share of "women's work"—copious quantities of paper grading once destined for educated spinsters and schoolmarms—he was too fatigued to fact-check them himself.

"And these liberal jokers who think we need more international help. True coalition? I'll show them a true coalition. Those French traitors sell out America to do business with the dictator, and now we're supposed to kiss their ass at the United Nations?"

It all eternally returns to this homophobic discourse, this unwillingness to smooch another man's behind. Duffy recalls a sharp, witty student who blurted out in class one day, "The liberals are the ones with their assholes open, the conservatives the ones who keep them closed." At the time, or the next day, Duffy considered that perhaps some liberals were merely those who respected the rights of other Americans to open any number of orifices as they so chose, but in class, he sat back stunned, as if scooped for a story by a sharp undergrad. The kid was a terrible writer, a top-shelf sentence fragmentist and first-rate comma splicer, but here in public, he made Duffy's sincere lesson seem pathetic and pointless.

"As soon as we make nice with the French they'll stab us in the back."

The stab in the back? That rhetoric sounds familiar. Hitler, right? Duffy admires the way this man, somewhat like old Adolf, is a resolved personality. He is entirely confident and consistent in his world view and most likely in his clothing too—gray slacks and charcoal striped Oxford; tie and shirt loosened to the second button. How Duffy wishes he could experience life this way, without the nagging doubt of conscience, the feeling he could be mistaken. Not just about some of it, but mistaken about all of it. It stems from the terms of employment, that the poorly paid nomad must fail to see the world correctly, and this explains why his pay is so low, his benefits so nonexistent. The harsh burden of his socioeconomic status includes the feeling of failure so deeply internalized that he knows he is at fault for his basic predicament. Whereas this man speaks securely in his views, Duffy deeply understands he could have it all wrong. Even when he has confidence in his moment behind the lectern, he doubts himself in private, after class or the next day.

"See, we need a man in charge. A man willing to do something about it. That's why this fall, we gotta do whatever we can to keep the man in charge on top."

Duffy's first impulse is to tell the man to go back to his own section. He doesn't appear homeless, or sympathetic to the indigent, so what is he doing here anyway? The instructor would command, "Go back to the conservative white-man's section," which he figures could be the train-station bar, the waiting area for the Acela Express, or some alternate means of transportation altogether, like a private jet or car. But from reading in his Business Communications textbook, he knows it is better to agree, to maintain civil ties, to never ever burn a bridge. So he pauses to uncover a few words that wouldn't start an argument. "I read the veep was captain of his high school football team. Free safety. All State."

"That's exactly what I'm talking about. We need natural leaders in charge."

The liberals must be Swiss cheese to this fellow—all of them, like Duffy, men with gaping holes of doubt and a suspicious odor of neutrality.

From above, a sudden burst interrupts. "Gentlemen, that's exactly why I'm here. I'm with voter registration. We must get out the vote."

Both instructor and reactionary look up to see before them the dark skin of a thick, squat fireplug. In his left hand he carries some papers and what appears to be a black desk stapler. A small black suitcase on wheels rests by his right side.

"Believe me, I'm registered," says the businessman.

"Me too." Despite his classroom show and even a failed trip to the polls last year, Duffy hasn't voted in five years. His political inertia is likely the result of mental depression—he cannot imagine it is the other way around—but he is still registered. Maintain residence in the same tiny two rooms and society keeps you in the political game, enfranchised and free to express apathy the first week of November.

"Man, we gotta get these niggas out of office, and quick." The newcomer is considerate enough to refer to the white men in power using the n-word for inclusion, but it's as if he hasn't registered these table dwellers' replies. He shifts the stapler to his free hand and holds it below his mouth like a microphone. "That's why I'm going through this whole muthafucka to get folks registered."

"Thank you, no." The businessman turns back to Duffy, trying to ignore man and stapler.

"So anyway, strong leaders are what this country needs, not these waffling guys you never know are with us or against us." Duffy feels himself incorporated into this man's idea of "us." Not sure if this is a good thing.

"Boy, you gonna ignore me?" The voter-registration man raises his voice, demanding a response. He waves the stapler at them, just slightly, but enough to see it could be used as a weapon. Duffy feels grateful it isn't a stapler gun, but only a common desk model. The businessman looks quickly at him, as a small annoyance, like a bothersome fly.

"See, this is what we get with liberals in charge." And the man nods quickly and slightly at the voter-registration guy. "This kind of thing is what's taking America downhill. Should this kind of guy have a right to vote?"

From the businessman's tone, Duffy can't decipher if he is saying this kind of guy, as in "this kind of belligerent guy" or "this kind of black guy." Perhaps the businessman did not see any difference at all.

But now the belligerent, black voter-registration guy is incensed. It is unclear if he has heard the businessman, or is merely upset at being ignored. He places the papers on the table and starts tossing the stapler from his right to his left hand, back and forth.

"Man, that ain't the way roun' heah! That ain't the way. You gotta show some respect, niggas. I'm the voter-registration Negro. I got contacts all over this mutha. Black Muslims control it up theah," and the man points, seemingly in the direction of the soul food and fish sandwich lunch carts outside the post office. "They ain't gonna take no crap from a white mutha tryin' to tell me what I can say."

At this point, the businessman turns directly to the gentleman and says, "Please, sir, could you let us be? We were having a private discussion."

"You gonna tell me where I can go? Who I can talk to? Mothafucka, that ain't the way roun' heah. Sheeet." Duffy tries to stay calm as possible. Again, he has wandered into an emotionally exhausting situation, and realizes that any expenditure of energy will make it more difficult to complete his long day, which is less than half over, with two more schools to go.

"Man, I drop a dime and Muslim brothas visit my crib. Just one word, mothafucka and I've got your ass! Your ass, mothafucka. Yeah you heard me." At this point, the man is screaming, but only occasionally looking at the businessman. It is as if he is shouting into the air for the whole station to hear. He pumps his arms up and down, shifting the stapler from right to left, all of his motions at a rapid pace, a tremendous exertion of energy. "I'll step outside right now mothafucka. You say go, I'll step outside right now mothafucka." Duffy remembers that "drop a dime" refers to the old charge of ten cents for local calls from public phones, and "step outside" means fighting will occur outside, as opposed to inside the bar.

In his rage, Voter Registration grabs his papers, checks his fly, tugs on his suitcase zipper, and then shoves off. He heads in the direction of a group of cops milling about thirty feet from the indigence section.

"Can you just explain to me what this country is coming to?" The businessman asks rhetorically, but it does inspire Duffy to speculate. He doesn't know what to say. He wonders what the businessman would think if he began to explain his nomad teaching for two or three grand a class all over the city. Would the businessman see Duffy's predicament as part of the problem with the current state of the United States? Or would he see Duffy as a heroic entrepreneur choosing the hard work required to make this country great? Duffy doubts very much that the businessman would be attracted to any of Marx's ideas about alienated labor or progressive approaches to improving health insurance for contract workers.

The two of them sit in silence with the businessman's last question lingering in the air. And then Duffy returns to his coffee and news, and his neighbor returns to his stock quotes and cola, and for a couple of minutes all is calm until a city cop strolls up to the two civilized sippers. He asks, "Which one of you fellows been using the n-word?" The cop is tall and rangy, pink and pale, a tiny head for such a long body. He twirls his billy club like a man at baton practice, expert in his approach, his eye on national competition.

The two stare back with perplexed looks.

"Fellow over there says one of you called him a 'nigger.'" The cop points the billy club back to his buddies in blue, who are now smiling and nodding, as the voter-registration man delivers his news in an animated fashion.

"That guy rudely interrupted our conversation. We asked him to leave."

"Hold on now, I'm the one who's conducting this investigation. Which one of you was it?" Now he holds the billy club stiffly, perpendicular to his package, six inches in front of and parallel to his waist. Assertion or protection, hard to say which.

Duffy looks at the cop, slightly unsure of how to handle this situation, despite the fact that half his job is to navigate through unusual communications with potentially hostile respondents.

So they both just blurt out: "We didn't use that word. He did." And they both point, and explain, and argue, and defend themselves until the cop says, "Okay, hold the phone."

"You're sayin' that guy called you niggers?"

"Yeah, he got angry, and started cursing us out," says the businessman. "We were just sitting here minding our business. Having a private conversation."

The cop eyes them suspiciously, as if he is waiting for one of them to fall apart and admit the truth. Duffy knows his guilty brow invites such thoughts.

"Look, I know Whitey Chinuski over at the 117th. He'll vouch for me. He'll tell you I'm a good guy." So this is what it has come to, fellow police officers who can testify on behalf of the accused. Freedom depends upon who you know, not what you said, or where you sat. Because he knows no one in the cops-and-robbers game, Duffy stays silent and tries to appear pleasant. As it turns out, this is enough.

"Okay, okay. Sounds like you guys had an argument. Just watch what you say in these parts. Temperatures are running hot." So the cop lets them off with a short reprimand, and strolls back to the other guys, who seem to be listening intently to the voter-registration man, the latter with a broad smile and wide gestures, stapler invisible, imitating various characters in some sort of song and dance. The cops seem genuinely amused by this diminutive man.

As soon as the investigator is out of earshot, the businessman says softly but aloud, "Goddamn niggers. They call you names and then complain it was you."

Duffy checks his watch. Past 2 p.m., he realizes it is time to get on with his long day. He begs a pardon from the businessman, downs the last half cup of his coffee in one shot, and gathers his belongings. Up and almost off, he hears a farewell.

"Say, buddy. You can't know enough good people. Take my card."

Duffy reads in a thick font "Educational Sales and Consulting." It figures and also heightens his need for release. As he turns back for a silent nod and to see if he has all of his belongings—the desert nomad's habit of double-checking after every oasis—his eyes wander to the old lady still seated with her bags, staring straight ahead, waiting for her second cup of coffee in Hollywood.

Unable to offer even the measliest bit part in any minor studio, Duffy sighs and leaves. The train station is beginning to fill up again with its normal load of people wandering through. He roams back past the Dunkin' Donuts, toward the large middle atrium of the train station. Amtrak is back in action, just a couple of hours after the assassination, the schedule sign shuffling its choices as the departing train gets removed and the remainder each move up a notch. As he presses on, past people in singles and pairs, he feels eyes on his back. Although accustomed to paranoia, feeling stared at but able to ignore it, he turns around and catches a glimpse of Voter Registration moving his way. The gleaming stapler is back in hand and the suitcase slides in tow. Duffy turns back around and hustles toward the bathroom. He can't help but feel that the guy is right behind him, tailing him, so he picks up his pace a bit. He glances back again, quickly this time, and sees the fellow is right behind him, striding wide, his right hand wheeling his suitcase with ease, his left hand swimming through the air, ghetto stylin'.

So this is it. Adjunct Duffleman's destiny is to get cornered in the can. But he can't break off the path now. It would be too embarrassing. He hopes the bathroom attendant is not one of Voter Registration's Black Muslim associates, a man who, for the sake of a nation, would look away while the damage goes down. Duffy plows ahead. He can feel this crazy man gaining ground. By the time he enters the bathroom, he hears the man's rolling valise sliding but paces behind. The restroom is almost empty save for a man in the corner, shaving over the sink with his shirt off and draped over his shopping bags full of homeless stuff. Duffy scurries ahead, as much as his inert form will allow, intent upon his last chance to grab a stall and lock the door. At the first one, he quickly heads in, terrified. But after being greeted by a shit explosion—brown sauce all over the bowl, the seat, the toilet paper, everywhere—he dashes back out, peeks in a second, and then a third stall, before finding reasonably clean harbor. He can hear Voter Registration's whistling right behind his ear. As he turns to shut the door, it is then that he knows it is coming, some sort of below-the-belt ending to his bleak life, cutting short his long day with an evil exchange in a public stall—Duffy's pride, what little is left if it even existed, destroyed by the black man's weapon, no doubt a brown and bluish thing he'd wagged at the white man before, many times in fact because voter registration involved squirting ink repeatedly on every page. To top him off, he'd use the stapler, no doubt—stapled to death in a public bathroom stall! In the briefest increment of time, a differential moment if you would, Duffy closes his mouth tight and prays that on impulse he doesn't stick out his tongue. Then he turns to face his fate, blankness beyond horror painted over his humility and shame.

As Voter Registration passes Duffy's stall, he turns, ceases his whistling for the briefest second, and smiles widely. "When I gotta go, I gots to go" is what he bellows to Duffy, whose jaw drops agape as the man proceeds onward to a further stall. So that is it. Duffy suffers neither a knifing, nor a licking with fists. There is no death or shameful fate worse; rather, the man offers his acknowledgment of their short-term shared ambition— the camaraderie of public evacuation in 30th Street Station. Relieved, and yet not yet relieving himself, Duffy resists a strange urge to follow the man to his chosen stall and check to see what colors of the rainbow best describe his private wares. But realizing this would be too time-consuming and just plain wrong, he instead shuts his own stall door, hangs his book bag on the hook at its top, undoes his trousers, with the toilet paper wipes the seat thoroughly, discards that sheaf in the toilet, and then lays two doubly folded-over fresh sections across the seat before lowering his worn, gray boxer-briefs to his ankles, turning around, and descending upon the can. At rest, he can hear loud whistling and other noises from the voter man's stall. Some prefatory La De Doos and Doodle De Las but then gruff rap lyrics: "Yo yo, bunny, hoot and hollah, twin-engine deplaned, raze two bitties for a dollah..." How Duffy envies the loud bowel movements of a happy man! Feeling an incredible sense of relief that he has been spared some horrible crime of nature or against it, Duffy feels sudden optimism, sitting shitting, that the day would come out right. It is then that the bright hopeful face of Allison Silverman passes through his brain as he privately and happily poops into the public, porcelain bowl. Yes, there were young hopeful minds, students who were kind and who genuinely enjoyed literature, the arts, life itself. He finds his left hand clamoring to stroke his heated beast, but just as quickly the urge softens as he loses concentration, and shifts faces to that of Frank Hamnett, the troubled boy who fought in Tikrit. Would Frank wind up like the voter-registration Negro, or the Hollywood actress, just another war vet, mingling among the homeless in the train station? Duffy's brief bit of optimism now fully evacuated, he sits and contemplates how he could ever help anyone like Frank.

CHAPTER 6

THE UNIVERSITY OF AMERICA

Back at the section of the train station for suburban lines, Duffleman submits to a second thorough search, this one already more like a routine event, and then heads to wait on the platform for trains passing through the city. Because he takes the train only to Center City's Suburban Station—he will walk from there to the downtown branch of America— it is no big deal that the Market-Frankford Elevated Line has been shut down. Besides, he isn't certain the El is any faster.

As he waits, Duffy imagines the arrow assassin slipping away from the crowd, calmly sliding his pass through as he passes through the turnstile. He could pass for some everyday schmiel no doubt, maybe unemployed, maybe even an adjunct. Would he be all out of sorts like Oswald, and wind up getting caught in a movie theater, or in an altercation with a cop? Could a Middle Eastern terrorist get away with such a public hit? The man had to be able to blend in with the crowd enough to escape. A domestic look. Why not a woman? That the person was an assassin and not a failed mass murderer was beyond doubt. Ramming a car onto the stage would be amateur hour and impossible with the surrounding thousands. But if he had wanted to take out hundreds of others, the killer could have easily done so; it was as easy as apple pie to purchase legal semiautomatic weaponry from discrete Web sources or to surf online for how-to information on homemade flame-throwers and other IEDs. Duffy isn't one for detective novels, but he can't help but play Poe's Dupin as he awaits the train.

Because the Blue Line is closed, hundreds of junior high and high schoolers stand with him on the platform, no doubt planning to access the El underground at 15th or catch the Broad Street subway. Despite Duffy's phobia of black male teens and of crowds in general, now he is taken aback by how innocent and fun-loving the youngsters seem. They are smiling and shouting, their worst crime teasing or pulling an innocent girl's hair. The children go on as if there is no war on terror or local assassination. Not blissfully ignorant but genuinely living is how he would prefer to see it.

The train arrives and Duffy boards after everyone else, like a patient parent or guardian, making sure all the kids clamor in safely. He's heard news reports of women and children rushing to trains, getting stuck in the doors, and losing limbs by consequence. And boarding last ensures he will be easily shoved out at the first downtown stop.

Suburban Station is a disaster. The underground shopping mall is a danger zone full of a frenzied mob looting at will. Chaos abounds; there are no American soldiers or spinach-fed cops with German Shepherds anywhere in sight. No man in charge to maintain authority, to keep order and people down.

Instead, Duffy sees customers jumping the counter at McDonald's; with as much alacrity as audacity, they steal mounds of fries straight from the fry-guy's bins, commandeer the burger cooker, and cook all manner of irregular, nonstandard burgers. Doubling, even tripling tomato and onion allotments, the marauding masses combine chicken and beef patties under one sesame seed but undersized bun. By the dollar store, he sees a gargantuan man carrying off dozens of rolls of Christmas wrapping paper, out of season but in stock. Fat Santa's opposite—tiny, frail, and aged—clutches as much plasticware as she can handle, semitransparent green and purple containers under her arms and against her chest. A homeless man appears to have set up a three-card monte stand right outside the store, shifting around new playing cards presumably plundered inside. A severe-looking white man in a business suit jumps the counter at the deli and begins passing out conical sections of lunch meat and cheese—salami, pastrami, corned or roasted beef with provolone, American, or Swiss. An amorphous blob bleats out, "Please sir, my babies love cooked ham." A teenager feeds Genoa salami to a hungry German Shepherd with a conscientious, cowering look. Duffy wonders if the dog were a traitor, a turncoat from the other side of the law. The teen senses the teacher staring, turns, and states, "Don't worry. It's kosher."

Meanwhile the school teens from the train have converted to smart mobs of the underworld, roving packs of looting thugs, shirts tucked out, book bags emptied of their contents and used to collect as much booty as possible. One boy smashes a thick textbook against a closet-sized candy dispenser while two others from below—arms up to the shoulder inside the bottom aperture of the vending machine—grab the chips and chocolate that, like lemmings, descend en masse. Over by an accessories store, two middle-aged women in dark skirt suits play tug of war with either handle strap of a leather Coach bag. Duffy surmises the black-and-pink checkered material could be synthetic—the bag a fake, the store's contents entirely counterfeit—but the Asian man beside them screaming foreign expletives and smacking his forehead is no doubt the shop's authentic owner.

With the assassination has come lawlessness, the people taking back the basement businesses. In true multicultural, post-racial America, every age, ethnicity, gender, and orientation is in on the action; this is no homogenous moment of young men—majority black with an overrepresentation of the impoverished—behaving badly for the camera. Speaking of which, your standard-issue, obese Eurasian in a pink golf shirt and plaid trousers, presumably a tourist, is using one hand to film with his handheld video camera while receiving magazines from his wife with his other. He glances down momentarily and reacts bitterly, "Eunice, I told you *Playboy*. I'm not a *Hustler* man, you know that! What would our kids think?" From this overheard exchange, Duffy feels a physiological reaction, a tingle down below.

And then he shudders, and then he is awake, out of his reverie. The train has stopped. The looting was all a daydream, just one of the many he experiences through his workday commutes. For some time now, he has been expecting to wake up at the end of his long day and learn that it was all a nightmare, but so far, no luck. Now, positioned at the train door, he hears the kids clamoring behind him, eager to resume their journey by walking underground to the green, orange, or blue lines. On the platform, Duffy can see the real Suburban Station, a crowd of eager people waiting to board and leave Center City. These are mostly office workers, the lucky ones who have been given an early afternoon due to the day's cuts in Homeland Defense.

Off the train, pushing through the masses of suburbanites, up the escalator, and into the afternoon crowds once more, he strides through the underground mall full of cheap merchandise and plastic food, through the teeming hordes of business people, shoppers, students, punkers, buskers, panhandlers, officers, and police dogs. The scene is hectic, perhaps chaotic, but everyone appears calm and law-abiding. Duffy has heard news of a slowdown, but below City Hall, it is hard to see this. People are milling about and moving ahead; he suspects some kind of vibrant economy pulls them to and fro. He peeks into the windows of passing shops, trying to ascertain if people are purchasing anything, if there are consumers—living, breathing, and buying—in the stores. Flowers, one. Sushi, some. Locksmith and shoe shine, a tiny shop, packed full with three. Dollar Store, lots of action. Burger King, every seat full albeit no few with homeless coffee sippers. But Duffy counts them because they always have coins. Plenty in the pizza joint as well. Yes, everything is as it should be. The people fill up restaurants and consume fast food and colas. They read newspapers, speak with associates, or shout into cell phones. They are boisterous and rude, not looking where they are walking or being polite enough to hold open doors. Duffy, trudging along toward the closest exit for his remedial tutoring job, experiences the vicarious thrill of everyday living. It is a distraction he rarely experiences, caught up as he is in the paper-grading game.

He spends perhaps a third of his waking day, particularly on his long day, commuting with the working herd, and so, when in Rome, Duffy tries to do as the commuters do. Sometimes the entire concourse would seem stuck in a mood, ebullient or glum, and then he found himself blending in, assuming the bliss or grief of the tribe. Today, the vibrant energy is contagious. The killing occurred only a few hours ago, and less than two miles from here, and yet it is as if the event has acted as a positive stimulant. Duffy sees no extreme displays of fear. Passing through some parts, it is as if nothing has happened at all. Have these Philadelphians become as steel-eyed as the Jews of Tel Aviv, able to overcome any devastating terrorist attack without blinking an eye? Or could it be that a city voting ninety-three percent Democrat might not care that its war-mongering President lost a capable Under-something man? Duffy finds it perplexing, and then amusing, and wonders at last if it is normal or healthy for any society to become energized from or even ignore such a murder.

As he trudges up the gray stone steps surrounding Philly's famous Clothespin, Duffy hears chanting from above. Certain it could not yet be the angels calling him from the heavens, toward the top he hears tambourines, but shaken not by Hare Krishnas or professional musicians. Above ground at last, before he can glance at City Hall and wonder if his city wages taxes would welcome a visit, he sees a mingling of protestors of every shape and size. In the middle front stands the familiar dreadlocks and face of the morning man of action, Julian Door. When Door sees Duffy, he hands the mike to a comrade, smiles widely, and walks over to him. "Professor! Glad you could join us!" Door looks sincerely pleased that his teacher has made it.

"Er, actually, I'm just on my way to work."

Adjunct Duffleman notes his student's puzzled look. Julian is unaware that Urban State alone is not responsible for his instructor's wages, but he shrugs it off and stays on message.

"Almost as soon as we heard, we knew the entire country would have its eyes peeled on Philadelphia. We knew we had to act, so we modified the original dead-deer protest to include the bigger picture. We all planned on meeting at three, and most made it out by two p.m. Call it another cell phone and Internet miracle."

Duffy has some idea that many of the protestors are students, unemployed, or homeless, and therefore, they have no capacity to fill or place to be, but he doesn't pursue this line of inquiry with Julian. Instead, he notices that Julian has changed shirts, literally, from eco-friendly forest green of the morning to a black tee shirt with a fluorescent green caricature of the President of the United States. Below it reads, "Like father, like son. One term and done." And then suddenly they begin chanting that very same couplet. Duffy looks up and sees all the usual suspects in the Philadelphia protesting game. The Free Baraka-istas. A GROW coalition. The Kingsessing Welfare Rights Union. The Public Schools Student Union appears rough around the edges of its rainbow colors. Julian's own group, wearing matching tee shirts, appears to be "Citywide Student Protest Live." Duffy is pretty sure he has seen these shirts at three of his campuses at least—Urban State, Liberty Tech, and Ivy Green.

Seeing Julian now reminds Duffy of the day's earlier concerns.

"Say, Julian, is the woman from class okay?"

"I wouldn't be here if she weren't professor. She rests peacefully at Collegetown Friends Hospital."

"Thank you," responds the grateful paper-grader. "Thank you so much, Julian." Duffy maintains eye contact until Julian gives a final shrug and his teacher nods in assent.

As he moves away from the protestors, the whole crowd begins to sing out the rhyme of Julian's shirt-message. "Like father, like son. One term and done." The entire motley crew chants in unison. They shake tambourines, beat home-made Tonga drums, and clop together their wooden sticks. All clamor along, almost in rhythm, and even lost-soul Duffy feels a momentary beat.

Working people and shoppers hustle back and forth around the protest; some of these passersby alternately cheer and whistle. Boos are distinctly a minority position but one rather boisterous group of true patriots—plus-sized white guys in work boots, blue jeans, and wife beaters, with red, white, and blue bandanas over balding heads—starts chanting "USA! USA! USA!" Just three against the masses, but their enthusiasm ensures that their voice gets heard.

Duffy finds it strange how these supporters of President Fern and His War feel that any protest against the man or the war is in fact a protest against the country. It is perplexing, yes, and even scary that these people cannot differentiate between a war and a country.

Duffy at least can separate the man and his politics. Although he disagrees with Fern's policies—what he understands of them both domestic and foreign—Duffy feels a strong bond with the man due to their shared experience. He could identify with Fern because he sees that both are middle-aged, white-male flunkies—that thus far, they have failed at most everything they have tried, that just as Duffy feels lucky to be hanging onto academic scraps, a few crummy jobs, so too had Fern become President only by some fluke butterfly-ballot snafu and the partisan practices of one state given a seal of approval by a biased Supreme Court. From Duffy's view, it was racist shenanigans, three-card monte with the voting count. Even Fern's victory in electoral-college votes was overshadowed by his failure to gain the majority of the overall voting population. Duffy wonders if this point of identification—the mediocre-white-guy vote—drove these working men to the polls. He imagines they love the way Fern pokes fun at the press, those uppity liberals with their "Washington talk." Perhaps some of his constituency enjoys the feeling of superiority they have over him. They'd rather have a joker in office, one they could poke fun at, than someone who makes them feel inferior by being able to speak about policy. For these men in work boots, it seems simpler than that. The President is their king.

Duffy lingers just a moment, taking in the scene. He is almost surprised to see so much political energy in the middle of Philadelphia. But ever since Election 2000, he has noticed that people have become more passionate about politics, that now, you could easily find people

who care. Random strangers want to talk. He wonders if he should praise
the heavens for this change, and turning toward the sky he sees what
appears to be a flying man come to save the day; upon squinting he
discerns his mistake. It is a black helicopter aloft—for national news or
war, to provide instant terror or defeat information.

When he shoves off, he strides past Center City business and bustle,
then enters a silvery skyscraper and, at the elevator, presses the number
12. He is headed upstairs to the downtown campus of University of
America, three floors of office space in a half-vacant high rise. Corporate
cost-cutting, city-wage taxes, and steep insurance costs for terrorist flight
school have sent the former white-collar professionals scurrying to
relocation in the suburbs. And of course, fear lingers that lightning could
strike twice.

Duffy began working for UAmerica back when it was a local independent called Johnson College. Then, overnight, the corporate chain
moved in and bought out the old school. They left their beautiful
brownstone mansion and moved the entire campus to these three floors
of Philly skyscraper. They began aggressively marketing continuing-ed
programs that included satellite classrooms; today, University of America
spreads its curriculum all over the city and with campuses in 147 counties,
they blanket the map of the United States as well. As the Wal-Mart of
higher education, U. of A. undercuts the market in every region, charges
less per credit, and pays less to its contract employees who provide all of
their educational services.

Even after the takeover, Duffy kept his four hours of tutoring each
week and accepted the dollar pay cut. Nine dollars flat is little more than
a retail wage, but he has spent decades convincing himself that education
is a good attainable by all, and thus should be likewise accessible and
affordable. At least some of his tutoring helps those on the lowest rung,
students struggling to stay afloat, treading water and flailing at the life
ropes thrown overboard, a quality education sailing ever out of reach.
And yet some U. of A. students are so challenged to concentrate, to
remember, to grasp meaning—too many of them diagnosed with

multiple complexes and learning disabilities—that he is left questioning if in fact these students could really learn at all.

At the Success Center, Duffy Tutorman is cordial with the staff assistant on duty. She hands him slips with his appointments. Linda Jones at 3:15 p.m. Hyuk Won Kuk at 4:15. No name, just six of seven phone digits at 4:45. As per his habit, he reads the wide letters of the white, red, and blue banner stuck high on the opposite wall: "Success Lives Here." He emits his patriotic sigh and then gathers some scrap sheets of paper, heads over to an empty table, lays his head down, and rests.

Linda Jones wakes him as she shuffles in at 3:10 p.m. Old school, she arrives five minutes early for her appointments.

Linda is one of his favorite students, and he genuinely enjoys working with her on her writing. Somewhere, someone else in the building, another adjunct, is assigning her essays and returning them without letter grades, but with goodwill in the form of detailed commentary— always with something positive to say first—and then a thorough elucidation of everything wrong with the structure, organization, clarity, grammar, spelling, ideas, and diction. Duffy suspects the teacher is a relative newcomer to the adjunct game, or a young person full of energy, because the written comments are so fresh and thorough, so full of aspiration for the student's improvement, so unjaded and not yet defeated. Perhaps this adjunct has a spouse or significant other supporting him or her, and could afford to teach a class or two as a labor of love?

"Howdy, Cyrus."

"Hey, Linda."

They exchange greetings like old friends. Duffy isn't sure if it's her middle age, the intimacy of tutoring, or the kindness and decency of working-class black women, but he feels genuine warmth in her words. He wonders briefly how the Afrocentrist would interact with him were they not surrounded by an audience.

Linda takes out her most recently returned essay, as well as a draft of a new one. They worked so arduously on the old one that Duffy is disappointed to see its margins filled up with the teacher's markings in soft green ink. For the returned essay, Duffy turned every sentence into a little game, asking Linda to say the full sentence aloud to try to see if she could hear the subject-verb disagreement, the run-on, or the fragment. And now, for all that hard work, they are returned a paper jam-packed with teacher's comments and an encouraging smiley face by the grade of C. At least the green is a less threatening color than black or red; at least she has a chance of passing the class.

"Linda, not bad at all, not bad at all. We're going to stay on this until we get it right. We're passing English 101 this time." From business writing, Duffy borrows the teamspeak of "we." "Let's take a look at the new one now."

The new essay is supposed to be on her American Dream, an expository essay, one that would explain her goals. Duffy knows this is her third time taking the class, and thus probably at least the third time she has been given such an assignment, and thus Linda's immediate American Dream is no doubt to pass English 101 and enjoy a future free of ever considering this essay assignment again.

They sit leaning toward each other, about sixty degrees apart on the circular table, an ideal distance for the intimate work of tutoring. The paper lies between them, so both can read the double-spaced typed print. Linda has chosen a funky font—squiggly-shaped characters—and lavender-colored ink. Duffy has noticed that sometimes the poorest writers seem to enjoy this artistic part of the writing process. Of course, he'll have to remind her to switch it to black ink and a standard font before handing in the final copy.

Together, they read the first sentence or two. "In my American Dream, my people is going to have all the nice things, the niceties, like a big house, TV, A/C, remote control DVD and stereo. And children won't have to work so hard cause they will be peace on earth. My husband will get hisself a job. A good job."

Duffy has been imagining getting "his [own] self a good job" for some time, but for now he is occupied by the daunting task at hand.

One problem is that the assignment is flaccid in the first place because the subject itself is about as tired and lifeless as "What I did last summer." The newbie adjunct teaching Linda must be stuck with departmental essay prompts from the required syllabus. But Duffy will have to let that go. Where to begin? How do you take a dying paragraph and breathe life into it, turn it into something fresh, entertaining, or worth reading? How do you create writing that a teacher required to grade the essay could tolerate or stand to read at all? He could write an entire novel about undeveloped ideas and poor sentence quality, and he knows some underserved citizen of the richest country on earth would make a fine protagonist—not that anyone in America could stand to read a book on such a broken people and their prose—but more importantly, for the sake of his current classes and contract renewals, he vows to keep his own bad sentences far from public view or at least his supervisors and peers.

With that in mind, he begins: "Linda, the good news is that I think I understand your American dream. Now let's take a closer look, sentence by sentence."

"Yes, let's do that." Maybe it is the maturity of an older person, maybe she knows she has to work twice as hard, or maybe she just wants it more, but Linda has a great attitude compared to most of the younger students. Duffy has visitors to this center who just sit there and stare at him, or even respond to his every encouragement with a skeptical shrug, as if to say, "You the man who want it corrected. Correct the shit yourself." The many ESL students offer polite silence, hoping reticence would lead Duffy to correct on his own. Foreign and domestic, too many want a proofreading service, not an interactive tutoring session. But Linda is an exception; she wants to improve.

"One thing we like to do is make an essay as specific and detailed as possible. We want the reader to know exactly what we want to communicate. With that in mind, when you say 'my people' of whom are you speaking, precisely?"

"You know, my people. My peeps as the younger generation say. My folks."

"Are you talking about your entire family?"

"Well, my husband and children mostly."

"How could we change the sentence to make it more precise?"

Linda stares at the page. But at least she knows how the game is played. She will rewrite the sentence for her tutor. And then she will look up anxiously, and ask of her work, "Is this right, Cyrus?"

Often Cyrus will make a couple of quick corrections of new mistakes added to the problem, but he'll almost invariably respond, "Good job, Linda. Let's take a look at the next line."

The two of them work their way through the five paragraphs. The intensity of writer-centered tutoring gets the best of Duffy, and soon sweat beads decorate his brow. With student and tutor both perspiring freely, they share audible sighs when Linda turns to the second page and Duffy sees just a third of it with typing. At 4:07, drowning in a salty ocean, he ends the session and wipes down the table. Normal sessions are one half hour, but he allows Linda to go longer whenever possible; for now, Duffy needs time to freshen up, drink the cool bottled spring water provided free of charge, literally listed as a "benefit" in the employee handbook, and regroup before the ESL student at 4:15 p.m.

"Thanks so much, Cyrus. You're really helping me."

Unaccustomed to student praise, Duffy blushes. "Please Linda. You're doing all the work."

"Well, have a nice weekend, Cyrus." A weekend was crashing early Friday evening, sleeping late and facing chores on Saturday, and then paper grading all day Sunday. Even Duffy wouldn't dare to write a novel about that. Now nearing forty, his mind drifts to an imagined marriage to Linda Jones; he pictures a row home, working-class black neighbors, family dinners, chitlins and latkes, borscht and fried chicken, and singing at the Church of Black Hebrews on Sunday. Every day is bliss save for their seven noisy children upsetting the Duffledad's delicate humors. In the dream, and yet as punishment for its ethno-eccentricity, Linda transmogrifies into the Afrocentrist who locks him in the basement and with his wet laundry has her way with his hairy behind. As the image resolves into a ménage a trios tug-of-war with the fried-chicken women and the Duffler's wishbone, Voter Registration pops in with his stapler and sends a shout out: "Waterboardin' ain't the way roun' heah."

"Whoa!"

"Cyrus?"

"Whah?"

"That look on your face, something special was on your mind. Just sayin' goodbye is all."

"Oh, of course. Goodbye to you, Linda. And give my regards to your husband." At the end of the fall semester, just before the holidays, Linda brought her husband to school and introduced him to everybody from the administrators to teachers to tutors. "Johnny, meet my English tutor, Cyrus Duffleman." He shook the big, soft paw of the enormous, silent man, catching a moment of shared sadness with a glance into his eyes. Johnny at least had Linda, thought Cyrus at the time.

"Take care, Linda."

After she leaves, Duffy walks over to the water cooler, and sucks down five paper cups of spring water. He feels so benefitted. Just past the fifth one, his 4:15 p.m. ESL student slinks in. As thin as Linda is full, she dresses midway between a business woman and a hooker, highly professional in purpose-statement mascara and heels. Her clothing is tight, her jeans somehow a shade off, something slightly out of style in them, maybe Shanghai or Seoul's fashions not quite in sync with New York City.

"Are you here for tutoring?" She nods quickly and politely, then hurriedly takes out her paper and hands it to him, still standing at the water fountain. He motions for her to follow him back to the table and then coordinates the seating, using hand gestures, so they wind up similarly arranged as he was with Linda Jones. She slides into her seat, moving as far from her essay as possible without moving her chair.

The tutoring session soon becomes a tense war in which the student says as little as possible in hopes that Duffy will correct the paper on his own. She stares and frowns slightly every time he asks her to try to say the sentence aloud. At last, they settle on their own new game. Before every noun, and even before pronouns, she stops and adds an arrow and an "a" and then looks quizzically at her tutor. If he nods yes, then she moves on, and if he nods no, then she erases the "a" and writes "an." If he says no again, then she erases the "an" and writes "the." If no, she erases, if yes, "the" stays, and either way she moves on to the next noun she can find. He has spoken to many different teachers of ESL, and not one of them has ever given him any specific advice on how to teach students raised in languages without articles such tiny nuisances as a, an, and the.

After a paragraph, Duffy looks up from their shared toil to find Absent Articles staring back at him. Her facial expression alternates between sorrowful and needy. Nothing happens so she throws in a sexy wink. He knows what she wants and he steels himself over, wills himself not to relent. But it is hopeless. He snatches the paper away, and proceeds to correct the whole thing on his own, adding the appropriate "a," "an," and "the" to every line, correcting subject-verb problems, and most of all, idioms. He hands the paper back to the student. She gives him a look like she will be forever grateful for his kindness, and would even consider marriage without intercourse after a car and courtship resulting in a green card. He feels shocked to think that a facial expression could imply that a meager man like himself could afford a lifetime of health benefits for a wife and family, but he returns her thanks with a gray gaze of scorn, letting her know they have committed some horrible wrong together, that his is a country of two-worker families that prides itself on individual effort, doing one's own work, not settling for plagiarism or forgeries of any kind— whether CDs, fast food, automobiles, or DVDs. Stolen pasta and gun powder aside, Duffy has allowed himself to believe in these overpopulated Eastern cities, Manhattan replicas with their entirely copied consumer societies, flashy American catchphrases on every billboard and sign. She nods her thank-you again and again, then grabs her purse and papers and dashes off, away from the look of us-versus-them awash over his face. His heavy sigh sends his scrap sheets floating to the floor.

At 4:48 p.m., anonymous six digits is nowhere to be found. Duffy decides to use his last twelve minutes to check e-mail and news online. A bit of paid leisure, the best time of his day, even if most of the messages would be from students.

He logs on using his University of America account—knowing full well this is precisely the kind of privatized campus that keeps track of worker e-mail. Despite tutoring just four hours per week, he had been required to attend the expensive, all-day, sexual-harassment training session, paid for by the University to protect its own interests, its own ass, that is, in a court of law with, "Well, we trained Professor B on the illegality of his actions, we taught him wrong from right in the workplace, and we cannot be responsible for his susceptibility to phishing scams."

But Duffy knows there is safety in numbers, and other affiliated parties—teachers, staff, and students—are probably receiving and sending all manner of easily misinterpreted or sketchy messages. When his inbox appears on screen, and he sees an e-mail from Allison Silverman, he clicks and reads:

University Towers Hotel. 10pm. Room 1007.

Be there, or be square, Professor. In fact, try to come cylindrical. ☺

Hah! Forget the long day of neuroses and paranoia. Terror and therapy. Work and fatigue. Extra flab, fallen arches, aching discs, and everything else. At last the Duffler has done it. He has taken the prize! He feels instantly transmogrified from sloppy contract slave to classy elder gent blessed with the bounty of birthday desserts. He sprouts hardwood that fights his zipper for freedom.

After years of wasting away in the teaching game, the sad celibate, his decency, his humanity, aye, his Dufflesex, has been recognized, and his efforts would pay off tonight with live, young flesh! With the creative, curious, and zaftig Allison Silverman no less! Hallelujah, hallelujah! A hundred times has he heard Fern's televised dictum, "Live your life"—his political propaganda for the greater good of the private sector—and now, finally, the Duffler would live his. Yes, see no Osama, fear no Osama. No teaching overload, no day-to-day drudgery of book-bag-lugging back pain. No worry for one of two black men without work or dole, and he could forget the weird visions haunting his working life. He would seize the day—er, the night that is. And the pale young premium label would all be legal, as he is certain she is a senior, a firm three years past the fighting age and allowed to imbibe. The Duffler sees himself naked, sitting in a lotus position, under the sun and atop a pile of nude Allison Silvermans. Dufflejunior stands tall, endowed well beyond any recent recollection or measurement.

Then, just as young flesh serves him an umbrella cocktail, he is startled out of his reverie. His euphoria dissipates and is replaced by guilt and shame. Although the staff assistant is the only other person in the room, and sitting by the door fifteen paces away—and in fact clicking her mouse and smiling at her own semiprivate screen—nonetheless, he immediately deletes the message, scrawling the hotel room number on a bit of scrap paper and shoving it into his sock. Ten tonight in Room 1007. Got it. To be extra cautious, he closes the window, logs off, shifts his head left and right searching for spies, and then logs back on.

When he gets back to his e-mail, he sees the only other message is from Frank Hamnett. Duffy reads:

Bark at the moon, die too soon.

Nice knowing you Professor.

A bit disturbing but Frank's usual correspondence more or less. Sometimes the childishness of his rebel spirit is a little overwhelming. Slightly annoyed, Duffy signs out of gmail, and checks the *NYTimes* online.

In big print, under an electronic masthead, he reads, "Cliff Down at Liberty Tech." He clicks the large font and reads:

Homeland Security Under Secretary Edward R. Cliff lies in extremely critical condition after being shot in the brain by a full-sized arrow, believed to have been launched from a long bow or cross bow. He is not expected to recover any brain function, and doctors are awaiting word from his family on how to proceed. Cliff, 51, did not have any material on his person relating to resuscitation directions or organ donations.

President Fern has already denounced the attack: "These terrorists are cowards who hide behind trees and shoot at us. Let's see just one of 'em come out of hiding and fight fair like a man."

Duffy muses briefly on the President's selective amnesia, forgetting the tanks and body armor of the American military, and how we can bomb from above anywhere we please. He then skims the details of the article, making sure his name doesn't appear anywhere—you can never be too cautious with the Patriot Act ruling the land—and then checks other headlines.

Seven American Soldiers Killed Near Fallujah

Australian Journalist Defenestrated from the Palestine Hotel

Arabs Denounce the Israeli Wall

Israeli PM No Go on Talks with Iran and Syria

Just the usual cycle of front-page pessimism in the age of terror, the up-to-date violence and obstinacy he has read dozens of times before.

Duffy shuts down the computer, gathers his net worth, waves goodbye to Success's staff assistant, and takes an empty elevator up one floor. He walks past a long line at the Financial Aid office—nontraditional students off early from work to question amounts received or submit new paperwork—much more of it required under Fern than ever before for the various

Federal grant programs that keep University of America afloat. He then passes the bursar's office and the payroll department—where every other Thursday they allow him to secure in advance his Friday payment, tearing the perforation betwixt check and stub one of the purest pleasures known to celibate man. After passing two stray, lonely classrooms, Duffy arrives at a small corner room with mailboxes on every wall where windows should be.

4:53 p.m. He is seven minutes early. Only Ed Saferi is ahead of him, sitting at the brown, faux-original-grain table—likely laminated, pressed wood chips—shelling nuts, and spoiling his appetite. Saferi is the only Republican adjunct Duffy knows he knows. Ed had been downsized from a good corporate marketing gig—six figures plus benes—and now teaches five sections of Introduction to Corporate Communications, two at University of America, and one each at Urban State, and two separate community colleges in South Jersey. He takes in a quarter of what he used to make. His wife divorced him a year after he lost his job, and now most of his adjunct pay goes to alimony and child support. Nonetheless, he doesn't seem bitter. Saferi believes in individual responsibility and free markets and even if the roaring economy has gobbled him up and spat him out to the backwaters of higher education, he still trusts Republicans to get the ball rolling again. And of course, in this age of terror, Ed has told Duffy too many times that we need solid men in charge who would fund our defense.

"How do, Cyrus?"

"Never better, Ed."

"So what ya think of those sick bastards, now? Still wanna let them off easy?"

He knows Ed sees him as a Democrat or worse yet, a liberal, which means he sees him handing terrorists a Get Out of Jail Free card.

"Whatever you say, Ed." To change the conversation, and needle him a little, Duff hands Ed a business card. "Hey Ed, here's the commercial health coverage I was talking about. It's really affordable for guys our age, particularly compared to what's out there." He is pretty sure Ed can't afford any health coverage at the moment, not even this cut-rate catastrophic plan Duffy found surfing the net. But he wants to remind Ed of how natural market forces can fuck the average working guy. Fern's solution leaves his voter-worker screwed.

Ed snatches the card and shoves it deep in his pocket. "I'll give the guy a call," he mutters, suspicion in his voice, as if it could be a multilevel marketing scheme, or as if health coverage is all just some socialist plot by freeloaders who'll do anything to avoid paying their fair share.

Just then, Deborah Grossberg bursts into the room, her usual noisy entrance enveloping the small space. "Gentlemen, gentlemen. And where pray tell is the pizza girl?"

Duffy checks his watch: 4:57 p.m. She still has three minutes.

"Have a seat Deborah. Talk to your fellow Americans." Ed pushes a chair out and pats it. Although Ed considers Deborah a communist agent because she has been trying to organize the adjuncts into a citywide labor union, Deborah smiles at Ed's invitation. She disagrees with his politics but doesn't mind being treated like a lady.

"The movement to unionize is getting big, Ed. Hop on now while the bus still has room."

"I thought the union bus was supposed to take any poor slob who begged entrance. I didn't realize there were limits to the hospitality."

"Please, Ed. We're going to be a professional union. We are going to mandate a master's degree as required for entrance to the union, and we'll boycott and picket any universities that replace us with bachelor's level teachers, or undergraduate TAs and tutors."

"I bet there are sharpies out there already better prepared to teach than some of us."

"And you think it's a good thing to just sit peacefully while we get replaced? What are we supposed to do then? Does a society owe its citizens anything at all?"

"If you pay your taxes, you deserve clean streets and cops. The rest government should let alone."

Duffy imagines Ed as President outlawing most of government. And yet, he admires Saferi's consistency. The Republican solution is his solution one hundred percent. Social Security. Public education. Welfare. Subsidized health coverage. Shrink it all down and drown it in a for-profit sink in the abandoned offices a floor above UAmerica. Despite Fern's cutbacks to government-funded student aid, the "campus" could skimp and save and survive. If worse came to worse, future tenants could put pressure on public water utilities, ensuring discounted bills would get paid; the sink would be working when business needed it next. Saferi moves over to the water cooler and gets himself a cold one.

Before partisan bickering can escalate any further, the pizza lady is here. Edna Hawkins bursts into the room, smiling wide, happily entering society. Perhaps in her mid-sixties, her spouse deceased and children grown, Edna seems to genuinely appreciate the constant company the adjunct's life provided. Always someone to explain or listen to, correct or otherwise communicate with concerning reading, writing, or life itself. "Spinach. Broccoli. Tomatoes. Mushrooms."

His inner carnivore roars for pepperoni, but Duff'll settle for veggies and the strong fumes of their fifth companion, Michael Vittinger, striding in right behind Edna.

Vittinger's heavy cologne and unwashed Italian suits are his calling card. He carries a stuffed, soft-leather briefcase, and a pipe protrudes from his corduroy breast pocket. In his late thirties, Vittinger has found himself as the local intro-to-philosophy guy, a much-coveted, post-fumous adjunct's joint chair, separating the seeds from the weeds at four or five schools around town. Depending on his or your mood, Vittinger is a brilliant if bitter man or an antisocial, pretentious whiner. Still, the others find his interjections entertaining—against the government, the universities, or institutions in general—and appreciate what seems to be his concern for working people's lives. A few years back, at Liberty Tech, when all the humanities were housed in one departmental shtetl, Duffy shared an office with Vittinger and eleven other mixed-discipline "scholars"; for his part, Vittinger was kind enough to pack lunch and add canned sardines in Dijon mustard to the olfactory mix.

Back to pizza, Duffy knows they make an unusual quintet—and that they never would have found each other as friends through any path other than work—but now they take turns buying an extra large pie every Thursday evening at five, and sharing it in the smallish common room at University of America. It is a weekly ritual they have maintained for over a year now, all of them opting for 5:30 to 9:30 p.m. Thursday night accelerated sections at America's main offices, or classrooms if you will. Duffy is the exception, but his Success Center tutoring makes it extremely convenient to pop upstairs for square pie and besides, his next class is not until 6 p.m. at Ivy Green.

He often recalls their missing sixth partner, Mrs. Emelia Lynn, a round, tiny woman of sixty-seven or so and Edna Hawkins's partner in the crime of composition. Last fall, she was tragically and brutally mowed down by a SEPTA bus on her way to morning classes at Liberty Tech. She was rushing to be there on time for the students and fell victim to a rude, barbaric driver, perched high above, barely glancing at crossing traffic, and refusing to give pedestrians the right of way. Duffy often thought of this tragedy in his spare moments riding his own trains and buses—a vibrant, witty old lady engaged in the classroom the one day, cut down by public transportation the next. It seemed too much to blame her misfortune on the adjunct's crazy hours and commuting life combined with the low wages that ensured a "working retirement," and yet where else could the blame be placed?

"So, Ed, sorry there's no red meat for the hunter!" Edna likes to chum around with Saferi's pro-gun position.

"Gun owners, hunters, all of them, should be shot and chopped up like feed, let them see what it's like to be an innocent animal in an evil man's world." Michael Vittinger eats meat himself—pork, beef, chicken, all of it—but he can't resist the bitter interjection.

"I don't have anything against spinach," says Ed. "If it was good enough for Popeye, it's good enough for me. This country needs more iron in its gut."

"The problem is we're too tough in the head. We're stupid. These corporate criminals in charge have sent us into this mess to line their pockets, and now we're in an impossible situation we can't get out of." Vittinger usually waits until after gobbling down at least one slice, but today he is on an early roll. Duffy and the others nod politely as Ed turns a bit pink, as if Michael's words have actually penetrated his Republican hide and had an effect, but conversation will have to wait.

With the others, Duffy digs in to enjoy the pizza. The men each get a second slice, the women settling for one plus company.

With her mouth wide open and crammed with red, green, and white pizza slosh, Deborah begins the rundown on the latest unionization activity. "Seattle has done it. New York City voted to form the union in three of five boroughs. The time is ripe for Philadelphia. The latest is we are planning a citywide strike for September. The overall rate of adjuncts teaching college courses in the Philadelphia area is forty-seven percent for undergrad, and that goes up to seventy-three percent if you just count freshman classes. We want to hit them where they're most vulnerable, freshman composition for instance, which is taught by an adjunct seventy-eight percent of the time and by full-time, nontenured staff another nineteen percent. That's a huge cash cow for the universities, and we can shut it down."

"It's easy for you to quit working, Deborah. Your husband can pay the bills." The irony of the radical union organizer living in a small mansion on the main line is not lost on Ed, Duffy, or anyone else.

Deborah is married to a vice president of one of Philadelphia's major insurance concerns. Duffy would think this would make a woman happy, but in Deborah's case, it makes her miserable. Her husband, with just an undergrad in business, takes home twenty times her salary despite her seven additional years of education, and the fact that her PhD in English literature was granted from what all her friends tell her is a top-tier program.

"There's no saying the leaders of the vanguard will not be rebels from the oppressing classes," adds Michael Vittinger, in an unusually diplomatic tone.

"Ed, I've been saving and am planning to start a fund for adjuncts in more desperate situations who would like to participate in the movement. If you want in Ed, we may be prepared to help with your bills and obligations."

Touché.

Duffy would love to linger and enjoy the feisty ruckus, and what he would love even more would be to blurt out his news of future conquest, but who could he tell?

He is almost certain he has seen Deborah deep in the cleavage—both home and away teams—but union talk aside, a latent lesbian as secret sharer seemed dubious if not dangerous. He could never tell anyone named Edna, and personal-responsibility Saferi would either respond, "Yeah, right," call the cops, or both. Vittinger no doubt enjoys such sweet tales of earthly delight, but he is unpredictable, a loose cannon, and who he would tell or how he'd blog about it is impossible to say. Alas, it is just too risky to speak of an affair with a student and a current one at that; and so for double-agent Duffy, "mum" must be the word. Besides, on his long day, he only has time to suck down his second slice, pop his two tablets of evening ibuprofen, thank Edna for delivering as promised, promise not to forget his turn in two weeks, and graciously depart.

Down the hall, descending by elevator, he strides out of the building with the crowds of people in professional suits, as if he were a normal white-collar worker leaving a beloved cubicle behind him at 5:30 p.m. He can see the day ending for so many, but the Duffler has only begun to fight. And yet, it is as if his future sexploits have changed his entire worldview. Unity rather than difference dominates his perceptions of the bustling throng of business suits surrounding him. He sees not competing individuals, or tribes of races, classes and genders warring against each other, but one sunny, multicultural citizenry, united in its pursuit of an honest version of the American dream. He can sense the professionals around him already thirsting for that tall, cool one in the local bar, but Duffy has loftier heights to thirst for in his evening's future. Just four and a half hours remain until his lucky appointment, and the treat of teaching Isaac Babel will tide him over in between. Forget terrorism fears and cynical and bitter peers. He has already escaped psychotherapy, an encounter with his boss, and all manner of apathetic, even belligerent, students. He was even spared stickup or sodomy in a public bathroom. His long day has become quite a remarkable day after all, the commute really not that bad compared to what he has heard. He has read stories about adjuncts in NYC hitting four of five boroughs in one day, middle-aged women supporting children on their own with over two hundred students and six hours of daily commuting. His late-night prize the Scooby Snack dangling under his nose, Duffy is whistling Dixie, a contagion caught from the voter-registration Negro no doubt, as he glides down busy Market Street. As he strides away from the University of America's downtown offices, nothing can wipe the wide, early evening bliss off the Duffler's honest face.

CHAPTER 7

AN EVENING SEMINAR AT IVY GREEN

Twenty-one minutes later, Duffy knows that those who fail to fall fail to rise again, although he has no recollection of where he read those lines. Nietzsche? Rimbaud? A freshman composition? An online blog? Now, as he ascends the steep incline of concrete steps leading up from the subway-surface line's 37th Street stop, he is thanked for his efforts by a beautiful setting sun, the evening's air cool with just a dash of leftover winter. The morning drizzle is long removed from what has been an outstanding, sun-drenched afternoon. From the top of the steps, he can see the Wawa Food Market, like a beacon of hope standing tall on the corner, and he knows immediately coffee will be the perfect complement to his newly won sexual optimism. Caffeine will see him through to the end.

At the crosswalk, he waits behind a gaggle of frosh flesh, not geese in any manner save for how they are squawking. Youth in bloom, first years of Ivy Green return to their famous dormitory, the quad, some of the oldest and most prestigious student housing in America. As the light changes from red to green, Duffy is mesmerized by the front-gate action, the children, nineteen-year-olds, young adults, whatever one terms them these days, milling about outside, taking in the day's last rays of sun, enjoying their wealth and freedom, as only the descendants of the monied can. Old or new cash or a combination of both, quite a few of them sport unseasonal outfits, or perhaps they were caught outside and are now back for a change, an additional layer for an April evening. But for now, Duffy notes that many, perhaps most, have achieved spring break tans, the ample visible areas of their bronze appendages in stark contrast to his own pale limbs. He catches himself staring at all the lost innocence before the light has fully changed, and so as fast as he can he flees the curb to cross the street, feeling his tight hamstrings tug maliciously as his lower back declares strike once more, refusing to man its fair share with all the other working muscles. Despite pain sharper than it should be—would he need to up his dosage of ibu or switch to the needle?—Duffy hurries across the street, captivated by a series of asses ahead of him, with light blue words in English written on navy terrycloth, hand-towels for miniskirts covering swishing behinds. Tier One University Grade A, the T—*au naturel* or augmented—no doubt top shelf as well. From left to right, he reads, "What" and "Looking" and "At" and "You." Hard to decipher until the last young woman drifts over to second from his left, lunging between girls one and three for the big sorority hug. What You Looking At. No question mark required for Duffy's shame to force his head down to the pavement for the ninety-degree right and sixty-yard advance to the store.

On his long march Duffy's conscience creeps up and bangs him on the brain; his own moral system is becoming as pliable as the worst element found among Ivy Green's tenured professors. From the daily papers, he knows one professor murdered his wife and another was convicted of testing the date-rape drug on a research assistant. A third came back from Southeast Asia with a laptop full of seven- to twelve-year-old smiles, torsos, and bare behinds, and a master of library science was caught in the hidden corridors of power with a male specimen aged eleven or fourteen. There were rumors scrawled on bathroom walls of secret Facebook agreements to exchange fellatio for A's in freshman seminars. A female professor was said to have flown her own pet frosh to Amsterdam and participated in a partnership ceremony attended by the elite academic establishment lesbians of Western Europe; this story, communicated to Duffy by an "in the loop" nontenured full-timer, sounded almost as absurd, if legal, as the rumors from Rural State that the 275K per annum athletic director had married his seventeen-year-old second cousin. Duffy could also dismiss the stories of Ivy Green's president bathing in thick wads of cash and gold coins in the bomb-proof bunker of her residential compensation, but the mounting evidence suggested the ivory tower was like any corporate structure; among the men in charge were criminals on the prowl while the women were cautious and yet profound in their expression of power. The majority, possibly, were beyond reproach—hardworking and so ostentatiously ethical that Duffy felt better whenever another felonious rumor or truth was leaked. If the rich were criminal, his celibacy and squalor could be celebrated as virtues. But what now? Argh! Close to the store, he demands that his associating faculties cease and desist ruining the evening ahead. He has a class to teach and Allison Silverman to meet.

Five paces from cheap caffeine he is distracted by a fervent discussion of business attire and interview manners. He looks up to see it is none other than Wawa Ed, holding court with three listeners in front of the convenience store. Ed is "on" today, as they say, in dramatic fashion expounding on the virtues of purchasing the most expensive suit one can afford. "See, you have to invest money to make money. Money talks and bullshit walks, and a man in meager threads is cow mud these days. So buy as much fashion as you can afford. Get your parents to pay, as an investment in your future. Or put it on credit if you gotta do it. In this sorry age, the clothes truly make the man."

Class time soon approaching, Duffy is nonetheless captivated by the lecture. Ed is a panhandler who has hustled outside the same Wawa for as long as Duffy can remember, perhaps a dozen years or so. More than a beggar, he returns coin offerings with career advice to these young professionals to be, a smile for the work-weary, silent reverence for the more reticent pitchers of coins. Duffy rarely has money for Ed, but they often exchange some brief conversation. If Ed isn't busy working, that is.

Now Ed supports specific points with his arms, as he goes into an explanation of proper sitting etiquette during the interview. "You see it is really all monkey see, monkey do. The man slouch, you slouch just a bit.

The man slouch, don't get caught sitting straight up. Don't you even dare lean forward. The man might feel like he is under psychological attack, particularly if you are bigger than he is."

The students listen intently to Ed's sage advice. In these words, Duffy can hear that Ed knows as much as the business communications textbook, maybe more, and certainly more than himself. During his interviews and interactions with bosses, Duffy sweats and slouches, the exact opposite of what he lectures to his students. Business communications is the perfect material for fulfilling the adage that he found most pleasingly ironic, that those who can't do, teach.

"Now, you get a woman behind that big oak desk, don't you dare get caught starin' at them titties!" The boys grin, enjoying Ed's show. "Back in the day, maybe, a man could assert himself as a titty watcher, even in the interview stage, but these days be careful. Times is tough, and takin' in just a little honest titty can get you fired, not hired, maybe just suspended, or worst case thrown in jail. Believe me, 'cause I been there, it's the pecker watchers in charge of that jail, boys." The students stop laughing and turn straight-faced and solemn, in consideration of the hierarchal sodomy of the workhouse. Duffy imagines all the men in jail, the darker men of America, so many of whom would be so-called black men. The young ones he fears, but the older ones seem to treat Duffy better than anyone else, particularly on his long day. Now listening to Ed, he remembers the quoted statistic from the Afrocentrist, supported by the newspaper article, that only one in two black men reported full-time, year-round work in 2002, and that a full quarter reported they were idle for the entire year. Here is Wawa Ed hustling, educating, helping society outside the convenience store, giving these wealthy students humor and wisdom, and yet he too is what society would term "idle year-round." It is a stark irony that the only time white America tolerated full employment of its African Americans was during the days of slavery. Duffy figures the collective white man must be a mean son of a bitch, but he finds himself too weary for strong emotion, particularly not hate and self-loathing, the most exhausting of all.

"Hey there, Duffy!" Ed snaps him out of it and smiles at him, like an old friend. "Coffee with milk and one sugar?"

"Yes sir, Ed. Yes sir."

"Good man, Duffy, you're a good man."

He is never quite sure of how to take Ed's insistence about his decency, and particularly not on an evening like this, when it would be perhaps his good fortune to finally experience some indecent exposure. What exactly about Adjunct Duffleman is good? Particularly compared to Wawa Ed? As he pushes the swinging door forward, and enters into the overly air-conditioned convenience store, he indulges in the guilt of his good fortune ahead, as it is Ed more than Duffy who is the nice guy busy finishing last. To the contrary, Cyrus Duffleman, at the coffee counter, stirs in extra milk and a salacious amount of brown sugar as he sips scalding hot liquid to measure the proper mix; he is a man beyond his own basic predicament, on his long day feeling slightly free and almost laid at last. And so, feeling he deserves it, he grabs a Snickers for the road.

Out of the store, large Styrofoam cup in hand, he tells Ed he has to run, crosses at the corner, and then enters Ivy Green's main campus. Duffy paces down a pedestrians-only path and into the two by four city blocks wide area of brick walkways, manicured lawns and elegant, aged stone and brick buildings upon many of which ivy, the vine in itself, grows. He crosses diagonally under one of the newest structures, the Halliburton Conference Center, a beautiful brick entity dedicated to further instruction in the art of imperial management and international growth. It fits perfectly with the other newer buildings on Ivy Green's campus; they are all parking garages, business-school additions, hotels, or strip malls selling overpriced goods—to Duffy, tributes to the oligarchal order of the times. He considers business a trade and decidedly not an art, or anything worthy of graduate-school training, and appreciates the fact that its finest practitioner in the land dropped out of Ivy Green during his sophomore year, unexposed to the greater flim-flam of continued education in the field of "management" or "business administration." Although Duffy knows his own poverty is no doubt related to his complete lack of financial wisdom, not even an "econ for artists" in his undergraduate days, he is adamant, nevertheless, in refusing to accept business as a field worthy of study for a graduate degree. That the MBA is President Fern's highest degree, and from the supposed best business school in the land, or at least a chief competitor to Ivy Green, further confirms the worthlessness of such education. And of course, the worthlessness of Fern himself.

But the building is formidable, and Duffy cannot help but admire the contemporary architecture of the conference center, its soothing lines and comfortable stones, one atop another, suggesting to any who pass here that this building is a welcoming one for all, rich and poor alike. The structure stands in stark contrast to the shoddy, frangible offices and furnishings of University of America. He cuts across the stone pathway, admiring the wooden benches and manicured bushes where squirrels and pigeons have found a wonderful, almost natural habitation for their play and feed. To the right and left, he notices that every person he sees looks happy. Is this merely his own projection of sexual optimism, an overcoming of his basic predicament? Or is it the weather? Or life itself? At some level, the people he sees are safe, attached to one of the finest names in business and education in the land. And then he walks past the Halliburton, and onto the widest path, Warren Walk, the main artery of Ivy Green's campus.

As he strides down the walkway, his hamstrings have loosened once again and so his confidence in his painkillers has returned in full force. Duffy feels alive and even slightly in place. Yes, this is what an academic career is supposed to be; this is who I am, Adjunct Duffleman, yes, but at the same time a professor of literature, not only business writing, diluted freshman comp, or remedial essay writing. Kafka. Babel. Schulz. Central Jews. Eastern Jews. Important Jews. Good men dying young. My destiny to bring their prose to the children! And get side action at the same time!

As he nears the dignified, aged, stone keep of the English literature building—yes, here literature has its own edifice—he passes through a student parking lot. He sees a few hand-me-downs from the parents—old

Toyotas and Nissans from the last century, but mostly what he notices are what appear to be new or recent models of expensive cars—BMW, Mercedes, Lexus, a sexy Mini or two. Beyond the student parking lot lies a smaller one, for faculty—full-time tenured faculty, that is—and he sees not the automobiles that would reflect some of the most important chairs in the humanities—but rather, the professors' six-figure salaries are reflected in the proud six-figure odometer readings of modest Volvo station wagons and Saab sedans that appear to have survived the entire ascent to greatness. Duffy surmises this befits liberals in power. They stick it to the big boys in Detroit but take care of the local working man, the mechanic, by returning again and again to repair the old model, if necessary even to restore the original engine.

Fifty grand a year for tuition, room, and board, and the full professors drive cars born before the students were. He wonders if Allison Silverman owns one of the automobiles in the student parking lot—would she be zipping him around in a European convertible, top down, getting fresh with the good professor by grabbing his kneecap instead of the stick shift?

It is all he can do to keep his own stick from shifting to a higher gear so close to his next class. *Pray, go down, good boy, please go down.* Duff wonders if it weren't better to show off the young puppy, boldly marching in with a full salute. He couldn't be certain this kind of message would appeal to today's youth, but could that be what Babel was talking about in "Guy De Maupassant"? To live full lives, experience every sensation, and afford the Ivy Green girls—the rich and the *zaftig*—a chance to stare at your full endowment, even in the middle of your years, in the middle of a seminar? And what if they notice nothing at all? Would he feel humiliated at their lack of vision? The implication of his smallness? His inability to command their attention? It is all too much to consider at once—boners, doubt, doubt about boners. The Duffler is past all that anyway. Tonight is his just due; he could feel it deep in his . . . skeleton.

He calms himself down enough to open a side door covered in ivy and slink into English Literature. On the bottom floor, it is all he can do to avoid coffee spillage while almost running over a crowd surrounding an elderly gent in blue corduroy with gray elbow patches. On closer inspection, Duffy can see it is the most prominent Melvillean in the mid-Atlantic region, the Amazon.com chair in the humanities, Professor Boethius Kenth.

Kenth is surrounded by a paparazzi-like swarm of sycophantic post-colonial grad students—talented, androgynous, ass-kissing careerists, of every diaspora known to have deplaned in the next America. These continental carpetbaggers recognize full well what it takes to bounce beyond graduate school, past the track toward tenure, and into prosperity and job security—a position so antithetical to the vast majority of American work experiences it could be termed anti-American, a little isle of guarantees in a sea of economic uncertainty. How Duffy envies that chance to rest for forty or fifty years on one's accomplishments and smiles from an earlier decade. But just as quickly, remembering his own evening's plans, he feels shame for how easily he slanders these humble slave-wage paper-graders attempting to forge ahead in an unforgiving world. They are realists, smart hardworkers who understand how bad the future could be for the less secure like Duffy. And besides, was he not post-colonial too? If both sides of his family hadn't drifted across the Atlantic, he'd be but five-eighths alive and trapped in poverty or working at a Hyundai assembly plant in Slovakia. He thanks the other three-eighths for the gift of guilty conscience and rallies to the occasion of awkward conversation.

But in the dim light, Duffy soon sees that Kenth and his crowd don't recognize him as a colleague or as anyone at all. He feels like a ghost, slinking in for the second shift, the late-night adjunct game. In the narrow entrance, he cannot help but block the exit, so he mutters profuse apologies, as Kenth and his entourage, visibly startled, squint to see what has interfered with their escape to freedom. Despite his coffee, Duffy adds some Eastern-style bowing for good measure, popping up and down like a hiccupping Chinaman, as he backs away from the egressors, his left arm ahead of him, fingers searching hopelessly for the elevator button. He gets it, though, walks right in, avoids spillage, arrives in the basement, and recognizes that he must have pressed the wrong button.

By the time he wanders into the third-floor seminar room, Duffy sees the regulars, fourteen strong, waiting for him. They are lodged in their comfortable, contemporary blue-cloth swivel chairs, around the octagonal configuration of tables. Two are seated per side with the last throne free for instructor and book bag. He has the maximum fifteen students, but one never shows up, not since the first class when she acted profusely excited to be in attendance; now, she just keeps Duffy updated by e-mail on her world travels, the dead great uncles, and unavoidable reunions of a wealthy family that owns a private jet, zooming her from California to Texas to this cape to that ocean and back.

After placing the coffee on his side of the octagon and removing Isaac Babel from his book bag, he sits down and immediately senses Allison Silverman to his right, at a forty-five degree angle. She catches his eye, and shifts in her seat, stretching to fully arch her back, and then flings her body forward so her twin towers collapse upon the table. It feels like an early offering, and Duffy blushes, having half a mind to pass a note down, *Not 'til later, naughty one.* Opposite Allison, notably to the left, sits the atheist communist, beady-eyed Gary, pessimistic and dour before his time, his eyes full of judgment and scorn. Duffy assumes Gary takes him for some pathetic, petty-bourgeois cog in the capitalist wheel, a form at least as prerevolutionary and dispensable as the lumpen proletariat. A quorum of young Zionist Republicans, or young Republican Zionists, congregate directly opposite their teacher; they are the three little dwarves of the seminar's neocon club. They were reared separately in Great Neck, Scarsdale, and Greenwich, Connecticut but wear the same grim expressions on their clean-shaven faces. Their texts out and lined up, they are ready to go. American undergraduates with political identities, inspiring and ridiculous all at once.

"Glad you could all make it despite the disturbances of earlier in the day. I really appreciate your attendance." He decides to start graciously. "So maybe we could start with 'Guy De Maupassant'?"

"It was sensual. So beautiful." Allison eagerly inputs first.

"It made me horny as hell," adds her raunchier neighbor. At Ivy Green, many more students freely espouse or expose their views, not for class laughs but from early years of positive reinforcement. Counselor Michael might attribute it all to mommy and daddy applauding every pee-pee and poopy, but Duffy prefers to move on, knowing to avoid certain topics in light of current circumstances. Discretion, after all, is the greater part of getting laid.

"Clearly should be read as an indictment of the capitalist system." Gary is never far behind, and always eager to steer the conversation away from the overly commodified sex of late capitalism, and toward something that Marx would approve of.

"Okay, Gary, I'll take the bait. How do we read this as a critique of capitalism?"

"Well, at the core of the story we have the wealthy Jewess. She is obviously a symbol of capitalist enterprise, the buxom trophy wife. The narrator is getting his ass kicked by the free market, sharing a few floorboards with another man in a rundown section of town. He is forced to suck from the capitalist's teat, or the capitalist's wife's teat rather, for his meager livelihood. Now, furthermore, her inability to translate is proof of how the capitalist system wastes its wealth on the undeserving."

"Pardon me, Gary, but before the full critique, should it be relevant that the story takes place in Tsarist Russia?"

"Yes, highly relevant, and the revolution will come."

"But doesn't it take place during a reign of despotism, not capitalism?"

"Well, yes and no. The Jews were the capitalists of this despotic reign, given unfair monopoly over the common folk. In charge of business ownership. Taxation. The usual."

At this point, the neocons start braying a bit loudly. They need to shoot down this communist antisemite, and quick.

"The story is an antisemetic attack on a reputable Jewish merchant class. That's what the story is."

"It's an attack on monogamous marriage as well, another critical tenet of Judaism."

"There may even be evidence of deviant sexuality at the flop house where the narrator stays. Two grown men share a room, so who knows where they slept!"

The young Zionists often talk in a team like this, three in sequence. They nod to affirm each other's points, and then glare at Gary, a half breed from the same town as the middle neocon. From student journals, Duffy has learned that Gary and the middleman were sworn enemies in suburban Scarsdale High's advanced placement European history, and now all over again at Ivy Green.

"Jewish intellectuals have been at the forefront of critique of the Jewish merchant class, the exploiters. It makes them honest, not antisemetic." Gary has no trouble defending his position. For his first paper in Duffy's class he wrote a comparison and contrast of his father to the father figure in several Kafka stories, a searing indictment of the patriarchal roots of the exploitive system. In it, he even linked the Prague ghetto to the quartering of Jews in Scarsdale and Tel Aviv, and described how capitalist practices encouraged racism, tribalism, and segregation, as opposed to ending them.

"Please boys. Can't we all just get along?" It is Allison Silverman again. When she is not discussing the poetry or the passion of the stories, she tries to play moderator. She seems to earnestly want all the Jews to get along. Live in peace together. Not in Israel, but in Duffleman's seminar. Duffy appreciates the thought as he looks around the room, trying to determine if anyone present is less of a Jew than he. There is one very blonde girl who rarely speaks, and he was certain she was the standard-issue, reticent gentile—smart and tactful—until one day she happened to mention that her parents adopted, but she was still Bat Mitzvahed.

Duffy, his just due upcoming, sympathizes with his sexual savior's quest for unity or at least some form of more moderate debate, but nonetheless he enjoys the fray, listening to the ideological opposites exhume their frustrations over the battlefield of Babel. Duffy can only imagine that their four years of college would be hardly enough time for resolving their own sexual inadequacies and celibacies. At times, the heated fight between the Zionist capitalists and the atheist communist is difficult for Duffy to follow. The verbal jabs are swift and scathing, the kind of stuff you hear from smart young people. They appear too young to have such definable positions, but then, he thinks again, it is experience in the world that will break their ideologies and anything solid they've learned to lean on as truth.

Too soon, the Duffler, worn down from his long day on the one hand, and on the other, unable to draw his mind away for any period of time from Allison Silverman's cleavage, finds himself drifting in and out of the debate. It has a life of its own, discussion that could sustain itself without a moderator. The students might not care for a moderator at all, particularly not a weary, folded-up 37.5 percenter like Duffy. So he sips his large coffee as he catches brief bits of attack and parry; with the seminar on autopilot, he is tangential to his very own life.

"I don't think Babel is arguing for an Israeli military superpower. That is not the point of 'The Story of My Dovecote,' not what it is about at all."

"Yes, and for that reason Babel has it all wrong. The Jews will get 'constitutioned' just like his grandfather in the story . . ."

"Yes, unless we fight back," one neocon serves to another, fighting the communist revolution, feeling no shame in outnumbering him three to one.

"Remember, Israel was founded as a socialist state. Remember the kibbutz? Herzl's promise of Jewish unity? It was never supposed to be an imperial superpower in its region." Duffy notes Gary has read his Chomsky.

"What are you, some sort of self-loathing Jew? I bet you support Mel Gibson!" The Zionists have been to the movies.

"Gibson is an idiot, a religious zealot. I have nothing to do with him. Your views are more like his than mine. Religious zealotry one and the same, your reflection in the Catholic mirror."

"You refuse to accept us because of your own self-loathing nature. Look at your heroes. Karl Marx? A self-loathing Jew! Noam Chomsky?

A self-loathing Jew! Babel rode with the Cossacks, probably self-loathing too! And Kafka, for refusing to accept the laws of his father! And Schulz too! His capitalized 'The Book' is blasphemous; such emphasis is dismissive of the Talmud."

"If we don't defend ourselves, who will? The Arabs? The terrorists? They'll kill us all, drive us into the sea, just as they planned in 1948. Ever since the first settlers arrived. These countries were Hitler's allies in World War II, and nothing has changed. We need to defend ourselves! And you too!"

The middle Zionist turns to regard his exhausted instructor who has been paying attention, sort of, despite blatant oogling of Allison Silverman's cleavage. Under normal circumstances, Duffy would admit to being four points over a third self-loathing, but tonight he is full of optimism. The promise of the breast is granted only to good boys, so he has no reason to hate himself at all in the near term. He is beyond his basic predicament, and his long day will soon be forgotten once his young Mommy surrogate grants him a wish.

Back to work, Duffy tries to redirect the conversation.

"So maybe the political angles are a little overplayed. Did anyone notice the number of mentions to flesh in the story?"

"Yeah, I noticed Babel is a sick fuck who can't stop staring at women's breasts."

Not quite what Duffy is looking for—and hopefully not an indirect attack on his own viewing habits—but at least it came from a gentile. Or so he suspects, as he is thankful to remember, that yes, there is at least one. He fears being termed exclusionary in the student-run website for rating teachers, but now he has awakened Amanda Thorn, the angry feminist—at elite colleges much less common than conservative TV talking heads claim.

"It is really a little overwhelming. Here on line thirty-seven, and then here again on line fifty-four and then again at eighty-three, and one hundred three, and one ninety-seven . . . " adds the other gentile, a sharp young woman proving she has once more taken meticulous notes. She is the other feminist in the room, one who prefers pithy textual analysis and subjugation to mere rage against the male author or the man.

Duffy has all of these "good parts" highlighted already, as if the Babel were merely the back issue of *Penthouse* he found in the alleyway at age twelve. Other women in the room nod in support, and add their two cents. The three neocons seem somewhat sympathetic to their concerns about Babel's sexism, his objectification of the Jewess. They may need these women as vessels for their Isaacs and Jacobs down the road. Communist Gary seems not to hear them at all, as if the current conversation does not appeal to him; he stares with disdain at the neocons, but his beady eyes also dart over to the teacher at times, as if to say, "So whose side are you on anyway?" During his brief respites from Silverman's cleavage, Duffy gets the full eyeball from Gary—cool, analytical, and austere; a solid black iris like his unwavering ideology.

Because it is a two-hour seminar, Adjunct Duffleman orders a ten-minute break in the middle. Everyone leaves the room save for Allison, and the beady-eyed Marxist. He remains seated, in his dark camouflage jacket, coolly staring at Duffy or glancing down at his book. When Gary begins twirling a front lock of hair—madly, like Dmitry in *The Brothers Karamazov*—it reminds Duffy of his bout of psychotherapy from earlier in the day.

Duffy shotguns the remains of his Wawa coffee before Allison walks over and with her thumbs and knuckles begins to knead his lower neck. In his state of bliss, he can recall nothing at all from his sexual-harassment training sessions. He knows he must have been exposed to language strongly discouraging the reception of massage therapy, but his upper back is so thankful, his mind draws a blank. And even with the ascetic atheist in the room, he lets her have her way with his unfavorably tight muscles and tendons.

"Poor, Duffy, you shouldn't have to handle all of that, particularly not on your special day."

Duffy generally tries to lay low about his quantity of work as it seems unfair to complain to his students. Now he wonders if he has let it slip out by e-mail that Thursday is his busiest day.

As she massages deeply into his neck and shoulders, she leans into him, and Duffy can feel the heat of her bosoms on his back. He can also feel the Marxist is staring over at them, but when he shoots a glance back, Gary's eyes are aimed straight down at his text. Just before a few culminating thumbs deep into the recesses of his grateful upper torso, Allison presses even closer and whispers into his ear, "Tenth floor at ten. Don't forget."

Duffy is almost relieved she ceases massaging and returns to her place in the octagon, even more relieved that he can feel no discharge below. The students file back in, and so the second half begins.

He allows the ideologues to take over where they left off, and soon the seminar is on autopilot, a noisy Knesset with no need for a king. Nevertheless, Duffy nods often, raises an eyebrow here and there, and once in an odd while adds, "Is that so?" or, "And what do you think?" In general, so many of the students volunteer to communicate, that the seminar really needs no facilitator at all. It is a genuine discussion of the meaning of the text. He loses himself in his own thoughts, which, when not of sex, are to his credit at least related to the discussion. Of Eastern Jews. Important Jews. Lives of literature led as literature. Dead Jews, all of them, before their time. One finally escaped his father, only to die frail and sickly in a sanitarium. Another was stolen away and murdered by Stalin's evil agents, the exact date unknown. A third was gunned down in broad daylight by one of Hitler's psychopathic henchmen on the streets of a city conquered and reconquered again. Kafka. Babel. Schulz. They were survived and resuscitated by meek, watered-down followers like Duffleman, 37.5 percenters, accustomed to climate-controlled lives, teaching the words of great ones to affluent American Jews and half breeds, a literary inheritance idly perused in security and comfort, between IM chit-chat and cell phone text-messaging. This is as close as he gets to the thing in itself. Literature.

Although Duffy is grateful for the opportunity to teach at Ivy Green, he cannot help but find himself envious of the ideal lives he imagines these students lead. They seem to have all that he lacks, in particular a hearty confidence that comes from economic security. They come to campus complete with credit cards carrying huge limits; they can afford to do as they please, and Mom and Dad will pick up the tab. He imagines them having no worries. They can eat whatever, fuck whomever, and live wherever with no repercussions; Mom and Dad will pay, and with Ivy Green's aid, sweep any nasty leftovers under the rug. No worries, at least no base-level worries in Maslow's Hierarchy of Needs. Their survival needs, safety needs—air, food, water, shelter, yes, nice free shelter with central air—all of it taken care of by their parents. Despite his impending dessert of Allison's flesh, Duffy finds himself distracted by envy. Staring at their suede moccasins and leather sandals. Their designer fabrics. Rolex watches. Armani rims. And the cleavage. He found the quality of cleavage on the Ivy Green campus amazing. So perfectly disproportional, it could overwhelm. Milky white breasts, two thirds or half-hidden, sometimes with religious adornment, perhaps to recognize the minor miracle betwixt which it lay, a gold cross or silver six-sided star gently resting midbosom, the perfect complement to perfection.

As Duffy disappears further into the depths of cleavage, and further away from the seminar room, he finds it bizarre, almost overwhelmingly perplexing, that the young men of his seminars, appear to be not the least bit interested in the breasts at hand. Or rather, *in view*, he should say. How could they not at least occasionally steal glances, and why has he never caught one of them openly leering, the honest display of pure lust? How could their values be so misplaced? How could they be so ignorant? Are they that serious? Could they just be successful in tricking him into thinking they aren't also staring? All perfectly polite gentlemen? Or all gay? It is a mystery he could not solve. Not tonight, or any evening, and thankfully tonight, yes, finally tonight, he need not envy so much, as it was now his own solid flesh to melt and thaw itself unto a dew of Allison Silverman's creamy delights.

Duffy kicks himself in the brain for allowing his thinking to sink so untowardly low. He gathers his thoughts, regains himself. Not back to the discussion really, but at least toward the authors discussed. He wonders briefly what Babel and Schulz would make of this current American age. Would they find the fear and paranoia abounding at all sincere? Indicative of a world like their own, the forces of evil surrounding civilization, bearing down, intent on destroying it all? Or would the authors see the current antiterrorism politics as an intense propaganda campaign, the Iraq war an imperialist venture that would merely succeed in making terrorism worse. He could imagine what Joseph Roth would say, a Galician Jew, the first to mention Hitler in a novel, in 1923. Duffy has read Roth's essay condemning Jews latching on to the German militarism and imperialism of Bismarck, how he saw Hitler as the natural conclusion, Bismarck the first premise. Duffy holds the romantic notion that men like Roth, Schulz, and Babel could smell Hitler and Stalin in the air. They knew the end was coming long before its approach. And what kind of smell is in the air now?

Duffy breathes in deeply through his nose, to see what scents are available to him. He smells properly deodorized undergraduates, the odor of new cloth swivel chairs, laminated wooden tables, and all the wondrous plastics of the age.

Gazing about the room, at this sharp-witted, boisterous, at times bilious crew of feminists, communists, Zionists, and converts, all he can know for sure is that the Jews are hardly a unified people. The cabal will have to be put on hold, the *Protocols of Zion* still fit for nothing more than the mulch pile. But at the same time, there is no denying, there they are, the dominant voices of his literature class, taking up most of the seats at a seminar at an elite American university. Duffy has read that Ivy Green is about thirty-four percent Jewish, more or less his own percentage, and just slightly above average for American first-tier schools. Because his seminar is full of Jews, he wonders where all the non-Jews are; he imagines them sitting in much more preprofessional classes, business and nursing and engineering. Far too concerned with surviving in the real world to care about a few spare if finely crafted books. Although his coed, orthodox, reconstructed, and secular quorum can sound alternately officious, omniscient, or merely spoiled, Duffy likes to imagine they have inherited the dreaminess of their forebears, Kafka, Babel, and Schulz. And yet when he looks at the Zionists in their striped Oxfords, he sees not the dreamy romanticism of the sons, but the practical drudgery of their fathers. How sad. The thoughts of drudgery remind him of the first week, when he passed out a copy of Shalamov's "Through the Snow," the opening marching through the snows of the Siberian gulag, contrasted ultimately to the author or writer of a book. Now Duffy feels lucky, not to be freezing in Siberian cold, but to be comfortable as a secondary man, a reader on another continent, blessed with free speech, spring weather, and a seminar room with advanced air-conditioning technology. He feels grateful for all of this, and the more to come. He feels grateful for all of the class participation too, as ideological as it may be. He is even more grateful that time passes quickly, and most grateful when the last class of his long day finally ends.

Allison Silverman is the last to depart the seminar room. Still seated as the last lingerers move on, she stretches freely, extending her young but fully adult body, every curve and crevice of her upper half available for perusal by his sad, soggy-bagged retinas and sockets. Eyeballing her now, he feels his manhood retrenching, peeping out of the left side of his boxers, clinging to his left thigh, like a thief pressing against a wall under the cover of darkness. Duffy has some distant, abstract understanding that this girl may be only a B+ at best in the world of twenty-one-year-olds, but he can hardly dream of better.

Allison approaches her teacher but stays a yard away this time. He hopes this doesn't mean she requires an audience for all her touchy-feeliness.

"So you won't forget now, will you Duffy?"

As easy as it is to get lost in her ripe melons during class time, now Duffy has trouble looking anywhere but the floor. At last, he overcomes his shyness, to peel his eyes off the carpet, and directly states, "Of course not. I'm looking forward to seeing you later." He hopes for a quotidian sound to his words, the unremarkable utterance of a professor accustomed to meeting female students in hotel rooms.

"Good boy." She smiles and giggles slightly; she pirouettes, and then she is gone, out the door.

Duffy takes a moment to himself before proceeding with his next adventure. The seminar clock says 7:57 p.m. He has a minute or two. He closes his eyes, and slumps down deep in his chair, realizing that the point he feels himself losing consciousness, falling asleep, is exactly when he must rise and depart. And that point then arrives, and so he is up and ambulant once more.

CHAPTER 8

SHIFT WORK

Adjunct Duffleman hustles over to the security building for his last task of the day. He is surprised at the lack of increased security here, but he soon fingers the usual suspects for reasons why. Because no current employees are allowed to work more than twenty hours per week, there's no time-and-a-half for extra night guards in an emergency; in addition, the higher-ups would resist any increased spending for more workers, and new hires couldn't be "deputized" on the spot and installed on the street corners. Besides, the Collegetown Guard is third-tier at best in keeping students safe—just unarmed guys who passed a basic physical, eyesight in range with spectacles on. Liberty Tech has its own force of rent-a-cops, and Ivy Green even deploys officers with fixed pensions, full health coverage, and semiautomatic weaponry. Of course, it's the job of real cops and the FBI to hunt killers and assassins.

So he flashes his worker ID and nods slightly to the elderly gentleman enjoying his dotage by mumbling expletives as he shadow boxes at the easiest company post. "Don't mess wit me, no sir, no-sama . . ." Past the geezer guard, he climbs down the rusted metal steps to the men's locker room. Downstairs, low ceiling, the light grows dim, the air cools, and Duffy can hear the faint pling, pling of water dripping. As usual, he is the last one in for the 8 p.m. shift; the others are half-dressed, nearly in uniform, almost ready to go.

"Yo, Duff. How ya doin' tonight?" Invariably, Dupree is the first to greet him with words. Tu Nguyen and Smitty nod while Johnston adds a serious hello.

"I'm good Dupree. I'm good."

Duffy finds his locker, remembers his combination, and begins the process of turning from quasi-faculty member to pseudo-security guard. He works the eight-to-midnight shift three nights a week, Thursday through Saturday, twelve hours at seven bucks per hour. It keeps him out of trouble, and from ruining his sleeping patterns by napping too late in the evening. What's more, with most of his course pay coming at the end of the month, or the end of the term, as with his tutoring gig, he appreciates the biweekly paycheck. Minimum wage is grocery money when he is conservative in his purchases. No direct deposit for part-time workers, but Duffy enjoys the thrill of taking his paychecks to the bank late every other Friday, waiting in the long line of shift workers living hand to mouth, weekly pay to weekly pay. Unlike these poor folk, he could deposit it all if he wanted to, and he feels a pang of guilt and embarrassment when he dwells too long on this difference. After the bank, he journeys to the cleaners, where he throws it all together in a cold cycle; his take-out dinner is followed by a short nap and then his Friday-night security-guard shift.

"Man, Duff, you look more than good. Somethin's changed. What's wrong? Or by the looks of it, should I say, what's right?"

Despite his attempt at business as usual—his poker-faced play of the usual sighs and sadness—Duffy's date with Allison Silverman is strewn across his face.

"Nothing at all, Dupree."

"Weird day to be smiling." Smitty speaks. He's a working-class white man with three kids, two dogs, and an obese wife who stays at home, and, as with Duffy, this is his moonlighting gig. In fact, it is extra work for all of them. They survive in the society of Americans overworking together. He has read in a business communications textbook that more than fifty hours is now the norm, but the Department of Labor has the average work week down close to thirty. So working America is on unpaid overtime while the underemployed are idle a full working day, but Duffy is too exhausted to ascertain how this anomaly came to be; he knows only that, for this group, the average hours worked per week approaches fifty-five or sixty.

"I heard that," adds Johnston.

"I heard that," echoes Tu Nguyen, a sinewy Vietnamese, the only one of their posse to be called by two names.

"Rough day for Philly," is all Duffy can think to say.

"Rough day for America, you mean," corrects Dupree.

"Every day a rough day with that asshole in office. Can't wait to get that mutha out, and get a man who fought for his country back in charge."

Duffy doesn't mind that Johnston, a Vietnam vet, is enraged by Fern's questionable military record and reckless use of current armed forces, but he is amazed the alienated worker can resist focusing on his own plight in favor of geopolitical concerns. That Johnston is fucked by Fern's trickle-down pisser of an economic policy is only his secondary concern.

"Men, you're right on target. It was a rough day for Philadelphia, and a rough day for America." A take-charge type, Smitty is paid an extra dollar an hour for the title of shift supervisor; it is not exactly a boost to the next tax bracket, but Duffy suspects Smitty may be a Republican due to how often he interrupts Johnston's long rants against the government, the stolen election, the war for oil, and everything else. "This is no time for smiling. We've got to be on extra alert. We've got our cell phones. If we see something suspicious, we need to call it in, right away. Our call-ins were sloping downward before today's incident. It's going to look bad in the assessment. Forget about our lack of resources. Our lack of weaponry. Our lack of paid training. We can still make a difference in the war on terror. We have to."

Solemnity hangs in the air. Duffy observes his surroundings. Johnston appears poised for one of his breakdowns, begging forgiveness to Tu Nguyen for what he did to his country. Dupree senses this, so he breaks the ice.

"Man, what we gonna do with cell phones! Smitty, we just rent-a-cops. No need to play it for more than it is." Dupree needs his extra cash too, just like the rest of them, but he isn't going to let a tragic mood dominate. Working as an indoor custodian another thirty hours a week, he appreciates the late shift for the moon, the stars, and the cool night air.

"Come on, Dupree. The man in charge. Let the man have his say." Johnston knows that Smitty receives no benefits, just like the rest of them, and so in a way it is hard to take his leadership seriously. At the same time, it means Smitty is in the same boat as the others. And Johnston likes everyone in the boat to stay in the boat together. They are grown men, tired men, and the shift would go smoothly if everyone follows the leader. Even without his new-found prosperity, Duffy could agree to that.

"The shit go down in my territory, and the terrorist gonna pay a price." Tu Nguyen, from out of his left shoe, produces a sharp, gleaming Chinese star.

"Goddamn, you two-winnin' motherfucker," shouts Dupree. "What you plannin' on doing with that?"

Johnston delivers a low whistle. Duffy eyes the sharp edges warily. It's all fun and games until someone loses an ear. Or worse.

"Tu Nguyen, you know I can't have you on the street with that." Smitty adds a touch of solemnity to his cool-headed approach. "Hand it over."

"How I'm gonna protect the students! Huh? Huh?"

Tu Nguyen provided a reasonable explanation when he first showed up to work as a security guard. Just a year before, he had been running his own food truck on campus, his native Vietnamese cuisine, with tasty coffees and desserts. It was a prosperous business, and one of Duffy's favorites, until Ivy Green undercut the competition to its university-owned properties of corporate-chain food courts and institutionalized cafeteria food. The administration outlawed food trucks and carts all over campus, save for in small designated areas with astronomical parking-space rental fees. Plus, space was limited so only the wealthiest trucks could survive. Tu Nguyen tried to reopen a few blocks off campus, far enough to avoid the fees, but the university shut him down there too. With a straight face, Ivy Green announced that all the changes were due to student safety concerns. Never mind that they were steering the students to higher-fat options of the overly French-fried food courts, the PR department said that the changes were made to protect students from darting out from behind the trucks and getting hit by city-street drivers in speeding cars. In a memo sent to every member of the university community, concerns about the sanitation of the carts were also mentioned. As if business owners taking their livelihood seriously, men and women like Tu Nguyen and his wife, would refuse to wash their hands. Anyone with eyes could see it was more likely the alienated, uninsured minimum wagers of the food courts and cafeterias who were the ones who cared little for the health of the customers. (Duffy has even read freshman essays about summer-jobbing juvenile delinquents—from the wealthy suburbs no less—choking the chicken right into the batter.) Alas, the American Dream of entrepreneurial success is over for Tu Nguyen, at least for now. His wife is cleaning houses, and he is left sweeping floors of science labs, and putting in extra time as a guard at night. He works as many hours a week as he can get for hourly pay. From boat people to business people to no-benefits people, three generations of his family had escaped communist centralized planning for capitalism's corporate imperialism; any way you slice the fresh fruit for dessert, he and his wife are left on the waiting list for health insurance while their children inherit student loans and credit-card debt.

Duffy hears their American Dream frying in the wok, fat sizzling away, until they are left to subsist on lemon grass and disposable wooden chopsticks. He watches Tu Nguyen admire his weapon and then calmly hand it over to Smitty.

"Atta boy," says Smitty. With no verbal or visual cue this could be construed as a slur. "Our task is a simple one. We keep our eyes open. And use the phones to alert the authorities. Now let's get out there."

Duffy is now fully changed into his work uniform; he feels lucky it is casual so security could blend into the crowd. He could wear the black pants, dark-green polo, and rainproof jacket to the hotel room, walk right in, dim the lights if they aren't already, and Allison Silverman would merely think he has changed into something more comfortable. Everything, even his clothing, is fitting together quite nicely.

In fact, the evening is fast becoming antithetical to his entire existence. The experience of not belonging—so central to his basic predicament—is now in the past. At the adjunct pizza party at U. of A., it is as if the five instructors share not belonging together, each in his or her way, not belonging to the group separately. They are a group of *isolatoes*, sharing anchovies and tomatoes.

But in the changing room, with two African Americans, a Vietnamese, and a regular white working guy, Duffy would occasionally get this vague notion that he does indeed belong to this group—together a thousand-plus pounds of flab and fatigue, adding to their daily toil by taking on the early end of a graveyard shift. They were lost in the funhouse of capitalism's creative destruction in an economy so elastic it could expand with the optimism of a televised blimp floating above corporate-sponsored stadiums and then contract like saran wrap to the size of a man's genitals and squeeze out the last productive drop.

Speaking of elastic around the middle section, Duffy remembers his attempt at bonding with his security squad coworkers and how he bounded in one evening with a wide smile and news of staggering discounts on Haines and Fruit of the Loom at the new Collegetown big-box superstore. What happened next was a twenty-first century lesson in textiles and retail. It came from Tu Nguyen, Dupree, Johnston, and even Smitty but starred Calvin Klein, Polo, and Ralph Lauren. Each man bragged and dished on online-only specials and close-out sales—stripes and silk and leopard-skin, boxer briefs and bikini thin. Each claimed to have purchased designer brands for less than the Duffler's deal. Guerilla tactics and Internet strategies had replaced simple discount shopping. It was shock and awe. His whole life had been built upon a shattered concept, and he would have to learn first principles over again. If there were no point to hunting down bargains for Fruit of the Loom, what other knowledge did he lack for staying afloat and content in the newest new world? He was paid like a prole, that he knew, but with his head lost in two decades' worth of books, he'd have to learn from his coworkers how to shop like one.

Duffy returns to the surface and nods at Dupree and Johnston, at Tu Nguyen, and then at Smitty. Shiny, silver cell phones stuck snugly into their forest-green jackets, the troops are ready to move. As they split up to man their territories, his partners in crime prevention walk off in policing styles learned from Clint Eastwood and Steve McQueen, but definitely not Fern or National Security Advisor Laverna Pap, or any others in power whose bold, wide strides elide past vote discrepancies but serve to remind the masses that they in fact hold office. Johnston and Dupree each offer their own version of the comic black detective in action, Johnston adding some fake fright and weird kung-fu hand positions as he parts. And then they are out of sight.

Duffy's spirits are high as he wanders around the Northeast section of the University of Ivy Green. The temperature has dropped, but students are out en masse—heading for libraries, coffee shops, study sessions, food, frat parties, and all manner of evening soirées ranging from lectures on celibacy to one-night stands. Thursday night can be the beginning of the long weekend for undergrads, so Duffy is alert to the fact that thieves may also know this. The idea of keeping an eye out for terrorists and assassins seems odd, unusual, and even somewhat ridiculous if not blatantly absurd, but he eyeballs his territory for these villains as well. He wonders what a terrorist assassin would look like. Somewhat deranged with a sick leer as his expression? Or just drugged-out red eyes and a blank face? Maybe the cold stare of mathematical genius, someone who could target with precision from any angle, any distance?

In the papers, he has read about terrorist sleeper cells. Men in these groups are quiet; they lead normal lives for years in America, and then in less than a blink of an eye, become actualized and intent on completing their mission. They peddle fruit one day and blow up an airport the next. In a way, they are like a normal man in a global economy who could move in an instant from employed with benefits to laid off, locked out of his office, or worse. A sudden career change could be thrust upon anyone. This move to the next chapter feels not unlike Duffy's own life, for he has often thought that were he a novel, he would be an episodic novel. No fruit stand in the morning and skyscraper razed at night, no, but each job completes a chapter in his daily book; his day's journey makes him an episodic man.

Moving further into his own next scene, Duffy circles the Ivy Green Library, an expansive stone and brick structure worthy of a tier-one university. Some evenings, he will go in and spend over an hour or more on his e-mail, haggling with students over grades from last term, trying to explain assignments detailed in the English language of his syllabus, answering the stupidest questions imaginable, wishing no teacher had ever said that there were in fact no stupid questions. He often wonders what idiot thought that one up. He discourages his students from thinking in such absolutes; in fact, he has counted at least 10,013 of his own dumb questions, and so he can imagine millions of others lurking out there in the deep seas of the national psyche, the collective ignorance and stupidity of an entire nation.

Tonight, he decides to forego this long version of Internet addiction, yet he cannot resist a peek and perusal. Plus, he can do the once-over of every floor, catch a terrorist in the act of planting his bomb, intent on burning up Ivy Green's vast store of unread books, imagining how foiling this plot could secretly displease the more reactionary holders of high office here in the states. Past library security, a slight nod to his rent-a-cop colleague, Duffy decides a thorough security sweep is in order. He walks to the first-floor Internet station and sees that nearly every chair is occupied. The Ivy Green Library Internet station is a great resource used by students and locals alike, and tonight he can see that nearly half the occupants are older people, possibly grad students but most likely townies, the irregular adults of the Collegetown community. He finds a place between an overt Philadelphian, nearing sixty and reeking of tobacco, and a middle-aged woman in a tank top, healthy hair growth protruding from her armpits, with loud purple and pink tattoos up and down her arms. Local anarchist or grad-student import, it is hard to tell which. Seated in front of the sleek, black flat-screen display, he impulsively contrasts it to the older models at Urban State, Liberty Tech, and University of America. For the latter two, their comparatively aged equipment is in particularly poor taste when both universities advertise themselves as "leaders in technology" possessing "top-line hardware" that of course opens "the doors to conquering the twenty-first century." But it is well-endowed Ivy Green that has the newest monitors.

As usual, first he checks the front page of the *NYTimes* online. He knows other adjuncts who eagerly dismiss this paper as too mainstream, nothing more than a corporate functionary, an apparatus of the state. But he likes the respectable font and layout, and the immediacy of the Associated Press, so he forgives them for their misleading articles. How much of their news from Iraq turned out to be based almost entirely on rumor if not the writer's imagination, disseminated from Fern's inner circle, or planted by the White House in the friendly confines of the press room? Duffy couldn't say, but as far as he could tell, this means that rumor and story—yes, fiction and by consequence perhaps even literature—are alive and well in the contemporary zeitgeist. Maybe the newspapers were complicit in the rush to war, but it was not as if their journalists were the ones voting in Congress, counting votes in Florida, or playing golf all August long. Tonight, Fern is on the home page, appearing stern, his grim pose looking a bit too mean for the role. Whenever he sees the President's face, his first thoughts are of sadness that he is a passenger under this man's piloting, and then he thinks of envy, as Fern gets more than twice as much vacation—fully funded, of course, unlike his brief breaks between teaching contracts. The man exercises every morning, ends his day at five, and rarely works weekends; he takes all of August at the ranch while peons like Duffy keep busy teaching summer school and grading compositions used to assess and place incoming freshmen. Now he reads Fern's own composed words. "We will kill the terrorists who are killing our men. We will hunt them down and defeat them." Underneath the photograph and quotation, he sees a link to an article titled, "Authorities not ruling out Philadelphia arrow assassin's links to Al Qaeda." Enough is enough; he has appointments down the road, and so decides to switch to e-mail.

Over at gmail, he sifts through spam to find three messages: a follow-up from Allison Silverman, one from Frank Hamnett, and a third from a Maureen Saporowitz. Allison's message comes first.

We need yo' body. Don't forget. 10th floor, 10pm!

The Duffler feels his third leg stiffen. He quickly moves back to the inbox, paranoid some e-mail eavesdropper would read over his shoulder and report him to the authorities, after which he'd lose it all, both his Ivy Green class and the security gig. If the story were to end badly and in public he could conceivably lose all of his classes. He is thankful that Ivy Green's computers, unlike those at his other schools, do not demand a login and password. In court, he could argue that someone must have stolen his gmail password, that while it does seem as if his inbox were the recipient, it was not he who responded or even read the messages.

So he clicks Frank's message.

Yo, Prof. The heat is on, but don't forget. Midnight meeting. The new Defense Building.

Yes, warned or advised of such a congregation, a midnight mass for the marginalized of Liberty Tech, indeed how could Duffy forget? He is positive it was Frank Hamnett lurking in the stairwell after class, and in a strange way, through these evasive e-mails, it is as if the boy lurks in the background of his entire day. Duffy clicks Reply, and types, "I'll try to be there." He returns to the message and skims through the entire string. He reads some of Frank's thoughts from earlier in the year. "Exactly right. In Tikrit, it was like a rush. I got juiced. Nothin' like that back home." And then, "Compared to battle, it's like nothing seems real. Nothing matters."

And, "I can't focus. I can't concentrate." To these his teacherly replies were always, "Try to adjust," and "It'll take time," and "I know it's hard but stay in school." Duffy feels regret reading his weak responses. How the hell could he know how to help a young man who fought in Tikrit? Duffy's only battle takes place in classroom after classroom, college after college, day after day. This boy has seen men dying, with ears, toes, and innards blown apart by emotionless IEDs. How the hell could Duffy advise anyone to stay in school? This is what he did, for years longer than he should have, and here he is, working security and teaching all over town.

But damn if Duffy will let his status-quo guilt and futility ruin his evening ahead. To boost his morale, he returns to and rereads Allison Silverman's e-mail. The amazing idea that this female undergraduate requires his physical wares is enough to lift the cloud of Frank Hamnett's messages and his own limp replies. In his giddy state of expectation, he cannot avoid opening a second window for a sneak preview of tonight's feature performance.

The pornography filters are good for mainstream corporate porn, but only so-so for the less-perused and often free amateur sites. At www. bustimpressions.com, he chooses the slideshow and lets his mouse wander over the cleavage, flat but perky to huge sag-harbor houseboats. He shrugs off the ample and uplifting possibly under-eighteen stuff and stays firm and committed in his awards of sevens and sixes to these novices, confident that a nine point five or ten awaits him tonight. If they were to exercise their freedom *for* the government with Patriot-Act alacrity—that is, snag him for the statutory-rape staring the way they pinch and imprison domestic-terrorist wannabes surfing across America—he'd plead "ambiguous contest" or "no birth certificate."

So with pleasure he clicks through the brown and yellow and pink and beige of the breast garden; but then, interrupting his perusal of mammary and teat stands a hulking tree trunk of phallus attached beneath two silicone battleships. In fear, he clicks the upper right X to remove the vision. He slides deep in the chair, shifts right and left for spies, and checks his trousers for secreted turncoats. He feels some relief that the beast was decidedly adult-sized, the certain proof he has not inadvertently endangered a minor. Aye, Icarus, too close to the sun and the Dufflebags will burn!

To move his mind from shame and transexuality, he clicks the last message that might be work-related. From Maureen Saporowitz, he reads:

Dear Professor Duffleman,

It looks like you were the teacher present when my daughter had a disturbing incident earlier in the day. I apologize for any inconvenience to your classroom. My daughter, Eileen, has been under a lot of stress, the culmination of which was today's episode. She is resting peacefully right now at Collegetown Friends Hospital. Thank you for your efforts and concern.

Sincerely,
Maureen Saporowitz

The formality and decency of the note makes Duffy inhale deeply, gratefully, and yet as he stares at the screen, for the moment, he cannot recall any Maureen Saporowitz from earlier in the day. It finally slaps him on the noggin that Eileen must presumably be the Eileen from his morning Urban State class. Insane Eileen. Such is his long day, with its multitude of students and responsibilities, that Duffy could barely remember what has happened in the morning by eight or nine at night. Maureen then would be the mother although he remembers this morning's Eileen has a different last name, at least on his student roll. Just another irregular approach to family, he presumes, thankful he hasn't the money or time to screw one up himself. Duffy appreciates the letter and is pleased to know that Eileen is currently resting and recuperating.

Rest for the wounded, but action for others, so Duffy signs out, restarts as is his habit on a public computer, and submits himself to a walk in the library. He paces around the periphery of the first floor, not really casing the area as much as he is trying to maintain that his uniform did indeed imply a certain guarding function. He begins to check for isolated packages left in odd places—indicative of the so-called briefcase bomb— but there are so many book bags and such left unguarded that it is impossible to sort the wheat from the chaff, or in this case, the genuine article of terror from the everyday satchels abandoned by students. He often notices that, in the Ivy Green library, students seem more trustful of others not taking their possessions. In the Urban State library, one would infrequently see bags left unattended, and if so, not for very long. But at Ivy Green, Duffy could not help but notice book bags left alone for hours on end. Perhaps the library really is safer? Maybe the library guards really were paid more to guard? Or perhaps the unattended book bags only signify student habit, and that the Ivy Green students have grown up in areas where stealing is a rarity, and so, from custom, they are used to leaving their possessions in full public view. Or maybe they are so well off they could afford to be careless? This may explain why there are so many car break-ins and snatch-n-grab crimes on Ivy Green's campus. The students leave tantalizing goods on full display in the backseats of sporty automobiles, where the nonworking poor could see the items, and take their chances.

Strangely enough, when reading the weekly crime blotter, Duffy would find mention of shoplifting committed by the Ivy Green students themselves. Coeds steal skirts and tops from the corporate chains on campus. Gender-neutral undergrads leave the Ivy Green bookstore with a bag full of unpurchased merchandise, sweatshirts and towels with the Ivy Green logo, even books upon occasion. Shoplifting must be a game for these wealthy undergrads. Something they do not go to jail for, something a grandparent or uncle can make disappear. Something society would forgive them for, whereas the poor, for similar thefts, would suffer scars for life in the form of a permanent record. And so such "criminals" would be counted as part of the quarter idle all year. After graduation, the only idleness the students would experience would be of their own choosing—a year through Europe, or with their parents paying their rent, writing a novel.

Now, in the library, the Duffleguard sees nothing unusual save for the fact that so few students seem to be using the library's resources on a weekday evening. He knows Thursday is the traditional start of the weekend bacchanalia on campus, and so he imagines the Ivy Green undergrads already preparing for wanton abuses later on at night. There'd be keggers, quarters, and funnels; frats charge two bucks for guys while girls get wrecked free with campus ID.

Up the narrow dark stairwell, on the second floor, he wanders in through a portion of the library designated for student cell phone conversations. From a table, Duffy picks up a stranded copy of *Newsweek* and shoves it deep in his back, left pocket. He leaves the second floor shaking his head, wishing these students could put books and magazines back where they belong. He ascends the narrow stairs to his favorite floor, the third, where the literature section serves as the land for free spirits and home of brave authors. He knows his favorites would be on the shelves; they aren't the ones anyone around here seems to be touching. So, instead of mimicking his bookstore procedure, he goes once around the entire floor. He counts students as he goes: seven readers, three sleepers, and two couples—one cuddling and the other engaged in foreplay of a pay-per-view caliber. At the end of all the shelves, in a far corner, he sees an elderly man, deep tan skin, perhaps from some midlatitudinal origin between Lisbon and New Delhi. The man stands by a cart full of books, presumably a shelver, arduously plucking bronze and green from his cavernous nose. The man catches Duffy staring at him and shoos him away, adding some singsong venom, "Feel lucky I wasn't jerking off."

He does feel lucky but not for long, because on the opposite side of the third floor, tucked away deep in the foreign-text section, he finds a young man who appears to be engaged in the wackier sin. Just below the aged, bound editions of Nietzsche's entire *Werke*, guilt and shame washed all over his face despite the freedom to move beyond lurking above. Oh what an ass I am to have made myself an adjunct instructor is all that sticks to Duffy here, as he hurriedly removes himself from the scene of this boy's bonding with genius.

The fourth floor offers only three students, all of them asleep at the same common table, as if they had come together for a Thursday-night slumber party. Duffy, weary, slouches down in a dark, firm but cushioned couch seat, withdraws the *Newsweek* he pocketed earlier, and idly passes some time. It is the April college-admissions issue no less, every national, general-interest magazine's chance to profit from educational advertising. He quickly pages through all the miracle software and university propaganda—huge financial aid awards and sunny faces on graduation day—until the centerfold catches his eye. It is a multicolored chart of the fifty most selective colleges in the country, with Ivy Green easily making the list. For each school, it shows the full room plus board plus tuition costs, and then, based on the individual college's awards, the cash amount the average student at each university actually pays. The vast majority of the colleges report that fifty to sixty percent of the students receive financial aid, and that hence, the average student pays but eighteen to twenty-four thousand, compared to a full tuition typically around forty or forty-five. For a brief moment, Duffy relaxes and considers the fairness and decency of his democratic America. Then he notices the specific line for Ivy Green. The possessor of the chair he presently endows gives financial aid to thirty-seven percent of its students, and thus the average student on campus pays closer to thirty grand to attend. So Ivy Green may not only claim the wealthiest students in Philadelphia, but also the wealthiest in the entire country. Or at least the ones who pay the most for college. Even Stanford and Princeton, known preppy country clubs, are giving out more money in student awards.

Is there any correlation between this statistic and the distinct chance that he would be getting laid later on by a generous Ivy Green girl? He cannot say, so he ignores the possible connection because he needs to push on. He leaves the *Newsweek* in open view, smack in the middle of the slumbering undergrads. Before abandoning the print source, he removes a pen from his right front pocket—he never fails to carry a pen at all times, even with the threat of an ink explosion—and circles the Ivy Green numbers, and adds a few huge exclamation points after the facts. That ought to be enough to get these students to take notice. He pictures Julian Door on Ivy Green's campus, trying to arouse passion and get the students active about demanding the administration accept more students from financial hardship. It would in essence be wealthy kids demanding the university admissions office sacrifice their own. Could Ivy Green stay true to its stated mission as a demotic force, the elite university as a beacon of hope for democracy and equality? Duffy has his doubts.

Leaving the library at a quarter past nine, he strides over, and into, the Ivy Green University Bookstore. Passing through the store is indeed included in his nightly itinerary. Like any other single, lumpish, if liberated, man in search of bright lights, and the stimulants of coffee and literature, he has turned this duty into a thirty to forty-five minute ritual during at least one of his three shifts a week. The way he sees it, the world owes him—heck, he owes himself—some meager feeding time; this half hour or so is the only sustained reading he partakes of on his long day. With a dissertation imagined in an all but completed state, advanced years of academic grazing in the fields of literature, he deserves time for paid reading.

Up the escalator of the open-ceilinged airplane hangar of a building, the second floor in a sense only around the edges of the first, he must pace halfway around the entire circumference before ordering his godly Tall half and half, a mixture of regular and decaf, properly supplying it with the minor deities of brown sugar and two-percent milk, and then descending again to browse the literature section.

Realizing he is a half hour away from very possibly getting laid, an amazing thought too overwhelming to contemplate, Duffy feels odd taking up his usual ritual. As a rule, at this point in his life, he gravitates only to the narratives of failed men—in memoir, essay, or novel form. Not even failed family situations would do in his dwelling on solitary man's demise.

Because he has lost hope of ever finding new translations of Shalamov and Schulz, in print and for sale at the contemporary superbookstore, and because Kafka and Babel were always available in bulk, Duffy's first task is to protect the Americans he can protect—the boys represented by a single stranded copy on the corporate shelf, breathing faintly but alive, still in print. So he moves to the Es and Fs of the literature section, where he squints to find *A Fan's Notes*, by Frederick Exley, to make sure there is at least one copy on the shelf. He knows the Modern Library hardcover is out of print, but he can still fight for visibility for the Vintage edition. If this trade paperback is missing, he would immediately inform an attendant, a "bookseller" as the name tag suggested, and have them check to make sure the book has been reordered. Because many who work in these chain-store book warehouses, the so-called superbookstores, are decidedly not readers of novels, never mind classics, he would occasionally need to urge the bookseller to complete his duty or her job function, as a copy of the book is a necessity for any store that sells books with a straight face. And of course, most of these clerks see the Duffler as a full-blown kook. Once, he even got in a nasty quarrel with a pouty female attendant flipping through *Cosmopolitan*, and threatening to call the manager if he dared to dart behind the information desk and fill out the form himself. She would get to it just after her hour she said. He was livid. Eventually, the manager was called, by another attendant observing the security guard's pink to red to purple glare. The result was the girl was publicly reprimanded, the manager himself completed the inventory-replacement order form, and Duffy was summarily kicked out of the store. *Shouldn't you be on duty, sir?* Oh yes, oh yes, my duty. And he left the store that night, escorted out by the manager, a frail, older, pesky foppish sort, with a look of sincere superiority on his face. But even that night, his duty had been completed, and so he congratulated himself. *Fine guard work, Duff.*

For Exley had earned a permanent place, and these preprofessional institutions still referred to as universities require that such books loiter on their grounds. Even if ignored, *A Fan's Notes* would be there lurking in the background. A student might stumble upon the novel on his way to purchase his b-school textbooks, or trip over a fallen copy on the way to the personal-finance section. Find the book, and reconsider the course; not only the course schedule, but the course of a life. In his weakest moments, Duffy could be an awful sentimentalist and a literary snob—the broke kind, the worst kind—a barely professional, pretentious fuck. But Exley must endure.

Duffleman found his own copy on remainder, many years ago. This was before the days of Amazon searches for penny used books plus $3.99 for shipping and handling; it was back when a dollar bought a trade paperback with a single black-marker stripe. He had never heard of Exley, but he purchased the book based upon back-cover reviews—"the basic business of life and literature" and "American, true, one of a kind." He gulped it down over the next three days. Whenever he returned to it, the scent of roast beef, provolone, brown mustard, and pickles wafted up and into his brain, what he was eating then on his first voyage through *A Fan's Notes.* If he recalls, he left his apartment only once during that reading. Since then, he has reread the book at least three times.

The book so overpowers Duffy, that just when its memory seems to escape him, it would come fighting back fiercely into his life. For instance, several years ago, when he was wandering away from his graduate-school cave of criticism and squalor, and adjusting his eyes to the bright ice of the frozen job market, he wandered into the real-estate game, back when a few affordable homes still existed, an outsider curious as to what was available for little or no money down. In one tiny, overpriced, two-bedroom boxhouse, closer to the 'hood than any vibrant hub of the economy, he was told the place belonged to an up-and-coming corporate lawyer, a young man moving on to bigger and better. This wasn't the kind of selling tactic that appealed to him at all—frankly, it made Duffy even more depressed. Up the narrow, five-foot-tall staircase, and on the second floor, he saw the two tiny bedrooms were adjoining with no door for separation, the smaller one used only as a walk-in closet by the owning attorney, his dark-colored suits and shirts lined up neatly on a clothing rack, the kind you see in department stores. Shiny shoes below them, at least seven pairs. But in the other room, a queen-sized bed the only apparent furniture, he saw but one book in an aged orange milk crate by the bed, a tattered and beaten copy of *A Fan's Notes*, its cover half torn and mangled. Duffy took this as a sign that even the corporate lawyer on the rise, the man with no worries and sundry sexual opportunities, up and coming as he might be, had once dreamed larger. The powerful opiate of literature, drawn in by the possibility of fame, that *swich liquor* stronger than earthly wealth or power. Stronger even than the wind from the west. The tattered, worn copy, the only book visible to the naked eye, like a *Gideon's Bible* in a hotel room, was a sign that he ought to reread his own copy.

Duffy's ur-text is one he dare not assign to the mean masses of undergraduates. God knows how they would denigrate and defeat old Ex, decry his sexism and debunk him not as a literary star but as a loser and closet queer. And of course, they would mock their instructor's flab and fagged life in the process. He does, however, maintain a perfect syllabus in his head, and has even listed its texts on scratch paper. The title is Post-War American Literature of Male Loneliness and Despair. History might be written by the winners, but Duffy's lit is written by the losers. His authors include the classics of course, like Salinger, Yates, and Exley. But he also has more recent discoveries added to this imaginary curriculum, both versions of *Case Quartered* for instance.

Yes, in his loose-coin life, one summer afternoon, to escape suffocating heat and humidity, he wandered into the air conditioning of the Ivy Green superbookstore to examine the midday shelves of book, and there on either side of the Exley, just a shelf or two apart, were two novels sharing the same title. Written by Eddy David and Italo Dante and published two years apart, their styles were opposite but their themes enduring.

Italo Dante's *Case Quartered*, with its bitter alienation and bicoastal despair, is in fact Duffy's favorite of the two. Dante is the son of a famous novelist, so his alcoholic's life is lived in the shadow of a dominant father's printed pages; the first-person failed male speaks from sheer desperation. Which, despite Allison's advances, is exactly Duffy's point of view and passion and why he heads for Dante's shelf again.

Now, at the shelf, the Ds through Fs, Duffy finds the single, required copy of Exley first, and then Dante, resting snug against his father's books. Back down by Eddy David, lower left, bottom shelf, he squints and can't seem to see anything between Dakar and Day. So he bends all the way over, not as he should by squatting with his knees, but with his back entirely, to fully see what is going on below. Sure enough, the copy has gotten dislodged, and is presently stuck behind the row of books. Duffy suspects a shelver had come along, not noticed the David *Case Quartered* shoved behind the others, and added a couple mass-market copies of Dassel's best-selling *Isle of Lesbos*, so the shelf was as tight as could be. The bottom shelf is the worst fate in every business, so many bad knees and so few browsing customers, but Duffy does the best thing he can, which is to remove a copy of Dassel, and place David's *Case Quartered* back where the novel belongs, visible to at least some of the perusing public. He can see from the tiny blue dot, from his ballpoint pen of two summer's last, that it is indeed the same copy he marked back then. But one day, he hopes, another customer would come and claim the lonely paperback and provide a warm shelf and good home for the novel. And then Duffy will go to the information desk, and insist that the alienated laborer behind the counter order a replacement copy.

Duffy pats himself on the back for his fine detective work, telling himself softly that he'd make a fine security guard. But tonight, his moment of conquest thirty minutes away, he recognizes he is no mortal shift worker but a chosen one on the verge of fondling undergraduate flesh. How could he connect to such suffering literature with such earthly delights for an evening repast? Soon sodden with guilt, he excises it in the best way he can. Roaming the literature like a rabid mammal, he scrambles on twos and fours as he checks and double-checks for perfect attendance in his loser-male canon. He kneels and hugs and pets and presses warm hands to all of his titles, a dusting here and spine-scratch there. As acolyte, he apologizes to his authors for his newly won wealth and promises to remain humble after his own narrative climax. As he fights off a final impulse to check under D for Duffleman, Cyrus—his hidden hopes have led him to this missing shelf of self many times before—Duffy notes an associate staring suspiciously. He smiles like a lunatic, raises his arms to express surrender, grabs the Dante *Case Quartered*, and heads for a cushioned seat.

The only soft chair available is facing a thin, ragged fellow in aged jeans and a black concert tee shirt cut off at the sleeves. The man, perhaps ten years his junior and giving up a good seventy-five pounds, donates an irritated look as Duffy plops down. The greeting is not enough to interrupt the man's constant scratching, moving his hands from his pale, sinewy arms up to his brown matted curls. The sight so disturbs Duffy that he shields his eyes by shoving the Dante right at his nose. He removes his glasses and begins to read.

Two minutes later, he tires of his face-blocking strategy, lowers the books, but continues reading.

"That's a strange title, dude."

Duffy looks up to see that Concert Tee speaks, so he grunts affirmation.

The man is still ruthlessly scratching, low behind the left knee, then high behind the right ear. Duffy would ordinarily become fascinated with and then fearful of the extent to which he could relate to this chigger scratcher, but not now, with his just due less than twenty minutes away. This skin scraper clings to the bottom rung of Maslow's hierarchy—seeking out shelter in the bookstore and no doubt returning to some flea-infested bed after closing—whereas the Duffler is on the verge of actual intercourse— the unpaid kind at that! He gets lost in thought trying to determine if free sex with Allison Silverman would fulfill a belonging need, or self esteem and status, or would it be genuine self actualization, the highest stage of man? An entirely self-developed want, hardly a need at all.

He decides he can overanalyze the whole thing tomorrow, but for tonight, Duff would stand atop Maslow's pyramid and beat his chest.

"Dude, with a title like that, I gotta ask what you do for a living."

Duff, taking pity on the man, the prelaid condescending to answer the rabble, decides to give the whole truth, or most of it, "I'm an adjunct instructor at several universities." Explaining the security-guard gig would be just too complicated.

"Cool. Where at?"

"Liberty Tech and Ivy Green. I'm an adjunct at both." It is too much trouble to list all of his employers.

"What's an adjunct?"

"It means I just get paid to teach the class. No tenure. No permanent job. Low pay. No benefits. No status."

"Weird."

The man seems satisfied so Duffy returns to his *Case Quartered,* wondering momentarily that, if his lot were to guard the loose change of others, what then could he call the few lonely coins in his own pockets?

"Mind if I ask what that book is about?"

"It's a novel about a guy whose dad is dying on the other side of the country. He goes to see his dying Dad, and he gets drunk instead. Wasted. So he pays to fuck a fifteen-year-old stutterer instead of spending time with family. Father-and-son book."

"Sounds kinda like my life, but I never drank around the old man."

Duffy is caught off guard, intrigued by the clarity of the chigger-scratcher's sentence.

"He kicked me out long before I became a chronic user."

Duffy nods. With his good fortune ahead of him, he finds it easier than usual to produce an earnest look, a sympathetic nod.

"Well, truth be told, he didn't really kick me out the first time. I ran away before it got to that. So you say you teach at Ivy Green?"

Another nod. Yes, he did say that. Just a course a year. Nothing special. Part-time status.

"Funny thing is that you might know my mother."

"What department is she in?"

"Literature. Not English exactly. World fiction or something like that."

Duffy is hired through the College of General Studies, and even paid less than he would be were his appointment from the literature department. He does take pride that his evening class is almost always full of true full-time undergrads.

"Oh. What's her name?"

"Sarah Berg-Appaloosa."

He hasn't spoken six words to her, but Duffy knows Berg-Appaloosa well enough. She was a guest poet for a week during his first year of his MFA in creative writing at Urban State. (Yes, that weak degree is the highest one he holds. In private, in parentheses, he could admit to that. For some it is a Masters in Fucking Around, but for Duffy, the degree stands for Masturbatory and Flatulent Art.) He had been encouraged to attend her poetry reading, the culmination of her week as writer-in-residence. At the event, she read loudly one obscure, incomprehensible poem after another, and Duffy still isn't certain the words were in English. But she would laugh with excitement and expectation after each poem—and sometimes after a stanza or even between lines—and say things like, "Oh, this is really excellent," or "Oh, I've hit a whole new level here," or "Joyce would envy this one." It was over-the-top, blind narcissism, like the taunting and showmanship of professional football, the dances and trash talking after big hits and quarterback sacks in the NFL. Perhaps such heroic acts of violence are worthy of such conceits because they could command the attention of millions. Duffy left the reading that night reminding himself why he liked quieter writers.

"I do know your mother. She's the major poet of the Ivy Green department."

"Figures."

Duffy can't quite comprehend the math.

"My old man is over at Urban State in history."

He knows Appaloosa too. He met this rather kind man at the Berg-Appaloosa residence in the suburbs, where the wife had decided to host her own party as poet-in-residence at Urban State. She didn't skimp on hors d'oeuvres and wine. Duffy found Appaloosa to be one of the more approachable professors in attendance, and they soon got into a heated discussion of European and Russian history during the reigns of Hitler and Stalin. It was impressive that Appaloosa, a historian, could speak eloquently about Babel, Roth, Musil, Schulz, and many other writers relevant to the time and place. At the time, Duffy felt shame his own knowledge of history was so weak.

"So you didn't get along well?"

"Well, you could say that. You see, I was adopted when I was nine. I think I was just their high-minded, liberal experiment or something. I couldn't live up to their standards. You could say the adoption never really took." A wry wince and snicker is his concluding thought.

Duffy sees he is talking to no regular flea-infested fellow; rather, this is the alienated, adopted son of two of the most important tenured professors he knows. He looks to be a homeless man at present.

"I first ran off when I was thirteen. By sixteen, I just told them flat out I didn't want to live there anymore. They didn't seem to mind. I told them I was going to find my real mother, and they let me go. She was down in Florida."

Nod.

"Well, that didn't really work out. I got the invite down there, but my real mom was pretty messed up and couldn't take me in permanent. So I came back to Bryn Mawr for a few days but it didn't sit right. Just couldn't take all the standards and uppity bull. So I split but stayed in the area. They knew I was around, but they never hunted me down. I was never invited back."

Duffy remembers going to the big house in Bryn Mawr, with all the other graduate students, young wannabe poets and writers, not yet failures, strangers invited into a mansion of tenured prosperity. But the son was spurned. There was nothing permanent or prosperous about the son in fact.

"I remember it got cold that winter. One early morning, when I woke in the park, there was already a coat of snow covering my sleeping bag. Snow was falling on me, the thick wet kind that makes the best snowballs. I could see this man come trudging up through the square, boots, winter coat, scarf tight around his neck, the works. He was the only other person in the park that early. He must have been out for bagels or a paper. It was him, so I yelled out, 'Dad, good morning, dad!'"

Duffy listens intently now.

"And he just walked on by. Pretended he didn't hear me. Didn't turn at all. He ignored his son, freezing his ass out in the cold. Getting snowed on."

The tale is alive with authenticity; it reminds Duffy of Shalamov's "Through the Snow," yet another vicarious chill while the speaker lives it.

"I quickly balled up a big fat one, but I didn't have the guts to hurl it. Didn't seem like it would do much good. So I just lobbed it at a tree and missed."

Duffy appreciates the irony of these two professors, having chosen teaching, a helping field, so willingly refusing to save their son. He makes the inescapable analogy that just as the university leaves its students to the poorly trained, poorly paid, unprotected, and overworked, so too had these tenured professors left their child to the wolves. Of course, it is not a perfect analogy, perhaps a false analogy but maybe also in a way partly true. The university students are paying customers whereas the boy is a son adopted late, perhaps only an "experiment" conducted by idealists, a chance to see if one could revive a life tarnished in its early stages, and sadly it seems the results point to no. Duffy stares at the scrawny, disheveled man, with the infinite attack of mites storming his skin. For a moment, he feels relieved to have been given a fair enough chance to fail entirely on his own. Two parents who never smacked him, and even stayed together until he entered graduate school against their better judgment. No one did to Duffy what had perhaps predetermined this man's fate. And so, it is no surprise when the question comes.

"Dude, you know, I hate to ask." Chiggerman interrupts Duffy's dwelling on his own relative good fortune. "But I'm kind of in a jam right now. Down on my luck. You see, I spent the last three nights in a homeless shelter."

Duffy now sees clearly where this is going.

"I've got a friend in Baltimore. She'll put me up if I can just get down there. I've got some clean clothes at her place. She lets me use the shower, the works. I just need some bucks to get there. The bus fare is only eighteen dollars. Could you help me out?"

Duffy hesitates but then relents. He reaches deep in his pocket to see what remains of the clean twenty that went unchanged for the Hollywood actress. He pulls out the bills and finds a five with eight of the most worn, tired singles he has ever been associated with—the money that was returned to him at the convenience store before he stiffed Wawa Ed.

Duffy cannot explain why he does it. Perhaps it is the giddiness of his good fortune, the fact that, at least for tonight, he will not be the loneliest, loser male in Philadelphia. Or maybe he wants to connect with this young man. He wants him to know that although his brilliant, self-focused parents were worthy of tenure, in fact, it is the adjuncts like himself who could offer a human connection, who are willing to lend a helping hand. And so he hands the man all of the bills, the fiver and the forlorn dollars. As he does so, he is crushed with guilt for not helping Wawa Ed or the Hollywood Actress earlier in the day.

"I can get the money for you in a week. Just give me an address."

He scribbles down some lines for the man. A final act of decency so the poor fellow can complete the exchange feeling it is only a temporary loan. The man sticks out a hand which Duffy is obliged to shake. A few slight nods and then Duffy's adopted debtor wanders away. Over the loudspeakers, the bookstore blares the five-minute warning for its 10 p.m. closing, and Duff remembers his date with destiny. The Ivy Green Hotel. Room 1007. His heart pounds in expectation.

CHAPTER 9

AT THE IVORY TOWER, RISE AND FALL

Duffleman pauses at the door. He admires its rich, reddish-brown mahogany. Laminated and secure, it is nothing at all like the single-lock old wooden defender, easily destroyed, at his own two-room studio. Lingering so, he is reminded of those long-winded sections from classic novels, three or more pages about the door, the entrance, a warning against further study in the field, the boredom of reading and the blackened death bags under the eyes; and then finally, "Before the Law," Kafka's most damning poetic justice, the best text in the universe for denying possibility. Duffy considers his own situation in light of the Kafka. He could grow old here, make a few friends of fleas—not that this was their feasting place—never dare to knock, to open, to pass through. Of course, at present, his dick is running the show, so he pushes hard on the bell. He hears giggles, from more than one nose and throat; three is a crowd but also a ménage à trois, and a quartet or pentagonal array is not so far beyond his imagination. In a brief fit of despair, he realizes that he hasn't brought protection. He has read the news that up to half of sixteen to twenty-one-year-olds in America have had some kind of STD, and after such a long, weary, run-on celibacy, the thought of a delayed death from his sole moment of bliss disturbingly crosses his mind. And thankfully just as soon departs.

Allison Silverman opens the door. She is wearing some sort of sexy, blue, silver-sparkled miniskirt and spaghetti-strap top, enough material to cover the three basic food groups but no more. Duffy holds his neck stiffly, desperately trying to avert his eyes, refusing to stare only at these forbidden fruits. "Hi, professor, come on in."

The room is dark, save for some faint sparkling across the mauve rug; out of instinct, he moves toward the light, and as he does so, he can see candles aflame atop a birthday cake.

Still standing by the door in her silvery-blue washcloth and hand towel, Allison offers a seductive, "Make a wish, professor."

Dufflejunior sprouts up to say hello, despite the fact that somehow Allison has learned he turns forty in two days.

"How'd you find out it was my birthday?" Duffy feels his inflatable friend wilt just a tad, as the acknowledgment of his age marches to the forefront.

"Internet." And she giggles slightly. It sounds different from the earlier giggling, somehow more nasal, less innocent, and more fun.

Ah, humanity. Ah, what matter of it? Duffy sees the sum total of the situation. He is in a hotel room with a woman just past half his age, covered in nothing but a skinned skunk's worth of cloth, her fragrance anything but skunk-like, and so he turns to the cake, wishes for a world peace that might include in his own life a lot less teaching and more fucking, any fucking at all that he didn't have to try too hard for, and then, with all his might, overcoming his long day's worth of wasted breath, he blows out the candles, thankfully just four of them, an image of Allison, nude, riding on a horse, a Clydesdale no less, trampling over his fat lump of a figure, the horse treading over the smile on his face, this the last wishful thinking blasting his brain as he blows and blows.

The lights shoot on, leaving Duffy momentarily stunned, facing the cake that rests on the television, behind which stands a huge mirror. The full effect is that a split second after his wish, Duffy is left standing, staring at his upper half near the end of his long day. The Botox-free forehead, the bags of coal under the eyes, the five-o'clock shadow turned to patches of bristle. The ever-present pale soldiers boldly reposition themselves for the evening shift of his hair.

Just then, from behind him, a loud, "Surprise!" And Duffy jerks his head around, and sees three other girls, two of them as scantily clad as Allison, and a young man, none other than the brooding Marxist, all of them from the evening seminar save for one girl he recognizes as a student from a previous class. One plus one plus three plus one. Equals six and Duffy isn't sure he'll have enough energy for a full dinner with dessert. He wonders if Allison understands the full implications of his age; even if he were to try as hard as he could, he doubts he could satisfy them all. Of course, only three of the girls are dressed like pop-song sluts so who is to know what will be required of his person. He looks about to see if this is in fact a suite, maybe another bedroom where the brooding atheist can take one or two of them off his hands? No luck. It appears to be your standard luxury single in the hotel Ivory Tower. Before he can dwell further on these problematic sexual-ratio concerns, Allison approaches and gives him a warm, full body hug, "Happy birthday, professor." It sounds sincere more than sexual, and the hug feels more like a friendly favor than a seduction. The other girls approach and alternately hug him lightly, stick out a cheek quickly for his lips to graze, and the last gives him a firm handshake. "I hope you remember me, Professor. Allison is in my sorority. I recommended she take your class." Duffy recognizes her as Linda Olinger, from last year's seminar. Could this be the custom? That previous students wear a full complement of clothing while current ones dress in washcloths and potholders?

But Duffy rains tears from hearing his course has been recommended. Somehow, something about his mostly Eastern Jews, his short story writers, has gotten through. His first impulse is to bend to all fours, and politely kiss each toe—pinky to big—of the young woman, but he sees this would be a bit much. Better to hold his position and request a tissue to wipe away the joy.

The Marxist maintains his reserved posture and doesn't move close enough to touch Duffy at all. But from behind his back he produces a bottle, and says about as cheerfully as a Communist can, "Champagne?" Pronounced with an exaggerated extra syllable by the "g" and "n."

He proceeds to unpeel the black wrapper around the cork, untwist the metal wire, and then handle the cork like an old pro. Duffy imagines course credits for such handiwork.

The Duffler finds himself in the middle of a full-fledged party, one at which he is the center of attention. It is his birthday bash. He can't recall anything quite like this, save for his failed final chance at passing his doctoral exams—yes, the oral portion—in which he publically choked, the three men and two women eyeballing him—in order, apprehensive, annoyed, solemn, disgusted, and sad—as he forgot his chain of thought again and again. As for parties, the 5 p.m. pizza gathering aside, he can't recall anything quite like this in years. He certainly has associates, but he has long since fallen out of the loop with what he might have called his friends. They all paired up, married off, moved out to the suburbs while he was left in the relative squalor of part-time academic work. Honest work, yes, he reminds himself, as he prepares to reenter society as a mingler.

"So what did you wish for Professor? World peace?" Allison smiles and winks as if she knows full well what was on his mind. Duffy has enough good sense not to mention the horse.

Instead, he accepts a paper Dixie cup of champagne, and with his free hand wipes a solitary tear descending down his left cheek. "Thank you very much, thank you very much. This means a lot to me. Yes, it does." Before he can lower the mood to the level of humble thanks, self pity, and tears, another girl produces a small cream-colored CD player, one of those three-inch, curved models they sell in fancy magazines. "Dancing!"

She pops a CD out of its jewel case, and soon all four girls have the Duffler surrounded, doing what were once extremely sexual gyrations but these days are merely modest moves. Duffy has seen movie trailers for dirty-dancing films, and he has heard TV reports about full-frontal exposure at raves and clubs and such, so he knows enough to know he is getting a PG-13 version here. Still, the way they swivel, arch, shimmy, and shake is overwhelming; even the one dressed in conservative dark jeans piques his curiosity. As they turn about, giving him the full display of shifting rump, he realizes he should try to move a bit himself. He tries to shake his left leg a little. Nothing seems to happen. Stiff. Dead. The right one he can more easily maneuver, but he jerks it out too far and nearly kicks one of the scantily clad maidens. His hands he finds a bit easier to navigate although he still has half a Dixie cup of champagne, and so can't do much.

Allison saves him with a "Drink up and get down, professor," and so after he downs his cup, she takes it from him and places it on the TV stand. Then she returns to him, takes both his hands, and moves him away from the others where there is more room on the opposite side of the bed. She directs his hands easily, maintains eye contact, and smiles the whole time. Soon she is doing things that he has never had happen to him before. He is not sure of what they call it but is almost certain it costs extra if you get it done by a professional. It varies in rhythm and intensity. It feels good. Duffy loses himself in the bopping, the accidental bumping, the ambiguous causality of the grinding, the beat itself. For a few minutes of his day, time passes without worry, without second thoughts, without concern for his basic predicament, his classrooms full of student cases, the one of two without full-time work, the worn down and defeated he meets in the train stations and subway stops each day. Duffy converts to the faith of the carefree dancing fool.

Lost in bop, hip-hop, the beat box, or whatever the young and informed call it, Duffy doesn't know if it is five or twenty-five minutes later when Allison stops gyrating, turns to face him, and then grabs and drags him toward the bathroom. She closes the door behind them; he hears the pronounced click of a quality lock. Now is his moment. The two of them alone. His Solomon O'Shea time! Would this encounter include sensual torture or other water sports? She stares up at him; he stares down at her, desperately trying to maintain eye contact, but his eyes keep drifting down to the mouth-watering melons below.

"I have something to tell you," she says, almost singing it in an audible whisper.

Duffy feels grateful for the forward-thinking nature of youth, this girl unafraid of action, unafraid to seize the object of her lust. A shy man, he'd never have gotten close to this far had she not led the way. With her help he is storming the keep of undergraduate knowledge, not cowering behind, like a cultural illiterate tied to the customs of his own generation. Now, her eyes are upon him. Serious. Bathroom eyes for when the bedroom is full.

"Professor, Gary wants you."

Duffy isn't sure he hears right. Gary wants you. "Er, what's that? Gary wants me for what?"

"He wants you, Duffy. It's your birthday. You can have him if you want."

Duffy cannot quite understand what she is talking about. There they are, father and daughter alone, about to engage in the most poetic, pornographic, inter-seminar incest imaginable, and she says something about a Gary he could have. Gary who? Or is it Gary whom? It occurs to him that Gary could be the cold, calculating communist Gary, with his beady eyes in the corner of the next room. Not partaking of any naughty gyrating Gary.

"You mean he needs a literature advisor for his senior thesis?" Duffy can't quite imagine working closely with such a cool, analytical mind, not in his present state, but he has an excuse handy. "You must tell him, I'm only an adjunct. They don't give adjuncts any credit-hour bonus remuneration for taking on honors-thesis students. I suspect we're not allowed. He'll have to find a full-timer."

"Professor, he doesn't want you to advise him on anything. He knows what he wants. *He wants yo' body.*" These last four words she sings out, twirling about, ecstatically grinning at the birthday boy. Present circumstances excluded, the idea of anyone wanting Duffy's body seems preposterous. His mind, maybe, but doubtfully, and definitely not on his long day, as the Dufflebrains turn to midnight mulch five hours early. But then it smacks him square in the mulch pile. He gets it. She is here helping to "hook up" her friend. She is offering him Gary, not her own ample goods, but the twine and sack of another. A male other. "Ah hah," his thoughts so close upon his lips he nearly says aloud, "You think I'm gay!"

Duffy can't help but just stare down at her, away from her supersized bosom, but at her gentle eyes, swimming in anticipation of his "yes," but now slowly greeted with his saddening look.

"But what about us?"

"Us?"

Duffy nods solemnly, tuning into the fact that this concept may have never occurred to her. Now he takes a long look at her silver-starred cleavage, a deep gulp from her C cups, to be sure she understands. Last chance he might get and he wants to be clear. To communicate with clarity is always the goal of the effective instructor.

"Oh, god." Allison moves back, no longer pressing against him below the belt. She smacks her hand to her forehead. "I think I messed up. I thought for sure you were . . . "

It hangs in the air, the unspoken word looming over them, to Duffy's mind damning and ruining the moment forever, but of course, he realizes now, to Allison the moment never was.

She stares up at him. "I'm sorry, sweetie."

He nods because he knows.

"I'm sorry, professor. You're forty. No wedding ring. What would you think if you were in my position?"

His shoulders droop; he turns silent and sad.

"Oh dear. So all this time, I've been leading you on." Allison looks genuinely concerned; Duffy can tell she cares about his feelings. "I'm sorry, sweetie. I've got a boyfriend at Stanford. He's in grad school there for a joint MD/PhD. He doesn't even know about the guy I see here in Philly. I just can't take on more guys right now." She says this as if she is genuinely considering the possibility of dating her teacher. He hears pity and concern in her voice.

A can of beans for a consolation prize.

The downcast Duffler retreats. He leaves his private audience and heads for the exit, his face wearing the day's last defeat. He checks his watch. 10:37 p.m. He needs to get back on duty, back to work. To man the guard. Protect students all over the area from criminals and predators, even the odd lecherous preyer upon young flesh. Back to reality, back to his life.

As he opens the door to depart, he looks back, sighing as he does so, trying to manage a weak smile of thanks. The music ceases; he sees Allison whispering to the others, apparently explaining the mix up, his mortifying mistake—or hers. He glances at Gary, the aloof intellectual by day, a red-hot, gay lover at night he can only suppose, but Duffy catches a look of both reprimand and sympathy. Gary's expression seems to say, "Sorry, old man. That stripe doesn't come so easy. We can't expect to get our rocks off on a young lass half our age unless we've got the goods, no?"

Duffy nods and leaves.

Into the hallway with its floor-to-ceiling mirrors, he is forced tragically, in defeat, to stare at his multiple reflections. A Duffleman on every wall, he looks fragmented, diffuse, and of late-night fame. Captive in a captioned life, he cannot decide among "duffled down and undone," "the walking wounded," or "pathetically lost"; whichever, the basic predicament dominates once more.

Around a bend, at the elevator, he presses down and waits.

It is just as well, he rationalizes. God knows it would have ended badly. Solomon O'Shea might have tenured security and union protection, but Duffy's contract jobs come with no such condoms of collective power. Sex with students may be okay for the mid-fiftyish fatter man, but for Duffy it could lead to job-costing troubles. It is the obvious big no-no, and yet Allison seemed sympathetic to his plight. She felt badly for him, enough so to have momentarily contemplated a mercy hump. Almost but not quite, but throwing the old Doberman a bone is worth imagining while waiting for the doghouse to arrive. She expressed genuine pity for his evening's dashed dreams, and so presumably, his job is safe.

And of course, the basic predicament means he has four companies, five jobs, five separate supervisors, and so losing the Ivy Green seminar would have been losing his leg in literature, but he'd still have plenty of remedial tutoring, business writing, and freshman comp to survive upon. Never mind the security-guard work.

The elevator arrives, and its matching walls of endless mirrors haunt his descent. Behold the man. Yes, you, Duffleman. And you too. And you. From all sides they are on to him. No other. Do you think we pity your measly part-time ass? Look at yourself. We admit the ass is not so measly; in fact, it's rather large and sloppy. And there you are slobbering all over a young child, owner of the fat sloppy ass, and expecting a mercy hump? And you even got some undeserved pity, you pervert. Compare yourself to the likes of tenured turds like O'Shea, and this is what you get. She is your student. They are all your students. They may see you as an authority. Someone to look up to. Unlikely, yes, but possible. Eileen the psychotic. Lost Frank. Jonathan Somebody, paralyzed with fear. Even the back-row Republicans and the domineering Afrocentrist. Do they deserve this from their professor? Do they deserve someone ostensibly on watch, his guard work, but truly only self-serving? Yes, someone like you!?

The mirrors are too much, and Duffy closes his eyes and bends his head down, trying to avoid any view at all. He desperately tries to avoid his own gaze, not to see himself as he stands. For once, he wants to live without any reflection.

When the elevator doors open, with his inner elbow over his eyes, he is caught midreverie, wondering how he would do himself in a movie; he decides against a Philip Seymour Hoffman or Kevin Smith in favor of a moist towel or Saturday night special. When he raises his head he sees that the all-marble lobby, a swirl of sand and roan, is crowded for a Thursday night. He finds this odd because the chophouse on the main floor has changed hands three times in the past two years and is now closed down. It was sunk by underage drinking violations and a hotel labor dispute. A union has been picketing for months on end; six to ten fat guys with signs rotate shifts, so a former employee is always present.

Duffy remembers a surprisingly temperate February afternoon, when he passed by the corporate chain, and got into a discussion with the man passing out pamphlets. He found out that the bartender with seventeen years of seniority was fired because he had been paid too much. He was due twenty-five dollars per hour according to the union man. "Plus tips?" asked Duffy. Yes, customers can thank the man for quality service too. Duffy left the conversation a bit baffled. He'd figured out his own average wages, including paper grading and lesson planning but not transportation time, to be about ten bucks per hour. How was it that a guy who served drinks for a living was worth so much more than a guy who taught school? College courses, no less. He took the union leader's literature. He said he'd be sure to vote pro-union, anti-Fern, in the next election. As he walked away, he felt like he needed someone to pour him a stiff one to wash it all away. Maybe the bartender really was worth more.

He doesn't see any of the union picketers in the lobby, but he notices several meaty cops, like the ones he saw earlier in the train station, and also a couple of firefighters waddling around like oversized rubber duckies in their full regalia.

"You! Over here." A beefcake in blue points and motions him over. "What floor were you on?" His stare reduces Duffy's last ruins of self to ashes frozen against the desert sun. But the sun has been down for several hours now, and his years in the desert never were. He knows for sure he is a goner and has half a mind to confess right on the spot. Get it off his chest before they let him know they know. It seems unlikely Allison would have cell-phoned the cops, but if she had done so it would have been for his benefit. He was getting tired of his long day anyway, his long life, in fact. Prison would be a fine chance to catch up on sleep with three squares per day; sex, yes, an unfortunate brutal sex he'd rather not think about, but he'd trade that for a temporary layoff and permanent relief from instructing.

So Duffy responds straight up and honest. "The tenth floor, sir." He gives the cop a nod of "you've nabbed the right man," and awaits the next stage in the process. Read him his rights? On with the cuffs?

The cop stares at him, piercing eyes searching for character flaws. "Okay, then. Out there." And he points his night stick at the door.

Duffy walks out of the hotel, and it seems as if hundreds of people, young people mostly, are staring at him, whispering at him from beyond a cordoned-off area that extends directly into Chestnut Street. Crowds are milling about. Waiting. Watching. Wondering if Duffy will be the evening news. But as he moves closer to the masses, he can see they lose interest in him. As usual, then. A nobody. No one cares. Then it occurs to him that something else has happened. To somebody else. In the hotel, that he, by coincidence, just failed to get laid in. Another assassination? A terrorist event? Are they all inhaling anthrax dust at the very moment of his neurotic concern that this could be it?

A cop with a bullhorn announces: "Please move out of the street. Please return to your rooms. Your dorms. Your libraries. Wherever you belong. We need to get traffic moving again. You are all safe. What happened here has nothing to do with the assassination." The assassination, ah, yes. His day is so long, he hasn't considered this prior tragedy in more than an hour. How strangely inappropriate, this lack of vigilance. Unpatriotic. An inadequate response for a security guard of all citizens, even one as pseudo and unarmed as he.

He notices he still has his outer jacket off, tucked under his armpit. He feels a breeze, so he pulls it back on, once more assuming the full uniform of his job. He checks the cell phone. Just one message. From Frank Hamnett, text mail only. "I stayed on duty late when I saw you took time off. Meet me at the new machine at midnight." Duffy is baffled by the message and by how Frank got his cell phone number. It occurs to him that he could have given him a wrong work number by mistake, in his fatigue producing the wrong ten digits.

Duffy moves into the crowd. He meanders but fails to mingle. Among the wandering masses, few of whom seem to be heeding the policeman's bullhorn, he thinks he sees the homeless movie star, the Republican businessman, and finally the voter-registration Negro, the way he would if his long day could end like an airtight novel. But alas, as he approaches each one of these familiar faces, to establish eye contact, say hello, touch them gently on the hand, feel them, feel their pain, and apologize for any

Fight for Your Long Day

mishandling of earlier affairs on his behalf or that of his associates, the images fade away and a stranger appears. The person is invariably disturbed by this odd, tired, out-of-sorts middle-aged man stumbling too close, invading personal space. A woman clutches her pocketbook more closely, gives Duffy a mean look, turns and marches away. He can't help but feel rebuffed, even if the mistaken identity was no one he knew in the first place.

So when he sees the tall, thin, bald form of the Urban State counselor, Michael Zuegma, standing by an officer, Duffy assumes again it's a mirage, some other lean, hair-deprived therapist with a direct approach and piercing stare. But as he approaches, he sees the same hand gestures from earlier in the day, the occasional finger pointing and wagging of certainty. It is in fact Counselor Michael.

Duffy is just a few yards off when the officer moves on and Zuegma turns to face his morning's patient. He recognizes him immediately and asks, "What are you doing here?"

Duffy isn't sure if the term applies to a man earning his living part time all over town, but he replies, "Moonlighting."

"Same here," replies Counselor Michael.

"You need a second job?"

"Not desperately, but I try to help where I can. Liberty Tech needed a second shift professional counselor to oversee the students it uses for its call-in lines."

"They have students work as counselors?"

"Efficient, isn't it? At minimum wage, work study, you get as many heads as you need. No worries ever about no one on duty to take the call. No benefits for any of them, and you bring in a supervisor—in this case, me—who is paid part-time, no benes as well. Good business model."

Duffy isn't surprised the corporate university is paying students seven bucks an hour for a job requiring professional training. Toward the future, he sees undergraduate seniors replacing adjuncts as the college advertises opportunities for hands-on training. Once idled, he could retire to a homeless shelter and sleep off the rest of his life.

"Wow."

"Over at Ivy Green, they replaced their entire unit of psych grad students running the suicide prevention hotlines. From classes, labs, TA-ships, and night-shift work, they were just so exhausted from being overworked that they would arrive at their phone desk bitter and resentful. To say the least, they were losing the common touch with the caller. Too many problems of their own with oppressive graduate-school schedules. So the problem-solvers in administration cut the entire group. So guess who replaced them?"

"Who," hoots Duffy, his quiet monotone imperceptibly interrogative.

"Not the cowboys, but the Indians, my friend. They are wide awake when we should all be settling down or sleeping—perfect for handling the stressed-out caller at three in the morning. They speak fluent English and can be taught to listen and sound compassionate according to Western models. And of course, they're dirt cheap. A master's in psych from the best schools in Mumbai and New Delhi for a fraction of the American price."

"So what happens to the grad students?"

"No worries. Ivy Green still has some teaching and research assistantship slots on campus. So they cut costs but didn't eliminate the program. And many of the students can get part-time work off campus. Psych grad students make great bartenders."

Duffy wishes one would pour him a drink.

"At other schools with smaller endowments, entire grad programs have proved unnecessary. Didn't you hear what happened to the graduate program of Midland State?"

"No."

"They eliminated everybody in the humanities. No profit in academic articles no one reads. Frankly, administration saw all the advanced work as one big waste of paper and data-storage space. All they needed was the English comp cash cow. Keep the freshmen rolling in."

Duffy has doubt but has heard this before.

"They canned the whole grad school. Now they have satellite hook-ups and TVs in every classroom. PhDs in composition and rhetoric from the finest Indian universities are teaching virtual classes long-distance. They even have tech equipment for high-quality one-on-one tutoring. Writing workshops from around the world. The fifteen grand a year they were paying the graduate student has become fifteen hundred for a hungrier South Asian. And they're whip smart. A friend of mine sat in on a Shakespeare seminar and said it was excellent. Fharard knew the Bard, better than most Aussies and many Brits. That's globalization and progress."

The shift is under way. The future looks bleak. Duffy looks up at the roof, and then over across the street, where it appears a tribe of rubber duckies amasses around two ambulances. Bleaker yet. He is almost certain "Fharard" is an ethnic slur, and an inaccurate one at that. He suppresses a need to move away from the therapist.

Duffy considers calling Deborah, the adjunct union organizer, but he isn't certain his cell phone is a private number. Security guard in Collegetown used to be high-paying union work itself, and so he wouldn't want anyone in authority to overhear. He briefly imagines bitter Deborah settling in for the evening. Night time, a time when it is bad enough that the undereducated fool in the bed beside her still wants his cock sucked this late in the marriage, but now he has the nerve to do work barely professional, barely legal perhaps, and take home twenty times more than she. Calling now would be a bad idea.

"So with all the layoffs and outsourcing, you'll know they'll need more people in my line of work," Michael says. "Maybe you should look into it. I'm sure you've got the listening skills."

Duffy drifts away. He recalls an evening not long ago, back in his apartment, aimlessly searching the radio dial, when he came upon conspiracy conversation on the local all-talk station. Ivy Green and Liberty Tech were the focus; the rumor was that they were employing only illegal immigrants for the unskilled construction positions. Under the cover of darkness they had even used the Israeli Mossad to ship in a truck full of illiterate Pakistanis who had once worked for Blackwater in Iraq. They brought them to Collegetown in the middle of the night and paid them room and board to work on the new Missile Defense Building at Liberty Tech. "Globalization ain't shit. That's just how they do a brother," was the final lament of late-night caller X. At the time, Duffy was dismissive of the information; the ridiculous conspiracy sounded too scandalous to be true. Could indentured servitude exist in twenty-first century Philadelphia? But now, according to Counselor Michael, outsourcing is hitting much closer to home. Duffy doesn't know what to doubt, worry about, believe in, or ignore.

Thankful when his brain returns to the counselor's kind words, he wonders if Zuegma sizes him up as another poorly paid employee, or one capable of becoming a full-time professional in the field. It is too much to ponder, so he changes the subject.

"So what happened here?"

"Tonight, we let one get away."

"I'm sorry to hear that."

"Yeah, me too."

"What happened?"

"The boy was a regular caller. Our kids worked with him. They did a good job. Did the best they could. The way I see it, the boy is gone, but it's my job to make sure the girls, my student workers, are okay. They're gonna take it hard. They have to know it's not their fault."

Duffy nods. This is serious stuff. He tries to appear solemn. Sensitive. Caring. On duty. Ignore his imminent outsourcing. Ignore the most recent defeat. Care about the child.

"So what did he do?"

"Off the roof."

Michael extends his long, right arm, and points to the top of the hotel.

"He fell. Rather, most likely, he jumped. Sometimes, true, they teeter-totter on the edge, and go down by accident when they are still in a contemplating phase, and yes, a contemplating phase is something many healthy people go through. But most of the time, if they make it that far, they know what they're doing. This boy leaped off, I'm pretty sure. You can tell by the trajectory."

Counselor Michael moves his pointing arm over to the ambulances, fire red and virgin white, and their school of yellow and black rubber duckies. Duffy squints to see that the ducks are firefighters and medics, swarming like it's feeding time at the pond.

"That's awful." Duffy tries to sound sincere, with some emotion, but not enough to give away his panic. He was trying to make it with an undergrad, and even offered a male of the species, when another boy leaped from the building. Guilt stabs him in the heart. Shame droops over his soul like the oversized garments his mother habituated him to buy, as if midsection blubber were not the only growth left in the man. He bends down, coughs repeatedly, but Zuegma continues.

"Ain't it though. The kid gets stuck in the hotel for his freshman year housing because the dorms are full. So he is alienated from his class to begin with. Half a hotel floor just isn't the same as dorm life. They didn't even have the kids in entirely adjacent rooms. So he's eighteen, struggling in college, and living by himself in a hotel."

Duffy, recovering, can't help but find irony in the fact that he wishes he could afford a night at the hotel. Full retail on a weeknight must be close to two hundred, over half his monthly take-home from a single course. He marvels, then, at how generous Allison Silverman was; could it be that for this giving student—or her parents—the rent for room 1007 was a mere drop in the bucket? He wonders what the college receives for a group rate before returning to conversation.

"So he's a freshman."

"Yeah, he was. Most of them are, except for the seniors terrified to enter the real world. Competition is brutal, and they know it."

Duffy knows it, oh yeah. This Counselor Michael is starting to grow on him. Maybe it couldn't hurt to visit him again? Discuss his problems, tangential to, but in a way relating to Eileen the psychotic student.

"What was his name?" Duffy realizes that only a small percentage of Liberty Tech freshmen have passed through his writing classes, but there's a chance he could have taught the boy.

"There's patient confidentiality of course."

"Of course." And just as soon, he recognizes that ignorance can offer more peace of mind.

"But heck, we've been through one battle together. You're a soldier I can trust."

Duffy isn't sure he wants therapy to be included in the war front. And yet, the metaphor is inescapable. Terrorism. Drugs. Fat. Cancer. Isn't there even a war on education in this country? He could hope he has the slogan wrong. Was it No Terrorist Left Behind? Drugs and Opportunity? The Fight to Make Cancer a Personal Choice? Fern's propaganda blurs together in Duffy's brain. Could he call it Fern's if Fern is on vacation half the time, if the speech slogans are created by significant underlings— or is it abovelings?—or maybe outsourced, made not in the USA but by knowledge-cogs in other countries? Fern is no longer merely a figurehead, but the lead figurine in a fake society, where Made in the USA might mean a few pieces or parts are assembled here. Even if the work is owned by American companies and shareholders, it is performed far away, by foreigners overseas. One nation, indivisible, under an economy of just pretend. A make-believe cowboy leads a nation of imposters and imaginary friends; the world's leader flies with his hat pulled over his eyes. Who ever heard of a Texas fern anyway? A cactus, yes. A bush perhaps, and a desert shrub for sure. But a fern? The Duffler feels lost, confused by it all. It gives him a headache. He loses track of where he is standing and why.

"Jonathan Doah. Spelled D-O-A-H."

Jonathan Doah. Pronounced like doe or dough. Not Jonathan Money or Jonathan Deer. Just some obscure, meaningless John Doe. He asks for a name and receives two words. Nothing registers at first save for the long and short of it now; not facsimiles or clones, but real students are leaping off buildings all over the United States of college dreams. They require no Arab or otherwise otherized terrorist to blow them up or shoot them down, no menacing methed-up felon to push them off. This boy needed no help at all. Perhaps globalization and the movement of capital were enough? Or the anxiety of job placement in the age of terror, information, McDonaldization, and Fern. No doubt the obituary would omit the part about the roster full of adjunct instructors busy failing to get laid. Or so Duffy hopes as he returns to earth to hear Michael continue:

"First year business student. Just looking for an education. A break with the co-op program. A chance at middle-class subsistence, as part of a two-worker family, in the greatest country on earth."

It slams him in the brain like an opponent's overhead. A haymaker sent down from the administration offices high above. Jason Something, Jonathan Somebody is Jonathan Doah. The boy who sat petrified and paralyzed in the middle of his English 103 class, not ten hours ago.

Off the building. He leaped.

Duffy feels woozy. For balance, he grasps at Counselor Michael's shoulder, whose eyes flash briefly both perplexity and horror. The therapist instinctually steps back, as he would with any strange man trying to grab him, leaving Duffy's extended hand and full weight falling down on nothing. He momentarily loses his balance as his palm falls flat to the asphalt. His legs bend to a crouch, and he teeters but doesn't totter, a weeble, wobbling but not falling down. Duffy is positioned like a football lineman before the snap of the ball. There he stays, in a three-point stance, although no team in their right mind would want him on their offensive line, protecting their quarterback. Not with his record for the day.

"Are you okay? Let's have you sit down." Counselor Michael recovers quickly, resuming his role as friendly therapist.

Duffy concentrates, gathers his brain parts together, does a mental count of appendages. He is almost certain they all remain attached, even the left leg frequently asleep at its post, and the other that has gone unfed during guard work. He pushes hard against the pavement and rises again.

"Yeah, yeah, I'm fine." He makes a show of checking his palm for scratches, dusting off his front areas, gut, and upper thighs as far down as he can reach. He suppresses, "I need to be away from you now," and instead offers, "Just a long day, just a very long day."

Counselor Zuegma and Adjunct Duffleman share a grim look, an acknowledgment of the sadness of it all. Or so Duffy hopes this is what he communicates, and not the despair of a morally weak marginal man recently refused the most robust of desserts. And so he proffers his palm, their final communication, this nonverbal act, fulfilling a belonging need, the shaking of hands. Zuegma grasps the wet fish heartily, ignoring its conference with the filthy street.

As Duffy walks away and through the crowd, he can't help but veer toward the ambulances. He needs to see, so he can know for sure. The large crowd of rubber duckies hides almost everything from view. But Duffy inches as close as he can, serpentining and asstwisting around as many as possible, even physically nudging away a couple of smaller onlookers, just gossiphounds, no doubt, craving dirty laundry. He gets as close as he can, so he could almost reach out and touch one of the paramedics. Through the brightly lit street night and the comingling of ambulance and fire authorities, he sees a mass on a stretcher. But it is covered up completely, so he will have to trust Counselor Michael's word. Or hold out hope that he could be mistaken.

And now he wants away from the masses. If his long day were lived in a European novel, he'd become "D" when on the run or near disappeared. But Adjunct Duffleman has no time for such literary bullshit! He is still on duty, still guarding, but he finds himself walking in the direction of Collegetown Friends Hospital, several blocks away from his territory. As he exceeds the periphery of the crowd, beyond the pairs and threesomes chattering at the edges, he is almost certain he hears familiar conversation.

"You know they ain't tellin' the truth about this one."

"Man, that boy ain't jump."

"Word."

"Terrorists pushed him off."

"How you know that?"

"I called Earl on my cell phone. He watchin' on cable news. Safe behind his bars. He tell me the authorities suspect foul play."

"Mmmm-hmmmm."

"So while we out here, breathin' God know what anthrax mess, he safe at home. He got them terrorist-proof bars. He told me it may not be Al Qaeda, but now they got splinter groups. Al Coulda and Al Woulda. Copycat criminals. Wannabes. All out to push an innocent boy to his demise."

"I heard that."

Duffy recognizes the voices. They sound like the fried-chicken women from his late-morning train. He turns to face the crowd but can't connect any of the faces to the words. Is he hearing things? Real or imagined, he cannot convince his conscience that the conversation counts as the final judgment on the event. The women say it's a terrorist group, but as Duffy skulks away, he cannot shake the idea that his teaching is to blame; his critical readings of America led a young man to throw himself off the roof and smash his face on the asphalt. Truth itself is a ruthless murderer, and thousands like Duffy her co-conspiratorial henchmen. As he drifts further and further from the crowd, he is left with an unwavering sense of guilt for this crime.

CHAPTER 10

NIGHT WANDERING

They press in from all sides now. Terrorists into buildings. Assassins killing deer and political appointees. Students off the roof tops. Choose your evil. World devils or inner demons. Collegetown needs protecting more than ever, and yet Duffleman heads in the wrong direction.

As he drifts away from the peripheral lingerers, in their own way, the last evidence of Jonathan Somebody's tragic leap, Duffy indulges in the solitude, a nearly full moon and street-lamp-lit spring sky. He looks up at the high roofs all over—parking garages built vertical, office buildings, some floors still with lights on, The Ivory Tower, and a particularly faceless structure he knows to be international-student housing. When he gazes at tall buildings now, he can't help but imagine the terrorists flying planes into each one, destroying all of America's phallic supremacy. These brief images are now stuck in his deranged psyche. From where would failed Americans leap if all of our towering buildings were razed to the ground? He envisions inflated airfare prices to Niagara Falls; renewed interest in the nation's dams and gorges; long lines at the Grand Canyon, potential suicides being asked to take a numbered ticket, to wait their turn. Couldn't Al Qaeda see that we are killing our own well enough? Competitive society creates deep-rooted feelings of failure. On our own, we succeed at self-termination; America needs no foreign aid from these murderers.

As usual when walking alone late at night, guard duty or no, Duffy peers down slim side streets he passes, not wanting to be surprised by lurkers in the darkness, intent on grabbing his few soft dollars. The terrorist threat adds to his paranoia. Of course, he knows he has nothing in his pockets save for photo identification, and perhaps some loose change, coins kept after he gave up his five and ones. Yes, a grown man, a so-called "professional in his field," walking the streets with barely a dime to his name. Could have used the hotel ATM, but of course, he wanted to avoid the fat tourist surcharge—gotta pay to play, and particularly so if playing in other people's cities.

Nothing to the right, but from the left, he hears noise. Some sort of clicking, thankfully not enough for the sound of a gun's safety, and yet, too little for a ballpoint pen. Just two hundred yards from the accident and all is quiet save for this soft clicking noise. Duffy listens intently, trapped in his paranoiac expectations, unsure if the thief, the terrorist, or the final stages of his lunacy—hearing noises—are with him now. Tonight, he decides to fully embrace fate. To find out for sure. The noise appears to be coming from behind a dumpster. He feels strange, adventurous, and even a little as if his life doesn't matter anymore—presuming, in fact, at some point it did. So he quietly approaches, and from behind the dumpster, he can hear the faint mouthing of sounds. Words. He inches forward, close enough to hear a voice clearly. "Goddamn." Pause. "Goddamn." Terrorist or thief? Possible but doubtful—wait. The voice sounds familiar. Most likely that of an African American man, but not at all like the deep, throaty quality of the voter-registration Negro. It is a voice Duffy has heard recently, a sound from his long day. Less than three yards from the dull blue dumpster, he loses it. He wonders aloud, "So this is what it has come to. On your long day, you're losing it. You're hearing voices, going out of your mind. You can't take the heat. You drive one student to the emergency room, another out of her mind, and a third from the hotel roof. You witness an assassination and go with business as usual, expecting to get supremely laid at the end of it all. You're a fine one, Duffy. Can't take the heat so now, you decide to flake out entirely. Is that all you can say for yourself?"

"Man, chill out. Chill the fuck out. Cut out that racket." From behind the dumpster, out pops Wawa Ed, pipe in one hand, lighter in the other.

A red sea of shame washes over Duffleman. He is embarrassed that this homeless instructor has heard him, a paid—albeit poorly—professional, mouthing off at the moon.

"Why aren't you at the Wawa, Ed?" The comma's pause feels misplaced.

"Man, Duffy, you think I live there? It's slow over there right now. Everyone went to the hotel, so I decided to cut out and catch some sleep."

Duffy hears "sleep" but stares at the lighter and pipe.

"I see what you lookin' at." In Ed's voice, Duffy hears it is okay to ask.

"Ed, is that for tobacco or marijuana?"

"Crack cocaine."

Duffy knows Ed may see him as a foolish white boy and now he knows why. He knows crack is still around, behind the scenes, in the crevices and back alleys of Collegetown civilization, where the African Americans have been bought out and deposited farther west each time Liberty Tech and Ivy Green expanded over the past fifty years. But this is the closest he has ever come to this evil wah—. He catches himself, recognizing it is not a weed at all; perhaps its distant cousin is the cocoa leaf, but that was many pickings and processes ago. Now the physical proof of Ed's pipe conquers everything Duffy has read online about epidemics of hillbilly heroin, medicinal marijuana, ecstasy, K2, and drank. But in Philadelphia, his ugly sister of a city, he sees it is the crack pipe that still loves you back.

"I'm sorry, Ed," is all he can offer.

"Man, what you sorry for? I should be sorry for you. You the one talkin' to hisself and it ain't hardly a full moon. I was just cussin' this broken lighter. The muthafucka has fluid in it, but it won't catch."

He listens to private Ed, a different voice not at all like the public Ed outside the Wawa. Encourage a young person, straighten a tie Ed. Duffy doubts he even bothers to enunciate as well as the public Ed, for he has let the public and private Duffleman blur together, as if the long day is any excuse. Ed no doubt hustles a long day too, a longer day perhaps.

Duffy stands and stares. He takes in the man. He sees fatigue below Ed's eyes and deep creases of addiction in the cheeks—the night shift of reality where rosy optimism guided the young several hours ago. He senses that Ed is staring back at him, absorbing the whole of the man or the broken halves. He feels his halves splinter into fragments. *Right back at you, Duff.*

"Brotha, you look worn down." He hears empathy in Ed's voice. Here is a homeless man, a crack-addicted hustler living off winnings gained from Wawa panhandling, telling Duffy that he looks rundown and defeated.

So Adjunct Duffleman blurts it out. The tell all, the short version of his long day. It takes about twenty minutes, includes all of it, in no particular order, the sex, the violence, the analysis, the pain. It culminates with the expressed conviction that he has caused the death of at least one child and the certain disappointment of many more.

As Duffy's last rambling subsides, Ed's face turns soft. He smiles and says gently, "Well, look on the bright side. You're not dead *yet.*"

Duffy grows teary-eyed receiving these words. Grateful. Perhaps the most sensible phrase he has heard all day. Three true words for the road. Not dead yet. So he moves toward Ed, one shoe inching past the other, until he realizes, catching himself, that an alleyway hug would be awkward.

"Thanks, Ed," becomes his soft reply.

"Say, Duff, could you spare a couple dollars? I can get you back later in the week, when things calm down. With all the commotion today, the Wawa was a bit low for work."

Duffy reaches into his pockets and is once more reminded there is nothing available for withdrawal. He gave it all away already. He pulls out the inner lining, so Ed can see the empty pockets. "I'm sorry Ed, I wish I could."

"Hey, Duffy, no problem. Another time, another time." Wawa Ed's smile lessens the shame.

All the same, Duffy feels the deep pangs of guilt that he cannot give anything to his friend. But just as soon, his conscience smacks him to the other side. If he gave all of his loose change and spare bills to Ed, would that not amount to some kind of insider trading or political cronyism—giving only to his friends among the homeless and not evenly to all in need? Could he denounce Fern's hypocrisy and ignore his own? With the rising wave of national poverty, perhaps it is time for the city to initiate open-bidding contracts for prime panhandling locations?

Duffy moves away, still freshly unlaid, and yet this late-night encounter with Wawa Ed reminds him how real talent—a genuine original—could be marginalized to the back alleys of this so-called civilization. Indeed, he should feel lucky to have not one but five solid jobs to perform on his long day. He teaches; he eats. Compared to the lives whose paths he has crossed, Duffy is doing quite well. Now a string of images floats through his brain. The Afrocentrist. Julian Door. Voter Registration. The Hollywood actress and the fried-chicken women. Allison Silverman. Gary the commie with whom he could have consummated a long-term gay future or at least shared a birthday quickie. And last but not least, there is Eileen the psychotic whom he is currently planning to visit and Frank Hamnett soon after that.

Did Al Qaeda have any idea that this is the motley crew they seek to destroy? That Fern is trying, perhaps poorly, to protect? Our streets are not paved with gold, far from it. Rather, the people of America are barely surviving—socially, emotionally, economically—trying to manage the arduous challenges of each day. To maintain balance and stay afloat was difficult enough. Are these then people worth targeting? Kidnapping? Oddly assassinating? Beheading? Duffy has some sense that the people who pass through his long day's toil are far removed from the true targets, the symbols of American finance and military might that the "terrorists"—whatever sort of amorphous, shifting, nonstatic tribe this term describes—truly want to damage or defeat. He has some idea what they want is to bring America humility, and yet all around him, he is surrounded with the broken and weak, people who deserve a chance to lift their head up out of humble circumstance precisely because they fail to participate and reap profit from a global empire in all its hubris. And yet the thought is inescapable, that if the dirty bomb should go off, the anthrax dumped and spread by the subway's motion, then these are the struggling, sad souls destined for doom. Duffy's daily associates were people who never did harm to anyone, anyone that is, save perhaps themselves.

And so his royal Duffleleupagus is seized with a megalomaniacal conceit that he is the contemporary Jesus, the man wandering through the lives of these forlorn people, beaten and broken down by the unbearable thirst of relative deprivation—unless it was all of capitalism, or terrorism, or loneliness, or time. Of course, to compare oneself to Jesus is at least ridiculous, and yet not uninspired extreme narcissism, and although he cannot explicitly remember reading it is symptomatic of a particularly overt form of latent homosexuality, he could not say for sure he has not read that either. On a cereal box top or as fortune cookie filler? Svevo or Zizek? A freshman composition?

Just who is Duffy compared to Jesus anyway? Nothing but a weaker strand, but a 37.5 percenter where Jesus was all Jew, a pure breed who broke bread and sipped wine only with other tribesmen. A man whose last supper was indeed a Passover. When was the last time Duffy even considered attending this religious ceremony, sipping the salty water, nibbling on the bitter root, the taste of life itself? Jesus, man or god, could surely help a lost soul like Wawa Ed, but transient Duffy has not a dollar in his pocket, and cannot summon any fishes or loaves, not even frozen bread or fish sticks, charged to Visa at Wawa, as he reached his limit long ago, late in the doctoral program, and these days could pay little more than the fifteen percent interest when his larger checks arrived at the end of the month. And finally, in a fit of honesty, he admits the APR is 14.99 percent.

Argh!!

No, Jesus would not let Wawa Ed down. Jesus would never pretend what he does is honest work, or pretend that he does it well and that he is not some foolish tool exploited by an overzealous marketing department at four different schools. Where Duffy is subject to recurrent and alternating bouts of self-pity and praise for his abundance of employment, Jesus, on the other hand, took responsibility, not just for his own life, but for every man's, in a way his father's too, and forgave the entire world. Duffy's specialty is in fact great feats of blaming others and the world itself, during down moods and sulking sessions that could last weeks on end, no mere seasonal affective disorder, but high-quality loser-itis. Yes, fat man, a swelling of the loser. Indeed, Wawa Ed is more the Christ figure, and Duffy but a wannabe, a cheap, tourist-trap figurine.

Awash with such crushing "compare and contrast," he is jerked back to reality by the neon time above the thick glass and steel bars of a locked and secured savings and loan. The sight of a brick-and-mortar bank distracts him from his crazed head games, and the time is enough to refocus his flagging body on current movement.

At the front desk of College Friends Hospital, he asks for the room for Eileen Zimmerman. There is some confusion, finally resolved when the administrator determines she has checked in with her mother's maiden name. Eileen Saporowitz. Duffy takes the elevator to the sixth floor. He experiences the austerity of the late-night, sanitized, ugly off-white hospital hallways; from his childhood he is reminded of the greenery of a local cemetery he would play in. How could it be that the place to cure people appears deathly ill, while where dead people lie appears green and alive? It is no matter at this late stage, and but slightly lost, he rounds a third bend to find himself at the door of 613. He is greeted by the sight of a tired, worn woman lingering in the hallway. A long cigarette befits her long black locks and deep mascara. Her own gray hairs outnumber his lonely pale veterans but he feels safe nonetheless. She appears to be his age, perhaps older. Eileen's mother. It must be.

From a distance, for a moment, they inspect the merchandise. But then she approaches. She smiles.

"I want you to know this isn't your fault." She stares intently at Duffy. "She has had these problems for some time now, but with the medication, she's functional."

"I see," is all he can think to say.

"She really wanted to go back to school after the first episodes. She was so happy when they finally found a med mix that made her reasonably stable. Before it all began, she was prelaw. Getting all A's and B's, and in the honor society. She had such a bright future." Eileen's mother sighs.

He figures it's time for another, "I see."

"Would you like to see her? She is resting peacefully."

Duffy finds himself shuddering internally—hopefully—at the thought of facing this Eileen Zimmerman-Saporowitz. Presumably, one of his own. Or is it three-eighths of his own or one of his three-eighths'? No matter. What he knows for certain is that the morning's experience was unusual. Scary. It freaked him out in its entirety. Nonetheless, he has come this far.

"Yes. I would."

The two of them walk in together. The mother moves disturbingly near. As his business communications textbook would say, she uses this intimate distance, up to eighteen inches apart, a distance reserved for close friends, relatives, and lovers. Would a visit to the hospital to see her daughter immediately qualify him for any of these categories? It's another scary thought, and he is eager to dismiss it. Above all, Duffy is a great believer in personal space, particularly his own, and wishes she would revert to the personal-distance category, defined by the book as from eighteen inches to four solid feet.

In the stale beige and off-white, sanitized, linoleum storage space known as a city hospital bedroom, Duffy stares at Eileen. She appears to be sleeping like a baby. No snoring, only steady breathing. It is the first time he has seen her looking calm and comfortable, her neck and posture relaxed, quite unlike the rigid, upright position she would assume in his class. It is comforting, even soothing, to see one of his students has found peace at last. He turns to the mother, and in his nod, tries to combine decency, sympathy, hope, and even progress.

Back in the hallway, the mother gains territory and in half-whispers continues to explain.

"Her traumatic event, the trigger for it all, was too intense. It ruined her. Believe me, it's not your fault, it's mine. He beat the hell out of me, but I swear I had no idea he was abusing her too."

She then delves deeply into the whole situation. The past. It pours out like the great flood itself. As she lays down her weary tune, chapter by chapter, the two ex husbands, one outright brutal and the other merely exceedingly dull, she moves in on Duffy. He feels the pressure of the full-court trap, the lasting impression of the intimate-distance category. He can feel the heat of her body just inches from his; her breath is in his nasal passages. He vows not to retch, but he fears some imminent collapse onto his person, a fallen face against his shoulder, or just an arm akimbo into his side. What could she want with his fatigue and gut? Just late-night desperation, a two-time loser, so why not strike out at the plate with the losingest of them all, Cyrus Duffleman, worn down and defeated fat guy, adjunct instructor and repeat loser of his flock. She had gobbled down the dull scientist for breakfast and the brutal truck driver for lunch. So for dinner, the last meal of her day, why not Adjunct Duffleman? The inconsequential man. The extra man. The man who knows too much about nothing anyone is interested in but writes too little—zilch in fact—in his field.

He feels her flesh now, her hand pressed against his wrist, and what could possibly be nipple brushing against his own flabby breast. A shock of fear sweeps through him even as Dufflejunior rises to request a parent-teacher conference. But the thought of getting caught up in this mess, this woman, this mother of a psychotic and ex-wife of a dullard and a brute, is too much. So Duffy begs her pardon, says he is late for another conference, and he has yet to use the Friends hospital automated teller. The ATM excuse, the most ridiculous one in the book, even if this one is surcharge-free.

Before departing, running scared from the scene of his long day's first victim, he takes a good look at Eileen's mother. The deep, purplish, black bags below the eyes. The blood-red lipstick screaming, "Fuck me if you dare, maybe when the orderly isn't looking, behind the curtain in the room where my daughter sleeps." The ample portions of dark mascara, hinting at God only knows what kind of past. The remains left for unmarried men. There are no Allison Silvermans in his future. Everything about her flirtation was too exaggerated to be true. Here stands the real option. Maybe fifty-one or forty-three, twice divorced, the heavy scars of life all about her person, visible nipple, designer jeans clinging like saran wrap to last week's leftovers. How could Duffy dare to hope for better?

He shudders in sheer terror, briefly blacks out, and then hallucinates. His late father—three-quarters Ashkenazi and thus almost an expert— returns to earth as a gynophobic patriarch and tells him Jewish women are trouble. Overbearing. Never satisfied and rarely sucking cock after the honeymoon. Duffy screams, "Save me, rabbi!" and then snaps out of it and into a recollection of reading that only sixteen percent of American men make it to age forty without ever tying the matrimonial knot. Now staring at this woman, he sees why he will be among this one in six or seven. And he has but two more days to go.

After a balance inquiry that shows $12.34 left in his account, he pushes buttons to command the bare minimum, and pockets a new, but already used ten-dollar bill. He stares momentarily at Alexander Hamilton, grateful for this familiar face, thankful he doesn't yet have to shove Wally Winsome into his pocket. At the thought of the fortieth President, Duffy feels the urge to micturate or defecate or somewhere in between, but the hospital offers such likelihood of the diseased using the lavatories that he can vividly imagine how that amplifies the negatives associated with the toilet seat. He determines to go without, and so he soldiers on.

Holding it in and visibly hustling, fast walking as it were, Duffy loses his way on the ground level. He finds himself in abandoned corridors, dimly lit, stale beige and off white, just like everything else. And then there are people, men and women in green and blue and white hospital garments, and he even sees rubber duckies again, EMTs, an occasional cop, crowds under bright lights. It must be the emergency room. He passes a large waiting area, where the masses sit. They are obese, old, worn-down, defeated, incontinent, and unable to control their children. On cellular phones, they talk too loudly or only in whispers; they sob real tears or wait in silence. In the middle of the full room, he sees a large black woman sitting with a thin young man in dreadlocks and goatee. The Afrocentrist and Julian Door. Her injuries occurred hours ago, and he is almost certain that Julian Door, at the protest, told him that she was resting and would be okay. And yet here they are, the only other option being that Duffy is losing his mind.

It is too much. He sees both of their facial expressions turning from blank stare to recognition and pleasant surprise, just as he ducks down below the glass. No time for more chat or fake concern when he is so desperate to locate a can. So he waddle-squats out of the hospital and into the area where they unload the ambulances and bring in the remains. He stands straight again, paces quickly, and then begins to run, maybe more like a slow scamper or jog, away from all the hurt and regret. Back to black night, and again in the wrong direction. Out of breath too soon, he slows to a stroll. Philadelphia shoves him down its open expansive streets, chewing him up and spitting him out. Duffy stops tracking his direction, as if he has been these past several years. He finds himself wandering up Lancaster Avenue, the so-called "bad part," the ghetto, the slums. It is Philadelphia's shtetl and Duffy's street of crocodiles, but also an area that undergrads have been encroaching upon, forced to do so by increased admissions office objectives and expanding student populations. These migrants drive up rents, and move more native residents deeper into West Philly. Ivy Green and Liberty Tech are such indefatigable centrifuges of economic might and destiny, they seem capable of expanding forever, obliterating Philadelphia's original grid of demotic intent to one day encompass and control the entire region. What would a Ben Franklin or William Penn make of Philly's current ethnographics? How would they understand the lay of the land in today's city of brotherly love?

As he paces westward, Duffy explores the great irony of this demographic shift, this further marginalization of the darker-skinned masses. The current mayor of Philadelphia, Wilson F. Rhodes, is an up-from-the-street-hustle African American whose most loyal constituents are these very same blacks being displaced and further ostracized by the city's nerve centers, its universities. The mayor has even partnered with Ivy Green to ensure that millions of dollars earmarked for the children of his poor constituents who attend the Philadelphia public schools would in fact go to a brand-new, state-of-the-art, contemporary laboratory school in the Collegetown neighborhood immediately west of Ivy Green, where faculty and administrators reside, many of whom could afford even the highest private-school tuitions for their own children. While the mayor's voters' kids roam the halls and rot away in dilapidated structures with rotting textbooks and broken heaters, these children of the elite enjoy the spoils of the mayor's election victory.

Meanwhile, over at the Philadelphia College of the Community, the best deal in town for two years of higher ed, and an institution the mayor's constituents could possibly afford to attend, one of Rhodes's close allies has been indicted in a scam to bilk hundreds of thousands of dollars from the school. The money was supposed to go to off-campus night classes, classes Duffy knows would have gladly been accepted and taught well by the kind, decent adjunct instructors of PCC—part-time professors committed to helping Philadelphia's poorest—for a mere forty or fifty dollars per credit hour, no extra charge for time-consuming lesson plans and paper grading. But the wife and son of the mayor's close friend—people he now dismisses as mere acquaintances—consorted with an administrator at PCC, took the money, and handed out no-show jobs, cash for no educational services rendered, to various friends and family members. Duffy sees the entire scam as one big *fuck you* to all the adjunct instructors of Philadelphia, women and men, who work overtime to grade papers for peasant wages and no benefits. Ironically, PCC, supposedly the lowest on the rung, is the only school in Philadelphia to offer health coverage to its adjuncts, and Duffy knows they attract a particularly strong core of instructors for this reason alone. If the money had gone to real courses, perhaps even Duffy could have taught one or two, maybe added the work to his current oversupply in exchange for a chance to visit the doctor.

To top it all off, the mayor had even attempted teaching, in his early years, and had been on record stating he left education because he felt constrained by the walls of just one classroom, limited in what he could do to assist the poor. He had in fact chosen politics to be a greater force of good in Philadelphia. His is an ambition of largesse and philanthropy, or so he says often in his favorite church stump speech. And of course, he promotes himself as pure: "No alcohol, no pornography, and no foul language" was Rhodes's refrain from the pew throughout the corruption investigation. Oh what a shyster! And of course, comparing his own failed adulthood to the successful mayor, Duffy feels like a stale turd for sticking it out in teaching.

The final irony of his rage against local machine politics, and the mayor in particular, lies in the fact that he almost voted for Rhodes's reelection. Last fall, it was the classic lesser of two criminals approach to American politics. The FBI investigation into the mayor's allies had been undertaken in secret and then discovered in the middle of the reelection fight when the mayor's personal guards uncovered planted listening devices in the mayor's office. So the evidence was there, and the mayor spun it some more, and the possibility was raised of dirty dealings by the RNC and undue politicizing of the local FBI office. So in the end, Duffy felt forced to hand Rhodes his vote. Besides, the moderate, socially liberal Republican running against him also had allegations of corruption hanging over his head. Illegal land deals in municipalities thousands of miles away. The mayor's opponent seemed like a nice man, albeit a bit reserved, maybe cold. Stiff as cardboard in fact. And he said nothing about what he would do to get health coverage for the hundreds of thousands of working Philadelphians, who like catastrophic-coverage Duffleless, at present, go only in emergency or entirely without. To top it off, the man was a Jew, and although Duffy is but 37.5 percent Hebraic himself, his instinct is for the preservation of his people, the so-called chosen people, to keep them out of public view, the conspicuous places, such as public office in particular, where they could be accused of ostentatious display, over-representation, or unfair political clout. For survival, it is safer to linger behind the scenes.

And so, armed with this final reason, he cancelled a class and ventured all the way to the polling station. Duffy came within fifteen yards of voting for Rhodes when a man dressed in camouflage and a black beret introduced himself as a former student and engaged his teacher in conversation. Even though they were both leaning toward Rhodes, despite his various failings, their discussion in line grew so heated that the two of them were summarily kicked out of the polling place for discussing their political choices too loudly. Weeks later Duffy would read that his student planned to sue the city for disenfranchisement, but the young man never called his former instructor to see if he wanted in on the action.

And so, in the middle of Lancaster Avenue, Rhodes territory, with black people parked and idled outside abandoned storefronts, just waiting for something, hard to say what but perhaps tonight waiting for the white man to wander down their way and wax insane, Duffy laughs and laughs and laughs, mad guffaws at all of his failings, his ridiculous comparisons to Jesus and Mayor Rhodes, his lack of funds and comprehensive health coverage, his inability to help a good man like Wawa Ed, or to prevent any of the student calamities of his long day. Oh, what a complete incompetent he is! Duffy experiences an intense feeling of *schadenfreude* now. He knows that word means laughter at another man's embarrassment or pain, but tonight Duffy is that other man, the original nincompoop, who through stupid self-interest he has deluded himself into calling generosity, has chosen academia, presently laughing at the marginalized jackass he has become.

Deep in Rhodes's territory, Duffy grows weary of laughing and so forgets. He regains his composure. He must press on. He passes through a transitional area, part slum, part student off-campus living. Marching onward over a mangled cement sidewalk, he sees dilapidated structures, empty husks of last-century architecture, some abandoned storefronts turned into churches and mosques. In the Wal-Martized economy, only the true masochists even attempted to sell a good or service, independently, as a store owner. Low-cost chains and high city-wage taxes ensured the only products immediately available to the shtetled were of low quality and high price. Only God, with his low overhead and unlimited marketing potential, could survive and turn a profit.

It is a beautiful, cool night. Philadelphia is out and about. He sees a man muttering to himself and another talking to invisible others. A heavyset woman with two babes clinging to her bosoms, and a third and fourth on either leg, tries to navigate the difficult, weighty walk of single motherhood. Teenage boys loom and lurk. Some look not so much mean as slightly disturbed; a large number stand by the barren real estate with no expression at all. They could be shy or even friendly. So many are thin, thus contradicting the current notion of overfed, couch-squash American children growing exponentially outward in every income bracket. Duffy sees no distended stomachs of malnourishment, and so he can only suppose the sinewy youths must be genuinely active. At least much more so than his own flabby ass.

Duffy finds it strange and unlikely that although it is in his character to be terrified of these teens during his underground commute, now he fears nothing at all. He looks right at them, observing their manner and posture, the opposite of his subway strategy, which is to avoid eye contact by any means necessary. And yet, they show no reaction. A few nod but most ignore him. Duffy wonders if because it is only Thursday, and well before midnight, it could be too early for the violent attack or ethnic intimidation one knows to expect from watching TV news. He lumbers on.

He passes a decrepit, rusted-out van, gray or brown, the original paint job impossible to discern. He approaches the opening on the side, curious about the evidence that it was once employed as a food truck. On another night it would remind him of Tu Nguyen's lost American Dream, but presently he remembers the truck parked downtown on a half-hidden side street where passport photos were discretely sold, and more obscure forms of identification could be had for the right price.

Even in the age of the Internet, with the world's oysters—aye, the entire ocean—seemingly available online, it was in that marginalized alleyway that Duffy waited to obtain the proper documents required for work as an instructor at Ivy Green. The credential he needed forged was in fact his transcript stating he held a PhD in English studies, comparative literature, composition and rhetoric, or a related field. ABD was no longer enough for new hires at Ivy Green, and technically, it was not a status Duffy enjoyed. Truth be told, he had flunked his exams three times in a row and was forbidden from extending his stay in graduate-school purgatory. When he saw the job ad, and saw it could mean teaching his favorites, the opportunity was too much to pass on; he knew he could babble on Isaac Babel and shuffle around Bruno Schulz more than most, and besides, how many PhDs could there be lining up for three grand a class with nothing on the fringe beyond false hopes for undergraduate flesh?

Waiting in that alleyway line with the immigrants and interna-tionals—legals, illegals, paralegals, what have you—he felt a tremendous oneness with humanity, a swelling not in the least stirred by the bosomy young Mexican woman six inches ahead. He knew his commoner's lust was pure. This was what people did; it was how they survived squeezed between the world's hegemonies—capitalists, tyrants, corporations, drug cartels, religions, universities, terrorists, democracies, free-trade agree-ments, and combinations thereof. The truck was co-owned by Aleksandar Amerika and Roberto Corolla, third- or second-world, white and Hispanic, and neither here nor there. They shared smiles, assumed names, and status as immigrants on the margins, offering sales and services from a mobile office; the company was named after the truck, GMC, as in "general mail and copying." It was Duffy's primer on the real global village, a visit to an area inhabited by most of the world's citizens. For years he had taught essays on such matters, but in line, he felt connected to a shared experience. The sexy Mexican turned out to be legal, and why yes, her status as fourth-generation American brought even more shame upon him for expecting anything less. She was intent on purchasing laminated transparencies for her college research papers, but these long-report prophylactics failed to ruin the romance of Duffy's exchange.

The piece of paper that said PhD cost him one hundred bucks and then Amerika charged another hundred to make it appear as if the forged transcripts were notarized, properly sealed, and acceptable if hand delivered. At the time, he knew it would cost twelve dollars to have real transcripts sent from Urban State, and he took pride in recognizing his net extra expense was only $188.00. In other words, he got a bargain at just a bit more than a week of his Liberty Tech pay. Corolla smiled as Duffy dealt half a deck of fives and tens and singles. "Cash only," whispered Roberto, but Cyrus was good for it.

He remembers fondly his rush to the Ivy Green Evening College and handing his fake documents to the departmental secretary. Both he and the woman at the desk knew no one ever bothered to check the legitimacy of adjunct paperwork—the pay was far too low to merit such concern, and if any problems arose the worker need only not be rehired. No firing or severance pay or legal entanglements ever occurred. But it was quite a thrill to hand over a forged passport for the purposes of teaching Isaac Babel's "Guy De Maupassant." You didn't have to be Nabokov to know America's English departments housed plenty of charlatans and phonies—and careerists and corporatists and lifers and losers—whose paper credentials nevertheless were official and in order. To Duffy, his "street cred" was but an extreme tactic for joining the club.

Now, under moonlight in the slum section of town, he forgives himself for being so delusional as to expect heterosexual relations from a teaching gig he gained through illegitimate means. He should have settled for celibacy and appreciation for the work.

Nowhere else to turn, he approaches the van and peers inside.

Expecting blank darkness, he is nevertheless not surprised to see four scenesters smoking what smells like midnight marijuana from a violet-tinted phallus. The leader gargles, "Dude, I'm not sayin' we can't spare a toke, but like could you knock first?"

Eight eyes are upon him as he stares back to see green sleeping bags and brown blankets and a full-sized camping cooler with a large, bright Liberty-Tech decal. Two girls and two guys are dressed like beatniks or peasants and Duffy can only assume this mobile home parked in a rough part of town is affordable housing for the young and enrolled. So this is a student dorm for the twenty-first century; it hits him like a pile of bricks that his meager allowance—termed "pay"—is extorted from these pot-smoking children despite whatever is said about grandparents and governments funding college for our young. Tuition so outrageous they are forced to dwell in such inhumane conditions and feel lucky for graduating with a retail gig lined up and less than twenty-five grand in loans.

The guilt is unbearable! He must away, so he runs and jogs and stumbles and pants and rests and when he regains whatever is left of his composure, from up ahead he spies what looks like an abandoned warehouse, the last structure standing on an empty block. From inside, he hears suffocated noises. Beating and thrashing and shrieking and screaming. It is like no kind of prayer session he has heard before. At the front, the first door is ajar, and behind it looms a massive bald man sitting on a stool.

"Two dollar cover," he mutters, not the least bit amused, intrigued, or threatened by Duffy's security digs.

Duffy reaches into his pocket for his freshly minted ten, and receives in return eight soggy ones. He passes through a vestibule or antechamber, and then down a long, dark corridor with a wall of old couches upon which half-clad teens and twenty-somethings amuse themselves with various balloons and water bubbles. Some look away while others return his stare with meanness, blankness, and even a sick leer from a red Mohawk in leather and chains. Exhibit A, a female, he is almost certain. At this late hour, he feels proud he can still discern and categorize by sex.

Gawking so, he stumbles upon and into the thick ropes of a noose; detangling himself, he notes two more on either side—intended as irony he imagines but creepy nevertheless. The noise is pounding, beating his brain down like a fall from a cliff. There are hundreds packed into the space. They move, throb, and grind. He sees all manner of physical act and obscenity; a few moves Duffy can recognize as dancing. The boys wear leather and jeans; many are topless, revealing tattoos and emaciation, perhaps not so much from starvation as skateboards and raves. The girls comprise a nation of midriff exposure: tank tops, half tops, spaghetti straps, bra only, or no bra at all under fishnet mesh. Duffy X-rays specks of nipple. Whites in all black, yes, but also a blur of color, the entire spectrum, angry reds, tranquil greens, purples, aqua, lemon, lime. Youth and energy bounce to the beat; it is exactly antithetical to the inertia of boring lectures and bald colleagues. Speaking of such, like the van tokers, they appear college-aged. They could be his students, mingling with the riffraff, the more off-the-beaten-trackers of their generation. Thrashers. Trashers. Scruffy punks and crusties. Stage and dumpster divers and for Muffy but not Duffy most likely as well. Where the real Kerouacs and Dantes would spring from no doubt.

He knows Jesus would never eyes, ears, nose, or throat race, but as a failed blind man, Duffy can't help but count the minority representation. He can discern a wide rainbow of young women of color but counts exactly six African American males. They are alternately dreadlocked, emaciated, spectacled, bald, garbed in neon, and glitter-dipped nude (Duffy feels a tingle but no extension); all have the look or manner of the kind of black boys who don't scare him shitless. The penultimate man, Pink Neon Tank Top, mimes to the beat, palms flat against the imaginary cube in which he is confined. Duffy wonders what these young men could think of the noose curtain. Could only one of the six escape alive and would that denied life be in physiological, emotional, or economic terms? Or are they living in the postracial environment he has seen on TV? Profiting from favorable odds, perhaps they were fulfilling their belonging needs through an ample supply of friends and women?

He dare not approach and ask. The scene perhaps five hundred strong, the black-male ratio is no worse than that of his three Thursday courses.

Duffy turns from race to air guitarists jamming above the moshpit. He sees bodies flying off stage. Male. Female. Every third or fourth kid's gender ambiguous, impossible to ascertain. Opposite the stage he sees two figures dancing on an empty bar. If he weren't already convinced he is outside of his mind, he'd be certain the two are his morning commute's "College is a Scam" purple-dreaded punk girl with the long-beard, barefoot hippie. They appeared apart on the trolley then, but tonight they are so intertwined they could be attached. But the roles have been reversed; she is barefoot and he wears the boots. When her camouflage tee shirt flies off, the reality of what his sizeable imagination produced in the a.m. is impossible not to note. At this late hour, he is thankful his eyes must be deceiving him.

The steady reverberations of unisex rock flood the entire warehouse structure, intensifying his need to urinate or poop. Still hard to say which, but world-weary Duffy imagines the worst. The band brings its final clamoring to a cascading halt. The lead singer seizes this moment to scream at the audience. "We are Al Jazeera, and we love you!" The audience roars back in appreciation. The love affair will continue. So this is what it has come to. American alternative bands name themselves after the Fox News of the Middle East.

Leaving the dance hall, intent upon an egress, Duffy runs smack into an old scent from earlier in the day. He looks up into the beard of the hippie commuter.

"Hey, man. You look familiar."

"I think we were on the same trolley."

"Dude! I was trying to get your attention this morning."

Duffy remembers the smile, its conspiracy, lewdness, or congeniality. "Why me?"

"Man, I thought I'd wound up smack in front of a fellow *landsman*; two lids stuffed together on a train seemed like cool cats at the time."

He needs time to place the terms. The hippie continues.

"You wear the lid on Friday nights?"

So that explains the wide morning smile. This kind of connection is not one he normally brushes off so quickly, but he needs to push on. The 37.5 percent seems far too difficult to explain at this hour, and he feels even more resentful of the questioner. He can only imagine the hippie speaks as a full Jew, and it seems unfair. Duffy is the one who has pounded the Babel and Schulz into his brain, enslaved himself to library stacks and computer screens while this one looks like he's been on leave since the end of the Carter administration. But he's trapped too and needs to get past.

"Half, on my father's side," is the easiest way to get close to the truth.

"Dude, that counts in my book," the hippie grins wide as he offers an open palm held high. His outsider's status once more revealed, he manages to raise his arm up to the hippie's and not wince in too much pain as his eager comrade crunches Duffy's fingers with his strong, moist grip.

"Harry Greenberg. Call me Hair."

"Cyrus Duffleman. Duff'll do."

"These kids are intense; they know how to party. Pedophilia up on the bar can dance my ass off; love that gal's energy."

"Pedawha?"

"Yeah, it's crazy the number her folks pulled on her, but she's a survivor. Double major at Ivy Green headed to med school in the fall. 'Call me Pedal' is how she plays it, and she likes to let loose. Be a good pooch and Pedal'll take you out on a leash loose enough for sniffin' the daisies."

Duffy has heard enough; he wants out. He looks away in search of fresh air, but Harry takes this as a sign he should change the conversation.

"I got in young and did my two tens and five in institutional food. It's crazy but college cafeterias set me free. Say, what's your racket?"

"Not feeling well" is as close as he can get to revealing his vocation.

He ignores Harry's spiel on same-sex food courts and cyberspatial nutrition for the institutionalized masses. He stumbles forward, gently pushing past the left side of retired and hip Harry and straight toward the nooses. He's pretty sure the nausea is believable and not so certain he is pretending malaise unless the entire exchange is hallucination. On the beaten couches beside the nooses, when he does or doesn't witness Professor Kenth snorting blow with a pair of administrators dressed in Armani, the three of them receiving the same from Kenth's finest doctoral candidates—the androgyny and middling hues intensified at this hour—Duffleman knows only for certain he needs air.

Out the door at last, failing once more to merge with the masses, he begins to idly compare his life to the bacchanal he has just witnessed. Whereas the young people tossing their bodies off the stage seem free, entirely in the moment, self-actualized, living, what could he say for his own life? Watered down composition classes, dull business writing, painfully tedious remedial tutoring? Deep down where it counted, on his bad days, he finds himself admitting that even his literature seminar could bore the hell out of him. Although he gobbled up what they wrote years ago, reading Kafka and Schulz has become a chore. The critics on their back covers might rave at their genius, but truth be told, Duffy's mind drifts while turning their pages. As much as he tries to concentrate, he finds their writing hard to follow, difficult to decipher, perhaps plain dull. To admit this now in his years of middle-aged malaise and tendon pain is in a way condemnatory of his entire hand-to-mouth existence on the margins of academia. All the same, he finds the irony of it all— the dullness of the sweet part of his day—not unamusing, and in fact thusly stimulating his interest in his own boredom, an almost wasted, half-over life of a half Heb less 12.5 percent. At himself, mocking, he laughs aloud.

Hah!

Who cares if it were the father or the son who turned into a bug and slithered away during old age or adolescence? Why doesn't Duffy have the good fortune for such an event to happen to him? Where do their plots really go anyway? Could Kafka have wanted to burn the whole mess because the stories were incomplete? Inconsistent? Plotless? Overly analytical nonlinear sketches? Maybe Schulz just didn't have that much to say—hence, the two slim volumes. His resurrection to fame is like some great politically correct movement. The canon requires that most oxymoronic of wanderers, a transnational Jew who never left home, and especially one shot by a Nazi sadist in the open street.

Speaking of murder, it was Comrade Stalin who did in Babel and did his best to kill Shalamov, two other members of Duffy's seminar syllabus. Their stories engross him, true stuff about life and suffering that makes anything American made at the time seem tame and inconsequential. "He's got me beat" is how Hemingway put it when he put down his Shalamov; nevertheless, Duffy has the bad habit of comparing his life, his achievements, his suffering to these canonical Russians. They led real lives, rode with Cossacks, witnessed pogroms, suffered in frigid labor camps, survived emaciation and freezing temperatures, one murdered quick, the other wasted away for seventeen years of Kolyma, only to survive long enough to denounce his own work. Duffy feels meaningless and soft contrasted with the murdered and frostbitten. What did Duffy know about suffering? He couldn't even survive his doctoral program in a private, air-conditioned library carousel. How could the fatigue of his long day be compared to Kolyma? So reading the stories makes him feel even worse.

He feels guilty and dirty for admitting to all this apostasy. Who is Adjunct Duffleman to proclaim such things? To criticize Kafka? To denigrate Schulz? Not even a half-breed, a false professor whose proletarian roast beef, provolone, and brown mustard on a Kaiser roll was as close as he would come to Proust's dip of biscuit into tea. For his is a watered-down olfactory association, and not even a kosher meal, his Judaism a meager, weak strand, his favorite book, *A Fan's Notes*, indeed written by a drunken gentile. Liberty Tech's student-run website for professor ratings has him pegged as a "wannabe," "a fake who fails to inspire," with a "voice worse than screeching chalk." He feels guilty and dirty, filthier even than the warehouse left him. Damp and dungy, the way he feels after leaving one of the many public stalls of his long day.

Speaking of which, it is nearly time to meet Frank Hamnett, but first he must find a toilet. He hates the pangs of alleviation interfering with any kind of student conference, even at this irregular hour. So off Duffy wanders to Liberty Tech's campus, hoping to find a quiet men's room among the spare concrete of the wired campus. He has the security codes for the main entrance of a couple buildings—enough to find the first hallway can, squat and shit, and surely the electricity and running water would stay on. If only he weren't afraid to go into these dimly lit buildings after hours. Who knows what graduate-student ghosts might be present to spook his world? What combined anxiety, guilt, and fear might ruin his lonely poop. No, for a bathroom break, he needs good lighting, a building still open to the public. True, he wouldn't find himself alone, but he would feel safer in these times of terror. He appreciates the situational irony of a security guard afraid of shitting alone in a building he is designated to guard. For scrub wages, they didn't ask during the interview.

So he rushes back to campus in a blur of self-doubt and shame. At the library—a brown brick structure with a third as many floors as Ivy Green—he finds his Liberty Tech ID, shows it to the guard at the front desk, who appears slightly bemused that Collegetown security flashes faculty ID. But she is also on the cell phone with a late-night chat buddy most likely working another second shift somewhere else in Philly, so rather than do her job and determine if there is a discrepancy—indeed, such dedication has disappeared with the health benefits—she looks quizzically at him, acknowledges a likeness, and then nods him through midchatter.

Duffy descends to the basement bathroom first, suspecting few would venture down here at so late an hour. Wrong again. As he descends to the bottom floor, he hears all kinds of noisy conversation. There are students organized in study groups—threes, fours, fives, and even six in some areas—surrounded by plugged-in notebook computers, fat textbooks open wide. Dense thousand-pagers, most likely for science and engineering, the kind he ran away from years ago. The students come in all flavors but the majority of them are hardly the most common vanilla and chocolate, but rather a kaleidoscope of complexion from the entire world. Most appear to be from South and East Asia, with Southeast Asia represented too, no doubt. Judging by their accents the sampling of whites are citizens of former Soviet socialist states hoping to become former citizens and settle in the new world. He passes a table of blacks whose cadences suggest a rough sea smacking rocks off the coast of the islands if not the motherland itself. He wonders where the regular white and black kids of Liberty Tech could be; they are decidedly not in the library past 11 p.m.

Duffy doubts this will be the right floor for sitting and shitting, but he wants to linger longer, absorb the intellectual energy of the place. He walks to the middle of the room and stares all around him. In the wide open space, scores of studying students are visible to the naked eye. Duffy feels like something is happening here. It is not at all like the dead feeling or babysitting experience of much of his tutoring and teaching, but something much closer to the true American ideal of education. Are we not destined to become a country of cooperative learners, educating by experience, and with industry and effort? The foreign students and falsely hyphenated take advantage of the opportunity; they teach us that higher education is still the well-lit expressway to the American Dream. In this coffee-colored plurality, he sees not Faulkner's howling madness but rather the utopia of Melville's "middling hues"—truly, few appear to be the descendants of slaves and slave masters—progressing together, destined to inherit a lion's portion of the country's career positions if not its considerable wealth. In graduate school, he idealized the diversity of the Austro-Hungarian Empire, *fin de siècle* Vienna; and now, its twenty-first century corollary has Herr Dufflemenschen reduced to tears. So caught up in the roar of America's mighty engines of immigration, the energy that fuels the country's power, he thanks God aloud for the tired, hungry, and poor. Thusly, he is pondering Emma Lazarus's position on this basement packed full of potential meritocracy when the stare of a stern-faced janitor returns him to this earth.

Feet back on the ground, he notices that some of the students nearby are fidgeting, turning around and looking up at him, wondering why the security guard stands in the middle of the open floor, staring at them. One young man, perhaps, has read stories of alienated security guards abruptly filling a room with gunfire—seven dead in Kansas, four critical and a suicide in Illinois—and Duffy can sense genuine fear in his look. So he tries to smile at the boy, and now the boy looks at him angrily, as if to say, "Dude, I'm from India. So what?" Duffy, failed globalist, feels the guilt pangs again for perceiving ethnicity. He has learned nothing on his long day; he has made no progress. But then again, maybe the student thinks Duffy is giving him the eye. A gay thing, the awkward, same-sex gawking of a security guard old enough to be his father. Either way, Duffy feels like even more of an ass. So he nods his head vigorously, turns away, and calmly proceeds to the elevator. He decides to try the other extreme, the second floor.

The slow elevator drops him off at the second floor. This is where Liberty Tech keeps the books. Actual bound volumes. Tech is a university but it is not a great acquirer of books, choosing instead to expand the budget of online electronic resources. The CEO has gone on record as saying, "The age of the printed word is over. Online research and education is the future." Duffy realizes that in this thinking, the CEO recognizes the adjunct instructor of freshman writing as just another middle man who could be eliminated. Like the book itself, a relic of the past, his quarterly "nonbinding noncontract" is just another waste of paper. The 1980 dollars of pay should be seen as a gift. No one paid the out-of-work monks in the monastery; no, one attached files, scanned, Cc-ed, made copies, and forgot about men of the cloth copying by hand.

Duffy promises himself a good hard browse after he's finished in the can.

The bathroom is silent. Although at times, he can hardly take seriously the idea that every American city is a major front in the War on Terror, as in real wars, at real fronts, Duffy's latrine time is the most peaceful time of the day. Or so he has read in *All Quiet on the Western Front*; once more, a vicarious excursion through literature is all he has for evidence.

First stall occupied, Duffy applies the all-American *avoid a next-door toe-tapper* rule, peeks in the third to find pee splash on the seat, but hits the jackpot with pristine dry clean the next stall over. As if his dump would be the first of the day, muses the Duffler, as he carefully lays down a fresh seat cover and then toilet-papers over it for good measure. He removes the two envelopes from his left pants pocket and uses his arm bent at the elbow to grip them in his left armpit. As he undoes his trousers, he tucks them in as best he can to keep any clothing from touching the floor; he then squats down to enjoy the tranquility of a stall of his own.

Seated on the can, with his left hand, he keeps Dufflejunior pointed down. With his right, he removes the letters from his armpit and balances them on his left knee. He opens the dark-green envelope first, and sure enough it is a birthday card. From his sister, with a personal check for forty dollars enclosed. "Wishing you all the best, Cyrus. A dollar for every year." Reading the note from his sister, his only immediate living relative, a tear fulfills its agreement with gravity and plops down upon the check, slightly moistening the signature. Duffy carefully rips a square of toilet tissue from the role and presses the note dry. He sees his sister rarely, off in the burbs as they are, and admittedly when he does see them, their materialist lifestyle could depress the hell out of him, but these rare snail mailings remind Duffy of his one real bond, a connection to another human on this planet.

He fondly remembers how his sister and brother-in-law, soon after the 9/11 attacks, began taking self-defense classes and also rifle practice. They became the increasingly common and yet paradoxical domestic liberals cum Zionists, or at least extremely sympathetic to Israel's defense of its ambiguous borders. For dinner, they doled out soup at the homeless shelter at least twice a year, but for breakfast, they ate never-again cereal fortified with iron and guilt. Duffy would get e-mails from his sister, talking up the shooting range. Sometimes the e-mails had photographs attached, and he could see his sister and her husband firing at terrorist images on the targets. Whereas her husband is a bit more of a conservative, stronger on Israel's right to protect its amorphous state, what she really enjoys is every other week's "liberal Wednesday" at the shooting range—apparently, not the oxymoron one would think. Then, you could shoot at images of President Fern, his evil veep, or even the Under Secretary of Homeland Defense. And so, as good Jews—his sister had converted—their good liberalism now no doubt caused severe feelings of guilt for having shot at the likeness of the dead man. Ah, yes. Too much ache of nostalgia for one bowel movement, so Duffy places the check back in the card and gently pushes it back in the envelope.

The second envelope, the light blue one, is of course, from Allison Silverman. Somehow she knows he works at Urban State as well. At this late hour, no need to bother figuring that one out. No money included, but why would there be? Just a note below two monkeys playing chess. "So we expect to see you later, alligator. Think of your day as a chessboard, and look forward to taking the queen tonight." So there it is, the phallic imagery of the most potent chess piece, and of course, it also makes sense knowing what he knows now. Duffy briefly ponders whether a bishop would have been a more apt piece to name, a reference to Gary's in-class asceticism, his devotion to orthodox Marxism or such. Then he feels ridiculous thinking of such things when all was over with. If only he had opened this letter earlier, but yes, he realizes it was quite possible he wouldn't have understood it at all. He shoves the card back in its envelope, and then returns both cards to his left knee.

All finished up, Duffy holds the cards in his armpit once more as he ensures that everything is satisfactorily wiped, allowing himself an ample supply of TP, and conscientiously securing each cheek thrice over. At the sinks, in good lighting, he sees the sweater's coffee stain from the day's early spill. Shaped more like Israel than the Virgin Mary, it is a pesky mark and one that will be hard to remove. While washing, he sees the other stall occupant is similarly rinsing off. Duffy watches the man use a paper towel to touch the hot and cold knobs so as to avoid any contact between skin and metal. He is African American, seemingly about Duffy's age, perhaps a bit younger, dressed either like a slightly preppy MBA candidate or a white-collar worker using the library after hours. Alumni perhaps. He speaks.

"See you took your time in there."

Duffy nods slightly. The guy looks exceedingly normal but Duffy has no idea of where this could be headed. Candid discussion of hemorrhoids? The final late-night fag out or a word about God? The library can get lonely late at night, but Duffy isn't ready for a heavenly climax.

"You can never be too cautious."

Duffy nods again.

"See, here's how I do it. First, I peel some paper off the roll. If available, I grab a hand towel and use that to peel off the first few squares." It takes Duffy a moment to understand the man speaks of the toilet-paper roll in the stall. The first stages of public bathroom hygiene. "I go at least twice around the roll for safety's sake. The way I see it, these are the squares most likely to be contaminated. Call them the primary contact squares. Must avoid these squares of tissue. So I discard them."

Another nod. He begins to take genuine interest in this hygiene specialist.

"I also do eye inspection. If there are physical stains on the side of the roll—particularly brown or yellow splotches—that's enough for me. I move to another stall. Of course, in a crowded, rush-hour public restroom there isn't always time. If I'm planning to pass through during rush hour, I cut back on fluids, allow myself a third of my normal allocation. Plus, I go twice before I leave the last clean stall area, be it at home or work. Not that the workplace is necessarily a clean-stall area, my friend."

Close to midnight, Duffy has gained a friend.

"I'm reducing my chances, you see?"

His new friend may have a point.

"I'll do whatever I can to avoid having only one dirty, public stall to choose from."

Yes, continue.

"So I'm very careful with everything. My bare hand doesn't touch anything in a public restroom. I grab toilet paper or paper towel for the sink, the toilet, the works. If I make a slip up at the end, and turn the sink off with my bare hand, guess what?"

What?

"I repeat the entire process. Rewash my entire hand first, fully up to the elbow, and make sure I get the paper ending right."

"So, all this to avoid germs?"

"Germs? Yes." The man nods vigorously, giving Duffy a heavy dose of affirmation in a day that has been one constant wagging of the head, up and down, the horizontal and the vertical, so many different responses to so many questions, in class and outside, and now this man's nod ripe with vigor. *Hell, yeah!* "But let's not stop at germs. That's your domestic problem. The dirty-drawered society we live in."

As if on cue, from the furthest stall, a flush is heard, and then a lean, shaggy-haired youth pops out of his silent can. Long hair, tee shirt, and faded jeans, he gives but the slightest nod at Duffy and the bathroom expert, ignoring the sinks entirely, as he hurries out of the room. A brief moment of disapproval washes over the lecturer's face as he arrives at the culminating point.

"But there's the international concern as well." He stares at Duffy, eyebrows raised knowingly.

Duffy feels blinded by the man's earnest, emphatic look but returns a squint, believing he understands but needing to hear more. "Terrorism?"

"Bingo!" The man smiles when Duffy guesses correctly. "The way I see it if there's anthrax in the toilet bowl, the sink, I've still got a chance. All you can do is ask for a chance." Already a survivor of his chalk-dust anthrax scare from earlier in the day, Duffy knows how it is used as a weapon—its spores breathed in, lodged in people's nasal cavities, or worse, deep in their stomachs, innards offering the perfect fertilizer for reproducing, growing, killing. Touching the stuff has little to do with its most deadly danger. He tries to nod slightly, politely, not wanting to disappoint.

Sensing his pupil's misapprehension, the man continues, "Oh, believe me, I wear the mask as much as I can. Just can't have it on during working hours. Company policy. Jones versus GE ruled forbidding the mask during working hours was not a threat to a worker's health unless an immediate hazard was present."

"Terrorism is not an immediate hazard?"

"My point exactly. How the man gonna tell us to be scared and then not let us feel comfortable in public? So what we got is the same jokers who tell us this is the age of terror, scare the living daylights out of us, elect these fellows to the Labor Board who rule against our expression of our greatest fears."

"Why would they do that?" Duffy appreciates the irony, but it still doesn't make sense. "Wouldn't they want a few to wear the mask, reminding the others around them to vote strong on defense in order to prevent terrorism?"

"You'd think, wouldn't you?" Merely rhetorical. "But the reality is the mask is bad business. You see an elevator man wearing it, well, who is gonna step on that elevator? Yeah, right. I've been running elevators all over Ivy Green and Liberty Tech, and this piece of shit university ain't gonna let me near the mask. What am I gonna do?"

Duffy looks at him, not saying anything, expecting more. He is surprised the well-spoken, well-dressed man is an elevator operator, but then again, he knows he shouldn't be. He thinks of Wawa Ed again, and institutionalized racism, and a bad economy. What the hell could the Duffler do about any of it? Would he hold any of his own jobs if competitions for careers were played on level fields? Just as Ed delivers free career advice, so too is this man offering life-saving guidance at no charge at all. Yes, what is Duffy going to do? Apologize for being terrified of young black men? Of course, he has seen Wawa Ed regard these teenagers with similar suspicion, and it could be that lift operations offers greater status and job security than paper-grading and chalk talk.

"Well, at least I still gots my paper towel system!" And the man bursts out laughing, thick convulsions of glee at the thought he still has them fooled. He grabs one last paper towel, holds it with thumb and pointer finger only, opens the bathroom door, and graciously lets Duffy through first.

As he passes ahead, Duffy feels downright appreciative the man is saving him a touch.

As the man strides through, he balls up and then tosses the spent paper towel back behind him, where it lands perfectly in the metal trash receptacle. He turns back to Duffy and winks.

Save for the fit of bizarre laughter at the end, the man seems so calm, sensible, rational. Duffy wishes he met more like him. A bit paranoid about this terrorist business, but frankly, he might be right. You never know who is around the bend to blow you up, destroy your symbols, set your embassy on fire, shit on your toilet seat, or send anthrax swimming into the subway air and everyone's lungs.

Duffy leaves the bathroom wishing he could shake hands with the man, genuine human touch to celebrate shared conversation and passion for hygiene. But of course, this would defeat the entire purpose of the antigerm ritual he has just been partner to.

He decides to settle on the books instead. The Liberty Tech literature section is as weak as they come. Although Liberty has recently begun offering a full-fledged English major—this no doubt, in response to market conditions and the surplus of young women of college age and ability—the library collection has remained small and out of date. A collection of stiff-spined, sallow hardcovers typically printed in '57 or '63. Last quarter, just for kicks, Duffy ambled through the stacks, oddly peeling off books from the shelves, and checking copyright dates. It seemed as if there was nothing dated after 1989, not when the book was written, but when the particular edition in question went to press. The books were left yellowing on the shelves for years and years, a selection of literature even more aged than that of the Free Library system. (Heck, Duffy has been to public branches that had plenty of new offerings.)

Aged and unread, these virgins linger and wait for first fingers to approach and gently leaf through; a kind reader who would avoid tearing pages or breaking their spines.

Duffy remembers back to his own undergraduate library—the literature section like a trap, a suction. He'd get stuck there for weeks at a time, immersed for hours, uncovering in his reading the shared eating and sexual experiences of others, discarded granola bar and condom wrappers stuck between the pages. The occasional wisp of a Chinese-cookie fortune left neatly as a placeholder.

Among the stacks, Duffy aimlessly wanders. Backward from Ts to Rs to Ms to Ds. Around the final bend of American literature—the world's lit at Liberty Tech is less than three shelves wide—he sees a lone coed seated in the aisle by what must be the beginning of the alphabet. Her ankles are crossed Indian style, and she appears engrossed in her book. Oh my. Oh my. Duffy stares. He watches her read. A tear slides down his cheek, admiring the lost art. He inches closer. He can see she has glasses, pig tails, and mousy hair. A small girl, perhaps petite. She stares intently at the page. Ever so closer he inches, so now he cannot quite see the printed type of the book, but he can see the open space above her. It is indeed from the A's, the top of the alphabet. He imagines Jane Austen or Sherwood Anderson, or a more recent popular writer, although he realizes it is unlikely Liberty Tech's collection would include any such "contemporary classic."

He admits he was wrong to press forward and reciprocate what he mistook as Allison's advances, but now he just wants to move closer. Oh, just a little closer, he longs to journey, to share with this girl an innocent taste in literature.

"One more step, buster, and I'll mace you and call the cops!"

Ouch.

"No one comes up here but me, so I've come prepared."

She doesn't even turn her eyes up to meet him, to see it is only Adjunct Duffleman, enduring his long day in the age of terror. He is harmless, no? A gentle soul garbed in the benign hues of part-time faculty member cum security guard. She matter-of-factly turns her page. He has thoughts of dropping to all fours, begging mercy, proclaiming his innocence, begging her to let him stay awhile, stand and loiter, and watch her take pleasure in reading. Then, his inner voice comes and smacks him across the brain. You sicko. You creep. Getting rejected in the hotel room, not two hours ago, isn't enough for you, is it? You want more. You have the nerve to admire a young innocent pleasuring herself with literature, when anyone can see, in fact, it is your own pedophilic predilections at play. Oh Duffy, you're as good as they come. Your long day is one long vicarious thrill. Even your misery is not your own but lived through train-station less-fortunates, student suicides, and psychotic outbursts. You don't even go to therapy for yourself! So leave the girl alone. Face it, you're a voyeur. A sick leer is your lone contribution to the world.

An image comes to him in a flash, that he is the new improved perp of the twenty-first century and that all the black teens are victims if in anyway relevant to the crime reports. He sees himself lined up among all the other pedophilosophers, middle-aged, multiethnic contract teachers whose guilt and exhaustion force their sallow flesh to sag to the cement floor.

He can no longer stand the self-flagellation; if his lot in life were to play the criminal educator, then why not go for broke? The Duffler has a sudden attack of pyromania. He is seized with the thought of setting fire to the library. Or better yet the bookstore. Death to chain-store monopolies, price gouging on textbooks, and unlimited accounts for tenured overseers. The thought of razing to the ground the oppressive corporate chain is not unappealing. He would be sticking it to the deconstructed, post-modern Man—the shareholders and CEO, that is, and hopefully not too many bystanders among the late-night latte crowd. Why stop with one location? The world's books aflame appeals to Cyrus Arsonman at this late hour. Destroy the evil that got him ensnared in the adjunct life. Maybe the Church, Hitler, and random dictators and wannabes already held copyright on these ideas, and contemporaries like Amazon and Google and all of network television were not so far apart in their attempt to destroy the printed page. Death to hardcovers! Death to mass market and trade paper! Death to Gutenberg! Death to Israel! Death to America! Lost so deep in homicidal rage, Duffy feels revived when the spray hits his face.

Its scent is more melony than macey, and in his eyes, the sting is momentarily severe but soon dissipates.

Still, he must escape this pungency as well as his recriminating conscience. Or at least get out of the library with enough self-esteem intact to stumble to his last appointment and then home to bed.

Because the girl blocks the aisle, he has no other recourse save to retreat. Seeking to avoid even the slightest sound, including the clumping of his heavy soles, he does what he remembers from his childhood, something he never did then, but would watch others engage in, the moonwalking of African American boys across the asphalt of West Philadelphia. He grew up on the outskirts of Collegetown, longing to try but always too intrepid and left watching alone. And now his brave, silent moment, and he learns he can!

Duffy hears the girl giggle as he moonwalks backward, slowly at first, sliding one shoe behind the other, amazed that he is able. Picking up speed, coasting back the way he came with ease, away from the reading beauty, he breathes again when he passes into the main aisle. Turning to the left, a library security woman, her bright yellow parka giving her away, is staring in his direction. At him in fact, a look partly perplexed and a tad fearful it seems. Ah, yes. He knows her from the movies; she is the law-abiding black woman staring at the strange and unusual ways of the white man. He tries to look innocent. She shifts her expression from questioning to judgmental to a final shrug, indicating fully she has no idea of how people operate today. And then she ambles away, down the steps.

A few minutes later, a voice over the loudspeaker: "Ladies and gentlemen, it is eleven forty-five. The library will be closing in fifteen minutes. Kindly gather your belongings and begin your departure. If you have books to check out, please proceed to the circulation desk immediately. Thank you for joining us this evening. We will reopen tomorrow at eight."

Duffy knows not where his long day has gone but realizes time is wasting. He intends to meet Frank Hamnett at the designated spot, although God knows the area is probably cordoned off by police. There is no way the new building will be free for visitors, not even the courtyard. No members of the public would be allowed, not even security guards with Liberty Tech faculty ID.

At the thought of security guards with faculty credentials, Duffy gives a loud guffaw that hangs in the air like a sow's oink after the boar's plowing.

Who is Adjunct Duffleman to decide what is realistic? Who has even imagined the strange, extreme day he currently lives? It reminds him of Karl Marx's utopian ideal, a section of *The German Ideology* he read as a young man, about living full and multifaceted lives. There would be painting pictures in the morning, teaching a class in the afternoon, hauling rubbish for an hour at most, building a chair in the evening. Marx's utopian vision offered a healthy, variegated existence, the nonspecialized life *par excellence*. Is this, his long day, his traipsing around to four different schools—a fulfillment of Marx's dream of a nonalienating future? Sure, he has taught three classes and tutored two students, but he doesn't feel as if he has done the same thing twice. He wonders what Marx would think of this pseudointellectual vagrancy known as adjunct teaching. This job of educating all of America's classes. Would Marx be rolling over in his grave at the thought of so many instructors working on a subsistence wage, living without health benefits, or job security of any kind? Come to think of it, he has read that Marx lived in a noisy apartment, his many kids in the next room, his days and nights spent in the poorly lit library of the London School of Economics. Did Karl Marx ever bother to worry about his own lack of health benefits or inability to pay a doctor? Most likely, Duffy surmises, Marx would consider such worries a distraction from his writing, a waste of his time.

Sigh, Cyrus—sigh and move on.

He leaves the library in a pack of stimulated foreign accents. The students speak rapidly in English and other tongues. He hears a smidgen about movies, music, and drink, but most of what he can discern sounds related to the unsolved academic problems they were team-solving in the basement.

The mousy girl is nowhere to be found. Perhaps she is camping in literature tonight.

He weaves through the students sparking midnight cigarettes on the front steps of the library. The building Frank designated will be his final destination. Time to get this long day over with. Duffy mumbles these words to himself but nearly aloud.

CHAPTER 11

THE LAST STUDENT CONFERENCE OF HIS LONG DAY

His long day has become a lifetime, and Duffleman thanks the faint stars it is almost midnight. He is not certain he would thank others if he knew who was responsible for the sum of it, but in the short term the astrology above reminds him he is close to the day's end. At the least, soon it would be another day. A new day, a Friday no less, is at best a chance for change and at least an end to the teaching week. For now, all he wants to do is find out for sure, from Frank Hamnett himself, and then go home and rest.

At the new building, the Institute for Homeland Security, Duffy can see a conflation of cops, soldiers, old and new media, and Liberty Tech security; the men in black are likely a mix of city detectives and university staff. Of course, this place would be swarming with men in uniform. He doubts very much that Frank is among them. Not yet at least.

He gazes at the crowd of intent-looking Americans. Some have weapons drawn, ready to go if need be. Big ones, little ones, fat ones, thin ones. Duffy blinks twice when he sees an army tank and is almost certain a few soldiers are armed with bazookas. All he hears is the low hum of electricity and violence. It occurs to him to look skyward where he sees a helicopter, strangely silent, hovering above, black and still. So they've figured out how to fly them without the noise pollution. Technological progress is a never-ending story that bookish Duffy tries his best to ignore. Scanning the rooftop of the building, he can't see much at all. But it is not as if army snipers would make themselves visible, so he presumes they are present.

His gaze returns to the building. Black glass and steel jut out of the darkness, hovering above the landscape of Liberty Tech. Duffy sighs as if the weight of the entire Graduate School of Defense Technology were on his shoulders. It is all just another promise of peace and protection from a society built on the erected phallus; two steel towers up north razed to the ground, but America punches the time clock and keeps building toward the sky. War contracts and quarter-million-dollar college educations would be the bounty won from this gargantuan, bloated shrine to death. Little Johnny would rest better knowing that completing his physics and calculus homework would never be in vain because America would keep growing noble professions protecting little Jane next door from all the evil axes and empires cultivating virtual and real viruses across the globe. Or maybe it was Jane protecting Johnny or trailblazing Juanita protecting innocent Jesus or the best and brightest skimmed off the global peaks or all and none of the above in thousands of other American languages and postnational lives. No worries either or any way because be it virtual, nuclear, guerilla, or just, warfare would expand and thrive and Duffleman would survive and serve as a gatekeeper of the death school, eking out a living by passing all the good, little glocals through their writing requirements.

Back to now, Duffy checks his watch. 11:53 p.m. So that's it; his shift ends in seven minutes. There will be no meeting with Frank Hamnett. His long day done, one hundred yards from the crowd of authority, he drifts away before anyone notices he was almost there. He doesn't want to get caught up in any kind of interrogation so close to final release. Not now, at the end of his long day. He backs away slowly and quietly, trying to stay under the trees, in as many shadows as possible. He does at least thirty yards of this sideward and backward walking—just exercising the calves and side muscles is what he hopes it looks like—and when he turns away from the crowd, up ahead twenty paces, just off the cement path, he sees his last student. Alone.

Frank is under a lamp no less, atop brown dirt and the odd clump of grass. Above his head he holds a blue thermos whose contents he now shakes into his mouth. Duffy squints and sees droplets of liquid smacking Frank in the face, a few splashing off his open mouth but then returning on the rebound. One prominent drop dangles from Frank's upper lip, either his orifice or the ground its final destination. Something tall and thin leans against Frank's leg. An umbrella? Duffy cannot remember where his own umbrella was forgotten on his long day. But no, this is not an umbrella. As he steps closer, and squints more, he nearly mutters aloud, "Why of course." A long bow and a quiver of arrows.

So this is how it ends, muses Duffy as he approaches his former student. A murder-suicide could be a fitting finale to his long day of terror, his day of disaster. He can hear the next morning's news anchor relaying the latest:

> As of right now, authorities are convinced the weapon is the same one used against the deer, but further tests must be performed before they can verify that it was also used against the Under Secretary of Homeland Defense. We expect the results to be in soon, and the likelihood of a match is said to be great. At this time, there appears to be some discrepancy over which man pulled the trigger—shot the arrow that is—for these crimes. It may be the case that we have a copycat version of the DC sniper. This is all speculation at the moment, but it is conceivable that the teacher may have brainwashed the student. At this time, we cannot substantiate allegations of same-sex sexual misconduct, but we can say the hotel room will be combed for evidence of prostitution and child pornography. A reminder—details are inconclusive at this time, and of course, we are all innocent until proven guilty by good TV watchers like you and me.

As tired as old programming, Duffy prepares to reduce the sound.

"Glad you could make it, professor." Frank's voice is gruff, like that of a much older man. Duffy knows he was in Iraq for nine months but believes the boy to be twenty-one at most. Hamnett has a way of sounding almost drunk, even when he is sober. Duffy is thankful the boy isn't wearing his army fatigues, as he was wont to do in the months leading up to his deployment. In the classroom, this patriotic clothing acted as a deterrent to critical readings of any country or text. But tonight it's just dark-green jacket and blue jeans. Strangely, he also matches Duffy's security outfit.

"So what's the deal, Frank?" The tired teacher blurts it out. "Why are we here?"

"It's been a long day, huh?"

So here he stands sharing questions and lamplight with a trained soldier who could be a madman and a murderer. The odd thought catches on and clings to Duffy, that this is his last chance of the day to help a student. If he could save just one, his teaching life might feel worthwhile, even necessary. But he needs answers first.

"So why'd you kill the Under Secretary?"

"He had a big jaw. I didn't like him."

"That's all?"

"Nah."

"What else?"

"I wasn't aiming at the Under Secretary."

"What were you aiming at?"

"The CEO."

"The CEO?"

"I wanted to take out the goddamned CEO of Liberty Tech. Show him the working man, the blue-collar ROTC student still has a say at this school. The so-called Liberty Technical University."

"You tried to kill the president of the college?" Duffleman finds himself less surprised than he should be by this revelation. How surprised should he be?

"Yeah, of course I wanted to kill the CEO. Doesn't everybody? He's a white-collar, big-shot, million-dollar asshole, building extra divisions onto his house while he jacks up the price of French fries in the cafeteria. Three dollars I pay. The CEO deserves to die for exploitation of everybody—the student, the teacher, everyone. Goddamn selfish pig. He ain't the America I fought to defend."

Duffy sees the long and short of it now. He of course has also envied the president's prosperity, considered him a selfish man, a bad man for being willing to take so much from the students and to provide so little in the classroom. At the least, the students deserve a fairly compensated teacher. And an affordable fry as well. In a way, as the man in charge, the CEO has turned Liberty Tech into a microcosmic parody of the entire world order—exorbitant tuition, rip-off meal plans, and hefty padding added to full-retail textbook prices. A course costs one student as much as they pay the instructor to teach it, and to top it off, an egregious fee appears for every new service on campus. Duffy, too, as a matter of fact, has not infrequently felt fucked by the CEO. But he cannot remember any genuine need to kill him. Is this just another example of his weak-minded, cowardly nature? His inability to fight back, his acceptance of his lowest-rung status? Again, an example of how he is entirely lazy and inconsequential theory while his students are young and vigorous practice?

He warily regards Frank Hamnett and feels the full force of his student's deranged leer—part haughty, part mean, a bit vacant, and maybe even fearful. In what feels like frozen-timed eternity, he shares a stare with a murderer.

And then it occurs to Duffy that this is the perfect ending to his long day. To go down at the hands of his pathological former student. To have it all end here and now, to have Frank administer to him the proper dosage of medicine so he could rest forever. Retirement with no worries of insufficient health coverage. Sleep. He'd be out of the adjunct game and on with the afterlife!

But it sounds too easy. Duffy once more regards the lunatic fringe standing and staring right back at him. It is then that he recognizes that Frank doesn't want to kill him. He would have done so already, right? He decides to press on.

"So why'd you request I meet you here?"

"So you could get it all down."

"Get all what down? Are we going to be eating?" For an instant, Duffy terrorizes himself by imagining Frank force-feeding him, one spoonful at a time, his own excrement. Did it have to end like some cheap horror flick?

"We ain't eatin' nothin'." Late at night, the g's are released from duty. "The 'it' I need you to get down is writin'. Sorry I wasn't clear with my pronoun." Frank sips again from his thermos and then burps loud and clear.

Now it makes some sense. Recruit your writing teacher if you have an editing job. A few years back, Duffy gave up on freelancing, with all its painstaking job hunting, pay negotiation, and proofreading. Perfect grammar and punctuation led to migraines and tension headaches. He is a little rusty he has to admit. Now he feels genuine fear. Not from the bow and arrow, but from the fact that in his overworked adjunct state, he hasn't written anything beyond email in several years. What if Frank notices he cannot write well? That he is out of practice and has trouble completing sentences, even dotting the T's and crossing the I's, and of course, it is the other way around!

But Frank is busy searching in his pocket. Duffy prays he doesn't pull out a gun and then feels exhilarating release when Frank produces a rough-looking sheet of lined paper, torn from a notebook, the frayed edges with little white side doohickeys still attached.

"Here's my rough draft, professor." Frank is in the act of handing over the crumpled sheet when he pauses. "Er, you want me to read it to you sentence by sentence, and see if I can make the corrections myself?" Tears slide down Duffy's cheeks because his lunatic has remembered how the student-centered approach is supposed to work. Yes, the student reads, thereby maintaining authorial control over the writing. We are tutors and teachers, not copyeditors and proofreaders.

"Yeah, you read it to me, Frank."

"OK, well, here's what I got so far." And Frank reads:

Dear Friends and Fellow Countrymen:

I am stunned and deeply saddened by our loss today. Those of you who know me know I am a deeply patriotic individual—my blind patriotism could even be part of my problem. God knows I got problems. So today is a tragic day for our nation. I am as stunned as you are. As a marksman trained by the U.S. Army, my lack of precision as evidenced by our Under Secretary's decline and fall is puzzling to me. I deeply regret the fact that I was not on target. Not on target today, rarely on target in many other ways too. I've made my mistakes. Ma, I'm sorry I can't pull more than a 1.969 GPA at this school. I try Ma, I try, but Liberty Tech is kicking my ass. So I can only offer my deepest apologies, and a prayer. May God judge us all. I bid you farewell.

Sincerely,
Frank Hamnett

A girl loses her mind, a boy leaps twenty floors, and now this, the final tragedy of his long day. He imagines Frank's signoff to the world as the crude scrawl of a madman. Suicide is following Duffy like rotten breath all day—clinging deep-down halitosis, the kind supposedly rare in toothpaste-deploying nations—and now it is to happen right before his eyes.

"So where do I gotta improve it?" Frank hands over his writing, asking his favorite professor to improve the quality of his last letter to the human race.

For a moment, Duffy gets lost in all the ways the note fails to follow proper business format. It is not persuasive, direct, or indirect. It rambles, bobs and weaves, and uses "I" too much. There are too many short sentences in a row. How could his textbook contain so many color photos of Fortune 500 products and CEOs but fail to include a good chapter on suicide notes? Is it too much to ask for a self-offing subsection within the termination of employment section? He ought to write to the editors on the matter.

But as his disillusionment subsides, he hears the student's voice.

Duffy fears he'll sound like an asshole, but he says anyway, "Frank, the letter is fine, but I think you need help."

"Professor, I'm past all that bullshit. I've made my mark, and it's time to deactivate."

At the end of his long day, Duffy assesses the state of the man. Is rehabilitation possible? When he looks at Frank Hamnett, he sees a young man glowing under the lamplight. His long bow has fallen off his leg and onto the ground. He holds the thermos with his left hand and twists its cap back and forth with his right.

"So why this building, Frank?"

"I wanted you to see what they are going to replace us with. The newest technology. Meticulous targeting device. The equivalent of human intelligence. Able to sense any enemy. Able to calculate and defend against any terrorist situation. The perfect all-in-one weapon of mass destruction." Frank leers as he pauses, his face awash with delight in anticipation of Duffy registering his finale. "They don't need us anymore."

Adjunct Duffleman isn't quite sure if Frank says "us" as in the immediate two of them, the peons of the armed forces, the alienated workers all across contract-slave America, or humanity in general. He certainly feels close to his final outsourcing although he is counting on a couple more monthly paychecks.

"You know, professor, I snuck in. I used my training, how they taught me. It worked. I got in there." Duffy now spies a strong hint of pride in Frank's smile. Less of a leer. Less lunatic-fringe.

"You got in where?"

"There. The building." And Frank points his thermos at the Department of Missile Technology.

"You got in this evening?"

"No, last week. Our conversation about the rush I felt in battle reminded me of what I wanted to do. I wanted adventure. I wanted to do something real. To feel alive."

Duffy hears their shared conversation and wonders if he has helped turn this boy into a murderer.

"I didn't mean for you to go kill someone."

"Professor, I ain't trying to lay this on you. It ain't your fault. I'm a man."

When Frank declares his manhood, his responsibility and agency, Duffy feels even smaller—shrunken to dependence, weakness, secondary status. Frank snaps him out of it.

"So anyway, professor, it was last week, and I was in there. Snooping around and crawling flat on the floor. My night vision goggles my ally. My bow strapped to my back, my only companion."

"And then you know what I did?"

"What."

"I dropped my drawers and defecated. I laid out the sausage links. Right on the floor, in the hallway outside the steel-tight locked door to the newest technology. I would have done it right on top if there was any way to get into that room."

Duffy pauses to admire Frank's original contribution to the field. He feels paltry and weak, never having made his own. Unpublished and wasting half his long day by playing it safe in the public stalls. His whole life Duffy has been neatly flushing down his draft work like good, harmless bourgeoisie. A mere mortal compared to this adventurer. He looks at Frank, whose expression has turned to a teary-eyed plea for acknowledgment. So this is what it has come to. His suicidal student wants positive reinforcement for his generous offering to the world.

"That's a good job, son." Frank appears gracious to receive these words.

"Now you gotta help me out. I just can't do it alone."

Duffy doesn't like the sound of this. "You mean with the letter writing?"

"No, you said that'll do. You meant it, right?" With a menacing stare, Frank makes sure that's the truth. "With this other thing here." And Frank nods down at the bow.

"What do you want me to do with that?"

"You need to help me get my final job done. I'm checkin' out."

"I don't think I'm qualified for that kind of work, son." Duffy's heart palpitates quickly and then misses a beat or three. He wonders if he is hyperventilating, on the verge of a heart attack, or both. "I mean, I'm just an adjunct. I don't even have a one-year appointment."

Franks returns a blank stare. Like most of America, he doesn't even know what an adjunct is.

"Professor, all I need you to do is hold it like so." Frank, in dramatic fashion, whips out an arrow, from a hidden quill that is possibly shoved down the backside of his jeans. He sets the arrow straight in the bow, and pulls back, demonstrating position. Then he releases. "That's all there is to it."

Duffy catches on now. Wryly, he muses, he has had them go down right and left on his watch today. But he is chilled to the bone at this boy's request.

"All you have to do is stride back a bit. Here, take the bow." Frank puts down the thermos, and limps over to Duffy, dropping the bow at his feet, along with the arrow, and a pair of black gardening gloves he produces from his back pocket. "I brought those in case they dust for prints."

Frank hops back to his lamplight, the shining star of this grim saga. His facial expression wavers between doubt, impatience, and grim readiness for the task at hand. All over town, they drop like lemmings, and now a student-soldier asks him to get in on the action. It is no wonder the students are ready for the end. Impressed into the army of undergraduate uncertainty, they hump their overpriced textbooks and credit-card debt, their adolescent angst and parental expectations, their student loans and our national deficit, their aspirations and dreams, their hangovers and bad highs, their unrequited lust and STDs. Could it all be blamed on America's ambivalence over its global obligation to create empire and capitalist democracy? The self-based system forced each individual to steal as much as possible from society and then pray the strong among us were willing and able to redistribute enough to maintain those who were too decent, drunk, uneducated, or disabled to steal on their own. Ugh! He feels stung in the brain by ideology; he has sifted through too much of history's rubbish pile to stand for this. The communisms and capitalisms and military complexes were enough. He must resist! An emotional jungle with snipers on all sides, the weight is too much to bear. Despite exhaustion and a piercing tension headache, he does his best to ignore nagging certainty that Fern and Rhodes and Hippy Harry and Wawa Ed and everyone else would know exactly how to resolve such a delicate situation. Whew! Lacking such clarity, he tries to sort through his choices.

As requested, if he strides backward ten paces, that would be enough to take out Frank Hamnett. Or he could no doubt use the weapon, at least the arrow, on himself. He is reminded of the Kolyma tale in which Varlam Shalamov describes a man hanging himself at the fork of two thick tree branches, no rope necessary. If that were possible, then the string of the long bow must be enough to get the job done. All he need do is to find the right tree. Duffy holds the long bow, moving his fingers up and down the wooden part, with his thumb occasionally plucking the string. Its reverberations make a noise like the dull twang of an unplugged electric guitar. He knows his fingerprints are now all over the murder weapon. But he likes them there. It could all be easily explained away in the interrogator's room. If he's lucky, it'll have a tiny window. For the police work, he's sure he'd get off at least a half day. He is looking at Frank, still five yards away. He assumes he has to move a bit further away for a fatal hit, but he has no expertise in arrow launches. Frank's look now is less vacant, less mean, and less proud. Doubt or fear or some other emotion discouraged by the textbook approach to business communications crawls across Frank's face. Is he afraid to die? Or is he afraid his professor will refuse to shoot the arrow?

Under the clear, moonlit sky, Cyrus Duffleman, comparativist, considers his options. He could drop the bow and run away, while hoping Frank doesn't shoot him in the back; his science lessons are so far in the past that he cannot remember if he would hear the final "twang" or not. Or he could simply follow directions, the easiest option in a life on auto-pilot; he could aim the arrow and shoot to kill, aid and abet Frank in his suicide. Or he could yell out the top of his lungs, scream until the cops, soldiers, detectives and others rush to his and Frank's rescue; with this option, he is certain of suffering a lasting view of Frank's anguish, a face flush with pain from this final betrayal. The professor fails the student once more.

He wouldn't be able to tell you later if it registered as actual strategy, but he begins to move toward Frank. Slowly, a quarter step at a time. Somehow, as he does so, he feels the weight of his long day lifting off of his shoulders. He hopes it is not merely because the roach-brown book bag is huddled at the bottom of his locker in the security-guard changing area. Frank's facial expression continues to vacillate between mere apprehension and actual fright. But the Duffler is hardly concerned with these minor details. He is intent on completing the mission. One quarter step at a time.

Because, yes, if he can reach Frank before he disappears, if he can hang on and finish up the shift the right way, if he can wake up tomorrow, not hit the snooze button, make the coffee, hop in the shower, remember to shave, get off his ass in a timely fashion, he'll have a chance again, yes, on a shorter day even, to teach his classes all over again. Yes, all over town in an encore performance, Adjunct Duffleman rises to the occasion in the age of terror, a lone soldier of the subway, bus, and elevated line and a failure of many in God knows how many ways. And yet from the bottom of his heart, he wants to believe that the outcome remains possible that for some student from his past, or perhaps one on the way, Cyrus Duffleman, educator, could make the difference. Yes, if he could reach Frank now.

CHAPTER 12

THE FLYING DUFFLER

He hears Frank scream in anguish as a shot from above tears into his side. Frank collapses. The Duffler shocks himself when he leaps forward and with his outstretched arms shields his student from the mean concrete. Body extended over the walking path, he suffers under the weight of this new responsibility. Elbow and ankle pain shoot through his nerves and flesh, and yet, at this late hour, he feels a momentary satisfaction, perhaps even self-congratulation, that he has reached out and shielded fallen Frank. He hears not a peep from above; he sighs. U.S. army sniper talent has taken down the last casualty of his long day and ensured that Duffy's Friday would be a day of answering the authorities. If he were lucky, the questioning would preempt his scheduled classes and give him a break from the teaching ahead. With more luck, he could return home at a normal hour and get some extra sleep. But now, lying prone on concrete, his arms underneath Frank's body and his head bent to the defense-technology side, Duffy can see the authorities approaching. Soldiers and suits march at him; America's leaders and defenders would get to the bottom of this. Weapons are drawn and pointed at Adjunct Duffleman. It is well past midnight when the instructor recognizes his next day has already begun.

ABOUT THE AUTHOR

Alex Kudera has survived a decade of adjunct-teaching overloads but in some circles is better known for his mysterious injuries. Driven by status and a thirst for fame, he has bussed dishes in two countries and has loitered in bookstores around the world. A lifelong Philadelphian, Alex currently teaches literature and writing at Clemson University in South Carolina.